FRAGILE GODS

RAGNARÖK: DOOM OF THE GODS

MELISSA SNARK   M. S. MACKNIGHT

LOKI'S WOLVES UNIVERSE

NORDIC
LIGHTS
PRESS

FRAGILE GODS

Universe: Loki's Wolves

Series: Ragnarök: Doom of the Gods

ISBN-13: 978-1-942193-22-7 (ebook)

ISBN-13: 978-1-942193-26-5 (paperback)

Nordic Lights Press

First Edition

Cover design by Ravenborn Covers

Contact Information:

Email: admin@nordiclightspress.com

Nordic Lights Press

P.O. Box 1347

Pleasanton, CA 94566

Published in the United States of America.

In loving memory of Laura Granger Newman
Always in our hearts, never forgotten;
Your spark burned bright and left us too soon.

ACKNOWLEDGMENTS

A great many people helped make Fragile Gods a reality. My many thanks go to my friend and developmental editor, Jennifer L. Carson, and my friend Sheryl R. Hayes. Thank you to my editors: Marjorie AJ Cooke, and Shay VanZwoll of EV Proofreading. Thank you to Anika Willmanns of Ravenborn Book Cover Designs. Thank you to my beta readers who provided valuable feedback: Rissa Watkins, Teri Carter Lloyd, and Becky Oviatt. And thanks to Shelley Tra Kimbrough for his guidance with composing a prayer to Freya.

Prince of Asgard. Heir to the Wild Hunt.

Sawyer Barrett grew up far from his divine birthright, raised as a hunter of monsters in Phoenix, Arizona. He failed in his duty as slayer and guardian. While in a berserker rage, he killed a wolf-shifter child of the Storm Pack.

Blood must be repaid in blood.

He pledges to protect the people he wronged, but enemies lurk on all sides—shape-changing shamans, an ancient witch, and the Norse Fates. Sawyer's downfall may come from within when the woman he's deceived for so long learns the truth about his murderous past.

Fragile gods endure loss... at the cost of a hand or a life.

In a treacherous world of lies and deceit, Sawyer must determine who to trust or destroy. Ice threatens to consume the world, and his most unlikely ally, Loki's son, represents Sawyer's best shot at saving those he loves.

CHAPTER 1

Helm of Awe: To Strike Fear into the Enemy

EARLY SATURDAY MORNING

Blood stained his hands and his soul. Sawyer Barrett gripped the edge of the coarse blanket and scrubbed his callused palms in yet another of countless attempts to wipe them clean. Then, he held his splayed fingers against the fiery halo as dying coals smoldered amongst the blackened ashes. He'd constructed the fire pit out of smooth river rock he'd hauled from the manmade beach along the lakeshore. He blinked to focus his blurry vision, but it did no good.

Dark red, wet gore still clung to his skin—Jasper's blood.

"It's not real. It's been proven that sleep deprivation causes hallucinations. It's a sign of madness." *So is talking to yourself. Get a grip, man.* Sawyer squeezed his eyes shut and folded his hands on his chest, mirroring a body laid out to rest. And the wistful thought persisted—*if only...* He never slept anymore. Unrelenting insomnia crushed him in its merciless grip, exacting its mental and physical toll. Right then, he wouldn't have minded dying if it meant eternal slumber. But nothing good, nothing peaceful, awaited him in the afterlife.

Quiet... *shush*. Sawyer breathed deeply and struggled to clear his troubled thoughts. He needed a few moments of blessed blankness, but his body ached to the bones. Even the hard steel of his shotgun pressed against his side proved distracting. Laboriously, he filtered out the disturbances and built a mental wall brick by brick. His turmoil eased but Lady Sleep spurned him, refusing to take him into her soothing embrace.

As dawn crept closer, hundreds of disagreeably cheerful birds launched into song. As grumpy as a bear, Sawyer turned over with a labored grunt. He might as well get up. He had work waiting for him. Today, he planned to raise the walls on the woodshed he'd spent the past forty-eight hours constructing.

He sat up, pulling on his boots, and settled his shotgun's carry strap across his shoulder. As a matter of habit, he fell into his morning routine: feeding the fire and making coffee. While it brewed, he performed the daily ritual of cleaning and checking his weapons, starting with the matching 9mm pistols he wore in a double shoulder holster. Blades in their scabbards: one secured to each forearm in a quick draw sheath, one on his belt, and tucked into each boot. He strapped a six-piece throwing knife set to his left thigh over his beaten jeans and a concealed revolver on his calf beneath his pant leg.

A soft rustle alerted Sawyer to an intruder behind him. He hesitated, a split-second glitch, in the act of reaching for his machete. Cold sweat ran down his back. Conditioned fight instincts kicked in. He dropped his hand to the shotgun and seated his finger on the stout trigger. As he pivoted, he brought the shotgun up, aiming it straight at his dead mother.

"There's no need for that," Sarah Barrett said, and Sawyer flinched. Her voice stung. It summoned painful childhood memories: the soft strains of lullabies and crooned reassurance. Her familiar scent—rose and sandalwood—flooded his nostrils, provoking a paralyzing surge of nostalgia and yearning.

"Mom?" Sawyer staggered. The muzzle of the shotgun dipped and slipped from his fingers. He caught the firearm and jerked it up again, but not at her. His instincts screamed this must be a trick, but he couldn't bring himself to point a loaded weapon at his mother... or her likeness.

"It's really me, Sawyer." Sarah offered a small, sad smile. An ethereal halo suffused her. She was as radiant and beautiful as she'd looked before the chemo treatments had taken their toll.

"It can't be. You're dead." He stepped back.

"Regardless, I'm here." She opened her arms, offering a hug, but left the decision up to him. It took everything he had not to rush to her.

"My mother died." Sawyer clung to the simple, stubborn defense. Inwardly, he fumed. *Why* did these sorts of supernatural shenanigans always strike before he got his first cup of coffee?

"I'm a goddess. Only my mortal incarnation died," Sarah countered with an enigmatic smile. Mistress of Mystery—his mother had a singular talent for making any answer, no matter how obscure or inane, sound reasonable.

"How do I know it's really you?" More than anything, he wanted this to be genuine. Hardened suspicion held him back.

"You don't believe it's me?" Sarah tilted her head. Hurt flitted across her face and she dropped her arms. Guilt dropkicked him in the gut.

"Let's just say this isn't the first time I've met the likeness of a deceased family member at this damn lake. Daniel tried to drown me." Reflexively, he tightened his grip on the gun. It wasn't magical. In his experience, however, a double-barrel shotgun unloaded at point-blank range solved all sorts of threats, mundane and supernatural.

"That wasn't Daniel. Your brother would never hurt you."

"I know that." Sawyer's gut cramped. Daniel's murder had been properly avenged, but Sawyer still lived in the shadow of grief.

"It is offensive that Daniel's likeness was used against you." She stiffened, and her tone acquired a flinty edge. "However, that isn't what truly angers me."

"No?"

"No. It's not. I am incensed that Freya *dared* demand *my son* be sacrificed in her name." Wrath burned in Sarah's gaze, but she wore the icy composure of a queen. She ruled her rage, and she was downright terrifying. His doubt regarding the truth of her identity toppled like a row of dominoes.

"Freya did that?" Sawyer asked, knocked off kilter.

"She did exactly that on the night *Den Valgte* attacked you and your friends."

"I was unconscious." Technically, he'd croaked. In keeping with the complex, contradictory rules that governed his life, he could die. It merely put him out of commission, however, while runic magic healed his injuries. Sawyer could slow or speed the process —to a limited degree—but he couldn't stop it. Unless his heart got destroyed; then he died and stayed dead.

He preferred not to nitpick.

"Freya ordered her priestess to cut out your heart and offer it to her."

He didn't know what to say, so he stood there in shocked silence while the implications sank in. Oh, he'd known *something* had upset Victoria. This explained everything—why she refused to look him in the eyes. Up until that moment, he'd clung to a shred of doubt. He told himself comforting lies—the *Den Valgte* attack had exhausted Victoria, and she needed time to recover. The truth was uglier, harder to swallow. Sawyer had dreaded the day Victoria learned about Jasper... and he yearned for it. Ironically, his worst fear remained unaddressed. Had Victoria only spared Sawyer's life because of the promise she'd made to Jake to forego revenge? She must've hungered to avenge the slain boy. Nausea churned in his gut.

"Do you understand what it means when one god is sacrificed to another?" Sarah asked in a soft voice.

"Yeah, I get it." He jerked his head in a curt nod. Abruptly, he got good and worried, though not for himself. He released the shotgun.

"It would've destroyed your immortal soul, Sawyer. This offense cannot go unaddressed. Freya must be held accountable. She *will* pay." Sarah raised her fist like a general about to order an army to war—not a casual analogy for a queen who had the might of Asgard's military at her beck and call.

"Mom, you can't blame Victoria. She refused, or I wouldn't still be standing here. Promise me you won't harm her." He caught Sarah's hand, hoping if he held on tightly enough, it'd drive home the force of his conviction.

Sarah lifted her brow. "Daniel already exacted that promise from me. Who is this woman that matters so much to my sons?"

Mortification turned Sawyer inside out. Sometimes, he forgot Victoria and Daniel had been lovers long before Sawyer entered the picture... Sometimes, he preferred to allow that awareness to lapse because it was easier. Now, beneath his mother's discerning gaze, he was an overturned snail. All his gooey, vulnerable innards exposed... He didn't care for the sensation in the least. But he wouldn't back down, not with Victoria's welfare at stake.

"I care for her and I owe her. *Promise me.*" Sawyer braced himself; he'd use the L-word if he had to. Most people considered Odin to be a harsh and merciless monarch, but the old man had nothing on the queen.

"What do you owe her?" Sarah made the question into a demand.

A terrible tightness constricted his chest so it hurt to breathe. He gathered his strength, pushing against the oppressive weight. Truth must be told. His voice sounded harsh to his own ears. "When Daniel died, I blamed Victoria. I believed she'd murdered him. I went mad with grief and rage, and I wouldn't listen to anyone. Not Dad, not Skinner... My thirst for revenge was vast and all-consuming. I destroyed everything and everyone who got in my way. Innocent people got killed—hunters, wolves... It's a long, complicated saga, and I suspect you already know most of it."

Light glinted in her eyes—confirmation. "All that is settled. Your father has paid the blood price. But that's not what you truly mean when you say you owe her."

"There was a boy, Jasper. He was maybe fifteen or sixteen... He was a member of the Storm Pack and under Victoria's protection. This was after Adair and Katherine died, and she assumed leadership." He glanced over her shoulder, noting the encroaching dawn. Once, he'd thought of Jasper as "the kid he'd shot". Living with—belonging to—the Storm Pack had changed all that.

"I met the young man once when he was a child," Sarah said.

"We picked him up in Albuquerque. Dad wanted to use him as leverage to force Victoria to surrender to us. He wanted to talk to her but I—"

"You needed to kill her."

Sawyer twitched and clenched his jaws. Hearing it that way cut deep, but his mother would forgive his sins whether he warranted it or not. More than anything, he despised the thought of how he'd failed her. He wanted to be good and worthy in her estimation. Not a coward or a child killer.

"Jasper made a break for it and ran. I shot him in the back. Just killed him in cold blood. Silver ammo, point-blank range. He died immediately." He hiccupped, a snotty inhalation.

"Oh, Sawyer..." Sorrow washed over Sarah. She reached for him, perhaps intending to brush her fingers over his cheek. He evaded her touch. He refused to accept her sympathy because he didn't deserve it.

"I have blood on my hands. Do you see?" In desperation, he shoved his red-stained, shaking hands into her face.

"Oh, my darling boy, I do see." Sarah looked down, staring, and caught his wrists. Tears shone bright in her eyes. She swiped her fingers across his palms. Where she touched, a pure blue X formed upon the crimson field. *Gebo*—the rune of love and forgiveness. It shone with sapphire brilliance, but then the hard edges eroded. The sigil fractured; blood filled the cracks. In a blink, it submersed beneath the ocean of blood. Even Frigg with all her immense influence couldn't remove the blight.

"I also perceive your father has awakened the runes within you," Sarah added in the tone she reserved for expressing criticism. She leveled a look that reminded him of the summer he'd stolen the keys to the Chevelle and gotten into a wreck.

"Dad said you wouldn't approve." Perspiration beaded on his upper lip. Agitated, Sawyer scrubbed his hands across his jeans but the ickiness remained.

That earned a frown from his mother... just as Sawyer had expected. His parents subscribed to old-fashioned parenting: the united front, et al. Even the suggestion of division—hence, weakness—displeased Sarah. It wasn't a trick he used but once in a blue moon. Every now and then, however, redirection proved highly effective.

Sarah pursed her lips. "Before we started a mortal family, your father and I agreed our children should live full *human* lives. Tell me, what else did Jake say?"

"That it was necessary—if we're going to live at all, we have to be able to die." As soon as he spoke, Sawyer regretted his vehemence. He should've softened his tone.

"You agree with your father." Sarah raised her brow in clear skepticism. Hardly surprising—Jake and Sawyer had a grand tradition of discord.

When it'd come to the runes, however, father and son had reached a swift and total accord. To start, Jake had lit the spark, igniting the magic dormant within the souls of Sawyer and his brothers, JD and Gage. Then, like tykes on trikes, they'd received a crash course in Runes 101. The most important takeaway had been the warrior's prowess bind rune, which heightened both physical and mental attributes and facilitated accelerated healing.

Sawyer didn't want to get trapped into playing he said/she said with his parents. From his lifetime of experience, this game never ended well. He would rather bare his soul in the hopes his mother could find some way to help him.

"You want to know the worst of all this—the really fucked-up part that doesn't make any sense no matter how hard I try?" Sawyer asked. "Murdering a kid isn't the worst of it. It's that Jasper's soul was condemned to Niflheimr because he got shot in the back. He died a coward's death."

Niflheimr: a land of mist and ice from which eleven rivers flowed. Home to the dragon Nidhogg; it bordered Helheimr where the goddess Hel ruled over the adjacent lands of the dead. While cold and dark, Helheimr wasn't a punishment, unlike Niflheimr where the damned suffered eternal punishment.

"Jasper's cowardice isn't on you," Sarah shot back.

"The hell it's not." Out of respect, Sawyer tried not to swear in his mother's presence, but this time anger overrode his inhibition. He tore free from her grasp and turned away, raising his fists. He desperately needed to kill something. "Tell me, Mother, what kind of value system punishes a kid for running away? What kind of gods are we?"

A thoughtful silence ensued. Sawyer started to wonder if she'd left but he couldn't quite muster the courage to turn around and face her. After a pronounced delay, Sarah replied in an even tone.

"Children are never sent to Niflheimr," she said. "But those laws were set down in a different era. Then, a sixteen-year-old was considered a man and expected to conduct himself as a warrior. Worth was measured in wisdom, cunning, and courage. I'll concede, many of the ancient edicts for how things are have outlived their usefulness... That isn't a cop out."

Sawyer sealed his lips. She'd beat him to it.

"It's simply how things are," Sarah continued. "I'm sorry. If I could save Jasper, I would do so for your sake, Sawyer. However, it's beyond your father's or my ability to change. Fair or not, *it is what it is.*"

He spun. "You just reduced the hereafter to a platitude."

"If it's any comfort to you, I promise no harm will come to your Victoria by my hand or my deed."

"Thank you."

She nodded.

Overcome with relief and exhaustion, he lacked the strength to stand. He strode over to the stump he used for chopping firewood and sank onto it before his rubbery legs could betray him. He heaved a tired sigh. "Why *are* you here, Mom?"

"I'm afraid," Sarah said in a trembling voice.

"Afraid." That made him sit up straighter. What could scare his mother? "Of what?"

Sarah clasped her hands together before her heart. "I'm a seer."

He grunted. "More powerful than Dad."

"Your father might disagree." Sarah smiled, but it faded fast. "I have seen your future. I have seen a future where you are trapped in the underworld."

Fear clenched his heart until it struggled to beat. When Frigg prophesied death, be it man or god, the question wasn't if —only when.

"We all die in the end," Sawyer said, striving for composure. He wasn't sure he wanted to know, but he was compelled to ask. "How will I die?"

"I am unsure..." Sarah frowned and gnawed her lower lip. "I have been unable to perceive your actual death, even though I have tried. When I look, I always see past the crux to the future of your soul."

"Not good, I take it?" Sawyer had a powerful premonition of his own, but he still hung on the hook of anticipation.

"Your soul will be lost to Niflheimr."

Ironic and apropos... Sawyer nodded in glum appreciation. "Maybe Niflheimr is where I belong."

"No! Don't talk like that, Sawyer. I forbid it." She flew across the clearing to grasp his shoulders with inhuman strength.

He gritted his teeth, enduring the pain. "I'm sorry. If it's any comfort, I don't intend to kill myself. What would you have me do?"

Sarah eased off, releasing him. "Come back to Valhalla with me. You'll be safe there where I can protect you."

"No!" Sawyer exploded to his feet.

"Sawyer, please. Daniel is there, as am I. You wouldn't be alone." Sarah paced, wringing her hands. "Now that I've talked to you, I'm more certain than ever. Guilt is destroying you. I fear Niflheimr will become your self-fulfilling prophecy. I've already lost one son to Hel's realm. I cannot lose another."

Baldur the Shining, Baldur the Beloved, had been Frigg's favorite son. To Sawyer, Baldur was just a name—the older brother he'd never met, who'd died centuries before his birth. His parents, however, still grieved for Baldur, their vanquished child.

"I'm not Baldur." Sawyer pressed his lips together to stop from adding, *I deserve whatever's coming to me.* To say it aloud would be cruel.

"No, you're not," she said, weeping. "For one, Baldur was never thick-headed or stubborn..."

"Now you're channeling Dad." Sawyer grimaced. It pained him to cause his mother grief but... "I can't return to Valhalla with you. I have to stand and fight."

"Now who sounds like his father?" Sarah pinned him with a beseeching stare. "Can you please tell me why?"

"Because..." Sawyer struggled to speak through gritted teeth. Anger overwhelmed and drove him. He fought but the words burst from him. "I'm a lot of things, but I'm not a coward. I won't run away and hide. I won't ever abandon the people I love!"

His shout blasted over them and on through the clear morning. Abrupt silence followed. Wide-eyed, Sawyer and Sarah stared at one another.

"Is that what you think? That I abandoned you and your brothers?" Sarah blinked, releasing a flood of tears. She pressed her hand to her mouth.

The depths of his resentment shook him to the core. Until he'd said it, he hadn't realized he harbored such a sentiment toward his mother. Sarah Barrett hadn't just gotten sick and passed away. As she'd pointed out so succinctly... she was a goddess. She'd allowed it to happen. She'd refused the magical intervention that would've cured her cancer. In essence, she'd chosen death over her husband and her sons...

Sawyer choked back a sob. He clung to his anger to keep grief at bay. "Dad needed you. Daniel and the twins needed you. *I* needed you, and you left."

"Oh, my baby. I'm so sorry." Sarah raised her hands to frame his face but didn't touch him. She shed enough tears for them both. "I didn't want to go. Leaving broke my heart, but it had to be done. Your father needed to learn how fragile and precious mortal life truly is. He is about to endure the greatest test he'll ever face."

"Dad is your excuse?" Sawyer barked with harsh laughter. His audacity shocked them both.

Sarah's ire sparked; a fuse with a slow burn. "Mock me, but know this. The fate of Yggdrasil and the Nine Worlds depends on your father."

Mother and son stared at each other. The breeze rattled the trees and an intrepid squirrel skittered boldly through the camp in its quest for pine nuts.

Sawyer hung his head. "I'm sorry. Please forgive me."

"Of course I forgive you. I'll always forgive you, but it's not my forgiveness you need." Sarah wrapped her arms around him and pulled him close. "Will you forgive me?"

"Yes." It shamed him that she even found it necessary to ask. He hugged his mother in return. "I love you."

"I love you, too." After they parted, she made one final plea. "You won't return to Valhalla?"

"I can't. I won't. Dad is counting on me. The twins have already lost so much. There are people here who need me..." He'd sooner hop the express train straight to Niflheimr than run out on Victoria, the Storm Pack, and his family. The prophecy of his death brought everything into sharp focus. "If I'm going to die, I want it to serve a greater purpose."

A sacrifice that mattered.

"Very well, I respect your decision." Shrouded in grief, Sarah squared her shoulders. "If you must follow in your father's foot-steps, then do so in style."

"What does that mean?" Sawyer suspected he was a fool to ask.

"I brought you a gift." Unceremoniously, Sarah thrust a solid object, which appeared out of thin air, against Sawyer's chest.

"Uh, thanks. You know my birthday's not till October." He grabbed it on reflex, wrapping his fingers around the smooth edges, and staggered under the impact. Defying appearances, his mother packed quite a punch.

"I know when you were born, Sawyer. I was there. Of all my children, your birth was the most difficult. You were breech." *Thunk*—the arrow struck the bullseye.

"I'm sorry." Sawyer winced, and delivered a mental slap to the back of his skull. Stupid—he should've known better than to fall into that trap.

"You're forgiven." His mother narrowed her eyes, her smile mean.

"I love you too, Mom," he said, groaning.

With a sigh, he held the gift up for inspection and pulled back in a double take. His goddess mother had brought him a round shield constructed of wood and steel. It measured thirty-six inches in diameter, and must've weighed at least sixty pounds. The hand-hammered center boss served as the hub for a black Helm of Awe upon a field of red. Sawyer had to bite his tongue against the impulse to shout, "It belongs in a museum."

Jokes aside, Sawyer had no idea what he was supposed to do with it. He never fought with a sword or an axe. Daggers and knives, sure, but firearms were his preferred weapons. A clunky, heavy shield would only slow him down in combat.

"Mom, you're aware this is the twenty-first century?"

"Don't get smart with me."

"Yes, ma'am."

"*Kappiskjǫld* was made by Thrust Tusk Ironforge," Sarah explained. "The wood was harvested from a Jötunheimr ironwood and the ore was smelted in the lava pools of Múspellsheimr. It is impervious to both cold and heat."

"Is it magical?" Sawyer's estimate of the artifact rose.

"Not yet."

And sank.

He frowned. "Not yet?"

"Take *Kappiskjǫld* with you to Arizona when you go."

"When am I going to Arizona?" Sawyer asked. Despite his incredulity, he tucked the warning away in the portion of his mind reserved for serious matters. Only fools and dead men failed to heed Frigg's warnings.

"Do you still have *Gnýrhorn*?"

"*Gnýrhorn*?" he echoed with a start of surprise. The tangent threw him for another loop. How had they gotten from Dwarven shields to enchanted ram's horns?

Gnýrhorn—when blown, the curved ram's horn summoned the Wild Hunt... or so the story went. Sawyer kept the Norse artifact packed away in an old captain's chest that he'd hauled halfway around the country and back. Ironically, but not coincidentally, *Gnýrhorn* was another gift from his mother, presented to him years ago on the eve of his high school graduation. No one had been more surprised, other than maybe Jake. Just a glance at his old man's face had told Sawyer his father disapproved.

"Where is it?" Sarah demanded.

"It's at the hunter's cabin here in Sierra Pines. Why?"

Sarah gripped his wrist. "You're going to need it soon. Remember, this is important. When you sound *Gnýrhorn,* stand at the center of a wide road and don't step off."

Sawyer's heart jolted with a heavy thud. "Or?"

"Or the Hunt will consume everyone in its path."

"You said when, not if. Is it a done deal?"

"Nothing is a done deal until you choose." Sarah stiffened. She jerked her head sharply aside, cocked as though listening to something.

"What is it?" Sawyer turned with her. He strained his ears but detected nothing amiss. Only the rustle of leaves and birds in the trees.

"There are strangers in the woods, Sawyer. Your pack is in danger."

CHAPTER 2

Ragnarök: The Doom of the Gods

THREE A.M. A fine hour for wolves.

Sylvie Thornton aspired to steal knowledge of the future from jealous gods. In deference and defiance, she raised the chest she carried overhead. Startled by her abrupt action, a swarm of fire-flies rose and vanished against the stars of the velvet-cool summer night. Beyond the reaches of the vast wilderness, nature's crown—the Sierra Nevada mountain range—thrust skyward.

She composed herself and called out in a clear voice that carried, "Hail Freya, Vanadis, wearer of Brísingamen... I pray that you'll bless me with insight to the depths of my soul. I ask your benevolence and guidance in this time of uncertainty and misdeed. Inspire me today."

Sylvie held the rune chest aloft until her muscles burned and her limbs trembled. Her sixty plus years had eroded her strength. Sylvie resented the weakness—her body's betrayal. Oh, her once-luxurious ebony hair had long since faded to the shade of winter. She remained agile and athletic, as befitted both her Native American and wolf-shifter heritage, but was not as robust as she'd been at twenty.

Silence resounded.

The goddess didn't answer, but then Vanadis never spoke to Sylvie despite years of faithful worship. There was no reason tonight should prove different. As always, her prayers passed into silence, no more than pebbles cast into a chasm. Since the death of her husband, Paul, a few months ago, an abyss yawned in her soul. In times of darkness and quiet, when her defenses weakened and her faith faltered, Sylvie wondered why she bothered with prayers and sacrifices anymore. She had more bitterness in her bones than hope in her heart.

"Well, then. I suppose I have my answer," Sylvie said with a small, ironic smile. She was on her own. But, if nothing else, being ignored taught self-reliance.

With a sigh, Sylvie lowered the rune chest. She surveyed her surroundings, seeking a suitable spot to set up. The task before her—a divination cast using Elder Futhark rune stones—required an appropriate forum. Fortunately, she didn't have far to look before she found what she sought.

Almost hidden within a briar patch, a battered picnic table hunkered close to the earth with one end pushed against the enormous trunk of a pine tree. A heavy branch overhung the top, as if the ancient living pine sought to wrap a comforting arm about its deceased brethren. A short distance away, a squat retaining wall divided the evergreen forest from the landscaped yard. The craftsman-style house topped a rise overlooking the pristine waters of Echo Lake, California.

She negotiated the thicket, stepping with care so none of the thorny branches tangled about her legs. The bench creaked beneath her weight; she sat facing north toward Asgard. With great care, she set down the rune chest made from a block of ash cut from Yggdrasil, the World Tree. She ran her fingers across the smooth grain. Centuries ago, a maternal ancestress of Sylvie's had carved it using bone tools and polished it with her bare fingers. Of all her worldly possessions, it was the only artifact Sylvie had managed to rescue from her life in Phoenix, before the massacre that destroyed most of the Storm Pack. She cherished it above all other possessions. It connected her to the cosmos.

She turned the rune box's lid over, revealing an intricate, hand-carved tree on the interior. The tree's trunk was the vertical axis of a sun cross. The cover served as the board upon which she'd cast the runes, the sun cross the template. A rush of excitement usually thrummed through her as she removed the rough leather pouch. Tonight, she acted with a burdened heart as she unwound the rawhide cords at the top of the bag and dipped her fingers inside. She'd rather be anywhere than here, but time had run out.

It might be too late already.

Wednesday, June 15th: the night of the full moon. For the first time in thirty years, the independent and scattered wolf-shifter tribes would meet in Desolation Wilderness, located in the Sierra Nevada Mountains. Formally, the gathering was called the Conclave; casually, the moot. From the fire of the forge, alliances would be shaped or shattered. Destinies determined. It could —would—change the course of the world. On the night of the Mead Moon, the earth would pass between Sol, the goddess of the sun, and her brother Mani, the god of the moon. All skalds acknowledged a lunar eclipse was the harbinger of ill omens.

The oval stones within were smooth and hard, perpetually chilly to the touch. Twenty-four in total, each carved from the rib of an ice giant—the story was a saga in and of itself, but a tale for another time—and had a single rune carved on one side. She moved the stones with her fingers so they created a lively melody as they clicked together.

"When shadows swallow the moon, how will it affect the

moot?" Sylvie asked. She kept the question framed in her mind and stirred the bones. Swiftly, a stone landed squarely upon the pad of her middle finger and she extracted it. In keeping with a five-rune cast, she set it to the right side of the field, taking great care to place it as it had come to hand.

The ivory had the distinct yellowish hue of age. Despite the near-full moon, the overhanging branches of the ancient pine tree blocked most of the light. Even with her nocturnal vision, Sylvie squinted and struggled to make out the symbol. Ancient trees swayed in the wind, needles rustling. The gibbous moon cast bright beams through the eaves, illuminating the board.

"*Jera*—the harvest."

Her divination had captured an audience. The nearby trees murmured in approval. As a general rule, *Jera* brought glad tidings.

Sylvie released a thin sigh, a tinny sound. The knots in her gut eased just a little. She returned her hand to the bag and resumed stirring the bones. Again, with surprising swiftness, her fingers found the next rune stone. With a quick motion, she set it in the center position.

"*Ansuz*, Odin's Rune. Right at the heart of the matter. Why am I not surprised?" Sylvie cleared her throat.

Sylvie cast a wry glance toward the canopy of branches. "Tell me, trees, how many ravens do your branches shelter?"

The forest offered no answer.

She found and placed the third stone to the left. It landed facedown—converse—with the symbol hidden.

Her breath departed her body. Sylvie knew this piece. Even in the spattering of moonlight, the aged chunk of ivory had a deeper yellow patina than its companions. Its

edges were sharp and chipped, and a crack
ran through the center. She'd always
suspected it wasn't part of the original set.

Sylvie smacked her hands flat against
the tabletop, one to either side of the line
of three runes. Her control over her wolf
slipped a little; claws sprang from her
fingertips. White knuckled, she dug into
the rough wood, gouging deep scratches. Stinging pain shot
through her middle finger. With a gasp, she yanked her hand away
and turned it over. A splinter protruded from the pad.

The snap of a breaking branch punctured the night. The harsh,
unmistakable light of an electronic device disrupted the natural
darkness as trampling footsteps approached. Sylvie shot upright,
spinning to face the intruder. The artificial illumination assailed
her nocturnal vision, so she threw up her arm to shield her face.

"*¡Mierda!* Sylvie! Is that you?" Morena's tone was pitched high.
The girl aimed her phone like a flashlight. "Mother Frigg! You
scared the crap out of me!"

"Yes, it's me, and don't abuse Frigg's name." Sylvie snapped
the reprimand by rote. She shifted her claws to hands and
clutched at empty air as she strove to recover her composure.
Morena posed no threat. As a matter of fact, Sylvie loved
Morena as though the girl were her own daughter. Her greatest
regret was that she and Paul had never had children of
their own.

"Sorry. What da Hel are you doing out here?" *Oh clever child...*
using Hel, the Norse goddess of the dead, as a play on words.

"Please stop aiming that light at my face." Sylvie hid a smile.

"Sorry," Morena said, sounding like she meant it this time.

As Morena lowered the phone, Sylvie caught a glimpse of an
open chat application. The werewolf teenager pressed the screen
against her breast so only a faint halo of light escaped. She wore
sleep clothes: a tank top and shorts set. Her short ever-changing
hair was an unkempt mess. As of this morning, bright cobalt

streaks ran through her dark tresses, but by tomorrow that might change to whatever whim seized the girl.

"What are you doing up?" Morena asked.

"Isn't that supposed to be my question? More to the point, why are you wandering around outside in the middle of the night in your pajamas?"

"I couldn't sleep."

"I couldn't either. Who were you texting with?"

"I never said I was texting." Morena flushed. She had flawless brown skin, the product of an ethnic heritage of more Hispanic blood than Norse. Her features were foxlike, but her pedigree was one hundred percent pure wolf. Within the pack, Morena was omega, the lowest-ranked wolf-shifter member.

Sylvie crossed her arms. "What's the boy's name?"

"Are you doing a rune casting?" Morena developed a sudden, avid interest in the picnic table behind Sylvie.

"I was." Sylvie offered the reply with great care. She had not the slightest desire to resume the divination. Perhaps this disruption was for the best. It provided her with all the excuse she needed to declare the ritual invalid and to pack up the runes. She could always begin anew on the morrow.

"You haven't cast the runes since Paul died."

"Paul." Her voice cracked on her dead husband's name. As a point in fact, Sylvie hadn't performed a divination in far longer than that. It'd been a couple days before war broke out between the Storm Pack and Jake Barrett's hunters. Sylvie had failed to catch even a glimpse of the ensuing massacre... and she hadn't taken up the bones since.

Morena grimaced, a mixture of hurt and regret on her face. "I'm sorry. I didn't mean to—"

"Oh, sweetie, don't apologize. We honor the memory of those we loved by speaking well and often of them. You know Paul loved you like a father."

Despite her brave words, the dagger of grief pierced Sylvie's heart. All too often, something would happen and Sylvie thought to herself—*I must tell Paul.* But then she recalled: Paul was deceased—his soul gone on to Valhalla. Even that glad news tormented her because conflicted desire divided her heart. Though Sylvie longed to be reunited with her lifemate, her soul belonged to Freya. Upon her death, Sylvie had always believed she would join her goddess in Sessrúmnir.

"I loved him, too." Morena gulped for air. Tears shone in the girl's eyes. She turned her gaze toward the ground.

Profound dissonance resonated through the pack bond. Morena lacked the maturity to deal with her grief, and the devastating loss remained too recent for Sylvie. When Morena coughed to clear her throat and changed the subject, Sylvie exhaled in relief.

"You're still worrying about the lunar eclipse, aren't you?" Morena played with one of the gold piercings that studded her ears.

Sylvie pressed her lips together. The girl knew her far too well.

"I'm sorry I even pointed it out." Morena threw up her hands.

"Shush, you. I'd have noticed myself." Sylvie had lost a lot of sleep over the issue. She didn't like discussing such sensitive matters with the teenager, though. Morena had already lost too much for one so young: her parents, her older brother, and her best friend, Jasper. To burden her with this was unfair.

Fortunately, Morena lacked the patience to dwell. As easily as a bee flitting from one blossom to the next, she moved on. She gestured to the runes behind Sylvie.

"Can I watch?" Morena asked.

"I'm not sure that would be a good idea. I need to concentrate."

"Oh, c'mon, I can be quiet."

"I've yet to see proof." Sylvie snorted.

"How am I supposed to learn when you never let me watch?"

"Fine, I'll make you a deal. Tell me the boy's name, and I'll consider letting you watch."

"Who said there's a boy?" Morena adopted an expression of angelic innocence.

Sylvie stifled a sigh. It never ceased to amaze her how every girl child between the ages of twelve and twenty assumed the adult brain shriveled away to a dried-out husk. Oh, Morena was a damn good liar, but familiarity was a two-way street. Sylvie knew the girl's tells.

"If you prefer, I can have Victoria check your chat history. Of course, that would result in her reading all your messages going back who-knows-how-far. Or you can just cooperate and tell me the boy's name."

"You wouldn't dare!" Morena gaped.

"Try me." Sylvie crossed her arms over her chest.

"I don't get any privacy!" Morena stomped her foot.

"You're seventeen. Now tell me his name." She left the *or else* hanging.

"Gage..." Morena mumbled something else vaguely B-sounding that got muffled against her shoulder. She developed a sudden, intense interest in the half-moon tattoo on the inside of her wrist.

Wheels turning, Sylvie gave Morena her full attention. Gage... Now why did that name sound familiar? While it wasn't uncommon, Morena didn't have that many friends, especially male friends, in the area. The Storm Pack had been settled in California for less than a year. Morena had lost her entire family and left all her childhood companions behind.

"Gage who?"

Morena threw her hands up, working her fists. *"¡Córcholis!* He's just a guy I know. What's the big deal already?"

"You're the one making a big deal of it. Tell me the boy's last name, and I'll let it drop," Sylvie said with a severe frown.

Morena stared in open defiance. Her blush grew hotter. Sylvie indulged in veiled amusement as the girl worked through her options, including a look of intense curiosity shot at the runes. Of course, Morena retained every teenage girl's Fifth Amendment right—a sullen refusal to engage in self-incrimination, followed by the mandatory flounce and the associated door slam. By leaving, though, she'd deprive herself of the opportunity to learn more about rune casting, a subject of acute interest to the girl.

Oh, the dilemma.

Morena's mouth worked, and then she spat the name, "Gage Barrett."

Sylvie rocked on her heels. "You're chatting in the middle of the night with Jake Barrett's son?"

"It's not a big deal. Geez, both Sawyer and his dad are members of our pack." Morena jutted her chin. "I'm friends with JD, too."

"I guess it's not. I simply wasn't aware you'd connected with them." Sylvie adopted a reluctantly conceding tone, designed solely to put the teenager at ease. Deep down, she was troubled over the teenager's association with the Barrett twins. It seemed the members of the Storm Pack grew increasingly mired in relationships with the hunter family. Although the alliance benefited them, Sylvie wasn't sure the continued intimacy was a good thing. An advantageous marriage with one of Odin's sons could improve Morena's station... or it might spell her doom.

"Well, I have." Stiff with rebelliousness, Morena cocked her head. Fleeting disappointment crossed her foxlike face, leading Sylvie to wonder how much of the teenager's performance had been crafted solely for show?

Determined not to be outdone, certainly not by a child a quarter her age, she adopted a beatific smile. "Either one would make a fine mate." She met Morena's wide eyes and smirked. "*After* you turn eighteen and graduate from high school."

"I turn eighteen before I graduate," Morena said with plenty of sass, but then she grinned and stuck out her tongue.

Sylvie raised an eyebrow and crossed her arms over her chest, as immoveable as a mountain.

"Fine, but I'm keeping my options open."

"Oh? Aren't you cocky?" Sylvie clucked her tongue.

"I prefer... confident." Quick and easy, Morena grinned. "So can I watch? You promised."

She pursed her lips, pretending to give the matter long and

careful consideration. "Well, you might distract me from giving my full attention to the divination." Sylvie tapped her finger on the tabletop. "On the other hand, you do have years of study under your belt. It's an ideal opportunity to test your comprehension of the skaldic arts."

Besides, Sylvie *had* to complete the divination.

"Fine, you may join me—"

"Yes!" Morena punched the air with her fist.

"Come sit beside me." Sylvie assumed her seat and patted the bench.

Morena plopped down onto the space. "What now?"

"This is a five-rune casting. Tell me what you see." Sylvie nodded toward the stones already laid out on the table.

"What's the question?" Intent, Morena studied the rune spread.

"When shadows swallow the moon, how will it affect the moot?" Sylvie placed her finger beneath the rune to the far right. "Begin here."

"You want me to...?" The teenager squirmed on the bench.

"Go on. You've been studying for years. You're ready."

Morena stilled. The gust of her breath marked her resolve. "*Jera* means success. Good spirits."

"Excellent. How does its position in the past position affect the reading?"

Morena hesitated, gnawing her lower lip. "It's the end of the season or the close of the year. It's mostly a good sign but sometimes it's not. It can mean justice is delivered too, right?"

"Yes, it can. Now relate it to the moot."

"For the moot, I guess it could mean that all those months of planning will finally pay off when it happens."

"Good." Sylvie hummed and swept her hand to indicate the center stone.

"*Ansuz*, Odin's Rune. Reversed, it represents Loki," Morena declared without prompting. Slowly, the girl tilted her head, scrutinizing the bone. "Is that upright or reversed? It's cockeyed."

"If it is not one, then assume it denotes the other," Sylvie said. "Often, when Odin and Loki have their fingers in the pie, it is the same difference. Whatever the case, this is our present."

"Sure... that makes perfect sense." Morena shrugged. "So... *Ansuz* is knowledge, power, and communication. At the moot, we could be facing a test that's somehow associated with the lunar eclipse?"

"You're guessing." Sylvie chuckled. "Not bad, though. *Ansuz* is the rune of prophecy and revelation. When taken in context with regard to the question asked, the lunar eclipse becomes an omen."

"Victoria always says, 'If you look for omens, you'll find them.'"

"Victoria says many things—not all of it is correct."

Morena shivered with boundless excitement. "The third rune. Can I turn it over?"

"Go ahead." Full of misgiving, Sylvie tipped her chin. She already knew the name of the rune waiting to be revealed. Delaying only prolonged the inevitable. She braced herself while Morena flipped the rune over.

"*Thurisaz*—the thorn. Thor's rune," Morena proclaimed without the proper reverence the name was due.

Sylvie shuddered but strove to hide her reaction. The thorn heralded a terrible hazard. No one she loved was safe.

Blithely, the teenager continued. "Since it's the future, we should expect threats from people with power. At the moot, that probably means the alphas of other packs. Something chaotic is gonna happen..." The girl smiled wide. "But then something always does. This could be a good omen."

"It could be, but it's far more likely our luck is running out. You're forgetting—the rune was facedown." Sylvie tapped her fingernail against the wood plank beside the rune. "Our people are in danger. *Thurisaz* tells us to be wary of hidden evil or an enemy disguised as an ally. Put it with *Ansuz*. What does it mean?

Morena fidgeted, but remained silent.

"It means," Sylvie said, "that we should consider rescheduling the moot."

"Victoria's gonna be thrilled," Morena said in a distinctly humoring tone. "Okay, so what's next?"

"I draw another." Sudden weariness weighed on Sylvie; she felt her age plus a few centuries in her back and her legs. Her hand shook as she returned it to the pouch and resumed tumbling the stones.

Beside her, Morena gasped, starting to speak, but didn't.

"You have a question?" Sylvie asked in a whisper while she stirred the bones.

"How do you know when to draw one?" Morena also kept her volume low.

"It is a certainty deep in your gut. You just know." At that exact moment, she found the next pebble. Glossy and warmer than its brethren, it settled upon the pad of her finger, however, before she drew it, a second landed square in her palm. It burned her bare skin, as cold as winter. Startled, she grasped both ice and fire. For a moment, her thoughts went blank, and an awful sense of foreboding filled her.

"Sylvie, are you okay?" Morena squeezed Sylvie's elbow. The teenager's scent was laced with worry.

"Yes, I'm fine." Jarred from her trance, Sylvie hastened to extract her hand from the felt sack. She didn't want to jostle the stones—had one turned over? Did she correctly recall which had come to her first or had she mixed them up?

Gnawing her lower lip, Sylvie settled the matter by touch. She placed the warmer of the two rune stones in the nadir position, the point closest to her, on the sun cross. A pleased smile touched her lips, and she announced it with pleasure.

"*Sowilo*—the sun."

The final bone turned her blood to ice. Eager to be rid of the

thing, Sylvie slapped it to the field, off-center from the vertical axis, but close enough. There it sat in the pinnacle point, completing the sun cross.

"*Isa*—ice," Sylvie said in a thick voice. She saw a flash of a world without the sun: an unending blizzard—a hungry, howling wind. She shuddered.

Morena wedged her thumbnail between her upper teeth. Then, without prompting, she launched into a speculative interpretation.

"Okay, so *Sowilo* is near the issue. It's light, energy, and *victory*—" The girl flashed an ironic grin. Victoria's childhood nickname was Victory.

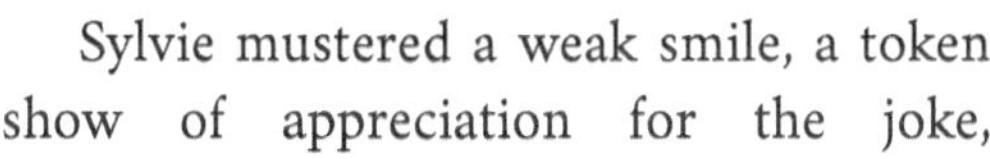

Sylvie mustered a weak smile, a token show of appreciation for the joke, however, she wasn't feeling it. She found herself unable to look away from *Isa*; she couldn't *see* the sun's rune for the terrible visions that flashed through her mind. Her lips were bone-dry as she spoke. "*Sowilo* is a positive sign, perhaps even a sign the challenges ahead will be overcome."

"See, you're worrying too much!"

"Am I?" Sylvie gazed into the innocent face of her foster daughter. She opened her mouth to offer an alternative explanation to the divination. Perhaps it was far simpler and more literal than that: the question pertained to the lunar eclipse, when the sun and the moon were separated by the earth. Her troubled gaze skipped to converse *Thurisaz*, harbinger of giants and monsters, and enemies who wore the false faces of friends.

"Not worrying enough?" Morena asked in a teeny-tiny voice.

Lastly, Sylvie considered *Isa*, the rune of stagnation. She shivered but nothing shook the vision of eternal winter. In a voice as grim as death, she said, "I must convince Victoria to cancel the moot."

Behind them, a twig broke beneath a man's footfall and a long shadow fell over the women. Sylvie twisted around and looked up. The man's silhouette loomed large, blocking out the moon.

CHAPTER 3

***Naudiz*: The Rune of Necessity**

HEADS BENT, Sylvie and Morena focused their attention on the rune stones arranged in a cross. Their low voices crackled with tension, and neither woman acknowledged Logan Koenig when he walked up behind them.

Few wolf-shifters took kindly to being caught unaware, so he blew out a gusty breath and crunched pine needles underfoot. Despite his heroic efforts, he went unnoticed. He opened his mouth to announce himself, but got caught on curiosity's hook. What were they discussing with such intensity? Cocking his head, Logan grabbed his balls through his cotton sweatpants. Only after he'd had a good scratch did he advance another pace closer, risking his hide if not his life.

"I must convince Victoria to cancel the moot," Sylvie swept the bones up and poured them into their leather pouch. "Or we are all doomed."

In astonishment, Logan rocked on his heels, breaking a branch beneath his bare feet. Both women jerked, releasing startled snarls. Yeah, *now* they heard him.

"Cancel the moot! Are you kidding? Victoria will have a fit." Normally, Logan didn't worry about upsetting people, but Victoria was pregnant with his sister. Technically, the unborn baby was his *half*-sister, a minor distinction that mattered, especially to him.

In unison, Sylvie and Morena rose and turned to face him. Snarling, Sylvie shifted her hands to claws. She glared, an entire murder of thrown knives aimed straight at his heart. Logan stepped back out of arm's reach.

"Asshole! Don't do that." Morena sprang forward and struck his shoulder.

"Oh. It's my fault you're oblivious?" Logan brought his arm up and blocked Morena's next blow; their forearms crossed. He'd trained in several martial arts disciplines, enough to judge. Morena's fighting style relied on speed and maneuverability. Her technique needed work, but it wasn't bad.

"Didn't anyone ever tell you it's rude to sneak up on people?" Morena came within a couple inches of looking him straight in the eye. No small feat since Logan stood well over six feet tall. His first and foremost impression of Morena had always been simple: the girl was a mouthy twerp. She annoyed him and amused him in turn, like the bratty little sister he'd never had. But she'd shot up what must be a full head-and-a-half since they'd first met.

"I couldn't have been more obvious if I'd walked in with a marching band," Logan fired back. In the periphery of his vision, he noted Sylvie bent over the picnic table, packing away the rune pouch.

"You're just pissed 'cause I caught you off guard."

"That's your fault too." Morena sneered, displaying a full swath of canines. Her eyes cast a golden glow across her fierce features. Somewhere along the way, the teenager had gone from being unable to shape change without the assistance of an adult to mastering a partial shift.

"Logan, did you need something?" Sylvie stepped between the two of them, acting in her customary role as housemother. Her inner turmoil showed through the cracks in her trademark composure. She clutched the ashwood rune box to her chest like a shield.

"Why do you want to cancel the moot?" Logan returned to the reason for his outburst with dogged determination. He wasn't sure whether Sylvie had dodged the question on purpose the first time he'd asked. The issue carried far too much importance to just let it drop.

"I performed a rune casting to discern how the lunar eclipse will affect the moot. The results were... unfavorable." Sylvie worried her lower lip. Her gaze strayed past him to the surrounding forest.

"Mercury's in retrograde, huh?" Logan subscribed to a broad philosophy of skepticism. Regardless, Sylvie's unease put him on edge. He pivoted, scanning the tranquil backyard for a discernable threat. The pool was dark and placid.

"You mock what you don't understand." Sylvie frowned.

"It's part of Logan's charm," Morena quipped with a smirk.

"Oh, c'mon. I mock everything. Understanding isn't required." Logan flashed a toothy grin, trying to coax a smile from her.

An indeterminate pause ensued. The proverbial chirp of crickets filled the air. Sylvie volunteered nothing further; she stood with her arms crossed, probably waiting for an apology. Logan assessed the skald's stern front—she wasn't going to budge. He cast an exasperated glance heavenward. Some people had no sense of humor.

"Look, I'm sorry. Tell me why? Maybe I can help?"

"It is difficult to expound upon the esoteric, especially to a novice." Sylvie wore formidable armor of disapproval and fore-boding. Translation: she didn't want to explain herself, especially to him.

Morena snickered. "That means you're ignorant."

"Yeah, I know what it means." Logan gnashed his teeth because his hands were tied. If the skald refused to provide solid reasons for her sudden opposition to the Conclave, he couldn't counter them. "Look, can you dumb it down for me? Use small words? Vic does it all the time."

Sylvie pursed her lips. "Perhaps—"

A rifle blast shattered the quiet. The boom resounded and then faded. The shot came from a half-mile off, originating from the vicinity of Sawyer Barrett's camp. The lake house topped the highest knoll in the immediate vicinity; the hunter's camp capped a lower rise to the north.

Ominous quiet descended. Terrible tension gripped Logan. In his gut, *he knew...* something wasn't right. Sylvie and Morena must've sensed the strangeness, too, because neither woman moved nor spoke. They waited, heads cocked, listening. Seconds dragged past like hours.

The rational explanation was that the hunter had shot a deer. The thing was, Sawyer preferred to hunt with a bow. Maybe paranoia was getting the better of him, but the pack had powerful enemies: *Den Valgte.* The last time they'd had a run-in with the shamanic shape changers, they'd almost lost. None of the pack's young had been present then, either. They had other enemies, too —the Necromancer and his undead army. Though, Logan considered it unlikely the Necromancer would launch an attack against the lake house.

Sylvie broke the brittle silence. "Morena, call Sawyer."

"Okay." Morena danced her fingers across the screen of her phone. She held it aloft so they could hear the continuous ringing. When it went to a prerecorded voicemail greeting, she hung up and said, "He's not answering."

"There's no reception out there." Irritation swept through Logan. He halfway suspected the hunter had built his camp outside of the mobile phone coverage area on purpose.

"I thought those newfangled satellite phones you passed out were supposed to solve that problem?" Sylvie asked.

"Newfangled." Morena snickered against her hand.

"They are," Logan muttered. "I just didn't give one to Sawyer."

"Oh, for the love of—" Sylvie released a great huff. "If you had an idea, it would die of loneliness."

"Hey!" Logan ducked his head. The insult stung but yeah, he sorta had that coming... As his father had always said, "Stupid is as stupid does."

"Here comes Sophia and the pups," Morena said.

On cue, the four gray wolves—Sophia and her three adolescent offspring—charged onto the pool deck. The French doors to the kitchen got left open all the time to accommodate the coming and going of the pack's nonshifter members. It'd reached the point where Logan was considering installing an extra-large doggie door. The little wolf family headed straight for Morena. She greeted them with open arms, offering verbal and physical reassurance.

"Victoria should be out here," Sylvie said from the side of her mouth.

"I know." Logan's gut turned leaden.

"So what are we gonna do now, Einstein?" Morena asked.

"Uhh..." Logan screwed up his face, wrestling with indecision. Should he howl to inquire as to Sawyer's status? Howling was the wolf thing to do, but the hunter was neither wolf-shifter nor wolf-kin. He might not even understand the language of lupines. Or maybe their enemies approached through the forest. Calling out would alert the enemy to the pack's presence and location.

Where the hell was Victoria when he needed her? Their petite alpha had "danger junkie" encoded in her DNA. Even in the unlikely event that she'd slept through the gunshot, the turmoil roiling through the pack bond would've pulled her from a coma. Only one explanation made sense for her continued absence—she hadn't come because she wasn't able.

"What should we do, oh fearless leader?" Sylvie looked straight at Logan.

"Wow, I didn't know you understood sarcasm." Logan refused

to drop his gaze, but it made hiding the uncertainty tearing him apart even more difficult.

"You'd be shocked at what I understand," Sylvie said. No false modesty there—and no respect.

"Guys, please," Morena pleaded. "Act like adults."

"Yeah, right." Logan bit his tongue. The words hurt worse than the wound.

Cold sweat trickled down his back. In Victoria's absence, the burden of leadership landed on Logan's shoulders. For foxes' sake, both women looked to *him* for answers. Hell, the whole pack had eyes on him, their acting-alpha in Victoria's absence. Their expectation weighed a metric ton. He didn't know what to say or do. He possessed no skill for leadership, only a talent for knee-jerk reactions that led to feats of sublime stupidity. His specialty. He stood at a total loss, asking himself: What would Victoria do?

"I can't sense Victoria within the pack bond. Can you?" Sylvie pitched the question to him alone. She exerted a rock-steady presence within the dynamic. Abruptly, Logan got why Victoria relied on the older woman so much. Sylvie's strength served as their foundation.

"I don't know. I'll try." Drawing a deep breath, Logan tried to center himself. He'd observed Victoria extend her awareness via mystical mumbo-jumbo across great distances to locate other members of the pack. Unfortunately, seeing wasn't the same as doing. Logan cast his conscious far and wide, searching for Victoria. He grappled with the psychic connection, struggling to get a handle on it, but the damn thing proved as slippery as a serpent. His failure to reach her didn't necessarily mean anything. The spiritual connection worked well in proximity and only then as a means of empathetic communication. In the purest sense of poetic irony, Victoria eluded all his attempts to pin her down... Just like in real life.

Trouble, though, he found in spades. A presence manifested within the bond—primal, predatory... danger on the prowl. His skin crawled but he couldn't quite get a handle on the source.

"What the...?"

"That's Sawyer. He's hunting something. Someone," Morena announced with confidence that barred argument.

"Right. Sawyer," Logan scoffed in raw disgust. Damn it, he disliked admitting to himself that the hunter was the source of his unease. And he hated finding out Morena shared a close-enough connection with the hunter to recognize his psychic signature across such a distance. It made his blood boil with resentment. A challenge curled in his throat. His wolf objected to the merest suggestion of Sawyer Barrett having an influence over the girl.

Sylvie pinned Logan with one of her signature stares. "Sawyer is a member of this pack."

"All I meant is Forrest Gump can take care of himself. I'll go check on him once we're squared away." Logan struggled with even the faintest praise. The words left a sour taste in his mouth.

"Right." Sylvie's glaring sarcasm delivered a much-needed boot to his posterior.

"From here on out, we're going to assume our territory is under attack until it's proven otherwise. Sylvie, check on Vic. I'm worried something has happened to her." Logan cast a glance toward the house. He advanced an involuntary pace before he stopped himself.

Sylvie tipped her chin in a nod. She frowned, clearly worried, but she probably chose to remain quiet for Morena's sake.

"Morena, call the sheriff's department and tell my uncle we need help," Logan said.

"Five by five." Morena threw out Logan's catch phrase. Tongue in cheek, she saluted, touching her fingertips to her temple. "I'll call Cali, too."

"That's a good idea," Logan said. The hunters had a cabin about ten minutes from the lake house, whereas the sheriff faced a thirty-minute trip from either his office or residence.

"I know." Morena frowned, and off she went without so much as a smart-ass remark. Logan took *that* as a sign the situation was serious.

"When I check on Victoria... if she's asleep, I'll wake her up and we'll retreat into Desolation Wilderness. If she's not..." Sylvie's stern face pinched at the possibility. "We'll go without her. If this is *Den Valgte*, we have the home team advantage. They won't know the terrain."

Logan grinned. *Ah, hell...* Both women had far more experience in dealing with emergencies than him. During the short but vicious wolf-hunter war, they spent months on the run, surviving by their wits and will.

"Vic can take care of herself." Logan fisted his hands. There must be a good half-dozen reasons Vic was incommunicado. His foremost instinct drove him to go check on her himself, even though Sylvie was more than competent. It galled him to no end that he'd gotten stuck with the odious task of following up on Sawyer.

The scald leveled a penetrating stare. "*I* don't need convincing, young man."

A mile distant, a rifle volley rang out through the night, and a barrage of weapons fired back. In unison, Sylvie and Logan pivoted northeast to face the racket.

"That was farther off than the first shot," Logan said. "He's leading them away from the lake house."

"Well, that answers that. We're under attack. Sawyer is out there alone." Sylvie turned an expectant glance on Logan.

He gnashed his teeth and threw up his hands in defeat. "Fine. I'll go save the jackass."

CHAPTER 4

Sisters Wyrd
Urðr: **The Past**
Verðandi: **The Present**
Skuld: **The Future**

THE DRAGON STAYED three feet ahead of the woman with the butterfly net. Undaunted, Victoria Storm chased through the freezing fog after the silhouette that floated low in the sky. Each beat of its massive wings produced the distinctive thwack of wind striking membranes. The beast banked left, and so she followed, plunging headlong down the hillside, dodging the spindly pine trees that leapt into her path with their arms spread wide to catch her.

At the bottom of the slope, the dragon hovered in place like a giant hummingbird. The resulting downdraft pummeled the earth. Victoria skidded to a halt beneath the drake. She pressed her elbows to her aching sides and gripped the post of the net so tightly the wood cut into her palms. Gritting her teeth, she fumed.

Damn, she hated how pregnancy sapped her strength and stamina. And what had she been thinking, bringing a tiny net on a dragon hunt? To catch him, she needed a much larger net! Giving up wasn't an option. She *had* to wrangle him or they'd be stuck here forever—

"Help! Please help!"

A high-pitched voice ripped her straight from her inane dream. A chilly draft nipped at her skin. She shivered and crossed her arms over her chest. Her fingers pressed against the soft cotton of the tank top she'd worn to bed. Beneath her bare feet, the earth was damp, and the familiar scents of the wilderness surrounded her. Right now, she *should* be at home in bed... except her darkened room was gone. In perspective, awakening from a sleepwalker's trance in the woods was weird but not *that* weird. As a rule, she attracted supernatural strangeness ranging from restless spirits to enigmatic gods. A one-woman trouble magnet—she ought to have her own bumper stickers.

The wind gusted, and a gnarly old tree swayed, reaching for her with thorny fingers. Hastily, she backed away from it. Her throat ached with thirst. She cleared it—so loud in the quiet—and tested her voice.

"I've a feeling we're not in Kansas anymore..." She croaked and pressed her lips together in thin amusement. She rubbed the sleep from her eyes, clearing the cobwebs of dreams. Now, what was it that'd woken her up? A voice.... She scanned the darkness, calling on her wolf's nocturnal vision.

"Help me!"

There! The boy's lonely shout echoed through the night. Her heart jolted; her blood raced in her veins. She sprinted toward the child's call. A crooked tree root grabbed her foot. She stumbled. Past her sweeping vision, the tall, twisted figures of thin men lurked in the gloomy fog. An army surrounded her; a menacing threat to her, her unborn child, and the boy who'd called for help.

She landed on her hands and knees. Unbidden, her wolf surged to the surface and propelled her through a partial shift.

With a pulverizing crunch, the bones broke and reformed while sinew and cartilage played tug-o-war beneath her skin where snow-white fur erupted.

A ferocious growl reverberated in her throat. She parted her jaws wide to accommodate the erupting canines and faced the nearest of the unnaturally slender creatures. Her eyes cast a glow of golden radiance that cut through the mist and better revealed the true nature of her sinister opponent—*a tree*. And not just any tree but a scraggly, drought-beaten pine, to be precise. Oh, of all the idiotic things! No army surrounded her, only a forest. Through the dense fog that engulfed the wooded valley, thick stands of evergreen trees thrust from the rocky mountainside like jagged spears.

Victoria released a mighty huff of disgust and collapsed into her human form. Fortunately, she'd come to her senses before she destroyed her clothing with a full transformation. So no real damage had been done, other than to her ego. Her ears burned to imagine what other members of her pack—Logan and Morena in particular—would say. Nothing flattering for sure.

Gathering herself and her wounded dignity, she rose and brushed herself off. Dew dampened the bare skin of her arms and made her cotton pajamas cling to her. Dead pine needles cushioned her bare feet. Broken, the spines released a toasted woody aroma that wafted upward to fill her nostrils. When she exhaled, her hot breath coalesced as thin streams of steam.

"Hello?" Victoria called out and then paused to listen. The boy didn't answer. Had she imagined that, too? To be on the safe side, she called out twice more.

Still no response.

To get her bearings, she turned in a tight circle and scanned her surroundings—trees in the mist but no distinctive landmarks. Next, she tilted back her head to look up. Low in the starry night sky, the gibbous moon shone bright, casting a fiery halo that filtered through the mist as stray beams and glancing shadows. To the east, a rosy haze on the horizon suggested the sun would rise in an hour. She breathed deep and inhaled the familiar scents of the pristine wilderness. The vast reservoir of primordial magic that lay dormant within the land affirmed her suspicions. She was somewhere in Desolation Wilderness.

Good—the territory belonged to her and her pack.

Not good—she tasted spiritual dissonance all around.

Her stomach turned leaden. Out in the cloying miasma, she sensed a great many lost souls wandering without direction or purpose. She suspected she'd somehow strayed into the realm of the restless dead. As a Valkyrie and a priestess of Freya—Victoria winced and corrected herself—*former* priestess of Freya, she possessed the ability to cross the veil from the material world to the spiritual. The world of the undead had a great many names, but to Victoria, like her mother before her, these were the Shadowlands.

Using the moon as her compass, Victoria took the easy route and headed south since she didn't know her exact location... or the path home. Even if she missed her house on Echo Lake, sooner or later south would bring her to civilization: the town of Sierra Pines or Broken Bend. Failing those, U.S. Route 50 bisected the rugged mountains, running through the range from Sacramento to Lake Tahoe. Eventually, she would find a place where the veil thinned, easing the difficulty of transitioning from the world of the dead to the living.

"Help!" The boy's plea, pitched high with distress, reverberated through the fog surrounding her.

Victoria halted. She adopted a defensive stance and searched the mist for hidden threats. At five months pregnant, she was vulnerable. She would do anything she could to help the boy, but she also had to consider the welfare of herself and her daughter. The lost child could be exactly what he seemed, or it might be a trap. In the Shadowlands, not everything was as it appeared.

"Can you hear me? I need help. I'm lost!"

"Where are you?" Her heart rose in her throat because the boy's voice sounded familiar. A niggling suspicion took root in her mind—she knew him from somewhere... Acting on her hunch, she added, "My name's Victoria. What's yours?"

"Victoria?" The child's voice lilted with surprise and recognition. "It's me—"

"Michael!" Victoria finished, speaking in unison with him.

Michael Allen Fraiser—a six-year-old boy whose life she'd saved months before in Albuquerque. She hadn't known him well or long, but the child had carved out a special place in her heart. During one of the bleakest times in her life, rescuing Michael had marked a rare and cherished success.

Together, they were silent. Simultaneously, they called each other's names again. Searching for a clue, Victoria inhaled through her mouth in hopes of catching the boy's scent. The olfactory brew, however, consisted entirely of natural wilderness creatures: skunk and deer, bear and raccoon. No boy.

"Help! It's coming for me!" Michael shrieked, a cry of terror that pierced Victoria's soul until her blood ran cold. It went on and on, longer than humanly possible.

Then it cut off.

"Michael!" A chill ran down her spine. She forgot caution.

Instinct overrode reason. Victoria launched into a headlong run through the fog. Her heart hammered within her chest, pounding with such force it threatened to punch through her breast. The mist concealed everything right up until the moment she collided with a solid object. She smacked her face, arm, and belly against the pole. The collision knocked her off her feet.

She wavered on the edge of consciousness. Once the world stopped spinning, she lifted her head. The motion sent lancing pain through her neck and shoulder. Groaning, she curled into a ball, gritted her teeth, and rode it out. In general, werewolves healed faster than most people. Only a few exceptional injuries defied their augmented regeneration—those inflicted by silver, the claws and fangs of supernatural creatures, or magical weapons.

Belatedly, she came fully to her senses and remembered her

unborn child. Gingerly, Victoria pressed her hands flat against her abdomen and concentrated her healing magic inward. To her immense relief, she found no injuries that endangered her daughter. Self-recrimination ate at her. Fervently, she vowed not to repeat the mistake. No more reckless or irrational behavior. It had gotten her nowhere and endangered her health as well as her baby.

Time to get smart.

She sat up, cross-legged on the frozen ground. Michael no longer called to her from somewhere within the fog. Victoria shouted his name. Only silence and darkness answered. The mist formed a canopy which blocked the moonbeams completely. It obscured her extended arm so she couldn't even make out her own hand in front of her face.

Concentrating, Victoria crafted a spell and extended her psychic awareness. As the alpha, she had mystical connections to people and places at her disposal. First, she turned to her wolf pack, but they weren't there. She didn't detect even a trace of their presence... which meant they were far away, dead, or she truly was beyond the veil. Alarm jolted her, but she surpassed it, clinging to hope. Next, she reached for the wild magic that resided within the land that made up her territory. Desolation Wilderness, however, proved equally elusive.

She was alone, without access to any magic other than her own. Except...

She narrowed her eyes in displeasure. She had another option open to her. As a Valkyrie, Victoria owed her allegiance to Odin, King of the Aesir, the All Father. Sometimes life—and the gods— had a cruel sense of humor. She also knew Odin in his mortal guise of Jake Barrett, the notorious Hunter King. He also happened to be Michael's adopted father... *and* the father of Victoria's murdered lover, Daniel, *and* a member of her pack. And a man she considered squarely in her doghouse.

The thought of praying to Jake hurt her pride, but Vitoria

ruthlessly sacrificed ego to Odin—a clean slice right across conceit's jugular. It sucked but it had to be done.

"Hey, Jake, are you there?" Spoken aloud, her voice sounded strange and strangled to her own ears.

"Victoria? What's up? I thought you were giving me the silent treatment." Jake answered without delay. His gravelly baritone conveyed concern and sarcasm in equal measure.

To her surprise, she heard him in both her mind and aloud. She'd expected to reach him via telepathy. Drawing a quick breath, she talked fast, "I'm making an exception for this. It's urgent. Is Michael okay? Is he safe?"

"Hold on." A loud thud and distinct footsteps followed. More sounds emanating from within the fog. Thoroughly disturbing, even downright creepy, until Victoria squeezed her eyes shut and pretended they were on the phone.

Following a short delay, a door creaked and Jake said, "Michael's fine. He's asleep in his bed."

"Oh, thank... Zeus." She fluttered her hands in relief.

He chuckled. "You're more pissed than I thought if you're leaving me for that pompous prick."

"I'm angry." The simple admission shocked her to the core. Of all the unremitting gall... Her ire exceeded her instinct for self-preservation. What right did *she*, a mere mortal, have to reproach a god? But then, this was Jake, too.

"Victoria, we'll have this talk, you and I. This isn't the right time."

"No. No, it's not. You're right." She heaved a sigh of frustration. "If we're being blunt and honest, the only reason I'm even talking to you is because I was worried about Michael."

"I believe you. Now tell me where you are."

"I'm lost."

"Lost where?"

"I don't know!" Victoria gestured, a wild sweep of her arms. "If I knew where, I wouldn't be lost."

He snorted. "Let me rephrase. Describe your surroundings. Better yet, give me a mental picture."

"I'm in a forest. The species of trees and the terrain are right for the Sierra Nevadas. When I first woke up, I assumed I'd been sleepwalking and was a mile or two from home, but then I suspected I'd crossed over into the Shadowlands...." She hesitated. Doubt robbed her certainty. A sneaking fear whispered that she'd strayed too far... Gotten lost *in between* and wound up someplace far worse.

"Victoria, there's no place in the Nine Worlds I haven't visited in my travels. There's nowhere I can't find you." Jake projected an aura of paternal protectiveness which washed over Victoria, soothing the worst of her fear.

Tension eased from her shoulders. She exhaled and concentrated on drawing the surrounding landscape in her head. After an indeterminate wait, she asked, "Is it working? What do you see?"

"I see fog."

"Yeah, there's a lot of that. Unfortunately. I suspect I'm trapped in the veil between the physical world and the spiritual, though I have no clue how or why I came to be here."

"Waking visions are a hazard of close association with me."

"Great. Another thing to thank you for."

Jake stayed silent long enough that Victoria succumbed to gnawing her lower lip. Anxiety needled her composure. She fretted. Up until a few days ago, she'd been a priestess of Freya, the Norse goddess of war and love. Victoria's stubborn pride had cost her that position and taught her a harsh lesson on the dangers of defying the gods. Jake had been good to her, but he could easily choose to take offense to her brashness. Odin wasn't a kindly king renowned for his mercy or tolerance. He demanded courage and valor from his followers...

Her slightest inclination to grovel dissipated. Victoria sealed her lips and straightened her spine. Beg? Apologize? She bared her teeth and snarled. No. *Hel, no.* He'd wronged her. The dishonor was his. She hadn't asked for his help. She'd wander through this fog-ridden land for the rest of eternity before she'd crawl.

"Valkyries don't crawl." Jake's chuckle rumbled through the forest about her, shook the trees, and quaked the earth. "I'm sending my ravens to search for you. It may take a while. I'll be offline while I'm in communion with them."

Stunned, Victoria felt her lips part. "Did you just say 'offline'?"

He hesitated and then sighed. "Hazard of having teenagers... Let's start over. From here on out, I'll be unavailable. Upon my return, you'll receive an oblique and obstructive answer."

"Better." A quick grin seized her lips before she stopped it. Laughter strangled her and love swelled her heart. Damn it. No matter how mad she might be, she adored the surly old fart... Him and his impossibly contrary sons.

"Hang tight, kid. Help is on its way."

"What am I supposed to do?" Victoria's nature wasn't geared to inactivity. As sure as cats were contrary, she had to *do* something.

"Try to figure out the meaning of the vision."

"Gee, thanks. I thought we established that's a hazard of—" Victoria bit off the complaint, sensing he'd severed communication on his end. It came with the abruptness of an old rotary phone being slammed down, an effect too vivid to be anything other than deliberate.

"Men..." Grumbling, she rose to her feet, keeping her movements slow and cautious. The worst of her injuries from the collision with the tree had healed, but soreness lingered in her neck and shoulders. She preferred not to take another tumble.

Turning in a slow circle, Victoria looked around. The fog remained so dense that even the outlines of the trees she knew must be there remained obscured. For an indecisive moment, she pondered the wisdom of wandering. Rule of thumb said she should stay put, however, she wasn't going to learn anything useful sitting on her thumbs. Besides, if Jake's ravens could find her here, they could find her anywhere.

With a satisfied nod, she reached the decision that suited her desire, neatly rationalized and worry-free. For lack of a better option, she chose a direction at random and she struck out again with measured steps, her arms held out in front of her. The ground sloped gently downward, and she covered at least a quarter mile.

The fog gradually thinned but the woods grew thicker. Tree trunks crowded closer together as though the army of the forest had closed ranks to block her path. Like a legion of foot soldiers, bushes and bramble filled up the spaces between.

Victoria forged on, raising her arms to shield her face from the thorny briar. As she pushed through a gnarly patch, something strong and sticky snagged her fingers. She yanked to free her arm but the binding held, and she succeeded only in wrenching her shoulder. She bit back a pained cry and channeled her discomfort, fuel for the forge of her will.

Sweaty and foul-tempered, covered in pine needles and sap, Victoria turned her head and narrowed her eyes, studying the silvery thread caught on her hand. The filament led upward, merging into a lustrous braid. A vast canopy hung suspended from the trees and blocked the sky. Sheer drapes descended to the earth, surrounding her on all sides.

Spider webs.

CHAPTER 5

***Huginn* and *Muninn*:**
Thought and Memory

VICTORIA YANKED on the sticky strand stuck to her fingers. It stretched and clung but didn't break. She pulled a face in distaste. "I swear, if this sort of shit keeps happening to me, I'm going to turn into Sawyer and start sleeping with knives." And *that* would mark her descent to a whole new level of paranoia...

Great, now she was talking to herself, too.

"Mother of all..." Victoria clenched her hands and then flicked them open. She transformed her hands to claws—needle-sharp points erupted from her fingertips and snow-white fur burst across her skin. She sliced through the spider silk with the sharp edge of her nail. Freeing her hand didn't even begin to solve her bigger problem, which was the prison built of spider webs. The tapestry filtered the faint light, casting a ghostly glow into the atmosphere. It tasted thin and watery and somewhat sour, like skim milk past its freshness date.

"Victoria Storm, today you will be judged." The female voice emanated from overhead, promising a grim verdict before the charges was even announced.

"Who said that?" Victoria jerked her head back so fast she gave herself whiplash. She threw up her claws in reflexive defense against the threat.

Movement drew her attention straight to three tarantula-sized spiders perched on a crystalized web that crackled with potent magic. At a glance, she identified them as the Norns, the Norse goddesses of fate. Each of them embodied an aspect of time: *Urðr*—the past, *Verðandi*—the present, and *Skuld*—the future.

"We are the Sisters Wyrd," Verðandi said in a voice vibrant with youth. The fist-sized spider was trim and sleek, covered in glossy, sable hairs. Attractive, even, so far as eight-legged creepy-crawly critters went.

"I know who you are," Victoria said in a snappish tone. Then she winced, regretting her rudeness. Off the top of her head, she couldn't name a trio of deities she wanted to see less, especially since the Norns had cursed her with an undesirable destiny. As she'd just lectured herself a short time ago, however, she couldn't afford to go around offending gods... or goddesses.

"Then why did you ask?" Urðr uttered a harsh croak. Her shriveled head and body were the color of old milk chocolate, cracked and chalky. One of her rear legs was bent and stuck out at an unnatural angle.

"Because—" Victoria stopped herself. Self-recrimination lectured in the back of her mind. Not three seconds after she cautioned herself, here she was about to mouth off. Better not to say anything, to keep her mouth shut, and listen.

"You are wise to be fearful." Verðandi nodded with a sad smile.

"She cringed like a cowardly cur." Urðr pointed with a crooked limb.

"Our verdict will determine whether you live or die," Skuld said in a voice both ancient and arcane. She was the largest of the three spiders, slick and ebony, with thick, bushy legs.

"What are you accusing me of? I demand you list the charges against me!" An icy bolt lanced through Victoria. She bristled and tensed to defend herself, but her limbs refused to obey. A raw cry of frustration tore from her.

"Don't struggle. You'll only hurt yourself more." A fourth, previously unknown woman spoke from close behind Victoria. She had a low, sultry voice designed for crooning blues lyrics in a smoky club.

"Let me go." Victoria resisted with all her strength, but whatever magic held her paralyzed proved too powerful. Worse, the harder she struggled, the tighter it got. Her chest ached under the constriction, and she labored for each breath.

"Grimhild, you're hurting her." Verðandi frowned, a sharp reprimand.

"Then grant me permission to end her suffering, my goddess." Grimhild chuckled and walked around Victoria. The woman was tall and statuesque with burgundy hair. She had pale blue eyes and hawkish features. Ageless beauty as sharp and brilliant as a diamond. She had a red leather clutch purse on her shoulder and carried an orange and white plastic bottle labeled "Diet Water".

"Are you kidding me?" Victoria damn near swallowed her tongue trying not to shout. With an effort, she stopped fighting physically and summoned her personal magic. But even that did no good. The pressure built until a pained whimper escaped her, and she feared for her baby.

"Grimhild, you will cease." Skuld dropped from the web and descended on a long line of white silk toward Victoria's head.

"Oh, very well." Grimhild huffed. Her water bottle swished as she took a pull off the spout.

The crushing pressure about Victoria eased, and she breathed easier again. Concentrating, she focused her attention on Grimhild. Who the hell was this woman? Ancient Norse literature made multiple mentions of a *seiðr* named Grimhild. From what little she recalled, they'd cast the meddling mother-in-law mold from Grimhild. This couldn't possibly be the same witch. Could it? She'd be centuries old. Nothing about the modern woman, from her bright-yellow halter top to her red 'n' blue elephant-print palazzo pants fit with Victoria's mental concept of what an ancient sorceress should look like. All else aside, the *seiðr's* attire was a completely impractical choice to wear in the middle of the wilderness.

"Where's your broom?" Victoria strained her vision trying to look up. Her eyeballs ached and watered. Nothing compared to how her skin crawled when Verðandi and Urðr dropped lines of silk from their spinners and descended, hanging over Victoria's head.

"Excuse me?" Grimhild sucked in her cheeks and pursed her lips.

"The broom you rode in on. I figure you didn't hike in on those stiletto heels," Victoria said with dripping sarcasm.

"Actually, I ride a Dyson. Now shut up!" Grimhild snapped her fingers. "I was kind enough to allow you to speak. That privilege is now rescinded."

Alarmed, Victoria tried to reply but only mustered a muffled noise. Her lips pressed together so tightly she feared they'd been sealed permanently. She wanted to kick herself. Stupid! Why hadn't she kept her damn mouth shut?

Skuld swept her rear legs in a scissor slice, severing the silk that supported herself. She plunked down on Victoria's shoulder. The big black spider drove her sharp hooks through cotton and skin.

Needle-sharp slivers of pain pierced Victoria, setting her nerves on fire. A snarl built in Victoria's throat but the *seiðr's* spell silenced her. Her sense of helplessness and frustration mounted until she feared for her sanity. She wanted to shout, *"Get off! Get off! Get off!"*

"Now—" Skuld began but piercing avian shrieks cut her off.

The Norns and Grimhild turned their attention skyward. Rawboned ravens descended out of the fog in an enormous unkindness. Countless swift night fliers darted here and there.

The night resounded with their raucous cries—the air shook and the spider webs trembled.

A pair of swift, eagle-sized ravens snagged ahold of a low-hanging branch with their talons. They clung to it, flapping wildly. Their lion-like roars drowned out the rest of the flock. Finally, the birds calmed and looked on with shiny gazes brimming with alien intelligence.

"Huginn and Muninn." Awe edged Grimhild's regard—the first crack to split her glacial facade.

Victoria's spirits lifted but only slightly. Jake had kept his promise. The pair of giant ravens served Odin. Every day, or so it was said, they flew all over the world and gathered information which they then returned to their master. She took care not to let her hopes rise too high.

For a long while, no one spoke.

Then, Verðandi said, "This is an omen."

"Bah, balderdash! Odin sent his hasty-witted harpies to frighten you, little sister." Venom gathered on the tips of Urðr's fangs until the fat droplets plopped to the ground.

"Huginn and Muninn only appear at truly momentous moments in history. Their task is to observe and report what they witness to Odin," Verðandi said in a stern tone.

"Our verdict today will have lasting and pervasive consequences. Victoria Storm's life or death will affect what is to come." Skuld handed down the pronouncement as the final word on the subject. End of discussion.

Urðr issued a rattling hiss.

Frozen in her magical prison, Victoria broke into a cold sweat as the implications sank in. Fear swirled in her gut like a sickness. The Norns intended to act as her judge, jury, and executioner, and now she couldn't even speak in her own defense. She directed a silent plea to Huginn and Muninn, hoping they would hear her.

The ravens remained silent and still.

"Come, sisters, you will join me so we may inspect the child." Skuld beckoned to Verðandi and Urðr.

The spiders dropped off their web and descended on threads. In spite of their sizes, they moved with surprising speed. One plunked atop Victoria's head and wriggled through her hair. The other latched onto her back and crawled beneath her tank top. Hairy legs writhed against the small of her back. The sensation filled her with revulsion.

A silent scream built within Victoria. Her composure unraveled. She prayed fervently to Odin, begging for his help, but Jake didn't answer.

"I can hear what you're thinking, Victoria," Grimhild said with a cruel smile. "Has the All Father abandoned you just like Freya? You can hardly blame them now that you're swag-bellied with your bastard child."

Unable to reply, Victoria forged her hatred into a spearhead and thrust it at the witch. She immersed her humanity in her wolf, allowing her primal nature to reign in the hopes of hiding her thoughts.

"The babe is a wild card," Verðandi said from her roost on Victoria's head.

"The babe will be as powerful as her brothers." Skuld clung to Victoria's top and climbed down to her belly.

Brothers—as in plural? Curiosity pricked Victoria even as she fought against the rising tide of fear. The Norns had already cursed mother and child. Their words were burned indelibly into Victoria's memory: *"Your daughter will be taken from you on the eve of her third birthday. The one you trust most, a member of your own pack, will give the child over to your greatest enemy."*

Grimhild leaned closer and whispered into Victoria's ear. Her breath reeked of spearmint. "Perhaps the Hanged God desires your end. After all, you're fated to free Fenrir, the great beast who will destroy him. Have you considered that?"

Victoria calmed. Clarity coalesced out the seething cauldron of her mind. She focused on Grimhild, crafting a mental smirk. *Fuck off, you nasty hedge witch. If Jake wanted me dead, he'd kill me himself.*

"Hedge witch!" Grimhild jerked her face back. "Do you know who I am?"

No, and I don't care. Victoria suspected Grimhild intended to illuminate her anyway. When Verðandi stuck one of her hairy spider feet inside Victoria's ear, it took everything she had not to erupt into a senseless, silent scream.

"*I* am the Queen of Burgundy and Ljosalfheim." The witch's gaze cut through Victoria like a scythe, piercing her soul. "I am the most accomplished practitioner of *seidre*. Mother and high priestess of the *iviðia*—"

Victoria leapt to the quick connection. *The troll women in the Ironwoods?*

Grimhild narrowed her eyes. Her face set to a hard mask. "Troll women—an unflattering kenning. We, *iviðia*, have served the Norns faithfully for centuries and the goddesses honor our loyalty. The Ironwood coven is charged with guardianship of the wolf-shifter bloodline that was prophesized to produce Hati and Sköll."

Hati and Sköll—the giant wolves fated to swallow the sun and moon.

None of this is news to me. Victoria strove to put forward a nonchalant front. Ironically, Grimhild provided her with a welcome distraction from the spiders crawling all over her.

"This silence is taxing," Verðandi said. "We need Victoria to answer our questions."

"Grimhild, you will permit Victoria to speak," Skuld said.

"As you command, my goddess." Grimhild clapped her hands.

Victoria's lips unsealed. She gasped for breath and could once again control the muscles in her face. She spoke up as soon as she could. "You can't murder me or my child," Victoria addressed the Future Norn. "You've already carved our destinies into Yggdrasil's trunk. Killing us would mess everything up."

Her words belly flopped into silence. The spiders didn't reply right away, but Grimhild grimaced in a telling fashion. Apparently, Victoria had lucked out and scored a direct hit. She wondered what exactly had forced the Norns to reconsider their plans. Whatever it was must be huge. Fate simply did not change her mind on a whim.

"We were fooled," Urðr admitted in a rattling hiss. "Tricked by that craven cheater. We didn't realize—"

"Your babe's father is Hróðvitnir, the great wolf." Verðandi stroked Victoria's cheek. The hairs on the spider's legs were surprisingly soft. She smelled dry and earthy.

"No! My child's father was Arik Koenig," Victoria blurted. The prior February, Arik had vanished—and was presumed dead—while battling an Ironwood *seiðr*.

"Arik Koenig was Hróðvitnir," Grimhild said with a mean stare. "He waged war on my coven and even succeeded in driving us from our homeland. He was a smug son of a bitch whose arrogance proved his undoing. He fathered twin sons on an Ironwood bitch."

"No. That's impossible..." Victoria reeled. Prior to his death, Arik had told her an abbreviated—but different—version of the story. For one, he'd never mentioned Logan having a twin brother. Could it be true? Had Arik lied to her? As much as she didn't want to believe Grimhild, the witch's story held a ring of truth.

"It's entirely possible. When Hróðvitnir learned the truth about his sons, he schemed to keep them from us. Our coven rescued one of the infant boys, but his infant brother was found murdered... Burnt to a crisp." Grimhild formed a cradle with her arms. Tear glistened in her eyes. "That poor babe. His charred little fingers disintegrated when I touched them."

Victoria's stomach turned over. She didn't want to think about where the infant corpse had come from, but she refused to accept that Arik had murdered a baby. Her cunning mate had been many things, but a child murderer wasn't one of them.

"You thought Logan was dead for eighteen years." Victoria's mind boggled while she put it all together. Logan had a twin brother—who, from the sounds of it—lived with the Ironwood coven. More impossible still, Grimhild *and* the Norns sincerely believed Logan and his brother were Hati and Sköll. What would Logan say when she told him? *If* she got that chance.... Would he be thrilled? Shocked? Angry? Yeah, she imagined the revelation of a prodigal brother would piss him off.

She nodded. "We grieved for his loss, and treasured the babe who remained with us." Grimhild nodded. "We nursed him on a witch's teats, schooled him in our faith and our magic."

"How did you find Logan?" Victoria asked.

"It was Hrafnar who found him," Urðr said from her nesting spot against the small of Victoria's back.

"Hrafnar?" Victoria froze. Arik had died fighting Hrafnar. The witch had tried to enslave the Storm Pack and turned them against each other.

"Hrafnar was my daughter." Grimhild glared at Victoria with pure hatred. "You murdered her, and now you will pay... or maybe, your daughter will. Yes, I think that would be just, don't you?"

The direct threat against her daughter's life galvanized Victoria. Resolve solidified in her heart. She *would* slay Grimhild. Right then and there, she swore it on the soul of her daughter and in Odin's name.

One of the great ravens spread his wings and shrilled. "Your vow is witnessed and blessed. The All Father will accept this sacrifice."

Brittle tension settled over those assembled. All turned paranoid stares to Huginn and Muninn.

"I'm going to rip you to shreds, witch." Victoria refused to simply wait and let fate decide whether she lived or died. She pitted the entirety of her will against Grimhild's enchantment. Her head throbbed; pressure built within her skull until she feared blood vessels would burst. She might as well have had her shoulder against a mountain. She labored for breath, her heart throbbed, and her muscles burned. Despite her best effort, nothing budged, and the exertion exhausted her.

"And you need to be taught your place, wolf." Grimhild raised her hand. Crackling magic swirled about her, lightning gathered upon the rod. It arched between her arched fingers.

"Stop! We need the child to live." Verðandi raised her front legs in a staying motion.

Grimhild flexed her hands but didn't lower them.

"Grimhild spoke correctly," Urðr said. "We must murder the wolf mother and her monstrous child."

"Finding is not the same as having," Verðandi countered. "Logan is strong-willed. He defies our mastery."

"True." Urðr huffed. "He resisted Hrafnar's enslavement and Grimhild's summoning."

"I believe it best to keep Victoria Storm alive and use her to influence Logan," Verðandi said.

"She would be a valuable tool," Skuld said.

"Goddesses, I know my first enchantment proved unsuccessful, but—and forgive me for reminding you—I did tell you the spell was cast across too great a distance." Grimhild held her head high. "This time, I will do better. I will be right there. I swear it."

"Perhaps you will redeem yourself." Skuld gave an ugly twist of her mandibles, flashing wicked venom-tipped fangs.

"We need Logan, especially now that Tristan knows his brother is alive. Imagine Tristan's reaction when he learns you murdered his baby sister." Verðandi cut through the dissension.

"He'd never know." Urðr produced another rattling hiss. The spider's stiff bristles lashed across the small of Victoria's back. It stung, but worse... *it itched.* Burning, unbearable irritation spread like wildfire along her nerve endings.

"Verðandi would tell him," Skuld said.

"She'd not dare," Urðr said with pronounced disbelief.

"Try me." Verðandi *lifted her chin.*

"Lady Skuld, it is split. Whether Victoria and her child live or die is up to you. What is your judgement?" Grimhild asked.

"I will not be rushed, Grimhild," Skuld said.

"Of course not." Grimhild bowed her head.

"We will decide now." Skuld sprang from her roost on Victoria's stomach. Four of the spider's limbs retracted into her body with a succulent pop. She wriggled like a bloated sack while her excess legs were absorbed, emitting a series of sharp cracks like the carcass of a beetle crushed underfoot. Mid-transformation, Skuld underwent a rapid enlargement and became an imposing woman in her middle years.

When Skuld crooked her finger, Verðandi and Urðr also leapt off Victoria. They remained arachnids, however, and clamored up their sister's robes to perch on her shoulders. The Sisters Wyrd—three in a row.

Great and terrible expectation brooded like a gathering storm.

"The wolf and her child will be allowed to live for now," Skuld proclaimed, and Victoria sagged in immediate relief.

"Good," Verðandi said. "Grimhild, collect the blood you will need for your spellcraft."

"As you wish, goddess," Grimhild said, sounding none too happy. The *seiðr* removed a small wooden bowl and a bone-handled knife from her clutch purse. "This won't hurt," Grimhild said, reaching for Victoria's hand. "Much."

"Stay away from me." Adrenaline surged through Victoria. She tried to evade but stayed stuck as a living statue.

Grimhild grasped Victoria's wrist and slashed open her palm with the blade. The witch then held Victoria's hand positioned over the bowl while her blood filled it. Helpless, Victoria endured the humiliation of being manhandled and bled like a sacrificial goat.

"You will forget all that has happened here tonight. All we have discussed." Grimhild tapped Victoria on the cheek three times. Her eyelids fell shut and she plunged into darkness. Before the last glimmer of Victoria's consciousness faded, she heard a strange woman's voice whisper in her ear.

"Sleep now."

CHAPTER 6

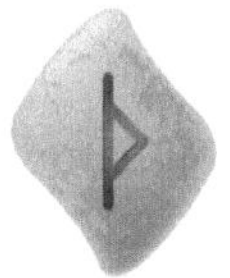

Thurisaz: The Rune of Chaos, Evil, and Temptation

SHRILL BIRDCALLS PIERCED the velvet serenity that preceded the dawn. Topping a rise, Logan plunged down the wooded hillside, swerving hard to dodge a stand of pines. His wolf dominated his mindset, shoving the human aspect into the background. As his beast took over, his color vision dulled while his sense of smell sharpened and his hearing grew more acute.

From the north, the strident howl of a wolf on the hunt rose into the twilight: an intruder in the Storm Pack territory. Before the call faded, more strangers answered—a rival pack.

Icy anger pushed up from Logan's core. A snarl resonated deep in his chest and his lips pulled back over his canines. Invaders in his territory offended his basest instincts. His kneejerk reflex: rush in and attack. _Kill, kill, kill..._ He fought the urge, struggling for discipline. The situation called for a cool head. The invaders had greater numbers and quite possibly superior strength. As much as it galled him to even admit, he needed to locate Sawyer and work with the hunter. With the pack's youngsters so close, the stakes were too high to let personal differences get in the way.

At the base of the hill, Logan burst from the brush into a small meadow lush with wildflowers. Startled sparrows sprang from the cover of summer grasses and winged away, and a rabbit raced for cover. Riding the edge of frenzy, he shoved his sweatpants down his long legs and kicked off his shoes. Fully naked, he leapt high and changed to his animal form while in flight. His body rippled and flowed, pouring like a liquid into a mold. He endured none of the bone-crunching agony other wolf-shifters experienced. Once through, he became a great black wolf, larger even than most of his kind.

He hit the ground on all fours and sprinted into the open field. On the other side of the meadow, trees formed a broken wall. Beyond it, the terrain sloped upward again. With the presence of intruders, the natural wilderness sounds had ceased. Instead, the forest crashed with the careless passage of several creatures. A bad wind blustered through the forest, carrying the distinctive aroma of men and foul magic. The familiar scent confirmed his suspicions—*Den Valgte*.

More howls went up, crossing miles. Logan paused to listen. The invaders' language lacked the universal grammar of the wolf-language. The words made sense but just barely—sloppy enunciation; bad syntax. He got the general gist of their conversation, though. The foreign pack ran together on a coordinated hunt, searching for a lone man with a rifle who'd ambushed and killed two of them.

Sawyer—these bozos lacked the sense to realize they were the hunted, not the hunters.

Logan paced the grasses flat beneath his paws. He wanted to run but didn't know where to head. He needed to find Sawyer. And while the enemy pack broadcast their locations, they lacked directionality. Meanwhile, the hunter remained as elusive as a tiger in the trees. Logan tried the pack bond again only to come up empty handed.

On the far side of the clearing, a fast-moving figure slipped wraith-silent from the brush. As though in answer to his thoughts, the cosmos supplied Sawyer, son of Jake Barrett, the ever-lovin' Hunter King, except there wasn't a single princely thing about the guy. He checked all the vagabond boxes, though. Mountain man: big and bold, matted dirty-blond hair tangled about his sun-leathered face, and bristling beard. A hardened frontiersman, pulled straight from the era of Davy Crockett. In pointed contrast, Sawyer wore modern clothing and carried a shotgun.

Across the meadow, man and wolf faced one another. Line of sight restored the pack bond which resonated with the hunter's anger. It blared like heavy metal music, drowning out everything else. When Sawyer adjusted his grip on his shotgun, Logan tensed. *Sonofabitch.* He swore if Sawyer aimed that gun at him, all bets were off. The bad guys could get in line because Logan would kill the hunter himself.

A raider's howl burst over them. Others followed. Logan stiffened; Sawyer hunched. *Close.* Too close and approaching fast from the ruckus of snarls and growls, and the snap of broken branches.

Two grizzled gray wolves with glowing eyes burst from the forest. Yep, they were *Den Valgte* all right. Logan's fur bristled, and a growl erupted from his throat. Their ragged hides hung from their taunt frames and no amount of magic could conceal the reek of dark sorcery. Death clung to the preserved wolf skins those bastards wore to shape shift.

The leader had yellow eyes and a ragged line at the base of a missing ear, which looked to have been bitten or torn off. Fleetingly, Logan wondered whether the defect belonged to the shaman or the wolf-hide shirt he wore, but he didn't have time to ponder further—the pair of grizzled gray wolves were bearing down on the hunter, and fast.

"Shit." Sawyer broke into a flat-out run, heading for Logan.

Primed for the fight, Logan barreled straight at Sawyer. His sides labored and his muscles burned from the exertion. He poured everything he had into the effort because his packmate's life hung in the balance... even if it was Sawyer. With every stride, the *Den Valgte* wolves shortened the distance between themselves and their quarry.

Race to the middle—the winner got the hunter.

Sawyer and Logan hurtled toward each other, a collision course that promised no winners. Slowing meant giving the enemy the edge so Logan held the course and crossed his mental fingers. At the last second, their gazes caught. A psychic sandstorm, the hunter's grating anger blasted over the wolf's mind. Logan balked and pushed back. They engaged in a short shoving match, no clear winner.

"Duck!" Logan shouted.

"You—you spoke!" Sawyer's eyes widened.

"Shut up and duck, you moron!" Logan barked... just as flabbergasted as Sawyer at having human words tumbling from his lupine mouth.

Sawyer dropped and rolled just as Logan launched into a leap that carried him over the hunter. He twisted so his shoulder rammed into One Ear's head. The impact altered their trajectories. He spun through the air in a crazy tumble, but catlike intuition anchored his center of gravity so he alighted on his feet.

The raider crashed to the ground. He lay where he landed.

Logan lunged for the enemy's exposed throat. His fangs penetrated fur and flesh, and foul-tasting blood flooded his mouth. Just a taste left him craving more. The vicious drive to kill ruled him. Digging his claws into the stony soil, Logan hauled back and ripped out a huge chunk of fur and flesh.

With a desperate effort, One Ear got his legs under him and pushed upright. He staggered sideways, trailing a river of red.

Beyond Logan's field of view, Sawyer fired a handgun on full auto until the clip emptied. *Den Valgte* wolves snarled, and the hunter roared a challenge at the top of his lungs.

Logan turned his head, intending to spit out the hunk of meat clutched in his teeth. His jaws refused to part. Visceral hunger exploded through Logan's gut and clawed at his sides. Thick ropes of drool ran from the sides of his mouth. Why spit out a perfectly fine meal? Easier to swallow it... *No!* He gagged and strangled at the thought of cannibalism. Reeling with disgust, Logan spun in a tight circle, wrestling with his wolf for control.

A few yards distant, Sawyer toppled beneath the assault of a lanky black *Den Valgte* wolf. With a great cough, Logan finally spat out the flesh, but strings and chunks got lodged between his teeth.

More wolves burst from the tree line—two tawny females that had slighter builds and a big red-furred male. He heard others, too. Yup, he and Sawyer had 'em surrounded. The bad guys were in big trouble now.

Head low, Logan circled in a deadly dance with One Ear, but the injured raider looked dead on his feet. A tawny blur charged Logan from his nine o'clock. He spun to face the new threat. His sharp turn brought him face-to-face with the pair of tawny females who he arbitrarily labeled Frick and Frack.

In tandem, Frick and Frack came at him in a coordinated attack. Divide and conquer. Smart, but he had tricks of his own. From his prior experience with *Den Valgte*, their shamans lacked the ability to perform partial shifts. He intended to use that to his advantage.

Logan sank onto his haunches, settling his center of gravity. He altered his front legs to arms, gaining full articulation, and his paws to claws. As the she-wolves bore down on top of him, he delivered an elbow strike to Frack's muzzle, knocking aside her barred jaws. Simultaneously, he presented his broad side to Frick and braced.

Frick locked her jaws onto his shoulder, her teeth buried deep. She hung on as tenacious as a hellhound, raking his torso with the claws of her front paws. Red bolts of pain lanced through him, and her bulk hampered his every movement.

Before Frack recovered, Logan raised his arm high and dropped the point of his elbow onto her skull. Stunned, she wobbled on her feet. He seized her jaws in both hands, thrusting his fingers into her mouth to secure a firm grip. Her fangs cut his flesh. Blood-tainted saliva coated his hands. Yelping in agony, Frack twisted and writhed while he pried her jaws apart. Bones crunched—the mandible hinge snapped. Resistance gone, she opened wide. Logan thrust his dagger-sharp claws through her soft palate, penetrating her brain case.

She died.

Frick released her bite hold and loosened an agonized howl. Her sister's death drove her into frenzy. Rabid with rage, she hurtled herself at Logan, attacking without an ounce of regard for self-preservation. With froth foaming from her mouth, she drove at his throat with the scent of madness on her breath.

Logan twisted, barely evading Frick's snapping jaws. He gathered himself to lunge for the she-wolf's throat when a silent attacker smashed into him from behind. Powerful jaws locked on the juncture of Logan's neck; claws raked gouges across his back and sides. A bright flash of pain. He bucked, attempting to throw off his assailant. As he twisted, he caught a glimpse of the *Den Valgte* wolf riding him.

The beast's crimson eyes cast fiendish light. Glistening white teeth like ice picks. Black overcoat, dark gray underside—a wicked scar ran along his broad snout to the top of his face. Scarface dwarfed every other member of the *Den Valgte* pack two or three times over, and maybe even Logan, too. It sure as hell felt like it. The bastard weighed a shit ton.

Frick came at Logan on his injured side. The she-wolf raked his ribcage, widening the wounds. Much deeper and she'd rip out his lung.

"Sawyer!" Logan called out using his newfound ability to speak while shifted. *Where had that bastard gone?*

Still struggling beneath Scarface's weight, Logan threw up his arm to block Frick, but she scored a direct hit and sank her incisors deep into his jaw. He knocked her back but lost a chunk of his cheek. Fireworks spun in his head. An enemy in front and behind—he had to get free, or they'd kill him.

"Sawyer, I could use a little help here!" Logan shouted. Just asking stung, but pride would heal whereas he wouldn't survive getting ripped in half.

"I hear yah. Hang on!" Sawyer's voice came from somewhere to Logan's left.

"Make it fast, you stupid—" Logan doubled over, heaving Scarface overhead. The raider collided with Frick, blocking her from attacking.

Scarface hung on to Logan with steel-trap jaws. Digging in, Logan hauled back against Scarface. Tug o' war. Every push and pull sent fiery stabs through his shoulder.

"Insulting the guy you're asking for help?" Sawyer yelled and a handgun boomed.

"You sonofabitch!" Gritting his teeth, Logan heaved the giant wolf off him. His shoulder wrenched. As he went, Scarface ripped a hunk out of Logan. Lancing agony blinded him. A howl tore from him in a torrent that decimated his thoughts.

Scarface finally dislodged. He landed on the she-wolf. They both went over.

Hemorrhaging from multiple wounds, Logan pressed his claw to his side so his insides didn't spill onto the earth. Whimpering, he stumbled in a direction that he hoped would take him closer to Sawyer. Retreat might buy him a few precious moments to heal. He regenerated fast, but the exertion of the past hour had drained his reserves. Hunger gnawed at his insides like a toothy beast determined to chew its way to freedom. Damn it, he regretted not having fed from One Ear when he had the chance. Cannibalism revolted him, but it was better than being dead.

Lighter and lither, Frick got out from under Scarface and recovered her stance first. Frothing at the mouth, she lumbered toward Logan. He threw his arm up as she lunged. She locked onto his forearm, snarling and shaking her head in fury.

Grinding his teeth, Logan twisted his arm, forcing her head aside to expose her throat. He drove at her and closed his jaws about her jugular. But her furious shaking threw him off, and he missed the major arteries. Instead, his canines sank deep, piercing thick fur, and embedded in the strong sinew of her neck. A gush of mothball blood filled his mouth. It tasted of bitterroots. Beneath the toxic sting, his tongue grew thick and his throat closed. He gagged, gasping for breath, and clamped down. He refused to let go.

Between his jaws, Frick struggled for air. She twisted and writhed, fighting to get loose, but her strength flagged with each passing second. Determined to end it, Logan jerked to the side. Her neck broke with a loud snap.

A crap ton of weight crashed down on Logan's back, knocking his feet out from under him. Fucking Scarface *again*. The raider's livid snarl filled his ears. Scarface bit into the open wound on Logan's neck, tearing out a mouthful of flesh. He ripped deep, right down to the shoulder blade.

Past the point of pain, Logan's sight faded. Distantly, he heard a man's voice, but the words blurred together.

Thunder boomed—the point-blank gust of a shotgun against Scarface's skull. A wet glob gushed across Logan's nape. Coagulated vitae soaked his fur. His ears rang from the deafening noise. When his hearing returned, he caught the tail end of Sawyer's sentence.

"...Last one."

Dirt crunched beneath the hunter's steps. Through pain-foggy vision, Logan peered up at his approaching packmate. He caught a blur of motion—a kick aimed at him. A warning snarl erupted from Logan's throat. No time to dodge. He braced, anticipating a solid blow and broken ribs.

The hunter's boot caught the underside of Scarface's ribcage. The raider rolled off Logan and crashed to the ground.

Freed of the burden, Logan transformed his arms to wolf legs and clamored to his feet. Gore dripped from his fur. As he took a step, a chunk of Scarface's flesh dislodged from his shoulders plopped to the forest floor. The rank odor made him offensive to his own nose. In disgust, he engaged in a whole body shakedown, sending forth a spray of meaty chunks, bone fragments, and blood drops. The foolhardy action sent lancing pain shooting through his entire body. He snarled deep in his throat to express his displeasure.

Oblivious, Sawyer advanced toward Scarface's corpse, favoring his left leg in a pronounced limp. A tear split the denim of his jeans from his hip to his knee. Blood soaked the fabric. His shirt hung in tatters. The hunter looked like he'd gone a few rounds with a professional boxer. Around every visible injury, the hunter's skin shone like glossy obsidian. His father's gift—powerful healing magic—made Sawyer invincible, as far as Logan could tell. Envy ate at Logan, but it was nothing compared to the ravenous hunger gnawing at his sides.

He needed to eat, and soon.

"Guess it's a good thing I was here to save your sorry ass." Sawyer turned to Logan and smiled. Beads of perspiration clung to the hunter's beard, and sweat tinged his basal odor. Not a hint of fear. If anything, from the sour apple 'n' cinnamon tartness surrounding him, the bastard was enjoying himself.

"Shut up, asshole." In the grip of raw resentment, Logan bristled. More than anything, he wanted to tell the hunter where he could shove it, but he was too damn tired to expend the energy.

"We need to get moving." Sawyer took a long stride as though to implement that bold plan but then halted. A spasm of pain crossed his face, and he dropped his hand to cover the injury on his thigh.

"Yeah, we'll get right on that." Logan twisted around, trying to get a better look at the nasty injury where Scarface had tried to chew his head off. Where there was once fur and flesh, a gaping hole lay open at the juncture of his neck and shoulder. A red glistening curved bone protruded from the wound. He was pretty sure it was his scapula. And it showed no visible signs of closing. He'd spent a lot of energy during the fight—shifting and healing had used up his reserves. He needed to eat soon or his shoulder wouldn't heal.

The forest resumed speaking. All around, the air reverberated with the voices of a dozen different bird species, blending into harmonious mountain music. The eastern sky brightened before the encroaching dawn, and the early morning air was cool and peaceful once again.

"Five minute break?" Sawyer cocked his head, his implication clear enough. If the rest of the pack was in immediate danger, they'd hear it.

"Five minutes?" Logan hesitated, wrestling with temptation. Exhaustion weighed on him. He wanted nothing more than to curl up in the summer grasses and take a nap. Of course he wouldn't, but what harm could come from a brief, well-deserved break? For the first time *ever*, Logan found himself in agreement with the hunter. Weird. Aside from that brief instance at the beginning, they hadn't worked together as a team during the fight with *Den Valgte*.

"Five minutes. I'll time it."

"Okay. Five minutes." Logan eased onto his stomach with his paws outstretched before him. Sawyer collapsed beside him, positioned with his legs splayed wide and his arms propped on his knees, hands dangling.

They sat like that.

Logan's gaze slid to the side, landing on his broody packmate. He found he couldn't sit beside the hunter without keeping a sharp eye on him. Dire straits might've forced him to work with the hunter to defeat *Den Valgte*, but that didn't mean Logan trusted the hunter in the slightest.

The flesh surrounding Sawyer's injuries was as smooth as stone and as black as the starless night. With mixed intrigue and revulsion, Logan studied a deep cut on the back of the hunter's forearm. The edges shimmered with slight but discernable motion. Beneath his skin, sigils swarmed like a busy colony of ants, working hard to repair the damage done to their vessel.

"Will those heal anything?" Logan spoke without intent. The words just slipped past his lowered guard.

"Pretty much. Why?" Sawyer turned his head, following Logan's stare.

Hunter magic derived from mystic runes—the language of the gods—or so Victoria said. When it came to magic, she usually knew what she was talking about, or at least she knew a lot more than Logan. Either way, no difference. She'd started to teach him the runic names and unique shapes. To his inexpert estimate, these symbols appeared identical to the ones on Sylvie's divination stones. And while he might not understand them, he could *smell* the power they carried. Real magic—a miracle and a shame it didn't rip the asshole apart.

"Just curious." Logan shrugged. "You came back from the dead after that bear ripped you a new one. I'm wondering what it takes to kill you for real."

Sawyer looked over at him and grinned. "Fuck if I'd tell *you*."

Logan snickered and then chortled, but it hurt too much so he settled for sniggering. Beside him, the hunter chuckled. Madness caught them in its feverish grip. Hysteria. Oh, beautiful, fucked-up irony. There they sat, the son of Loki beside the son of Odin, laughing their asses off.

"So how is it you can talk?" Sawyer shot him a sardonic smile.

"No fucking idea. Before today, I had no clue I could."

"No clue?" Sawyer wielded skepticism like a scythe.

"I'd never tried."

He'd never had reason to before. While fully shifted, he shouldn't be able to talk at all. No wolf-shifter possessed the ability... except, as he'd noted before, Logan wasn't like other wolves. He changed shape without difficulty or discomfort, and silver wasn't toxic to him. So now he fit the cliché talking-animal trope —one more difference to set him apart.

"Five minutes are up." Sawyer hauled himself to his feet. He looked about a hundred percent improved from the short break.

Jerkface. Logan stayed put, afraid the slightest motion would send his internal organs spilling out through the gaping hole in his side.

"Are you okay?" Sawyer pinned Logan with a piercing glance.

"I'm fine. I just need another minute."

"Fine. I'm going to take care of the bodies so they can't reanimate."

"Good idea."

Metal hissed over leather as Sawyer drew his machete. With a deft twist of his wrist, he spun the weapon and swung overhanded. He brought the blade down, beheading a corpse. Then the hunter worked his way around the meadow-turned-battlefield, lopping off heads. Logan performed a quick body count and arrived at eight dead... maybe nine. Hard to be sure, what with all the parts 'n' pieces strewn about the grassy field.

Logan hugged the ground in abject misery. A ravenous beast lived in his belly. Black flies had already found the bodies. Their obnoxious buzzing droned in the backdrop. With each passing second, the thick scent of carrion blanketing the air lured Logan farther from his humanity.

"You're not healing, are you?" Sawyer returned from his mission of decapitation and wiped the machete blade clean on the grass.

"I won't until I eat." Logan convulsed in the grip of excruciating pain. His teeth clattered and thick strings of salvia sieved from the sides of his mouth.

The hunter narrowed his eyes. "If you're hungry, then eat. I won't judge."

"I can't."

"Why not?" Sawyer cocked his head so blood-soaked blond hair fell into his face. Perspiration trickled down his cheeks and clung to his beard. He cracked the barrel on his shotgun and reloaded.

"Because," Logan grated, raw honesty ripped from him, "once I cross that line, I'm not sure I could stop. You should go after the rest of the pack. There could still be more raiders out there."

"Where are the others?" Sawyer turned his head in the direction of the house.

"Morena and the wolves are with Sylvie. She's supposed to lead them into Desolation Wilderness." Apprehension assailed Logan. He and Sawyer had barely survived *Den Valgte*. It made him sick to contemplate how Sylvie, Morena, and the rest of the wolves would fare alone. Sharp self-recrimination tore him apart. He never should've left them to save Sawyer. The hunter would've fared fine alone.

"Sylvie? What happened to Victoria?" Sawyer paused in the act of reloading his handguns and looked up with real concern.

Logan stiffened at the other male's interest in their alpha. He shoved the stupid reflex aside. "Missing. She didn't show when we gathered."

"You don't sound concerned." Sawyer shot him an accusatory look.

"I'm not. Vic can take care of herself." Logan lied through his teeth. He wallowed in worry, but he refused to share his doubts with the hunter.

Sawyer stared long and hard. "I won't leave a man behind even if it's a flea-bitten mongrel."

"That's stupid. Go, I'm fine." So long as he didn't attempt anything strenuous—like standing—none of his internal organs would fall out. He didn't want to test that theory, though. He felt like one of those tattered old wolf hides the *Den Valgte* shamans wore, except probably not as pretty.

"Stay here," Sawyer barked and hobbled off, dirt crunching beneath his boots. He disappeared into the trees, heading toward his campsite on the hilltop.

"Where do you think I'm gonna go? Damn it—" Logan bit off the rest when the trees swallowed the hunter. No sense in wasting energy on complaints that couldn't be heard.

In abject misery, he rested his head on his front legs and waited for Sawyer to return. *Stupid.* If life had taught Logan anything, it was not to count on anyone but family. For years, his father was the only person who'd stuck with him through thick and thin. All his supposed friends, even his so-called best buddy, had deserted him after his mother's murder.

Except Evan.

The footsteps of a man with a limp—Sawyer?—approached through the forest. Logan lifted his head, scenting the wind, and confirmed it was the hunter. He also picked up a salty, smoky aroma that set his mouth to watering. *Oh boy! Trout!* Still crouched on the earth, Logan slobbered and thumped his tail like an eager Labrador. The worst of it, he was too damn hungry to care about the penultimate humiliation.

Sawyer broke through the trees into the meadow, carrying a line of uncleaned fish suspended from their heads. The hunter halted and cocked his head, staring down at the ravenous wolf. His scathing smirk said it all as he pried a nineteen incher off the hook and tossed it.

Logan snatched the trout out of the air and swallowed it whole. It hit his belly, a drop in the bucket compared to his famine, but it took the edge off. When Sawyer threw the next fish, Logan gulped it down. A rush of energy flowed through him and his regeneration kicked in.

"Give me the rest." Logan lunged to his feet. He snatched the next trout from the hunter's hand... and almost took his fingers, too.

"Watch it." Sawyer yanked his arm away and held up his hand for inspection. Fresh blood glistened on his fingers. Tiny runes swarmed across his skin and engulfed the injury.

"Sorry." Logan winced at a pinch of shame.

"I was trying to make sure you didn't eat the hooks." With marked disgust, Sawyer hurled the remaining fish toward the ground. He swept his hand in a wide invitation. "Have at it."

"Sensitive, ain'tcha?" Logan snatched the fish from the air. Cautious now, he forced himself to slow down, taking care to jerk the fish from the hooks before he consumed them.

"That was my breakfast. You're welcome, by the way."

"It's my land," Logan returned between bites. He finished off the final four fish in less than a minute. His hunger remained unsated, but the meal made a world of difference. He grunted in satisfaction, strength and viability returning.

Sawyer sneered. "Did you piss on a tree? I must've missed it."

Logan bared his teeth and bristled. Peevish, sullen possessiveness pushed to the surface. By his wolf's basest instincts, he wanted to declare ownership—*his land, his lake, his fish...* and Victoria, too, *his...* A sudden grin gob smacked Logan when he envisioned Victoria's reaction to being named chattel... She would kick his ass so hard he'd be flossing with his shoelaces.

"What the hell...?" Sawyer jerked his head to the side, staring at a point in the distance. The hunter grew intent.

"What?" Logan looked over to see what the hunter was on about and found his answer. Scarface's corpse was smoking. Wisps rose from his skin at first, but within seconds a haze engulfed the wolf's body and his detached head.

All around the field, sooty fog swallowed the other slain *Den Valgte* wolves. Logan's nose itched something fierce. He snorted, blowing a spray of snot, as the reek of sulfurous magic burned his nostrils.

"What's happening?" Sawyer asked.

"It's the zombie apocalypse! Run!" Logan tipped up his muzzle in lieu of raised hands.

"You're an absolute ass." Sawyer gave him the side eye, but his ribcage heaved as he fought laughter.

"Thanks, I try." Logan snickered, his mood improving. A good meal made the world a better place. He even despised Sawyer slightly less. "Seriously, their mojo is wearing off. They're reverting to their true forms. This is how it happened when we killed the first raiders in Broken Bend. You missed it because you were down and out for the count."

Sawyer pressed his lips together.

The smoke dissipated, the remnants swept up into the arms of a brisk breeze, and the worst of the stench went with it. The human corpses of the deceased *Den Valgte* shamans remained. To the last, they wore the wolf-hide shirts that enabled them to transform into wolves. Otherwise, the men and women appeared unremarkable.

Logan pushed upright and headed over to the bodies of those he'd killed. *Huh.* One Ear's ratty wolf skin lacked an ear while the man had both. In contrast, the pronounced scar that gave Scarface his nickname belonged to the man. So, it appeared the *Den Valgte* wolves derived traits from both the cured hides *and* the shamans.

Lips curled in distaste, he ripped One Ear's wolf-skin shirt open. Heavy clumps of fur separated from the brittle, flaky hide. The garment reeked of age: years, or maybe even decades.

"Are you going to eat him, too?" Sawyer asked.

"No, fuckwit, I'm not."

"What're you doing then?"

"Checking to see if he has one of those wolf cross amulets the *Den Valgte* witch-bitch was wearing last week."

"Does he?"

"No."

One Ear didn't have any jewelry at all, enchanted or otherwise. Restless, Logan moved on to Scarface's headless body. He performed the same examination as he had on One Ear, tearing through the brittle hide shirt to get to the corpse's throat-chest area. When his search left him empty handed, he scanned the ground on the theory that a necklace might've slipped over the shaman's neck stump.

Again, he found nothing.

A rifle blast split the night; a bear roared. The commotion came from the south—the lake house.

Sawyer and Logan stopped. They looked at each other. A single, powerful sentiment traversed the pack bond, a shared thought.

Shit. Not again.

CHAPTER 7

Uruz: **The Rune of Strength**

AN INCREMENTAL ADJUSTMENT raised the rifle's tilt on its bipod and brought the enemy into sight. As tense a bowstring, Sylvie licked her parched lips. Her old bones ached from the strain. Perspiration beaded on her brow and a trickle of sweat ran down her temple. Her self-confidence wavered. She knew how to shoot. It'd been years since the last time when she'd held a rifle, and even longer since she pointed one at a man with the intention of ending his life. The Remington held 375 H&H caliber cartridges—one chambered round, and two more in its magazine. Now, three miles from home and with five lives depending on her, the stakes were high. She had to make every shot count.

In the box canyon below the ridge, seven *Den Valgte* raiders gathered at the end of the blind alley. Two men hunched over an open map. Ancient glaciers had sculpted the broken terrain of trough valleys and rocky ridges, creating a maze that challenged those familiar with its twists and turns, so it was unsurprising that the intruders had run into trouble.

The dark-haired man that stood there stabbing the map with his finger wore a shirt made of wolf fur. His blond companion had a bear-hide cloak. Based on secondhand accounts from both Victoria and Logan, the enchanted hides enabled the shamans to change their shape. Their followers, all wearing their stolen wolf's clothing, paced in restless circles around the men who were engaged in an intense discussion. Their exact words were lost across the distance, but there was no mistaking the contentious tone.

She aimed through the scope with both eyes open, switching between them while she acquired her target: the back of the brunet's head. Time slowed, measured in heartbeats, and she settled her finger against the rifle's trigger.

"What are they doing?" Morena asked in a hushed whisper. The teenager knelt beside Sylvie, peering through a pair of binoculars.

"I believe they are lost," Sylvie snapped in frustration over the interruption that broke her concentration.

"Lost?" Morena produced a rude sound. "How can they be lost? They were smart enough to get in front of us and cut off our retreat."

"Not smart—lucky." She clicked her tongue against the roof of her mouth. "I believe *Den Valgte* split their numbers to surround and ambush us at the lake house."

Morena snorted. "Right now, they don't look too lucky."

"No, the Fates did not favor them." Sylvie drew a sharp breath. "The Norns have not looked so kindly upon us, either. The ridge-line that runs along the edge of this box canyon is exposed. We cannot pass them without being seen, especially since doubling back is their only way out."

Sylvie stole a quick glance over her shoulder to verify her charges remained where they'd been instructed to wait. The Storm Pack's gray wolves gathered in a close-knit circle, Mother

Sophia at the center; her three adolescent pups pressed close. If they got backed into a corner, the wolves would fight, but the objective remained to keep them out of it until no other choice remained. Distressingly, their frantic search for Victoria had failed, and they'd been forced to leave the house without her.

"What are we going to do?" Morena dropped her hand to the holstered 9mm pistol she wore on her hip. Even with the attached laser scope, the enemy soldiers were well out of handgun range.

"I'm still thinking." Sylvie returned to the rifle scope again and made a slight adjustment to the resolution. The improved focus, however, didn't help her decision-making. She'd learned how to handle a rifle as a child and she'd fought in plenty of battles, but it'd been a long time since she'd aimed at anything other than an immobile target.

The dark-haired man jabbed at the map and then swept his arm toward the canyon's opening. He raised his voice loud enough to climb the canyon's steel walls. Sylvie couldn't quite make out what he said, but she got the gist well enough. *Ah, this dark-haired man must be the leader.* She started to target his head but then the man in the bear-hide said something at a volume too low to carry and made an adamant gesture. In response, the blond man jerked and stiffened, radiating defiance, but then he ducked his head in a show of submission.

Not the leader then. Sylvie's thoughts crystalized; she formulated a plan. Morena wouldn't like it; the girl would argue. Ultimately, Sylvie had no real choice in the matter. She needed the teenager's cooperation.

"Morena, I want you to take the others and double back to the house."

"But—"

"No buts. I'll delay firing on them as long as I can so you can get as far away as possible, but once they start moving again, I have to take the shot." Sylvie turned her head enough to meet the girl's worried gaze.

The teenager sank her teeth into her lower lip. "I don't want to leave you."

"Morie, you must." Sylvie smiled, allowing her love to shine through. "You and the pups are the future of the pack. Get them to safety. Cali should be at the house by now. Goddess willing, the sheriff and his men will be there soon, too."

"Fine, I'll go." Morena huffed, but then threw her arms around Sylvie. "Be careful."

"I will." Sylvie hugged the girl in return and pressed a quick kiss to her forehead. "Now go."

"Bye." Morena pulled away and rushed off. With a few quiet words, she gathered the four gray wolves. Swift and silent, they vanished into the woods.

Alone, Sylvie breathed a little easier. She returned her attention to the raiders. Stillness filled her, and nervousness drained away. Her focus narrowed to a single purpose: the task before her. The rest of the world fell away. Abruptly, she remembered what it meant to be a predator—the thrill of the hunt, the exhilaration of closing for the kill.

After a couple minutes, the men's discussion came to an end. The commander rose and turned to his followers, issuing orders. His second-in-command remained crouched, folding the map, his head in the crosshairs.

She squeezed the trigger. The brunet's head split—he toppled.

The sound of the gunshot cracked the canyon. Chaos erupted. The commander's angry shout filled the air along with the fearful growls of his wolf soldiers. While they scrambled for cover, Sylvie drew back on the bolt, ejecting the casing and chambering a new cartridge.

Her second shot hit one of the retreating wolves in the hind leg, destroying the joint. Yowling, he knocked over onto his side. None of his companions turned back to help him. Not a single one even slowed.

Sylvie operated the manual bolt again, loading the final cartridge into the chamber. When the raider she'd maimed rose onto unsteady legs, she shot him in the head. By the time the third gunshot faded, the enemy had taken cover. She had more cartridges crammed into her pocket but nothing to shoot at. Once the raiders exited the box canyon and reorganized, they would come after her. She would flee; unsuspecting, they'd pursue. Her calculated retreat would lead the enemy straight to their deaths.

She slid the rifle's strap over her shoulder and cast a final glance into the canyon, surveying her handiwork. The two dead bodies still littered the valley floor. Not bad for an old woman who preferred knitting to hunting. Ah, and what a glorious rush it was to once again assume the warrior mantle she'd set aside so long ago.

A slow smile split her lips. "And that, children, is why you don't bring a knife to a gunfight... Or assume wolves won't."

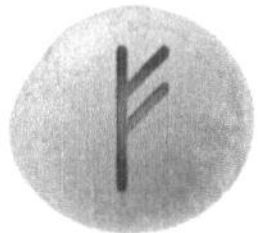

CHAPTER 8

Fehu: The Rune of Wealth

DAWN SLOWLY EDGED out the night. As the moon retreated behind the mountains, rose and gold painted the eastern horizon. The evergreen forest grew thick, standing close like a brotherhood, boughs interlocked. The forest ended a hundred feet from the road that led to the lake house where she hoped to rejoin Morena and the others. A strange white pickup was parked on the shoulder and the front yard was empty. Sylvie halted at the tree line, hesitant to depart from cover. The truck could belong to an ally or the enemy. Until she figured out which, she couldn't afford to take chances.

Precious minutes ticked past. Her patience barometer passed the red line. Just as she decided she couldn't afford to wait any longer, the front door swung open, revealing Morena. Cali Kinkaid—_Crazy Cali_ by her hunter nickname—stalked into view next. The female hunter wore fatigues and combat boots, a sidearm strapped to her hip, along with the usual assortment of knives. A cast covered her forearm, which had been broken a few days before during the first confrontation with *Den Valgte*. The hunters had lost a junior member in that battle, too, a young man who'd died fighting alongside Cali.

Sylvie stepped out and hurried toward them.

"Can I help?" Morena asked, dogging Cali.

"No, go back inside." Cali headed straight for the white truck.

"I have a gun." Morena followed on the hunter's heels. "I know how to shoot. Sawyer taught me—"

"Look, I don't have time for this, kid. I've got an unknown number of hostiles incoming, and I don't even know which direction to point my rifle." Callie dropped the tailgate and released one of the bungees securing the tarp that covered the bed.

"There are five raiders approaching from the northwest. They'll be here in less than ten minutes," Sylvie raised her voice to draw their attention. Both Morena and Cali turned toward her.

"Sylvie! You made it." Morena grinned and bounded to sweep Sylvie into a fierce hug. The impact almost knocked the skald off her feet.

"Was that ever in doubt?" Sylvie flashed a cocky smile and squeezed the teenager in return. "I killed two of the raiders, including one of their leaders."

"Nice work." Cali grinned but didn't pause. She kept working on loosening the remainder of the tie downs.

"Morena, where are the others?"

"Inside. I hid them in the basement." Morena cranked her head toward the house.

"Good," Sylvie said.

"Are the raiders armed?" The truck dipped as Cali jumped into the bed.

"Four wolves, one bear. The grizzly is the leader. They weren't armed. Not that I saw." Sylvie hefted her rifle.

"Good. That improves the odds." Cali grabbed the edge of the tarp and dragged it aside, revealing a small armory's worth of gun cases and ammunition.

"You came prepared." Sylvie stared in awe at a grenade launcher.

"This is just my standard arsenal. When I got your call, I rolled out of bed and came straight over." Cali shoved loose strands of frizzy brown bangs out of her eyes. A haphazard ponytail bound the rest of the wiry mop. She yanked a large black metal case from the tightly packed cargo.

"Thank you for that," Sylvie said in sincere gratitude. "Can I borrow a handgun?"

"Sure." Cali leveled an appraising glance, hovering over the weapons cache. "Is a Smith and Wesson 9mm semi-auto okay?"

"Perfect. Thank you."

"This one has a laser targeting scope." Cali passed over the pistol and two spare clips. Task complete, she returned her attention to the black case. Its clasps opened with a dramatic snap, a salute to suspense.

Sylvie resisted the urge to watch while Cali raised the lid. Instead, Sylvie performed a quick inspection of the pistol and found it fully loaded with the safety on. She tucked it into the waistband of her pants and set the spare magazines down within easy reach.

"Morena, go into the house and join the wolves in the basement. Be prepared to fight. If we fall, you're their final protector." Sylvie gave Morena a quick hug and then pushed her toward the house. "Now go."

"Already gone." Morena broke into a sprint and dashed off.

Sylvie turned and found Cali watching her with a raised brow. The skald pursed her lips. "Morena is seventeen. In wolf-shifter culture, she is already a woman."

She didn't speak of how much trauma Morena had endured in the past year: the deaths of her parents, her older brother, and so many other members of the pack. Because of it, Sylvie and Victoria sheltered the girl—overprotective to a fault.

"No skin off my nose. I killed my first vamp when I was thirteen." Cali shrugged and finished setting up a rifle tripod in the truck's bed. The hunter worked with impressive speed and efficiency despite her broken arm. She mounted an air rifle with a long barrel and a scope on it and unzipped a case full of pink-tailed darts.

"A tranquilizer gun?" Sylvie asked, unable to disguise her skepticism.

"Carfentanil. It's an elephant tranquilizer." Cali loaded the dart. Sourly, she added, "Jake told me to take a couple prisoners if they attacked again."

"We're taking prisoners?"

Cali shrugged. "Jake said he wants at least one of these guys taken captive. Who am *I* to argue with a direct order from the boss?"

"What's the rate of fire on that thing? Will it keep up with the charge of five raiders?" Sylvie asked.

"Slow. The same with the reload time." Cali looked up and scowled. "Look, I only need to take down one or two. We can kill the rest. Standing orders aside, I'd rather not get killed trying to take prisoners."

"It's a great honor to die for Odin," Sylvie said with dry sarcasm.

"Fuck that." Cali snorted. "It's a good thing you're here to provide support."

"Yes, a good thing." Sylvie set her Remington M700 up alongside the tranquilizer rifle. They aligned their firearms toward the tree line. The enemy would have to cross three hundred feet of open meadow to reach them.

As much as Sylvie admired and revered the All-Father, a fool she was not. Champions that triumphed in battle were said to curry the god's blessing; those who fell, his curse. Sooner or later, everyone died, including Odin's chosen warriors... especially his favored. Sylvie had always hoped her soul would go on to Freya's hall. But that was before Paul died in combat and entered Valhalla. Now she faced an impossible dilemma: Freya in Sessrúmnir or Paul in Valhalla? It divided Sylvie's heart.

Cali placed an automatic assault rifle beside her leg and gave it a reassuring pat as if she meant to comfort the gun. Then she placed a concussion grenade beside the firearm and petted it also to dispel any hint of favoritism. And *this*, Sylvie decided, was as good a reason as any for liking the hunter.

"Morena filled me in on the Logan-Sawyer situation," Cali said, adjusting the knobs on her scope. "Where the fuck do you suppose those two are?"

The Logan-Sawyer situation... Sylvie smiled despite the severe circumstances. "I don't know. Assuming they haven't killed each other yet, maybe they decided to take a break?"

Cali snorted. "Yeah, I wouldn't be surprised."

"Did you bring your skillet?"

"No, not this time." Cali chuckled and Sylvie joined her.

Deep in the woods, the branches of a tree cracked, marking the passage of something big. Other sounds signaled the approach of multiple creatures. Either the raiders considered stealth unimportant or they lacked sufficient familiarity with their stolen animal forms.

Both women stiffened. The noise grew nearer.

"Here they come." Sylvie bent over her scope, aiming with both eyes.

"Leave the bear to me," Cali hissed the words. Peppery heat sharpened her basal odor—the mark of a predator primed to fight.

"I will." Sylvie targeted an area of the trees that clattered and shook. Her grip steadied on the rifle and she slid straight back into the cool detachment of a trained warrior. Funny how her body remembered what her mind had long forgotten.

A dark brown wolf broke from the woods, emerging squarely into view of her scope. She fired—the rifle cracked. The raider released a pained yelp and staggered.

A few yards away from the wolf, a sapling toppled beneath the weight of the charging grizzly. A gray wolf followed on his heels. The raiders rushed toward the truck.

The air rifle released a powerful pop. A pink-feathered dart lodged in the bear's shoulder. He roared and kept coming.

"Jake, so help me..." Cali scrambled to reload.

Sylvie worked the bolt, loading the next cartridge. Without aiming, she took another shot at the brown wolf and hit him dead center in the chest. He dropped.

The bear reached the halfway mark at center field. The gray wolf passed the bear.

"You one-eyed sonofabitch, I'm going to rip you a new one if I get killed..." Cali twisted and snatched up the concussion grenade. She yanked the pin and lobbed the grenade into the field. It flew wide. In baseball, it would have been a foul ball.

Sylvie ducked down beside Cali, taking cover behind the wall of the bed. She hooked an arm over the hunter's shoulders, pressing down. To her surprise, she found Cali doing the same for her.

The grenade detonated, rocking the world. The explosion beat at her eardrums, leaving her deafened and stunned. To Sylvie's vexation, Cali recovered first. The hunter shot erect, seized the air rifle, and swiveled it on its mount. She squeezed the trigger. Sylvie felt the signature pop, saw the gun lift on the back kick, but she couldn't hear it.

Sylvie scrambled up to look out at the field of battle. The force of the explosion had knocked all four enemy raiders off their feet. Even the grizzly lay on his side, his head lolling; maybe the potent tranquilizer had finally kicked in. Behind the prone bear, the other two wolves remained down for the count.

The grizzled gray wolf hauled himself to his feet. His proximity to the truck made him the most immediate threat, especially to Cali, who was once again reloading tranquilizer darts into the air rifle.

Sylvie grabbed her rifle, cranked the bolt, and sprang over the side of the truck. She landed in a crouch. Her wolf ascended to dominance, the transition mental rather than physical. Predatory instinct took over, and she thirsted for blood.

The lanky gray wolf recovered from the grenade and raced across the rocky ground, his claws gouged the earth. Head high, he billowed forth great clouds of steam as his hot breath hit the cool air. His eyes glowed coal-red, and his parted jaws revealed dagger-sized teeth. He meant to rip out her throat.

"Eat this!" She fired point-blank into his open mouth. The bullet passed between his parted jaws, lanced through his head, and burst the back of his skull wide open. His head erupted, spewing forth a glorious gush of gore.

A huge, dark shaped loomed over her. Cold fear lanced through Sylvie. Gooseflesh rose on her back. She turned, staring up at the towering grizzly. He stood on his rear legs, his enormous paws raised, wicked claws brandished. She tensed in dreadful anticipation—too late to dodge or defend.

The bear moaned, a mournful, sour-bellied sound, and toppled over. He struck her as he fell, a ton of solid mass, and knocked her right off her feet. Sylvie landed square on her back; the impact forced the air from her lungs. A second later, the grizzly crashed down on top of her, trapping her beneath him.

Mangy brown fur smothered her face so she couldn't see or breathe. Her lungs ached and her legs were pinned flat. Infuriated, Sylvie pushed and pulled at the beast's underside, but his dead weight didn't budge.

Humiliation scorched her pride. She refused to end like this, suffocated beneath an obese, immobile bear. Gritting her teeth, she focused her efforts, a concentrated shove. At first, nothing gave but she kept at it with pure grit until her muscles burned and her arms threatened to pop from her shoulder sockets. The bear budged, only an inch, but enough to reinforce her resolve. She ground her teeth together with enough force to pulverize stones to powder. She sweated like a woman in a sauna, her limbs shook, and the burden lifted and moved, freeing her face.

Fresh air flooded her lungs; a renewal of strength. She heaved the crushing weight off her and rolled over into a crouch. It cost her precious seconds to get oriented. She scanned her surroundings and counted the downed bear and the two wolves she'd shot. Another wolf rested alongside the rear tire of the pickup truck, looking like he'd dropped midstride. The hot pink tassels of a tranq dart stuck out from the thick fur about his neck—another direct score for Cali Kinkaid. Unless Sylvie had her count wrong, that left one *Den Valgte* raider.

A ruckus arose from the back of the pickup truck: Cali shouted over the fierce growl of an angry wolf. From her position on the ground, Sylvie couldn't see what was happening, but it sounded like a life-or-death struggle. With a mighty effort, she hauled herself to her feet. Over the truck's sidewall, she spied both her ally and the enemy.

Cali sat with her knees to her chest, her back pressed to the crates that made up the cargo. She thrust her good arm into her attacker's face, clawing for his eyes while her broken arm doubled as a shield. A russet-furred male wolf stood over her, his jaws locked on the hunter's white cast. Growling, he jerked his head from side to side, shaking her arm like a toy.

"I'm coming!" Sylvie gathered herself and took a running start. She flew through the air and landed square in the bed of the truck behind the *Den Valgte* shaman. The vehicle rocked under her weight.

"Get this flea-bitten mutt off me!" Cali said through gritted teeth.

Sylvie leapt onto the wolf's back, and looped her arm around his throat, jerking the inside of her elbow taunt across his gullet. She hauled back, throwing all her weight into prying him off Cali, and lifted him off his feet.

The russet wolf growled furiously, struggling to break free. He held onto Cali with his stubborn jaws, dragging the hunter along with him.

"Not sure this is an improvement."

"Hang in there." Sylvie grunted. Her aged bones groaned under the strain of exertion. She feared one of her joints would pop before the wolf succumbed to strangulation, but she poured the entirety of her strength into the effort. Even her accelerated healing couldn't fully compensate for the rigors of aging. Later, if she survived, she'd gladly pay the price.

"Oh, you're funny." Expression contorted in agony, Cali ceased trying to gouge the raider's face. She twisted around, dangling from her broken arm, and groped for something on the bed of the truck.

"He's weakening," Sylvie said, crossing mental fingers that the wolf's slackening resistance wasn't her imagination.

The wolf thrashed and opened his jaws, releasing the hunter who crashed to the metal floor. In desperation, he twisted around. On the verge of losing her balance because of his shifting weight, Sylvie staggered backward. His jaws snapped together right beside her face. His whiskers tickled her cheek.

Sylvie caught a blur in her peripheral vision. Shouting at the top of her lungs, Cali surged toward them. The hunter swung her arm overhead. A flash of hot pink. She stabbed the wolf in the throat, driving the needle of the tranquilizer deep into his jugular. Blood squirted from the puncture wound, and the wolf collapsed.

Sylvie let go. The wolf crashed to the ground. Shaking, she doubled forward and crossed her arms over her gut. Before her, Cali swayed on her feet. Their gazes caught, and they stared at each other. For a long moment, the only sound came from their labored breathing.

A smile split Sylvie's face. Cali grinned in return.

The heavy pounding of footsteps marked the approach of new arrivals. Sylvie spun, expecting to confront yet more raiders, and greeted the arrival of Sawyer and Logan. Man and wolf skidded to a halt beside the truck. Perplexed, they rotated, searching for the enemy, but of course found nothing but dead or unconscious raiders.

"What the hell took you two so long?" Cali snapped.

"We were busy." Sawyer strode toward the bear and nudged its huge paw with the toe of its boot. Covered in blood and dirt, the hunter looked like a hellhound's toy that'd been chewed up and spat out. If she had to judge the sorriest of the pair, Logan got the blue ribbon. A gory, gaping wound split his neck and shoulder, exposing raw meat and bone.

"Did the two of you take out five guys by yourself?" Logan asked in an incredulous tone. "Including that bear?"

Startled, Sylvie glanced over at Logan. She blinked. Yes, he was still in his wolf form.

"Yeah, it speaks. I was shocked, too," Sawyer drawled.

"Shut up, asshole." Unmistakably, Logan's voice came from the wolf's mouth.

It took Sylvie a moment to process the abnormality but she dealt with it in short order. Given all the Storm Pack had endured these past several months—hunters, witches, vampires, and more —a talking wolf warranted little more than a raised brow. Besides, Logan had always been a little... off.

"We took out seven. These five and two more." Sylvie waved her arm the general direction of the canyon. She walked to the open tailgate and hopped down.

"It took longer than it should've. Jake wanted prisoners so we took three of them alive." Cali bent over the drugged wolf and jerked the dart from his neck. Mid-gesture, she paused, staring at her forearm. She twisted her limb, revealing a scrape near her elbow. "Look at that. I got cut."

"You're okay other than that?" Sawyer asked.

"Yeah, I'm peachy." Cali cocked her head. "How many raiders did you guys take out? From the looks of you, it must've been a couple dozen, huh?"

The men stayed quiet, but traded a significant look.

"Is that so?" Sylvie asked, clinging to her skepticism.

The question smacked into a pool of dead silence that went on for a few seconds too long. Sylvie's suspicions aroused the same as when Morena tried to deceive her. Sylvie frowned. She expected deception from teenagers, but Sawyer and Logan were adults. Just based on their mutual animosity, she failed to conceive of a scenario where they acted as partners in crime.

The silence endured. Sawyer, who she trusted to a certain degree, looked to Logan, and Logan, who she trusted less, assumed responsibility for his failure.

"We got our asses handed to us," Logan said, a grudging admission torn from him against his will.

"Did you?" Sylvie asked in marked surprise. Arik's spoiled, selfish son—an immature ingrate in her esteem—rose above her opinion of him. She sensed his attempt to assume leadership within the pack bond. And in that moment, her perception of him changed.

"Hell, yeah." Logan snorted and elbowed the hunter. "Tell 'em."

After a long, long pause, Sawyer chimed in with sheepish chagrin. "Yeah, that about covers it."

"It's all right, Private Snowflake." Cali smashed her elbow into Sawyer's side. "You aren't a marine like your old man 'n' me."

CHAPTER 9

Bifröst: **The Rainbow Bridge**

THE RED LASER dot locked on his chest the second he yanked open the basement door. Glancing down, Logan threw up his hands.

"Whoa, don't shoot! It's me!"

"Logan?" At the bottom of the stairs, Morena held the handgun with ease, maintaining a professional shooting stance. Her firearm technique bore an eerie similarity to Sawyer's, the same parallel he'd noticed in her fighting style. Apparently, the hunter had trained the girl in more than just hand-to-hand. The teenager had taken her job as guardian to heart. Sophia and the pups were hidden, but Logan detected their familiar scents.

"Who do you think? Will you stop pointing that thing at me?" Getting shot usually wouldn't kill him but right now, he wasn't so sure. On point, his stomach rumbled. The worst of his wounds still hadn't yet healed despite a shift from wolf to man. Yeah, better not risk it.

"Dunno, it's hard to tell. I almost didn't recognize you."

93

Morena kept the pistol trained on him for a moment longer. She scanned the area behind him, searching for hidden threats.

"Yeah, yeah," Logan groused. He knew he looked bad.

Before coming to release Morena and the wolves, he'd stopped off at his room. He threw on yesterday's shirt and jeans, scavenged off the top of the laundry hamper. A mixture of dried blood and grime coated his hair and skin. He offended himself and longed for a shower. Proper hygiene would've taken more time than he had to spare. He'd brushed away the bits of flesh and fur stuck between his teeth, though. It took three full rounds of flossing and Listerine to rid himself of the nasty aftertaste of magic-fouled blood.

"Is it over?" Morena asked.

"Yeah, it's over."

"Did we win?" The teenager cocked her head.

"Would I be standing here if we'd lost?"

"If you're a winner, I don't want to know what the losers look like."

"I guess that's the thanks I get for almost getting ripped in half while defending the pack."

"Aww, don't pout. You know you're my hero." With a sly smile, she lowered the handgun, thumbed the safety on, and holstered it in a practiced motion.

Logan's hackles rose. How much time—and physical intimacy—did that level of instruction require? He got weird and resentful just thinking about it. He'd only been gone what...? Four months? What the hell happened while he was away? It had to stop. As soon as the current mess resolved, Logan planned to do something about it. What, he wasn't quite sure yet. But something...

Morena turned to face a part of the basement off the landing which was out of Logan's line of sight. She beckoned and whistled. "It's safe. C'mon out!"

Wolfish barks rang out, and then panting and pounding paws as the four gray wolves rushed to join Morena. The formidable, furry cavalry charged up the steps. Logan took a hasty step backward, clearing a path; better than getting knocked flat on his ass. Mick, the only male pup, shot past. His sisters, Minnie and Gypsy, followed close on his heels, and then Sophia. Nipping, yipping, and tumbling, they crested the stairs and vanished into the upstairs hallway.

Morena brought up the rear.

Logan touched her shoulder as she passed. "Just so you know, Vic is still MIA."

"Victoria can take care of herself." Morena looked to him with wide eyes, pleading for reassurance.

"I'm worried, too, Morie." Oddly, Logan found confessing to Morena so much easier than admitting the same thing to Sawyer or Sylvie. Victoria's absence ate at him—a vague but persistent sensation he couldn't shake no matter what.

Stricken, Morena wrung her hands. "That's not what I wanted you to say."

"I'm sorry. I hate lying. You deserve the truth."

"Thanks... I think."

"You're welcome." He took a swipe at a maddeningly itchy patch behind his ear, freeing a shower of red dandruff from his scalp.

"Eww." Morena pulled a face.

"Yeah, I'll have you know this is *eau de man*. What a real man smells like!"

She gave Logan the old side eye. "You should shower."

"Can't. I have to go back out. The cops just arrived. It's a madhouse out there."

"The cops are here?" Morena turned deathly pale.

"Hey, what's wrong?" Logan caught her arm. She trembled beneath his touch and fear soured her scent.

"Your uncle brought the police?" Morena demanded.

"Of course he did. Why is this news? *You* called him." Logan shook his head, baffled at her reaction.

"I called him but I thought he'd come alone." Morena grabbed his forearms and shook him. "You really don't get it, do you?"

Logan shook his head.

"Cops mean men with guns poking around on our land. There are a crap ton of bodies out there." Morena waved her arm in a wild sweep meant to encompass the great outdoors. "If they figure out what we are..."

"Oh." Abruptly, Logan got it. Morena was scared... no, *terrified* of discovery. She perceived the deputies of the El Dorado County Sheriff's Department as a threat to the pack. "Don't worry, these guys work for my uncle. They know all about the supernatural—"

"*¡Increíble!*" Morena smacked his arm. "Did it ever occur to you to explain this to anyone? Hmm?"

"What's the big deal, squirt?"

"Sylvie? Victoria?" She redefined incredulous.

"No." Logan felt like a fool, but he refused to apologize. Morena and the rest of the Storm Pack had resided in Sierra Pines for months. How was he supposed to know what they did or didn't know? Besides, he'd only been home a few days and the subject had never come up.

"*¿Cómo puede un hombre tan hermoso ser tan estúpido?*" Morena walked away, talking with her hands, headed to the front of the house.

"I'll take that as a compliment!" Logan sauntered along at a sedate pace. Mindful of his gnawing hunger and unhealed wounds, he detoured through the kitchen and raided the fridge. He snatched half a cold pizza from the box, folded it, and crammed it down his throat. By the time he reached the front door, tomato sauce smudges on his hands were all that remained. Still starving, he polished off the container of breath mints he found in the front pocket of his jeans.

A commotion reached them through the walls of the house. Ever cautious, Sophia and her pups halted in the entryway. Morena, however, surged forward in a reckless advance.

"Morena," Logan said, a word of caution that came too late.

"What?" Without turning, Morena yanked open the front door.

"Never mind." Logan hesitated. He glanced back at the wolves. "Stay put, okay?"

Sophia ruffed in agreement.

Hurrying, Logan headed outside. Morena stood on the front porch, fenced in behind a pair of deputies who blocked the passageway. The officers faced out into the yard. Over their heads, Logan got a glimpse of the scene. The El Dorado County Sheriff's Department serviced the small community of Sierra Pines. Patrol vehicles as well as the official corner's van crowded the paved two-lane road. Officers in uniform and morgue personnel swarmed the area. Industrious deputies loaded the three unconscious *Den Valgte* shamans—reverted to their human forms—into a prisoner transport truck. For the moment, the bodies of the dead remained where they'd fallen.

"Look at that!" Full blast, Morena twisted sideways and slipped through the thin space between the two deputies.

"Hold up." Logan grabbed for the teenager's arm but was too late. She darted off, leaving him trapped behind the men. Fuming, Logan bit back a curse. Damn it, and people said *he* had no common sense.

His movement attracted the attention of Deputy Mark Gilman and Deputy Bryan Shaw, who worked as partners. Logan knew both men on a first-name basis as well as their wives and children. In a town the size of Sierra Pines, such innocuous intimacies made up the fabric of life. At Logan's disheveled appearance, both men gave a surprised second look.

"There you are," Gilman said to Logan. "Out picking posies while the womenfolk defend the homestead?"

"Thanks, but I've always been a pansy man myself." Logan smiled through gritted teeth, curbing the desire to flatten the burly jackass. The fact the burly jackass wore a gun and a badge helped. "What did I miss?"

"Damned if I know." Gilman ran his hand through his thinning hairline. The man had more girth in the gut than regulations allowed, but he was within nine months of retirement with a full pension. Logan knew for fact his uncle looked the other way when it came to certain rules.

"I'll tell you what it is. It's a damn mess." Shaw's sweeping gesture encompassed the whole of the front yard and road.

"Thank you, Deputy Shaw. I'll take over now." Mike Trash, Logan's uncle, emerged from the busy throng. He was a fit man in his late forties with piercing brown eyes set in a rectangular face. His ears stuck out a smidge too much, but he was passably good-looking for a guy his age. Thanks to his position in law enforcement, he wielded considerable influence in Sierra Pines. Like Logan, Mike was also a medium capable of seeing and speaking to ghosts, following in the traditions of the maternal side of Logan's family.

"Yes, sir." Shaw moved aside as did Gilman. They retreated to the walkway.

"Logan, how are you? You look like death warmed over." Mike tromped onto the porch, chuckling at his own joke.

"Thanks, Uncle Mike. I get that a lot." Logan bared his teeth in his best shit-eating grin. "What's happening?"

Mike released a mighty huff. "My people have secured the scene here at the lake house. We have two dead bodies and three unconscious suspects."

"You took away their hides, I hope?"

"What kind of fool do you take me for?" Mike curled his upper lip.

"Just checking. What about the other dead guys?"

"You mean the mess you boys left out by Sawyer's campsite?"

"That's what I mean." Logan sneered in his turn. Since when were Mike and Sawyer Barrett on a first-name basis? First Morena and now his uncle... the guy kept inserting himself into Logan's life, meddling with the people he cared about.

"We haven't gotten out to the second scene yet. From what Sawyer said, the cleanup is going to consume a lot of manpower. This is an all-hands-on-deck situation. I've already had to call in every off-duty officer. That's a lot of overtime in addition to the bribes it'll take to keep this out of the media."

"The outside world is going to hell in a handbasket. Who's going to care what happens in a remote mountain town?" Logan asked.

Mike leveled a significant stare.

"Fine, I'll write a check." If it placated his uncle, Logan would foot the bill. Of all the problems Daddy Dearest had left in the wake of his untimely death, money wasn't one of them.

"That'll do." Mike nodded and patted Logan's shoulder. "We've loaded the suspects into the prisoner transport. I'd like to get them into town before the sedatives wear off."

"Yeah, about that." Logan stuck up his hand in a staying motion. "Victoria is going to want to talk to them."

"Victoria isn't here, is she?" Mike hesitated, interlacing his fingers.

"Not now, but she'll be back." Logan refused to entertain any other possible outcome. "And when she is, she'll need to interrogate the *Den Valgte* leader."

"Then I'll work with her to make that happen." The sheriff exhaled, betraying his thinning patience. "Trust me, Logan. I'm not interested in complicating this matter. I don't want any more trouble with those raiders than you do. Right now, my primary concern is getting the suspects locked up before the tranquilizers wear off. We don't know what these shamans are capable of. The jail may very well be the only facility secure enough to hold them."

"All right." Logan jerked his chin in a curt nod.

"Good, we'll talk more later." The sheriff raised his voice. "Gilman, you're riding shotgun with me in the prisoner transport. Let's get a move on."

CHAPTER 10

Ráðgríðr: **The High Valkyrie**

ABSORBED IN HIS THOUGHTS, Sawyer tugged the corner of the tarp taut over the bed of Cali's pickup truck. The injuries he'd sustained in the fight had already fully healed. He operated on autopilot; his attention focused on the prisoner transport as it receded down the road. Mike Trash and two of his deputies had left to escort the prisoners to the county jail. Another dozen or so officers along with the coroner's staff remained behind to process the scene. Initially, the presence of so many local law enforcement officers had alarmed him. The sheriff's people, however, had handled the entire situation with laudable professionalism.

"Hey, are you listening?" Cali asked across the truck.

"Yeah, I'm listening." Sawyer secured the last tie down and checked his work. In truth, he hadn't heard a word she'd said. Other matters preoccupied his thoughts. Foremost, he worried about Victoria's continued absence. What if she'd had a run in with another faction of *Den Valgte* and been captured or killed?

Not to mention, the Storm Pack had other enemies, including the Necromancer and the Norns.

"Bull!" Cali jerked her arm in a throwing motion.

"Hey!" Acting on reflex, Sawyer dodged. A rock whizzed past his ear.

"Don't shit a shitter. You haven't heard a word I said." Cali hefted a second stone, holding it so he could see it.

"I heard you." Sawyer kept his hands raised to defend his face.

"Yeah?" The corners of her mouth contorted. "Then what's the answer—yes or no?"

Damn. What'd he gotten himself into now? He considered admitting he'd lied but discarded the thought immediately. He might as well guess. At least then he had a fifty-fifty chance at the correct answer. If he got it wrong, Cali would give him hell either way.

"Yes."

"That so?" Cali flashed a wide shit-eating grin.

Sawyer's stomach sank. *Wrong answer.*

Cali cackled like a hyena. "All right, Romeo, you have dibs. Logan is all yours but if you fuck this up—"

"Kinkaid, hell to the no." Sawyer snarled in warning and started around the rear of the truck, going after her. Laughing, Cali retreated.

A brilliant flash of light interrupted the chase. Both hunters halted in their tracks. All activity ceased as deputies and coroner personnel also turned toward the phenomenon that'd manifested on the far edge of the front lawn alongside the driveway.

A swirling portal hung suspended in midair. Bifröst, the rainbow bridge, burned with all the colors of fire. It connected Midgard, the world of humanity, with Asgard, the home of the gods. It could also open at Urd's Well, the base of Yggdrasil.

A pair of warrior women stepped off the bridge. They advanced and then split and marched in opposite directions. They were tall and athletic, armed with medieval weapons, and clad in armor that'd been polished until it shone. Two more female soldiers emerged from the portal and parted ways, mirroring the motion of their predecessors.

"Valkyries," Cali said it like a dirty word.

"Yep." Sawyer frowned. He harbored no innate objection to Valkyries. Or he hadn't before Freya had asked Victoria to sacrifice him. These Valkyries worked for Freya, which put them at the bottom of the list of people he wanted to see.

"Wonder what they want this time?" Cali reached for the rifle slung across her back and pulled it into her hands.

"Let's find out." Sawyer grabbed for his shotgun as well. Normally, he'd have preferred an empty-handed approach. Peace and respect, and all that... Ultimately, he kept circling back to the Vanir goddess having demanded the obliteration of his soul—the stumbling block he kept getting stuck on. It might be petty, but he had issues with the whole thing.

Together, the hunters started across the lawn, weaving through the crowd of onlookers. A great snort and the thunderous pounding of hooves heralded the arrival of four mounted horsewomen through the portal. The dapple-gray horses cantered atop a rolling road of mist. The riders carried short lances and round shields, short bows and raven-feather-fletched arrows. People in their path hurried to get out of the way, resulting in a mass retreat. It spoke well of the discipline of the sheriff's people that no one panicked or fired their sidearm.

Ráðgríðr, a raven-haired woman of extraordinary height, strode through the portal and Bifröst winked closed behind her. She brandished a spear and a shield as well as a sheathed sword and assorted knives. A woman after Sawyer's own heart: armed to the teeth... quite literally.

The High Valkyrie sported an ornate headdress made from a gleaming dragon skull. Fully articulated ridges swept back from the hollow eye sockets. Razor-sharp teeth clenched in a gruesome smile between the powerful reptilian jaws. A peacock's wealth of ivory feathers cascaded across her shoulders and back. Her gothic armor, shining as brilliantly as the morning sunshine, possessed rounded curves and gold fluting, the product of singular Dwarven craftsmanship.

"Cowabunga, look at that getup," Cali said with a snort. "Is there a cosplay contest no one told me about?"

"What's cosplay?" Sawyer asked.

"You don't get out much, do you?" Cali nudged Sawyer in the ribs with her elbow. She snickered up a storm.

"Hot damn. Does that woman have a dinosaur on her head?" Logan asked, sidling up to them. "What do you call that anyway? Dino Hat?"

Dino Hat. Sawyer's lips twitched despite himself. Damn it.

"Nice one, A-Hole." Cali flashed a grin at Logan.

"Thanks, Dixie." Logan moved to flank Cali so they formed a defensive line of three with Kinkaid in the middle. "Looks like it's time for round two with the Bitch Brigand."

Sawyer grunted and frowned. He didn't get Cali's friendliness toward the wolf. Just a few days ago, she'd clobbered Logan over the head with a hot skillet. Now, the two of 'em were yucking it up like old buddies.

Three hundred feet distant, the cavalry soldiers circled around to face their leader. Ráðgríðr issued a command and pointed northeast. The Valkyries whirled and spurred their mounts. The horses leapt high and took flight. Awe rocked the onlookers, who exclaimed and cranked their necks to follow the remarkable sight as the riders charged across the sky. The Valkyries were headed toward the meadow where he and Logan had fought and slain the other *Den Valgte* raiders. For Sawyer, the spectacle inspired a leaden weight in his gut. Doubtless, they intended to collect the worthy souls of the slain for transport to Valhalla.

"Should we stop them?" Logan asked in a low voice, a spooky parallel to Sawyer's thoughts. He kept moving toward Ráðgríðr, maintaining an even pace so as not to appear hesitant or hurried.

"How? This is what they do." Sawyer shook his head. He'd wanted to say yes, but common sense advised against it.

The few remaining deputies and coroner personnel continued

to withdraw, vacating the front yard. Their retreat made the wisdom of approaching Ráðgríðr all that much more questionable, but that's where Logan and Sawyer were heading. Smart had nothing to do with it.

"Vic will be pissed when she finds out they poached souls and we didn't do anything." Logan employed a deliberate, needling tone.

Sylvie strode toward them with Morena dogging her heels. The skald cut into the conversation with a severe rebuke, "Valkyries don't poach souls. It is their sacred duty to choose the slain worthy to enter Valhalla."

"*Den Valgte*—" Logan started to say, but was cut off.

"However objectionable we may find *Den Valgte,* they are Odin's followers. When they die with valor in battle, they are eligible to be chosen." Sylvie sounded none too pleased with the situation herself.

Ráðgríðr addressed her four followers, "Hervör, you and your sister are to cavass this field and collect the worthy souls of those who have fallen. As soon as you are finished, take your charges to Fólkvangr. Thrud, Rota, remain with me."

The four Valkyries responded with a collective, "Yes, my lady." Two split off and departed, presumably to attend to their duties. The others remained with Ráðgríðr.

"Thrud," Logan snorted, putting heavy emphasis on the UD. "That woman is a hundred times sexier than her name."

"Just a hundred?" Sawyer heard himself ask in defiance of good sense and respect for women everywhere.

"Thousand," Logan added after a thoughtful delay.

"I'll grant you, she's hot." Sawyer resolved to turn in his feminist membership card at the next opportunity.

"*I* will handle this." Determination shone in Sylvie's dark eyes. As mild as she might seem, the older woman kept iron fists concealed beneath those velvet gloves. She stepped forward, holding her head high.

Sawyer stood with Cali and the rest of his pack. Not bad

company, should the shit hit the fan... Even Morena lurked nearby, milling as though unsure of her place. For the moment, he deferred to Sylvie's authority while she spoke on their behalf. Their united front, however, made a statement. The skald had more than words backing her up.

"Lady Ráðgríðr," Sylvie said with the utmost deference. "I am Sylvie Thornton, Skald of the Storm Tribe. If you would explain your purpose here, I would gladly be at your service."

"I am not required to offer explanations." Ráðgríðr stared down her beaked nose. Her sharp features formed the spearhead on her contempt. She condemned with her stare.

"My lady, have I offended you?" Sylvie parted her lips and gasped. "If so, please tell me what I have done so I may make amends."

That—*right there*—set Sawyer on edge. If anyone deserved respect, it was Sylvie who, despite her formal proclivities, was one of the most considerate people he'd ever met. It took everything Sawyer had not to intervene on her behalf, and then he wondered at his restraint. Logan also stirred, his quick anger flaring across the pack bond. The two of them teetered on the verge of jumping to their packmate's defense. Ah, hell. Sawyer hated how life kept twisting things so he was forced to side with the hotheaded werewolf.

It had to stop.

Ráðgríðr opened her mouth but then hesitated. She appraised Sylvie. Thoughtful consideration overtook the High Valkyrie's outright contempt. "Perhaps I have been unnecessarily harsh. The offense offered was not yours. "

"Then who has offended you?" Sylvie compressed her lips and crossed her arms over her chest.

"It is your leader, Victoria Storm, who is the traitor." Ráðgríðr raised her sharp chin.

"Impossible!" Sylvie spat an immediate denial.

"Victoria betrayed Freya."

"No," Sylvie said, shaking her head. "She wouldn't. She couldn't—"

"She fails you even now. Don't believe me? Ask her yourself when she returns from her clandestine meeting." Ráðgríðr's tone softened with sympathy. "Sylvie Thornton, I'm telling you this so you can understand the danger of your association. Consider the path you wish to take with care."

Sawyer couldn't keep his mouth shut any longer. "That's enough. Victoria isn't a traitor. If anyone has committed treason, it's Freya."

"Oh snap! Look at her face. Nothing worse than being caught in a lie." Logan landed a congratulatory slap on Sawyer's shoulder.

Ráðgríðr paled to a ghastly hue, and then stiffened like a corpse in rigor. No matter what, she couldn't blow off a prince of Asgard. Sawyer never used the title. His entire life, he hadn't set foot in the Aesir homeland even once. He understood, however, the advantage his birthright granted him here. And he was far too practical not to put it to good use.

"Ráðgríðr, do you know who I am?" Sawyer stepped forward, hopefully out of reach, but Logan moved also. Sticky paper and fly.

Without a word, Sylvie stepped aside, beating a fast retreat. From the look on her face, she hadn't yet recovered from the shock of the accusation against Victoria. Sawyer worried for her, but he didn't have time to dwell on it.

"I know who you are." Ráðgríðr clenched her spear so tightly her knuckles turned white. "I would speak with you in private—"

"You saw fit to make the accusation against Victoria in public. Any response I make should be just as open," Sawyer countered. Anger burned through him white-hot. The intensity of it shocked him. He'd gone to bat against his own mother for Victoria. He sure as hell wouldn't back down for the likes of Dino Hat. "While you're advising others to consider their loyalties, you should think on your own."

"True loyalty is not open to consideration," Ráðgríðr said.

"Then you've got another thing comin'," Logan snarked from over Sawyer's shoulder.

"Think," Sylvie snapped.

"Not according to Judas Priest." Cali swiveled to argue with the skald.

"Judas *Who?*" Morena asked.

Sawyer increased his grip on his shotgun. He. Would. Not. Shoot. Them. All.

Ráðgríðr flushed to burnt umber. A smear of blood appeared on her lower lip. She squared her shoulders, pulling herself to her full height. She stood strong and proud, taller even than Sawyer. Rumor placed her heritage as half Jotun—a giant.

"I answer only to Freya," Ráðgríðr said. "She who commands all Valkyries."

"Freya is a general." Sawyer borrowed from his father's playbook, opting for stoicism over passion. Funny how the very thing he'd spent his life rebelling against had become his canon. "She may command Valkyries and the army at Fólkvangr, but her authority derives from the throne."

"While you are reminding me of my lady's place, you would do well to remember your own. You are neither the king nor the queen." Ráðgríðr narrowed her eyes. Unflinching, she returned his stare. He had to give her credit where it was due. The woman possessed nerves of steel.

"True enough." Sawyer bared his teeth.

"Freya is my sovereign. I have sworn my loyalty directly to her. It is my duty to defend her from any who would do her harm." Ráðgríðr pressed on as though he hadn't spoken. She tucked her chin against her chest, protecting her throat, so Sawyer wound up staring into the empty sockets of her dragon skull.

Dino Hat... Damn Logan to Helheimr and back.

"I'm not the one you should be worried about. Your lady ordered my execution. Have you stopped to wonder how my parents feel about that?" Sawyer left the question hanging in the ensuing silence. He had to admit—the drake's cranium was damn impressive. *Except...* his education encompassed the growth cycle of dragons. The poor beast couldn't have been much older than a hatchling when it died.

"I spoke with my mother this morning." Sawyer pitched his voice low and soft, sharing a confidence. Intimacy conveyed the significance far more effectively than any intimidation ever could.

"Frigg?" Color bled from Ráðgríðr's lips. The High Valkyrie glanced about as though the goddess was to be caught lurking just over his shoulder. But Ráðgríðr had better figure out fast that she should be looking over her own... or it'd be too late for her.

"Tell me, Ráðgríðr..." Sawyer lapsed into a pregnant pause. He advanced, invading her personal space. "Who's guarding Freya while you're here?"

CHAPTER 11

Perth: The Rune of Chance, Mystery, and Science

BLINKING OWLISHLY, Victoria stared at the long white van blocking her path. Its rear doors stood open; the gold-star logo on the side of the side of the vehicle read "El Dorado County Coroner." She couldn't quite process the how or the why, but it didn't belong any more than the half-dozen county sheriff patrol cars.

"Excuse us, miss. Coming through." The man's voice, polite but insistent, sliced through her reverie.

"Sorry." Victoria moved aside on reflex, and wound up stepping off the driveway onto the front lawn. The soft grass proved much easier on her bare feet than the sharp gravel.

Two uniformed men whisked past with a gurney that bore a zipped body bag and loaded it into the back of the van. Aside from that acknowledgement, they paid her no mind. The sun hung at a mid-morning position. The front of the lake house was the unmistakable aftermath of a battle. Uniformed personnel buzzed about the area, intent on their gruesome business of removing the dead. No one spared more than a brief glance for the rumpled woman in pajamas who wandered into their midst.

The whole hustle 'n' bustle exacerbated Victoria's sense of surrealism. She teetered on the edge of total freak out. Was she dreaming again? In a self-check, she ran her hands through her hair and dislodged a shower of pine needles and thistle. She recalled waking up in the Shadowlands, Michael's voice in the mist, and talking to Jake... After that, her thoughts encountered blankness.

It'd happened again. She'd lost time.

She wondered where her packmates were, but lacked the energy necessary to call on the pack bond. Cold fear crept through her. Were they injured... or worse? The field across the road was the focal point of the law enforcement effort. Sick with dread, Victoria stumbled across the pavement and ducked beneath the yellow crime scene tape into the clearing.

On the shoulder of the road, three deputies surrounded a body. They were engaged in a low discussion and stood with their backs to her, blocking her view. Victoria recognized Bryan Shaw, but not the other two men. In one of those rare instances when being short proved advantageous, she ducked beneath Deputy Shaw's arm and pushed past him.

"Hey! You're not allowed..." Shaw grabbed her elbow.

Victoria ignored Shaw to look down on the gristly, decapitated male corpse that lay on the dirt. Her stomach turned over, but she forced herself to study it until she was one-hundred percent positive the dead man wasn't a member of her pack. Her breath escaped in a gust. Alarm, however, followed on the heels of relief. The dead man's tattoos and wolf-skin shirt marked him as a member of *Den Valgte*.

"Victoria Storm?" Shaw adopted a much more kindly tone. "They've been searching for you. I was told you were missing."

"I'm fine, thank you. What happened here?" Victoria asked in what sounded like a rough croak to her own ears.

Shaw squirmed beneath her regard. "There was an attack—"

"Vic!" Logan's shout boomed through the air. Her heart leapt with gladness to hear a familiar voice.

Victoria turned just as Logan descended on her. His strong arms flung about her, snatched her off her feet, and held her safe. He swung her around in circles so her feet spun out.

She laughed. *Home*—not a place but people. These people. Her people.

"Vic, I—" The whirl of the wind snatched away the rest of his words. Logan slowed his spin but didn't set her down.

"Logan, stop." Victoria thumped her fist against the solid wall of his chest. Damn it, but it required far more of her will than she cared to admit to do other than melt against him.

If she worried about going unnoticed before, no need for that now. Everyone—absolutely everyone—was staring. Logan's *blitzkrieg* greeting had turned them into the center of attention. Distantly, she noted Deputy Shaw's retreat as he fell back to join his fellow officers.

"Are you okay? Where have you been?" Logan huffed against her ear, blowing breath flavored with citrusy sweetness. He'd been at the breath mints again. Otherwise, he reeked of dried blood and grit, the scents of violence and death.

"Yeah, I'm okay. Knock it off. Put me down." She kicked him in the shin. Lack of control ate at her. She needed to get her feet on the ground. No one could possibly take her seriously while she hung suspended two feet off the earth.

"Ouch. Well, good to see you're fighting-fit." Logan thunked her down.

"Logan, are the others okay? What happened?" Victoria demanded, determined someone would provide her with an explanation for the mayhem that'd gone on in her brief absence. Overcome with sudden suspense, she squinted. She'd only been gone for a few hours... or had she?

Logan screwed his face up. "Yeah, everyone is fine. Where were you? We searched but you were nowhere to be found. I couldn't reach you through the bond."

"Never mind where I was..." Although, damn it, she'd really like answers to that herself, but the presence of so many law enforcement officers alarmed her. "What are all these people doing here?"

"Yeah, about that..." Logan worked his face into a full-blown scowl. "Everything's fine. My uncle's people know about the supernatural."

"All of them?" Victoria burst out in sheer disbelief.

"They're trained to deal with these sorts of situations," Logan continued as though she hadn't spoken.

"You mean cover-ups?" She canted her disbelieving gaze across the many professionals working the scene in a business-as-usual fashion. Impossible, yet everything going on supported it as the truth. It begged the question—in this tiny town, how far did this conspiracy of secrets reach?

"Look, this is my fault. I probably should've mentioned it before."

"Ya think?" Victoria asked with only a sliver of her usual sarcasm.

"I'll give you a quick recap," Logan said, talking fast. "*Den Valgte* attacked. We killed most of them, captured three. My uncle has them in custody—"

Victoria opened her mouth, a flood of questions about to come pouring out. Her mind whirled with information overload.

Logan stayed her with his hand. "Ráðgríðr dropped in 'n' out with her Valkyrie brigand. They swiped some souls. Ol' Dino Hat got into a pissing contest with Sawyer."

"Dino Hat?" Victoria's brow jumped high. At the same time, trepidation tripped through her. No good could come of any interaction with Ráðgríðr. The High Valkyrie had a serious grudge against Victoria.

"Yeah, Sawyer read her the riot act—sent her running with her tail between her legs." Logan jerked his head over his shoulder. His tone held a grudging note of respect... for Sawyer?

Victoria frowned. What world had she woken up in?

"We're about to have company," Logan said. "We'll talk more later."

"Company?"

"Incoming—on your six." Logan tapped Victoria's shoulder and pointed.

Victoria performed a full about-face in time to see Morena charging straight at her. This time Victoria got her arms up and braced, meeting the teenager on her own terms. They flew straight into each other's arms.

"Are you okay?" Morena asked. "You look awful."

"I'm fine. And gee, thanks a lot." Victoria released the girl.

"De nada." Morena blew a breath that raised her cobalt bangs off her forehead.

"Where are Sophia and the pups?" Victoria asked.

"Inside." Morena tilted her head. Her bright eyes shone in her foxlike face. "Where the heck have you been?"

"Around. I swear, if one more person asks me that..." Victoria rose onto the balls of her feet, scanning the crowd. If things held true to pattern, the others ought to be along any second to—

Ah-ha.

Sylvie wove her way between parked sheriff vehicles. "Victory! Thank the goddess you're okay!"

"Sylvie!" Victoria greeted her friend with open arms and a wide smile. She expected them to unite with the intimacy of long-time friends, but then something weird happened.

Sylvie hesitated. And again, that damning question came in its enormity. "Where have you been?"

Confidence deserted Victoria like rats off a sinking ship. It sapped what little strength she'd recovered since reuniting with her pack. The gap in her memory remained. She didn't have answers, only confusion and fear. But this time, she couldn't blow off the inquiry or provide a smartass remark. Because this was Sylvie: the housemother, Victoria's mentor and best friend, and the one person Victoria trusted more than any other. The psychic bond between the two women was stronger than any other in the

Storm Pack; the foundation of their small, close-knit family. Over the course of the past several months, one crisis after another had tested it, but somehow they'd always pulled through, tougher for the course. Now, though, it grew brittle beneath the strain.

The others waited, too, in tense expectation. Poor Morena wore an expression of absolute bafflement.

"I don't know," Victoria stammered at last. She shook her head so the loose frizz of her hair flopped into her face. Tears stung her eyes. She clenched her fists and wished for a wall to beat.

"What do you mean, you don't know?" Sylvie demanded, as imperious as a mother speaking to a wayward child. She almost sounded suspicious, which bewildered Victoria even more.

"I don't remember." Victoria winced at the older woman's exacting tone. Guilt assailed her at being unable to provide real answers. How utterly humiliating to be interrogated before so many witnesses. Here she was supposed to be the alpha, but she lacked the gumption to even come to her own defense.

"Sylv, lighten up. I know it's scary but the whole world doesn't need to hear about Victoria's weird pregnancy sleepwalking. You gals can gossip later." Logan made the announcement at a volume that carried to the four corners of the yard. Crass but effective. Not too long ago, blinded by preconceptions and assumptions, Victoria had accepted Logan's brashness at face value.

The stop-motion scene broke. Gruff, patronizing laughter arose from the mostly male group. Then, motion resumed and people went about their business. Sylvie blanked with surprise, but then she flushed in anger. Her face froze in a mask of hostility as she stared at Victoria. Whatever she'd meant to state passed unsaid.

Victoria couldn't bear to look her friend in the face anymore. Sylvie's behavior was hurtful and confounding, but Victoria didn't have the energy to devote to solving the puzzle. Not now. Later. She reached for Logan. When he stepped close, wrapping a protective arm around her shoulders, she sagged against him. His strength flowed through the pack bond, propping her up. For once, she didn't mind accepting his help. Fact of the matter, gratitude damn near overwhelmed her.

"Thank you." Victoria pitched her voice for his ears only.

"You're welcome." He delayed a perfect beat. "Wait. That's not how this conversation goes. You're supposed to lose your temper and call me names."

"I'm too tired. Rain check?" Victoria patted his arm.

"Rain check." He chuckled; his signature on the truce. "C'mon, Vicky, let's get you up to the house. Once you have a chance to rest up—"

"Stop making me out to be an old lady."

"You're the youngest old person I know," he said with a smirk.

"Jackass." Victoria laughed even though it hurt. Their stupid banter grounded her in a sense of normalcy, assurance that at least one relationship in her life wasn't completely screwed up. She smacked his chest to show her appreciation and pulled away, standing on her own two feet again.

Gathering herself, she trudged toward the house, watching the ground for trip hazards. It became a matter of putting one front in front of the other, progressing an inch at a time. She crossed mental fingers that her reserves would hold long enough to make it into the house before she collapsed. Her ego wouldn't survive being carried.

Muddy black boots blocked her path.

Victoria stopped.

With a muttered curse, Logan ground to a halt behind her.

Braced for the most difficult confrontation yet, Victoria raised her face and gazed up into the remote visage of Sawyer. Like all the Barrett men, Sawyer had a grizzly's stature and brutish intimidation, too. The hunter carried a shotgun, the barrel aimed at the ground. Despite wearing the blood 'n' bone of his slain enemies, his long dirty-blond hair and untrimmed beard shone in the bright sunshine. His piercing eyes were hard and glossy, the same shade as his father's.

Faultless shininess: the superpower common to all of Odin's sons.

Her heart twisted in her breast. A vision filled her mind's eye. Jasper—the face of the teenage werewolf that Sawyer had murdered, a child of the Storm Pack. Would Jasper have condemned her for allowing his killer to join them?

Soul sick, Victoria crossed her arms over her chest. She had nothing to say to Sawyer. *Murderer. Betrayer.* The vicious accusations sat on the edge of her tongue, as bitter and toxic as arsenic. Victoria dared not speak them because the others didn't know what the hunter had done, and the truth served no purpose other than to hurt them further.

"Victoria," Sawyer began, faltering. Broken.

"No. I can't deal with you right now." Victoria gave a hard shake of her head and pushed past. Pretending Sawyer didn't exist gave her the strength to keep going. Anything else would've destroyed her.

The short journey into the house took forever. Victoria insisted on making it under her own power. Logan stuck by her side every step of the way. He witnessed her struggle, offered no unsolicited help, and stood ready to catch her if she fell. Right then, she couldn't have asked for a better friend.

"Go lie down," Logan began once they reached the bedroom door. When Victoria locked her hand on his wrist, he looked down, a question on his face.

"One thing, real quick..." Her voice sounded weak to her own ears.

"Yeah?"

"When Sawyer confronted Ráðgríðr..." She trailed off, swallowing convulsively, unsure how to continue. Fear played a real and unworthy part in her reluctance.

"Ráðgríðr accused you of betraying Freya." Logan's tone took a decided turn toward ugly. He bristled with unconcealed hostility for the High Valkyrie.

"In front of Sylvie?" Victoria would've sworn she *felt* the blood drain from her face. Leaden weight settled in her stomach.

"In front of everyone—the entire pack." Logan narrowed his eyes, which gleamed amber bright. Dangerous. Red streaks of murderous intent painted his aura.

"Shit." Victoria reeled, and suddenly she needed her grip on Logan to keep herself upright. Logan caught her elbow, steadying her.

"Sawyer defended you to Rags. It was one hell of a bitch fight —scratchin', hair pullin', titties flyin'..." Logan leered with exaggerated lasciviousness.

"Knock it off." She smacked his chest; the punch packed a pale echo of her usual strength. More like a kitten swatting at a fly than a werewolf expressing displeasure.

Logan snickered. "Too much?"

"Too much." Any other time, she would've laughed, but for now she lacked the strength to even crack a smile.

He snorted. "Sawyer turned it around. He called Freya the traitor because she tried to have him murdered. He made a pretty ominous threat, too. You know I don't think much of the guy, but I'll give him this. He handed that bitch her marching orders."

"Is that everything?" Victoria closed her eyes and pressed her fingers to her throbbing temples. The revelation painted things in a far worse light than she'd imagined.

Silence ensued. It went on long enough that Victoria pried her eyelids open and tilted her head back. Logan's face set into a granite mask, and he said, "It didn't come up that Freya ordered *you* to kill Sawyer, or that Freya cut you off when you refused."

"Good." Relief weakened her knees. Victoria gave silent thanks that not all her ugly little secrets had been exposed. Guilt nagged at her conscience because she could've said something sooner and hadn't. Sylvie had deserved better than to learn the truth on accident. She needed to hear it directly from her alpha. That delayed, much-dreaded conversation with Sylvie had just become imperative.

She gazed at Logan, wrestling with her inner demons. The question she dreaded asking sat on her tongue—did he know that Sawyer had murdered Jasper? The events of the evening Freya had severed her bond with Victoria remained a blur in her mind. She wasn't sure how much Logan had overheard or suspected.

"No one talked about why Freya wanted Sawyer killed, either," Logan added in a dark voice, alluding to the terrible secret that possessed the potential to destroy what was left of her fragile pack.

Victoria's gut cramped. One look into Logan's hard amber eyes told her all she needed. *He knew.* For days, she'd worried herself sick over how much Logan had figured out. Now, she wondered what he would do with the information. She understood him too well to think she could coerce him into silence. Logan hated Sawyer more than anyone. He should be jumping at the opportunity to get rid of the hunter.

"Why haven't you...?" Victoria grated out.

"Why have I kept my mouth shut?" Logan twisted his lips into a grim parody of a smile. He embodied the poster child of mockery.

"Your mouth is so seldom closed." Victoria clenched her hands in an unconscious gesture, ready for a fight.

Logan's malicious smirk melted into his equivalent of resting bitch face. He caught her raised fists and gently pushed her arms down. "When are you gonna get it, Vic? I'm not the enemy. No matter what, I've got your back."

Loki: **The God of Lies**

SUNDAY MORNING

Spices crowded an entire shelf of the walk-in pantry. More than Logan or anyone else needed for one lifetime. Sylvie or Victoria must've purchased them, because the collection had increased tenfold in the months Logan had been gone on walkabout. His fingers flew, sorting by muscle memory. He had a system down: lift, rotate, scan the label, and reject.

Sage, oregano, pepper, oregano, oregano...

His phone occupied the lion's share of his attention. In an act of digital gymnastics, he typed one-handed.

Without warning, Morena popped her head into the pantry. "What's taking so long? Sylvie still needs the onion powder."

"What's taking so long is this damn disaster. Why do we own so much oregano?" Logan asked, discarding what must've been the tenth bottle of the stuff.

"Dunno. Move." Morena slid between the thin gap between

Logan and the shelf, and then used her elbows—quite unnecessarily—as precision pokers to drive him away. He vacated posthaste.

Down the hall, the kitchen bustled with the song of Sunday morning breakfast. Pots clanged on the gas range, the refrigerator banged, and the faucet hummed. The aromatic scent of sizzling eggs and bacon set his stomach to rumbling.

Stepping into the hallway, Logan hit enter, sending his text into the virtual ether: *RU coming over?*

Morena's hands flew as she worked her way through the spice collection. After a minute, she emitted a satisfied cry, "Ah-ha, onion powder!"

"No way, I already checked that side." In disbelief, Logan reached for the bottle but Morena snatched it away.

"Tontos del culo." Morena rolled her eyes and took off with her trophy.

Logan pressed his lips together, wishing he'd paid more attention in high school Spanish. He didn't think she'd just called him her cool friend. He considered pulling up Google Translate, but then he got a reply.

Cali texted: *Yeah. Be there in 20.*

Logan: *K, see ya.*

He slid his phone into his pocket, and debated whether to return to the kitchen right away. If he went back too soon, Sylvie would doubtless assign him another task. The woman had no tolerance for idle hands... On cue, Logan's stomach rumbled; hunger stabbed at his insides. It made him think maybe chopping some onions wasn't such a bad thing after all if it put food in his stomach faster. Anticipation of a full belly put a spring in his step. He started toward the kitchen but before he got underway, a high-pitched squeak snagged his attention.

Logan pivoted on leaden feet. The sound had come from his "dead" father's office. Arik Koenig was also known as Loki, the Norse god of bullshit and bravado, AKA the Trickster... But Logan usually just called the sneaky bastard "Dad".

Uneasily, Logan studied the closed door. He'd only been inside the study twice since Arik had faked his own death, leaving Logan holding a big bag of lies. And what'd Logan done upon discovering his old man's true identity? Had he manned up and taken responsibility for the woman and child his father had abandoned?

No, he'd run like a coward.

While he watched, the knob turned and the door swung inward, creaking on its hinges. It stopped at the one-quarter point. The flesh on the back of Logan's arms crawled. He swallowed around a thick lump in his throat. Hardening his nerve, he leaned out and pressed his fingers against the hardwood and shoved it. The door swung open, revealing shadows at play.

"Son, come in. We need to talk." Arik Koenig's deep, resonant voice emerged from the darkness.

"I'm still not talking to you."

"Fair enough. While we're not speaking, I have a few things to say. That is unless you're too busy to spare a few minutes for your old man," Arik said with a chuckle. He occupied the leather executive chair behind the exquisite handcrafted desk tucked into the corner of the room. He wore a tailored suit with a silk shirt the same hue as the smattering of silver hairs that peppered his dark head. He had brown eyes the shade of dark honey and an aged scar on his cheek.

"Cut the B.S. Are you back?" Logan crossed the threshold. He shoved the door shut behind him to muffle their voices. Morena had big ears and an even bigger nosiness. The last thing he wanted or needed was to have the family skeletons dragged into the open.

"What if I am? What then?" Arik bared his teeth, placed his palms flat on the desk, and rose in a smooth motion. Taunting—a dare or a challenge? He exuded the charisma of intimidation from every inch of his powerful frame. Father and son reached about the same height, but Arik had a good twenty pounds of muscle on Logan.

"For starters, Vic will rip you eyeballs to entrails. Just as soon as she realizes you ran out on her, leaving her barefoot and pregnant..." Logan cocked his middle finger and swiped a dust bunny off the corner of the desk.

The parts and pieces of an antique computer were scattered across the surface. As long as Logan remembered—probably longer than he'd been alive—the machine had sat on a side table, the forgotten relic of a bygone era. In fact, the whole study reeked of stale air and grime. He made a mental note to hire a cleaning service... after he okay'd it with Sylvie, of course.

"Hmm, Victoria..." Arik hummed her name the way one spoke of ooey-gooey chocolate chip cookies straight from the oven. "To be fair, she went barefoot long before we met."

Logan gnashed his molars together so hard his jaws threatened to pop. "Are you back or not?"

"As much as I'd love to come home, it'd be far too dangerous. I'm just dropping in." The shiny leather of the executive chair squeaked beneath Arik's weight as he sank into it.

"Right." Logan sneered to conceal the blast of relief that loosened the grit in his gut. It sickened him, but he didn't want Arik to bust back into their lives. Logan had just begun to gain Victoria's trust. He didn't need the competition for her affection.

"Speaking of—how is Victoria?" Arik cleared his throat. It might've been his imagination, but Logan *almost* believed his father's concern was genuine.

"She's okay." Logan maintained his guard, however, for the sake of civility, he plopped into a shiny blue leather and stainless steel chair opposite the desk. Nostalgically, he inhaled. His mother had purchased it on one of her many overseas retreats. He could still detect her scent on the Italian leather.

"And the baby?" Arik surveyed the mess on the desktop. He picked up a screwdriver in one hand, a computer component in the other.

"She's okay, too."

"Just okay?" Arik glanced up. The corner of his mouth twisted into a cynical smile.

Logan huffed. Jealousy ate at him over having to share Victoria with anyone, but he owed his loyalty to his father. That conflict prompted him to volunteer more. "All the vitals are good. She's developing normally. We had a real scare last Wednesday night. Freya hurt Vic pretty bad. It was touch 'n' go for a couple days there, but she's back on her feet."

And those feet had newly acquired somnolent-locomotion tendencies, but he chose to withhold mention of Victoria's sleep-walking. He'd already given Arik more than he deserved.

"Freya is a real piece of work." Arik scowled at the electronics in his hand. His tone dipped to a vicious, vindictive hiss. "Rest assured, she'll get what's coming to her..."

"We'd better be talking about Freya." Logan rumbled his warning.

Arik raised his chin. His eyes glittered. "Of course we are."

Logan dashed off an acrimonious sneer. "I spent my entire life believing my father was a small-town attorney only to find out he's the god of lies. You can see how I might second-guess your motives, *Loki*."

With careful deliberation, Arik set down the items in his hands and planted them on the desk. Logan shot bolt upright. A long, drawn-out silence ensued. Father and son engaged a determined battle of wills. Stubborn determination cemented Logan's resolve. He'd sworn to protect Victoria and his sister from everything and everyone, up to and including his father.

Arik flared his nostrils, releasing his pent-up tension. "I understand this has been a difficult transition for you—"

"You've made me complicit in your lies!"

"You've made yourself complicit!" Arik smashed his palms upon the desktop. Every piece of electronics jumped under the impact. "If you don't like it, man up and tell Victoria."

Logan shut his mouth with an audible clash. His conscience nagged that he ought to do just that—come clean to Victoria. He would've already, except he was too damn scared of what she'd say once she learned the ugly, unvarnished truth. His reticence ran bone deep. He feared and loathed the prospect of disappointing her.

"Yeah, I didn't think so." Arik snorted and rocked back in his chair. He picked up the same component he'd been fiddling with earlier. "Look, I know my reputation, Son. It's nefarious, even well deserved. What you need to understand—and look past—is my ill-repute has no bearing on our relationship."

"It doesn't?" Logan wagged his brow.

"No. We're family. Everything I've done has been to protect you and your siblings." Arik opened his topmost desk drawer and extracted a black tool roll which he flipped open with a snap of his wrist. He fished out another screwdriver with a different shaped head.

"And Victoria...?"

"My past with Victoria is... complicated." Arik shuttered his gaze and returned to fiddling with the computer part.

"Complicated?" Logan thrust his hands into the air. "You orchestrated the murder of her lover. Her entire pack, including her parents, died."

"Complicated..." Arik dipped his chin. "I regret what happened, but her lover and the souls of everyone else she cared about are in Valhalla, so no real harm was done..."

"No real harm," Logan parroted in disbelief.

"The point being, I'm working on putting things right with Victoria. Besides, she's carrying your sister... my daughter. If that doesn't assure you, nothing will."

"You knocked her up—you're using her." Logan seethed with explosive resentment. Jealousy churned in his gut, because now they were down to the real cause of his anger. His father had tricked and seduced the woman Logan loved.

Arik grimaced. "The pregnancy wasn't planned. It was an accident."

"An accident! Did you trip and fall in?"

Arik bowed his head. His shoulders shook, and he wheezed as

though in the grips of terrible sobbing. Alarmed, Logan jerked his shoulders back.

"Damn, I've missed you, Logan." Arik wiped tears from his eyes with his fingers and grinned something fierce. Even through his mirth, he maintained his grip on what Logan had finally decided was a hard drive.

"I've missed you too, Dad." The recent past and all its unpleasant revelations vanished. They were father and son again. Bittersweet nostalgia filled Logan for what they'd lost. Their relationship hadn't been perfect, not by a long shot, but it'd been good. He stumbled into a wistful realization. "We can't ever go back, can we?"

"Don't waste time looking over your shoulder." Arik set the drive down dead center amidst the clutter. "Watch where you're going."

"Right. You gave me that speech when you were teaching me to drive." Logan thrust his arm out and snatched the hard drive up. It weighed far less than he'd expected.

"It worked, didn't it?" Arik shrugged

Out of curiosity, he shook it. Something rattled around inside it. "It's hollow."

"Careful! That's valuable."

"Is it?" Logan grasped either side of the component and exerted his strength. It snapped in half—something small fell out and landed on the desk.

"Irreplaceable."

Logan tossed the busted halves aside and squinted at the thing. A curved sliver of wood, sharp on one end, rested atop the hardwood. "It's a twig."

"It's a thorn." Arik plucked the sliver between his finger and thumb. He held it up for inspection as though it was a precious treasure. Reverence defined his expression...

"So, it's a thorn. What's the big deal?"

Arik beamed. "It's more than *a* thorn. This *is* Thorn.

"Come again?"

"Thorn is a part of Yggdrasil."

"The world tree has thorns?" Curiosity piqued, Logan stirred and bent forward.

"Just the one—Yggdrasil grew Thorn specifically for me. She is utterly unique—a weapon connected to the tree of life and touched by Fate. Thorn will slay any creature–mortal, monster, or marvelous. She strikes with a single true blow to the heart." Arik flicked his wrist—a swift, slender dagger sprang into his hand. The curved blade shone silver-bright. In keeping with its name, an imposing cluster of stylized thorns formed the guard.

"Is that why you're here—for Thorn?" Disappointment stabbed Logan in the back, catching him unaware: a wound to his ego and his heart. For a few minutes there, he'd allowed himself to believe his father had dropped by for a father-son chat. He should've known better.

"That and to deliver a warning."

"Which is?"

"There are witches in the woods." Arik's eyes glittered like gemstones.

"Again?" Anger blazed in Logan's soul—boundless hatred. He despised the Ironwood witches, and with good cause. The year he'd turned eighteen, a *seiðr* named Hrafnar had enslaved Logan's wolf and forced him to murder his mother.

"Again." Arik nodded with marked solemnness. "They're watching... listening... waiting for their opportunity to strike."

"We really need to do something about them once and for all." Logan clenched his hands to fists, shaking in the grip of strong emotions.

"Believe me, I've tried. Over twenty years ago, I gathered a war party of my wolf-shifter children and tried to destroy the Ironwood coven. I succeeded—for a time—until they reclaimed the town."

"How many people died in your turf war, Dad?"

Arik narrowed his eyes. "Casualties are an inevitable part of war, Logan. You'll learn that for yourself soon enough. Attacking

Ironwood was a necessary gambit. I almost won. I drove the mother spider from her nest, and destroyed three of her daughters."

"Hrafnar was a fake out."

"I wasn't counting Hrafnar. Besides, it's moot. Hrafnar is gone for good. I drove Thorn through her heart and bored a hole through her chest to be sure." Arik thrust and twisted the knife in his hand, demonstrating the killing blow.

Surprise flickered in Logan. Until now, his father had refused to discuss the distant or recent past. Presuming he could be trusted to tell the truth, this was the most he'd ever revealed. "Just to be clear—we're talking about last February. Right before you faked your own death."

"Yes, last February." Arik glanced heavenward.

"And what happened to all that 'only water will destroy the witch' nonsense?" Logan hollowed his voice for spooky effect.

Arik only smiled.

"Right." Logan coughed *"Bullshit"* into his hand. "So now we're dealing with a different witch?"

"The whole damn coven knows where you are, Son."

Terror seized Logan. His heart skipped a beat, and then hammered his chest with a heavy thud. "What do they want with me?"

"They sense your power. They desire to control you."

"Hrafnar was scary. How am I supposed to take on an entire coven alone?"

"You're not alone. I'm with you." Arik dropped his chin. His posture compacted as though readying for a fight.

Logan also grew tense. "Do you have a plan?"

"I always have a plan. Hundreds. Schemes and contingencies..."

"Cut the shit. No games." Logan thumped the desk with his fist. The assorted computer components strewn across it jumped again.

"I'm working on renewing an old alliance," Arik said with a sigh.

"Odin?"

His father stared. His lips parted.

Logan snorted. "I know how to read. Once I learned Jake Barrett's true identity, it's obvious."

"Let's hope it's not obvious to *ethay itchesway foay ronwoodiay*." Arik flashed a wicked, whimsical smile.

"Hope." Logan sneered. "If there's a fight brewing, I want in."

"For now, I need you to sit tight. Stick close to Victoria—protect her and the babe. If your uncle asks for your help, give it."

"In other words, you want me to sit on my hands."

"Be smart. Don't do anything to attract unnecessary attention to yourself. Oh, and stay away from the hospital basement."

"Why?"

"Logan..." Arik released a loud sigh.

"Yeah, Dad?" Logan donned a cloak of angelic innocence.

"Please?"

"Gotcha. Help Mike. Hospital basement is off limits." Logan etched an X over his heart while crossing his toes.

"Good." Arik nodded and tossed the knife, sending it into a quick spin. "Catch."

Of its own volition, Logan's arm shot up. He snatched the dagger from the air. The moment his hand closed about the hilt, warmth suffused his palm. Thorn vanished from his grasp. His skin tingled something fierce.

"Whoa!" Logan thrust his arm out for inspection. A bracelet tattoo of three braided thorny vines encircled his entire wrist. The artwork was delicate and intricate, and it radiated an aura of vitality.

Alive.

"Feels good?"

"Hell yeah!" Logan flexed his wrist experimentally. Magic resided within the tattoo but also sentience, distinctly feminine in flavor.

Arik rose from his chair in a smooth motion. "Thorn has four forms she's capable of assuming: the tattoo, the dagger, the thorn

—which is her true state. She's also capable of becoming a mistletoe dart, but that is only useful for a singular application."

Logan burst with questions. "Her? Is she self-aware? Does she talk? How do I get her to change?"

Before he even finished the last word, the enchantment within the tattoo jazzed with the lively strains of a verdant earth song. The bracelet of vines revolved, slow but then underwent rapid acceleration. Sprouts sprung from the main branches. Stabbing pain radiated from his palm. Logan hissed and turned his hand over, revealing a cluster of thorns ruptured from beneath his skin. The wound bled profusely.

"Easy, don't fight it," Arik said softly. "The first time is rough. Just go let it happen."

"What exactly am I letting happen?" Logan asked from between clenched teeth. The pain worsened.

"Patience." Arik's gaze fixed on the weapon in his son's hand. An incandescent, passionate glow lit his face.

Before Logan's eyes, the smaller spines merged into a greater single barb. It sucked up every ounce of his blood so not a single drop escaped. Thorn altered from a living plant to the dagger Loki had held. Even after the transformation completed, Logan remained connected to the weapon—an extension of himself.

Wonderment bedazzled him. Experimentally, Logan raised the blade, thrust and parried, getting a feel for it. The weapon had featherweight and sublime balance. It moved with him, as a part of him. As his comfort with the weapon increased, so did his confidence. His movements grew deft and more daring.

"Keep Thorn secret until you need her. You'll get one good shot at your enemy's heart," Arik said, speaking in a sudden rush. He clasped Logan's shoulder.

Perplexed, Logan frowned. "Who's my enemy?"

Pounding resounded on the closed door and Morena's voice came from outside, "Hey, Logan? Are you in there?"

"Yeah. What do you want?" Logan swung around. Unbidden,

Thorn vanished out of his hand. A pleasurable caress marked the return of the vine tattoo to his wrist.

Morena erupted into the study with the suddenness of a rogue twister. She thrust the door open and crossed the threshold, bellowing, "Breakfast is ready! Are you coming?"

"Live a good life, Logan," Arik said. "Protect our line. It all falls to you now."

"I will." Logan turned only to confront an empty room.

All trace of his father—gone.

"You will what?" Morena poked Logan in the side. "Who're you talking to?"

Logan scowled and glanced down, staring at the bracelet of vines encircling his wrist. "Nobody."

CHAPTER 13

Othila: The Rune of Family, Home, and Acquisition

DARKNESS ENGULFED THE MEDIA ROOM, and an off-screen news-caster provided an ongoing narration of how the world was ending while larger-than-life images played out on the flat-screen television. "...The Republic of India launched nuclear weapons against Pakistan..."

The leather recliner creaked when Victoria leaned over to snatch up the universal remote. Lately, live-streaming news reports carried nothing but stories of the chaos and destruction sweeping the planet. She was sick to death of listening to it. With a grimace, she changed the channel.

"...The president declared a national state of emergency. Congress is blaming the president..."

Click.

"Rioting continues in Los Angeles amid what Washington insiders are calling the invasion of U.S. soil by an unidentified terrorist organization. It is believed..."

A day had passed since the *Den Valgte* attack. The prior morning, Victoria had made it to her bed before she'd collapsed. She retained a hazy recollection of forcing food down her throat and then nothing until the alarm on her nightstand blasted her out of dead slumber. She awoke to find herself safe and sound in bed. Bleary-eyed, she lay there in absolute disorientation, bone-weary and starving. Blurry memories flooded back to her: being lost in the Shadowlands, the *Den Valgte* attack, and the missing gaps in her memory. She wondered if it'd all been a dream—and feared for her sanity.

It undermined her confidence that her entire pack had been treating her with kid gloves ever since her unexplained absence. Heavy, awkward silence fell when she entered a room, and the others watched her when they thought she wasn't aware. Sylvie, in particular, had been uncharacteristically cool and distant. She spoke to Victoria with marked restraint... and mistrust in her guarded gaze. Things had been so tense between the two women over Sunday breakfast that Victoria had retreated to the media room to ponder. That talk was long overdue. Victoria intended to make it happen just as soon as she could get Sylvie alone with some guarantee of privacy. She wasn't ready yet to drag those skeletons out of the closet in front of the others.

Machine gun fire blasted from the state-of-the-art sound system. The disruption jarred Victoria from her reverie and back to the present. With a mental start, she returned her attention to the wall-mounted screen again.

One horrific scene after another flashed past: crashed and overturned vehicles, smashed storefronts, burning buildings, rioting crowds. Combatants—both soldiers and civilians—armed with automatic weapons... Bedraggled refugees fled Los Angeles in droves. Exactly the disturbing imagery one expected from Hollywood disaster movies, except this wasn't fiction; this was the Necromancer, and he controlled the vampires in southern California and Arizona. With each passing day, the undead armies increased. The Necromancer's agents had murdered or turned over a million mortals and hundreds of hunters. They'd almost killed Sawyer and Victoria.

Maybe she was lucky Ragnarök hadn't started while she'd been comatose.

Victoria muted the sound system and cocked her head, listening to the world around her. The longer she lived in the lake house, the more she'd come to understand how isolated they were from civilization. The vast forests and towering mountains served as a natural barrier. Here, life followed its own rhythm. Primal music. The melody varied based on the time of day and the season, and incorporated natural elements from wind and weather to birdcalls and insect buzzing. At first, the members of the Storm Pack had constituted a discordant element—out of harmony with the tune. Gradually though, their voices blended with the melody, and lately their voices assumed the dominant roles. It happened naturally and as a matter-of-course, because everywhere wolves went, they sang.

Currently, the song centered in the kitchen with the clang of pots and pans competing with the clamor of joyous voices. It was a family song and a stomach song; the robust sizzle and hearty aroma of cooking bacon served as the bridge, uniting all diverse elements. Sylvie and Morena talked and laughed while the pups produced a racket with their tussling.

The clomping of footsteps in the hallway outside the media room caught her attention. Victoria switched off the television and set the remote down. The leather recliner squeaked beneath her shifting weight as she turned around.

Logan appeared in the entryway. Arms crossed over his chest, he propped himself against the jamb. "Hey, Vic. How're you doing?"

"Better." Victoria sat straighter.

"You busy?" Logan asked, and his oh-so-casual question belly-flopped into the pool of failed pretenses. Something in his manner immediately struck her as off. He had too much tension in the set of his shoulders and he clenched his jaws, so the corner of his mouth tugged.

Talk about a man on the make... What was he up to now?

"No, I was just watching the news." Victoria pinned him with a flat glare, though, really, she didn't mind having an excuse to gaze. And he was *so* worthy of female appreciation.

A study in masculine beauty, Logan had light brown hair, distinctive amber eyes, and the too-perfect bone structure of a model. His broad shoulders far outspanned his trim waist; a stature sculpted in lean sinew. At twenty, he gave every indication of not having fully filled out. Ah, too damn bad he was off-limits: her dead mate's son, and the half-brother of her unborn daughter. In surprise, she noted fresh ink on his right wrist: a bracelet of entwined vines covered in delicate thorns. It had to be new. She'd never noticed it before, and she wondered when he'd found time to visit a tattoo parlor.

Scuffing came from behind Logan, who blocked Victoria's view of the other person. But the pair of women's sized combat boots that she could see was a clue. They could belong to only one person, Cali Kinkaid.

"Get out of the way, A-Hole." Cali shoved Logan out of the way, an impressive feat given the difference in their respective sizes. Stature-wise, Cali was slightly larger than Victoria—a few inches and maybe fifteen or twenty pounds. But her extra weight owed to sinew not fat; a build like a leather strap—lean 'n' tight without stretch or excess.

"Watch it, Dixie," Logan said with an offended scowl.

"No, *you* watch it." Grinning, Cali assumed Logan's former place against the jamb. She wore fatigues, and carried a holstered arsenal of knives and firearms.

Victoria laughed, gripping her sides. Damn, but the irate look of wounded-ego on Logan's face was too good. It just cracked her up. "Hey, Cali."

"Hi, Victoria." Cali waved.

Harrumphing, Logan moved farther into the room,

approaching Victoria. Cool blue and green streaked his predominantly dark aura—all his grumbling for show. So, it begged the obvious and left her wondering again what had him on edge.

"Dixie?" Victoria looked to the hunter, seeking clarification. Kinkaid wasn't from the South—or at least her inflection had no trace of any particular regional accent. Then, as a matter of politeness, Victoria asked, "How's your arm?"

"It itches." Cali glanced down at the plaster cast on her arm, and reached across to grasp it in a telling gesture. "I grew up in Utah's Dixie."

"Ah." Victoria nodded. That made sense. Of course, it didn't explain, however, when or where the pair had acquired the familiarity necessary for Logan to have assigned Cali a nickname. Interesting, especially considering they'd only met a few days before.

"Yeah, Dixie's located in southwestern Utah. Washington County." Cali trailed off to awkward silence. The tough hunter almost fidgeted before her gaze canted to Logan. Her scent held ashy notes like mesquite and sage. Her aura presented a blue-gray slate wall of reticence.

Victoria's gaze skipped to Logan, but he wasn't where she expected. He hovered over her, blocking her perspective. She twitched, a ripple that traversed skin and sinew, traveling from her shoulder along her side. He'd been overprotective since her return. But then, the entire pack had been acting weird. They stole quick glances when she was looking and long stares when she wasn't.

"Logan, what're you up to?" Victoria tilted her head back to regard him with suspicion. In close proximity, she relied more on olfactory cues, a natural aspect of her wolf nature. She opened her mouth and breathed in, scenting him. His basal aroma consisted of blended chamomile-lemon notes from his shampoo, the distinctive sweet citrus from the breath mints he was addicted to; both overlaid the potent marker of a male wolf.

"*Moi?* Up to something?" He pantomimed shock.

She snorted. Evasion rather than outright deception... A while back, she'd come to the belated realization that she'd never actually caught Logan in a lie, not even one of the little ones people told as a matter of course, to be polite. Since then, she paid attention to how he used words and body language to his advantage. He possessed an innate talent for artifice that he must've inherited from his mother. Victoria hadn't known Lori Koenig well or long, but Arik had always been staunch and forthright.

Victoria looked back and forth between them, but neither met her eyes. She jabbed at Logan. "Okay, what's up with you two? Just spit it out."

"I told Cali you'd heal her arm." Logan narrowed his eyes. His face was set in a mask of determination, the pinch of his lips suggested uncertainty.

Victoria blanked out. Nervous ribbons swirled in her gut—the baby loosened a strong kick against her side. It wasn't that she didn't want to help Cali, but curative magic had always been such an obstacle to her. From a young age, she'd been a talented spiritualist, but she'd struggled with even the rudiments of healing. In many ways, that weakness had shaped her life, including the choices which led her to become a registered nurse. Much of her ability as a healer had stemmed from her status as Freya's priestess. The goddess often assisted in healing spells, bolstering Victoria's effectiveness many times over.

But, she had healed Cali's concussion after the severance with Freya. Her healing ability wasn't dependent on the goddess. Not entirely.

Victoria bit her lower lip. She wasn't sure she wanted to test herself. Not yet.

Cali broke the silence. "I told you this was a bad idea—"

"No, it's not that." Victoria rushed to reassure Cali. Gods, what must the other woman think? "I'm not sure I'll be able..." She trailed off into another awkward lapse. Damn it.

"Remember when you brought me back from the dead? This is

a broken bone." Logan smiled with tension in his jaws. The innocent-sounding question had sharp teeth... and so did he.

"That was Freya." Victoria stiffened. The barb stung, as it was no doubt intended. He'd nailed her soft spot, the wound she'd been nursing.

"Oh." He nodded, somehow forging pity into a sharp stick. "So are you saying you're too weak to do this?"

Victoria shot to her feet. Weak! How dare he? She'd show him. "There's a surgical cutter in with my set of medical tools in the broom closet. Get it."

Logan smirked.

"Huh..." Cali straightened, pushing away from the jamb. The brunette refused to retreat but from the look on her face—she sure as hell wanted to.

Victoria's heart went out to the hunter. Victoria understood what it meant to be an outsider. Deliberately, she softened her tone. "Cali, I'd be honored if you'd allow me to assist you. Hunters have been valued allies to my pack, and your injury was sustained defending my territory against invaders."

Cali stared at her. Disbelief gradually gave way to a grin. "Okay, I suppose if you put it that way..."

"I mean it." Victoria might not be kindly predisposed toward Jake or Sawyer at the moment, but her sense of fairness wouldn't allow her to tar and feather Kinkaid with the same brush. The female hunter had done right by them.

By mutual consent, they exited the media room and headed toward the kitchen. In the hallway, Victoria pulled Logan aside. She asked in a low voice, "When did you two get so chummy?"

"We've hung out," Logan returned without the slightest regard for volume control, and then he grinned. "I think she likes me."

"Not in a million years. You're not my type," Cali rifled over her shoulder.

"Yeah, what is your type?" Logan chased after the hunter.

"I don't have the time or the crayons to explain." Cali turned the corner with Logan hot on her tail.

"Logan, aren't you supposed to be getting the cutter?" Victoria asked, feeling distinctly like the odd man out.

"Yeah, go fetch!" Cali chuckled.

"I get no respect." Grumbling, Logan disappeared down the hall, headed toward the kitchen and the broom closet where the pack kept cleaning supplies, including their many brooms... and other witchy-type implements.

Cali followed him.

Victoria stopped and took a moment. She stared down at her shaking hands. She could do this—heal a broken bone—couldn't she? Her faltering courage dropped like a stone. It hit the bottom of a deep, dark canyon, and nothing returned except the hollow echo of self-doubt.

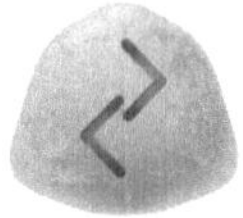

CHAPTER 14

Jera: The Rune of Success and Continuity

IN THE KITCHEN, Sylvie and Morena were in the process of cleaning up the breakfast mess. Morena stood in front of the sink, rinsing and loading dishes. Through the back window, the teenager had a clear view of the vista overlooking the lake. On the far side of the room, Sylvie returned dry goods to the cupboard. The French doors stood open to let in the cool morning air. Sophia and the three adolescent gray wolves were almost certainly somewhere out back. They spent little time indoors.

As she entered the kitchen, Victoria caught a glimpse of Mick, the leader of the pups, leaning over the edge of the in-ground swimming pool for a drink. She grimaced and shook her head in distaste. "Morena, is there fresh water out back?"

Morena frowned. "Yeah, there's a whole lake of it."

"That's not what I asked."

"I filled the bowls this morning!" Morena shot back. "Waste of time if you ask me. The pups would rather drink from a mud puddle..."

"Where do you want me?" Cali hung back, still very much the outsider.

"Please, have a seat." Victoria mustered a smile and gestured to the table. "I just need that saw..."

"Okay." Dropping a curt nod, Cali assumed a seat at the head of the table. By their nature, veteran hunters exuded confidence. Female hunters were rarer than their male counterparts, but Jake Barrett ran an egalitarian organization—those who could hold their own and prove themselves were welcomed.

"Do you need our assistance?" Sylvie asked, turning it into a formal inquiry. Clearly, the skald only offered from a sense of duty, not genuine desire.

Victoria deliberated, tempted to accept the offer. The pack often joined together when she performed healing magic. They put their combined strength at her disposal and boosted the spell. She hesitated, however, and sank into a bog of fear and doubt. If Victoria's abilities proved unequal to the task, the healing spell would fail, regardless of whether she had help. She had to face this trial alone, though, if for no other reason than to prove to herself that she could do it.

"Thank you. I appreciate the offer, but I can handle it." Victoria reinforced her expression of gratitude through the pack bond.

"We'll just get out of your way then." Sylvie reached behind to untie her apron which she folded and tucked away inside a drawer. She addressed Morena. "Morie, shut that off. I'll finish up later. I want to get going... I have a list of chores a mile long."

Groaning dramatically, Morena whacked the faucet to cut the water flow. She flipped around. "Do I have to—"

"Yes, you have to," Sylvie snapped, cutting the girl's protest off at the knees. "I don't want any lip from you. Run and get your shoes."

"Fine." With a final pouty huff, Morena flounced off toward her room—presumably to retrieve her footwear.

Sylvie hesitated in the entryway. "Victoria, there's an important matter we must discuss when you have time."

"Of course..." Victoria started to say more, but then Logan burst into the kitchen. With a lithe twist, Sylvie turned and slipped past him.

"Here you go." Logan tossed the medical kit to Victoria.

"Thanks." Victoria caught the kit. She followed Sylvie with her gaze and considered going after her friend. This awful gulf between them troubled Victoria even more than her selective amnesia.

"Hey, earth to Major Tom!" Logan snapped his fingers beneath Victoria's nose. "You there?"

"Yeah, I'm here. Knock it off." Victoria swatted Logan's hand aside. She turned and discovered Logan and Cali watching her with ill-disguised concern. Maybe they expected her to sprout a second head or totally lose it.

Hmm... Tempting—where was that butterfly net when she needed it?

"You okay?" Cali asked.

"Yeah, I'm fine." Victoria sighed. Oh mighty Tyr, but she was sick of being asked that! Their consternation, however, made one thing crystal clear. Victoria couldn't run out without exacerbating the situation. Her heart-to-heart with Sylvie would have to wait until things settled down.

"Good," Cali grunted.

Silence reigned for an awkward space. Victoria arched her brow and asked Logan, "Do you mind?"

Logan cocked his head. "Are you asking me to get lost?"

"No, she's telling you, dumbass." Cali jerked her thumb over her shoulder for emphasis.

"Fine, I know when I'm not wanted..." Logan threw up his hands.

"Apparently not," Cali said with a grin.

Grumbling, Logan left.

Victoria ambled over to the landline and turned off the ringer.

She was already nervous enough about attempting a healing spell without interruptions.

"So you're having a girl?" Cali cast a glance toward Victoria's stomach.

"Yep, I'm having a girl." Victoria covered the swell of her abdomen with both hands.

"Gosh, that's great..."

And that exhausted their social small talk. Awkward, stretchy silence...

"I'm going to remove your cast and then use magic to heal your arm." Victoria eased into the chair across from Cali. "If the bone was properly set, it won't hurt. You'll feel warmth—"

"Tingling like when you healed my concussion?" Cali jerked her chin toward her shoulder—troubles behind her—a neat way to deal with events already in the past.

"If that's what it was like before, then yeah..." She unzipped the pouch and removed the surgical medical tools within.

"I'm only used to dealing with other hunters. We have our own medics."

"I'm a hunter, too." Victoria tipped her chin toward her shoulder. She had a hot pink dagger tattoo on her upper arm that was identical to Kinkaid's... except for the color. The hunter's mark served as a symbol of unity and belonging to the men and women who worked for the Hunter King.

"Oh. Yeah." Cali spared Victoria's mark a glance, gawking as though she didn't know what the hell to make of it. After a second, her mouth compressed but she otherwise offered no comment.

Epic failure—so much for trying to be inclusive.

Victoria scrunched her nose. "Please place your arm on the table."

"Have you ever removed a cast before?" The hunter sat as stiff as a board. Her suspicion tasted acidic, like unripe green tomatoes.

"I'm a registered nurse." A touch of impatience crept into her tone, which she regretted... but damn it, hadn't she earned this woman's trust? Why must it remain such a tenuous thing between them?

"Yeah, but have you removed a cast?" The hunter's tone lifted, hinting at what may've been offbeat humor. It was difficult to tell.

"Once. The lady lost her arm but the cast definitely came off."

Cali's face went blank, but then a wide smile split the sides of her mouth. She chuckled. "You had me there for a second."

Victoria smiled. "Yeah, I've got this. Not only have I removed a cast, I healed Jake Barrett's heart when his own follower betrayed him. When a vampire bit Sawyer, I reversed the necrosis and stopped him from turning—*and* brought him back, too."

"Guess I'm in good company then." With a grin, Cali plunked her broken forearm down onto the table.

Victoria glanced at the cast, and then performed a sharp double take. She boggled. Bite marks covered the cast, which was only a few days old. Incisor-sized holes riddled the plaster and chunks were missing in a couple spots. It looked like a huge wolf had used the hunter's arm as a chew toy.

"It served as a surprisingly effective shield," Cali said, perfectly droll.

"You've got the strangest sense of humor." Chuckling, Victoria chose a cutting tool and bent over the hunter's forearm. Despite the nervous flutter in her stomach, her hands were steady when she made the first incision lengthwise across the outside of the cast. Whoever had put it on had done a good job. Aside from the assault damage, it showed no signs of wear and tear.

"From what I've heard, you do too."

"Sawyer told you that?"

"You wouldn't know it to look at him, but Sawyer's a real Chatty Cathy when he gets going." Cali held her arm perfectly still while Victoria worked on it, but beneath the table the hunter's foot tapped against the floor. It sent a faint vibration through the wood.

"Really? I'd never have guessed..." Victoria trailed off, a friendly invitation.

Cali stepped right into the opening. "Oh hell, yeah. Compared to the rest of the Barrett men, he's a fucking social butterfly. Pardon my French."

"No worries." She brushed away filings, eyed the slit, and then went back to work. "Is there a reason for that?"

The hunter blew bangs out of her face. The strands lifted, briefly revealing her knit eyebrows, before they dropped again. "Sawyer takes after his mom more than his dad. He's got her hot temper—"

"Sarah Barrett had a bad temper?" Victoria asked in real surprise.

"Not bad. Just hot." Cali smiled at some fond remembrance. "She was passionate—she was also compassionate and charming. Gage is like her, too, but he got more of her diplomatic traits."

"I've only met the twins briefly..."

The cast split. Victoria put the tools away. Then she grasped the two halves, pried them apart at the incision, and set them aside. Cali's forearm was a montage of deep bruises: black and blue along with patches of yellow.

"So what do you think, Doc?" Cali asked.

"It ain't pretty."

The hunter snorted. "Well, no shit, Sherlock."

"Now comes the hard part." Victoria cracked her knuckles. Nervousness swirled inside her like a dust devil that'd picked up all the insecurities and fears she normally kept hidden. It dragged her self-doubt out into the open, exposing dark places to the rays of introspection. She was afraid to try to heal Cali because she might fail. *Gah!* With a quick shake of her head, she admonished herself not to be a coward.

"If you're not up to this..." Cali's hand twitched.

"I'm up for it. I *will* do it."

"Okay." The hunter subsided, but hunched forward and braced as though in anticipation of a storm.

Victoria leaned into the task and braced herself. She fell into prayer and reached out to Freya... Nothing. Only the deep, cold void in her soul. She was forsaken—a priestess shunned by her goddess. The weight of abandonment sat heavy on her shoulders. Pressure built in her chest. She wanted to cry out, give voice to her grief and loss, but she silenced herself with ruthless efficiency. She wasn't Freya's priestess anymore... and Victoria possessed the strength and skill necessary to heal a broken bone on her own. She really needed to start remembering *that*.

Plan B. Gathering herself, Victoria summoned her personal magic. Verve sputtered through her—it gunned and died, and then revved again—a tired transmission turning over as it struggled for that spark. Right then and there, she could've given up and allowed it to die. Fade out forever, a relic of her time as a priestess. Letting go would've been easy.

A howl of frustration built in her throat, and it required all her discipline not to give it voice. Victoria hated easy—despised it with a passion. Laziness and surrender weren't in her nature. She refused to just give up... As her wolf ascended, her skin rippled across the back of her hands and forearms. Victoria grabbed hold of that surge, mastered and directed it. The white-hot energy of small suns radiated from her palms; an identical glow would also shine from her eyes and mouth, obscuring her facial features.

"For the record, you're freaking me out," Cali said. The dagger on her arm cast a fiery aura, and the atmosphere charged with arcane forces.

"Hold on, almost there..." Victoria held her breath as the magic fluctuated. She perched on the razor's edge while it wobbled like a slowing top. The accessible throb of hunter's magic proved too much of a temptation. With a flicker of her will, Victoria summoned it.

Power flowed into her, and her own dagger tattoo flared with heat and light. Rays radiated from her hands, bathing Cali's skin. Their auras touched through the hunter's bond. The fog of doubt hanging over Victoria lifted, and hope cut through the murki-ness. She was doing it—performing healing magic—and on her own.

"Holy shit! Look at your tat! That fucker's pinker than a monkey's bits!" Cali whooped and slapped the tabletop so hard it jumped.

"That's it. I'm going to kill Jake." Face on fire, Victoria grinned and grumbled, but she was secretly glad for the diversion. While Cali laughed, Victoria swiped her face against her shoulder to remove an embarrassing trickle of tears. The thrill of exhilaration sang through her, but the blessed relief was even greater. She'd been so damn scared—no, terrified—that she'd fail. But this proved it—she was still a healer.

Victoria focused her efforts at the core of the hunter's frac-tured ulna. Under her direction, cells multiplied at an accelerated rate, speeding the natural process of bone repair several times over. It altered her awareness, so she could observe the energy patterns living cells generated.

"You already have a good collagen buildup around the fracture. If I didn't know better, I'd say your arm was broken a couple weeks ago."

Cali grunted. "Yeah. We heal fast. Hunters."

"You probably didn't need my help. This would've been fully healed in another week on its own."

"Another week would've been too long. Not with the moot coming up."

"Good point." Victoria wasn't looking forward to the moot. Monday morning, the other alphas and their entourages would start arriving in her territory. The honor of the Storm Pack depended on keeping her guests comfortable and safe. Safe... what a joke. She couldn't even prevent *Den Valgte's* incursions. How was she supposed to protect sixty additional wolf-shifters?

"Is all this talking a distraction?" Cali cast a dubious glance toward her broken forearm, still steeped in the radiance of the healing magic.

Victoria grinned. "Nah. It's fine. But if you feel an extra finger sprout, let me know—"

"Hah, very funny." The hunter fought for a frown, but the corners of her mouth turned up.

Victoria performed a final inspection of the hunter's forearm and allowed the healing magic to subside. "There you go—as good as new. Better. I doubt an X-ray would even show it was ever broken."

"Thanks." Cali flexed the fingers of her formerly broken arm and lifted it.

"You're welcome." Victoria smiled, though her pleasure sprang as much from relief as the joy of helping another. The small success went a long way toward bolstering her confidence.

Cali grasped her forearm, squeezed, and twisted.

"Uh, the skin is going to be tender from the cast," Victoria cautioned too late.

The hunter grimaced but then waved off her discomfort. "It's nothing. I'm happy to have it off. It's handy knowing a healer."

"You should've dropped by sooner."

"Sawyer said to give you space." Cali shuttered her gaze.

"Did he?"

"Yeah, he did." Cali cocked her head. "Maybe it's none of my business, but did you two have a fight?"

"No," Victoria answered, a bit too fast.

"I thought werewolves didn't lie." Cali grinned.

"We don't lie to each other. Only because we don't usually get away with it and getting caught means losing face..." Victoria ducked her head. Warmth crept up her throat. She'd said more than she'd intended.

"Good to know. I'll remember that."

"I'm upset with Sawyer," Victoria admitted. "We haven't spoken since the ambush—the first one. I'm angry with Jake, too, but at least he and I are talking."

"Look, whatever this is about, don't overthink it. Jake ain't a mouth breather. If he's pissed, you'll hear about it. If you're pissed, then you ought to rip him a new one. Don't engage in any of that passive-aggressive bullshit."

Oh burn. Anger and embarrassment choked Victoria. She doubted the zinger was intentional, but it hit the target dead center nonetheless.

Victoria took a deep breath and retrenched. Opportunities for establishing trust were rare. She didn't want to blow this because her ego was bruised. "Thanks, I'll try to take your advice."

"In the future, you don't have to pussyfoot about for my sake. All the Barrett men have their moments." Cali flashed a conspiratorial smile, making an obvious effort to smooth things over. "Sawyer can be a total jackass."

"Too true." No dispute there.

"Let me tell you, Daniel used to piss me off to no end. Every single damn thing somehow became a sports metaphor with that guy. And he wouldn't call or text for days. You'd be left thinking he was dead or worse, but then he'd just turn up like a stray cat, acting all cool." Cali laughed, but her voice broke in the middle, heart-wrenchingly close to a tiny sob.

"I remember." Victoria lacked the heart to smile; a sad little parody twisted her lips. Sorrow wrung her heart. Daniel Barrett, Victoria's lover and Jake's eldest son, had died the prior year. She missed Daniel. Mourned for him. Even with the closure of rescuing his soul, her grief endured.

Lips parted, Cali considered Victoria with a long look. Chagrin passed fleetingly over her face and she groaned, smacking her forehead. "Shit. That was insensitive as all fuck. Excuse my French. I really suck at this relating thing."

"It's okay—" Victoria waved her hand but Cali kept talking over her.

"Somehow, with all the other shit that's happened, I managed to forget about you and Daniel. Star-crossed lovers..." The hunter's inflection conveyed disgust—judgment and anger. Cali stopped herself from saying anything else.

"You can say it—it was my fault he died." Victoria preferred the blunt truth to prevarication for the sake of politeness. If she had any hope of becoming friends with Cali, then they both needed to lay their cards on the table. "The whole damn werewolf-hunter war was our fault. If Daniel and I hadn't kept our relationship a secret, our enemies wouldn't have been able to use it to turn us against each other. A whole lot of people on both sides are dead because of me."

She'd been too damn inexperienced.

Cali flushed beet red. She stayed tongued-tied silent, but then cleared her throat. The sharp, salty tang of unshed tears flavored her basal scent. "I shouldn't have said that. It was out of line. Jake spelled it all out for us—"

"Us?"

"Hunters." Cali crafted an inclusive rotation with her hands. "Everyone who knew Daniel got the same basic lecture. It wasn't your fault. No recrimination. No blame casting. It's just... Daniel was my friend—and my partner—for a long time before you arrived on the scene."

"I know. He talked about you all the time. When we first started dating, I was a bit jealous."

"No reason to be." Cali snickered. "We weren't romantically involved. I loved Daniel like a brother."

"He cared about you, too. I could tell."

The hunter nodded, conveying gratitude. "I'm guessing you two started seeing each other on the sly around November, two-and-a-half years ago?"

"It was more like mid-October." Her guilt eased, and she found it easier to share. In fact, she savored the odd, bittersweet joy of being able to discuss Daniel with someone who'd known and loved him. When—if—she resumed communicating with Jake and Sawyer, it was something to bear in mind.

Cali snapped her fingers. "I *knew* something was up when Daniel started making excuses for why he needed to go off alone. He was apologetic, but it was pretty damn clear he had a new partner who'd taken my place."

"I loved him." Victoria hoped the declaration bridged the divide between them. No matter what, even with 20/20 hindsight to their disastrous end, she refused to regret her relationship with Daniel. "If I could go back, I'd do things differently..."

"Yeah, me too." The hunter's regard had a razor-sharp edge. "You're not the only one who wishes for a second chance. I should've pressed him harder for the truth. Shouldn't have let him get away with it. A part of me is always gonna blame myself."

"Don't," Victoria said in an adamant tone. "I've been down that road. It's a waste of time, and it only wears you down. All you can do is learn from your mistakes and move forward."

"Yeah." The corner of Cali's mouth tugged down in a sharp, unhappy slant.

An unexpected stab of sympathy drew Victoria outside of her comfort zone. She brushed her fingers over Cali's wrist. "Have you shared any of this with Sawyer?"

"Sawyer?" Cali's voice hit a funny high. "No! Oh, no. I talk about three things with Sawyer—sports, hunting, and guns... in that order."

"He's hurting. You're hurting." Victoria rolled her shoulder. "You should try talking to him."

"Sawyer," Cali parroted.

"You should try opening up to him."

"Opening up—what does that even mean?"

"You know..." Victoria grinned. "It's when you take a risk."

"A risk... on Sawyer."

"Put yourself out there. Take your own advice and try some emotional honesty. You never know, it might really help the both of you." The gods only knew how much Sawyer needed it. Victoria hoped Cali could offer him the support he needed, because she never could. "Oh, c'mon. What've you got to lose?"

Cali's jaw moved sideways while she considered. Victoria gnawed her lower lip with mounting anxiety. Weird, she hadn't understood how important the matter was until this very moment. She hoped Sawyer and Cali could help each other.

"All right. Yeah, sure. Hell, what've I got to lose?" Cali smiled and nodded, the poster child of doubt. She gave Victoria the side eye. "Open up... Emotional honesty?"

"You've got this." Victoria gave her two thumbs up.

Approaching footsteps brought their conversation to an abrupt end. The women looked over just as Logan burst into the kitchen. Waves of aggression rolled off the male wolf—he was primed for a fight.

"What is it?" Victoria shot to her feet. Cali did, too.

"Uncle Mike called," Logan announced. "The *Den Valgte* leader has agreed to talk to you."

CHAPTER 15

Hagalaz: The Rune of Disruption

WITH A HUFF AND A PUFF, Morena smashed the lid flat on the yard waste bin until it closed. She smacked her gloved hands together, loosening a shower of dead leaves and twigs. Her sweat-slick skin shone beneath the late morning sun.

"Okay, that's it!" Morena announced. "The back of the truck is full. Both bins are full. I'm hot. I'm sweaty. I'm gross. Can I go now?"

Sylvie smiled at the girl's impatience and adjusted the brim of her wide Tilley hat. She surveyed the area about the old pine picnic table and nodded in satisfaction. They'd spent the past couple hours clearing overgrowth, but left the surrounding trees undisturbed, removing only weeds and briar. An earthy aroma permeated the atmosphere—the sappy thickness of cut bushes and overturned loamy soil. The path was unobstructed now.

A few yards distant, Sophia and the pups stretched out in the shade beneath the patio awning over the outdoor kitchen.

155

"You've been a huge help, thank you."

Morena took a step but hitched. "Yeah, but can I go now?"

"You may go."

A quiver passed through Morena; a thoroughbred eager to burst from the gate. Instead of racing off, however, she dallied. "You know that thing we were talking about earlier?"

"We discussed a great many things earlier." Sylvie removed her own gloves and set them aside. She sipped iced tea from her thermos and then placed it on the table again. Babying the aching muscles in her shoulders and back, she eased onto the bench and leaned back.

"About Gage." Morena kicked the ground with her formerly white sneakers, which were now an unappetizing shade of light brown. Not that it mattered much, since both shoes had holes in the toes.

"What about Gage?" Sylvie heaved a sigh, and added taking Morena into Reno for new footwear to her long to-do list.

"He's graduating on Monday."

"Good for him. Is his brother graduating also?"

"They're twins." Morena rolled her eyes, but left the "Duh" implied.

"I've heard Sawyer talk about his brothers. I suffer from no illusions that the twins are equivalent in their academic achievements."

"Gah! You're trolling me!" Morena threw up her hands and performed an elaborate pantomime, grabbing the sides of her head.

"I'm doing no such thing. I don't even know what that means." Sylvie offered a serene smile.

"*¡Mierda!*"

"*¡Mira tu lengua!*" Sylvie clapped once, a powerful stroke. "You want to be treated like an adult, then act like one. Stop beating around the bush. State your desire upfront—plain and to the point."

The teenager squared her shoulders and pulled herself fully upright, the rare act of achieving her full height. Within the girl was an imposing woman in the making. "We're planning on getting together this summer."

"Getting together? Does that mean what I think it means? Is that a euphuism for casual sex?" Sylvie sat straighter in burgeoning alarm. For a rare change, she cursed her ignorance of current slang.

"No! This is why I don't tell you anything!" Morena threw off palpable heat, burning with embarrassment. Her arms performed wild gesticulations. "It means we want to meet. Hang out."

"Oh, well." Sylvie collapsed again. Thank the goddess she was already seated or she'd have tumbled over. "I suppose that's okay then."

"I'm going to take *another* shower." Morena stalked off. Precisely at the outer edge of Sylvie's hearing range, the girl muttered, "I don't want *casual* sex," before she sprinted off.

"That child will be the end of me." Sylvie stared after the girl and then shook her head. She sipped her iced tea in the shade and sat for a time.

After the crisis that morning, she needed the break. Despite the restfulness of the forest, however, her soul remained troubled. *Guilt pinched Sylvie's conscience over the harsh treatment she'd bestowed upon Victoria. Ráðgríðr's accusations had gotten under Sylvie's skin and made her foolish. She envied Logan and Morena, who appeared to have shrugged off everything the High Valkyrie had said... Sawyer's scathing rebuke of Freya, however, provided even more reason to worry.*

As though answering Sylvie's distress, Victoria appeared on the edge of the enclosed patio off the kitchen. The blonde scanned the area, and approached with sluggish determination. She gave the impression of a woman kept upright via sheer stubbornness alone.

Sylvie sat straighter, gathering herself. This time, she resolved to handle things properly. Communication meant a conversation rather than a confrontation. Given the opportunity, Sylvie firmly believed that she and Victoria could work out their differences. They'd always been the fastest of friends.

"Hey." Victoria wagged her hand.

"Hello." Sylvie scooted over, patting the bench beside her in an unspoken invitation. She didn't have to ask twice. With a groan, Victoria plopped down and slouched into a shapeless lump.

For a conspicuous lapse, they remained quiet. Then they both talked. Sylvie said, "I'm sorry for how I behaved—"

Simultaneously, Victoria exclaimed. "Sylvie, I think we should have that—"

They cut each other off, traded a glance, and then laughed together. It helped ease the worst of the tension. Suddenly, Sylvie felt pretty silly for having allowed the whole matter to inflate into a big deal.

"Please, you go first." Sylvie flexed her hands in a smooth, sliding motion.

Victoria nodded. "The sheriff called. The *Den Valgte* prisoners are awake. I plan to head into town to interrogate them. Before I go, I wanted to touch base. We haven't had much time to ourselves lately."

"True enough. This past week has been a trial." Sylvie quelled the urge to lecture. In her state of exhaustion, Victoria belonged in bed, not gallivanting off on another adventure. Nagging would accomplish nothing, though. The threat to the pack remained. As the alpha, it was Victoria's job to deal with it.

"No, there's not." Victoria mustered a quick grin, but it faded fast. She thinned her lips in a telling gesture. Plainly, the alpha wanted to say something more, but refrained.

Victoria was keeping secrets from Sylvie—her mentor, best friend, and advisor. An outraged shout gathered in Sylvie's throat, but she swallowed it. Why, oh why? How had they come to this? Not so long ago—three days by Sylvie's estimate—the two women had shared everything.

Sylvie sensed the change in Victoria. The skald felt it in her bones. It started with the first *Den Valgte* ambush, when millions of ravens blacked out the sky, and Victoria challenged Ráðgríðr's authority for the first time. Both Victoria and Logan had recounted different but equally sketchy accounts of that fateful eve. Sawyer refused to speak of it at all. Initially, Sylvie had focused the entirety of her attention on what had been said, but now she wondered about the omissions. Adding in Ráðgríðr's harsh accusations, iron dread rusted in Sylvie's chest. She wanted to ask but suddenly she was afraid to hear the answer. She retreated to another topic which was far more urgent right now, anyway.

The moot.

"So, what's on your mind?' Victoria asked.

Fortifying herself, Sylvie plunged straight into the cold waters of bluntness. "We must cancel the Conclave."

"What? No!" Victoria shot to her feet. She rocked on the balls of her feet. The two women stared at each other. Victoria asked in a quieter voice, "What are you saying?"

Sylvie rose, but with care. "I understand you've worked long and hard on the Conclave. Perhaps my choice of words was unwise. I meant to say, it should be rescheduled."

"Why?" Victoria beseeched with her hands and eyes. Clearly, she found the advice being offered as difficult to hear as it was for Sylvie to say.

"There is going to be a lunar eclipse this Wednesday. The same night the Conclave convenes." Sylvie tipped her chin and crossed her arms, pushing her conviction through the pack bond. She met the sort of solid barricade only a determined alpha could erect.

"Lunar eclipses aren't *that* rare..."

"I am well aware that not every lunar eclipse is significant. I am a skaldic scholar—schooled in both the sagas and the art of *seidre*." Sylvie lifted her chin and held Vitoria's gaze. "Mark my words. No good can come of holding the Conclave on the night of this lunar eclipse."

"Sylvie, I don't want to dismiss your concerns, but *why?*"

"I cast the runes early yesterday morning prior to the attack."

"What did you see?" Victoria grasped at the air with her hands, perhaps clinging to the immense labor she envisioned slipping through her fingers.

"The divination was... ill-omened."

"How so?"

Sylvie drew in a deep breath, centering herself. "A season is coming to a close; the next season beginning. Prophecies and portents abound. We will face a great test or a trial of some sort. Odin is at the center of an elaborate structure..."

Victoria snorted. "I could've told you that."

"Don't treat me with such blatant disrespect!" Sylvie snapped. The young woman's sarcasm offended her. Sylvie was the skaldic elder; she was entitled to respect.

"I apologize," Victoria said, stiff with formality. Her face reddened but she kept her gaze level. "What I meant was—those meddling gods have been messing with our lives, using us as their pawns, all along. It's unlikely that's going to change anytime soon."

Sylvie nodded. "Odin and Loki are well known for their scheming and deception. My intuition says they both have a hand in the mechanism—*dues ex machina...*"

Victoria frowned. "Do you have proof?"

"No, I don't. The runes don't work that way." Sylvie pursed her lips. "But *Thurisaz* presented in the future position. We face a hidden enemy, possibly posing as a false ally. *Sowilo*, the sun, is close to the danger, and the final outcome is *Isa*. Ice."

"You think the moot will mark the start of Ragnarök?"

"Yes. During the lunar eclipse, the earth will come between the sun and the moon, but I fear it is an omen, a reflection of the trial we will face."

"That's a very literal interpretation." Victoria obviously tried to sound reasonable, but she wore her skepticism on her face. "Please consider how many different ways a divination can be construed. Just as for instance, *Sowilo* means Victory. It could be that the trial faced will be mine—should I fail, I'll fall into terrible stagnation."

"It's true. Divinations can be taken many ways, and normally I'd be the first to warn against jumping to conclusions." Sylvie grimaced in frustration as her own patience wore thin. She longed to reach over and shake some sense into Victoria.

"But?"

"But, I'm not wrong. I had a vision of a terrible blizzard, of the world swallowed by snow." Sylvie grabbed her friend's hand and held fast. The skald's entire body shook in the grip of fierce emotion. "*I know.* Victoria, you must cancel the Conclave."

"I can't." Victoria shook her head, as set and unmovable as a boulder.

"You must." A whirlwind of hurt and confusion tumbled through Sylvie. She stared at her alpha, trying to discern the reason for Victoria's unreasonable intransigence.

"I promised Jake the moot would go forward as planned." Victoria shook her head. "Even if the portents are unfavorable, he wouldn't insist unless there was a good reason. Whatever trials we face, we'll do so head on. If there's one thing I've learned this past year, it's that I can't run from my problems. They always seem to chase me down and ambush me."

Sylvie sucked in a harsh breath. She had one last card to play. "Have you prayed to Freya for guidance? Her opinion matters more than even Jake Barrett's."

"There's no easy way to say this, but I no longer serve Freya." Victoria said as though it was the most natural and effortless thing. "The goddess has severed her spiritual tie with me. I'm no longer her priestess."

"So, it is true, then." Sylvie yanked her hand away and crossed her arms over her chest. "I didn't want to believe it."

"You're referring to the accusations Ráðgríðr made against me?" Victoria stiffened, and all color drained from her face.

"You're aware?" Denial echoed through the emptiness of Sylvie's soul. Her chest ached in what must be a heart attack... or break?

Victoria tipped her chin. "Logan told me, but let's go over

exactly what she said just to be sure we're on the same page. Tell me what Ráðgríðr said."

Brittle silence endured for a long time; the two women walked the cracking surface of a frozen, depthless lake. Sylvie struggled to muster the fortitude to speak.

"Ráðgríðr called you a traitor. She said you betrayed Freya." Frost spread through her insides. She feared a solid blow would shatter her body into a thousand pieces, but she had to ask. She must hear Victoria affirm or deny it. "Is it true?"

"No!" Victoria shouted the denial but then quieted. "Listen, please. You don't understand. Freya gave me an order I couldn't obey. Yes, I openly defied her. It wasn't the first time I'd disobeyed her, but obviously it was to be the last."

"What was it? What was this order you couldn't obey?" Sylvie tried and failed to envision a scenario wherein Victoria was actually *unable* to follow Freya's commands. On the other hand, she had no trouble imagining Victoria rebelling simply because she didn't want to obey.

But then Sylvie recalled the heated confrontation between *Ráðgríðr* and Sawyer. The hunter had accused Freya of ordering his murder, but he hadn't named his would be killer. Sylvie gasped and raised her fist to her heart as she finally put two and two together. *No.*

"Freya demanded that I sacrifice Sawyer to her," Victoria spat out harshly.

"Why would the goddess do such a thing?" Sylvie's mind blurred, unable to reconcile the shocking revelation with what she believed to be true. Freya might not be perfect, but the goddess was good and wise.

Victoria pressed her lips together. She donned an all-too-familiar mask of stubbornness. "I can't tell you that."

"Can't or won't?"

"Does it matter?" A cynical smile tugged at Victoria's mouth.

"Of course it matters, Victoria." Sylvie garbled her answer. She remained preoccupied with the conundrum that challenged the foundation of her faith.

A test of faith.

Abruptly, everything clicked into place and it all made sense again. A gust of relief blew past her lips. *Of course.* Freya had meant to assess the fealty of her priestess. If Victoria had acted as an obedient priestess should, Freya would've rescinded the command before Sawyer met with harm.

Sylvie marshalled her resolve. "This was a test of faith."

"Killing Sawyer was a test of faith?" Victoria's tone dripped skepticism.

"Yes. A test you failed." Sylvie's anger returned ten times over, but her ire was unmatched by the enormity of her sorrow.

"Did I?" Victoria asked coldly.

"Surely you can't be blind to your own arrogance. It's led you astray. You must repent and plead for forgiveness. If you atone, I'm sure the goddess will forgive you. She is kind and wise."

"I won't repent because I'm not sorry. If I had a redo, I'd make the exact same choice," Victoria said in a steely tone. "Ráðgríðr called me a traitor, but if anyone is a traitor, it's Freya."

"That's blasphemy." Sylvie stumbled backward. Aghast, she stared, wondering who—or what—awful imposter had taken Victoria's place.

"It's the truth. Sylvie." Victoria reached, seeking to recover their connection, but Sylvie once again withdrew.

"I can't accept this." Sylvie crossed her arms over her chest again. She blinked, releasing tears that streamed down her cheeks.

"It's not your decision. It's mine." Victoria dropped her hands, giving up.

"You're making an awful mistake." Sylvie reeled in shock but refused to accept Victoria's adamant decision. Some part of her remained convinced that the younger woman could be shown the error of her ways. Could still be saved.

"It was the only choice I could make." Victoria turned on her heel and walked away. End of the discussion, and—quite possibly —their friendship.

Sylvie pressed a hand over her breaking heart, but no strength or force could keep it from shattering apart.

CHAPTER 16

Warrior's Prowess:
Bind Rune Granting Enhanced Speed, Strength, and Stamina

VICTORIA PROWLED THROUGH THE TREES. She lacked a destination but feared that if she stayed still, her demons would catch up to her. Hollowness filled the place in her chest that'd once held her heart. She crossed her arms over her chest, praying her depression wouldn't harm her baby. As she paced, the sound of a man chopping wood echoed through the forest.

Sawyer.

Her first impulse turned her in the opposite direction, but pragmatism halted her retreat. For days, she'd avoided Sawyer, refusing to deal with the problem he presented. Well, her time had run out. *Den Valgte* had snatched the choice from her. Strange. When she'd envisioned this confrontation, she imagined choking on her own rage. Not drowning is sorrow. The disagreement with Sylvie had drained the fight right out of Victoria, though, leaving her empty.

She came upon him silently, hiding among the trees—a wolf stalking the hunter. Like the predator she was, she watched.

Sawyer heaved the axe overhead in a two-handed swing and brought it down upon a log perched atop the stump. The blade struck dead center and split it. Twin halves fell to join the scattered logs on the ground. The hunter was tall and strong—broad in shoulders, narrow in the hips. He wore no shirt—only the sheen of sweat on his tanned skin—glove-tight jeans, and short black work boots. His toned muscles rippled as his long limbs flowed through the repetitive motions.

Without breaking, Sawyer seized another piece of firewood with one hand, the haft grasped in his other. He kept to his task: position, swing, and repeat. The steady thwack of the axe set the rhythm to the song's refrain. A flurry of small songbirds shook the branches of the surrounding trees, producing a frenzied but cheerful verse. Discordant squabbling scrub jays sang the bridge.

Victoria stepped out from behind the cover of the twin trees into the open. At the same time, she released her rein on the pack bond. Quite unintentionally, she smashed through the ambient aura with all the finesse of a sledgehammer. *Shit.* She might as well have fired a gun.

Sawyer whirled about, bringing the axe overhead in a two-handed swing. A tree at her back blocked Victoria's retreat. She surged closer to the hunter and thrust up her forearm to block both of his. He bore down on her, the steel axe blade mere inches from her head.

Sweat drenched Victoria. Her muscles burned from the strain of the contest. *Fuck.* Either he'd gotten stronger, or she'd gotten weaker. Had the runes changed him that much? She endured an eternity of real fear that her arms would give before he came to his senses.

"Victoria," Sawyer gasped, and ceased pressing his attack. His breath blew hot across her skin.

"Remind me never to sneak up you while you're holding a

weapon." Out of—wholly justified—paranoia, Victoria secured a grip on his wrists and took the axe from him. He let go.

"Sorry, I'm on edge." A tangle of damp, dirty blond hair hung in his face, obscuring his eyes, but she sensed the press of his gaze on her face.

"We all are." After what'd happened on Saturday, Victoria questioned the wisdom of keeping the pack at the lake house. They weren't safe in their own home anymore, and *that* pissed her off.

A snarl erupted from her throat. Victoria whirled and buried the axe in the wood-chopping stump with a forceful stroke, burying the blade deep. Trembling, she released the handle and shuffled her feet, struggling to recover her cool. Seeking a distraction, she surveyed Sawyer's campsite with marked interest since it was the first time she'd set foot there since he'd begun construction.

The hunter had chosen an excellent location to settle—atop the second highest rise in the area. The hilltop offered an excellent vantage point, and it was closer to the freshwater lake than the house. It also overlooked the meadow where Logan and Sawyer had fought and killed one of the two *Den Valgte* raiding parties. The campsite included a fire pit which was currently banked. A round red-and-black shield leaned against a smooth-topped stump that doubled as a stool. The antique shield stuck out like Thor's thumb amongst the modern implements surrounding it. Victoria had never seen it before. She would've assumed it was a prop for historical reenactments... *if* it'd belonged to anyone other than a Barrett. As much as it bugged her, she bit her tongue.

Bricks and posts were stacked side-by-side; more material than one man should've been able to haul in on foot in such a short time. His in-progress construction project piqued her curiosity the most. Four walls made of solid oak boards flanked the completed foundation. She wondered whether he intended to raise them alone or would finally ask for help. They had so many more pressing issues to deal with, but the mystery building just begged the question.

Besides, she was running out of bitable tongue.

"What's it for?" Victoria asked Sawyer who stood at her elbow, observing her inspection. She gestured at the structure to remove doubt.

"It's a wood shed," he said in a voice rough from disuse. He dragged the tip of his tongue across his upper lip. A haggard pall hung over him, including dark circles under his eyes. The hunter wore the potent cologne of sweat and wooden scents, including a highlight of pinesap. As his norm, the man pulled off an air of perpetual scruffiness with a certain *je ne sais quoi*. His apathy toward his appearance, however, had finally allowed his scruffy Hollywood chic to slip into the realm of mountain man.

"We have a perfectly serviceable shed beside the house."

"We're going to need a lot more firewood than that." Sawyer snatched a water bottle off the ground and tilted back his head. The strong column of his throat worked as he downed the whole thing at once. Water sloshed from the sides of his mouth, running in rivulets along his throat and across his chest.

A chill ran down Victoria's spine, and her skin performed a goosestep march across her flesh. She stared... no, gaped until Sawyer looked up and caught her in the act.

"What?" Sawyer wiped his mouth on the back of his forearm, then crushed and cast the empty bottle aside to where others littered the ground, waiting to be collected and recycled.

"You intend to build more than just one shed, don't you?"

He squinted. "Yeah, how'd you know?"

"Two things," Victoria said. "There are more building materials than one wood shed warrants. And the way you're clear cutting."

"I plan to sink a well over there." He pointed and then, he swept his arm across the northern expanse of the vista. "A row of cabins there and a main lodge through here..."

Unable to help herself, Victoria grimaced. When Morena had accused Sawyer of having totally lost his sanity—a far politer version of what the teenager had actually said—Victoria had chalked it up to dramatic exaggeration. Now, she wasn't so sure.

"You're not here to discuss the camp, are you?" Sawyer asked, demonstrating uncanny insight.

"No, I'm not."

Victoria gnawed her lower lip. Crunch time: should she confront Sawyer over Jasper's murder or give priority to *Den Valgte*? She dreaded the former, acknowledged the urgency of the latter, and didn't have time for both. Maybe it wasn't so hard after all... No matter how great her hurt and anger with Sawyer, Victoria still trusted him to fight in the pack's defense. The bastard's guilty conscience condemned him to it, and she had no qualms about using it on him.

"Yeah, I get it," Sawyer said in his husky baritone.

The bond resonated with his anger and sympathy. His force of personality exerted gravity, pulling her into alignment with him. The psychic connection operated as it should to reinforce the unity of the pack, but she resisted. She didn't want to share that intimacy with Sawyer. Not after what he'd done. Even so, she turned to face him anyway. Their gazes locked. The man held a world of torment in his warm brown eyes.

Her scalp prickled. Suspicion transformed to certainty. In that instance, without a shred of proof and beyond a shadow of a doubt, she *knew*. He knew that she knew... his ugly secret was out.

"Victoria," Sawyer raised his hand, reaching for her like a drowning man for a lifeline. His aura roiled; dense storm clouds that completely covered the primary reddish hues that characterized his chakras.

"No." She flinched from his touch.

"No?" Sawyer held his hand suspended. The roughness of his voice grated on her nerves, all but begging.

"No. Just no." Victoria shook her head and hardened her heart. She only intended to grant him the simple refusal, but once she started talking, words poured out of her. "I don't have the strength to spare. Not right now, maybe never. I'm the alpha. My duty is to the pack—keeping them safe. Sawyer, you're a problem that has no resolution. And I trusted you; you betrayed me. You murdered Jasper!"

Sawyer flinched. "I'm sorry."

"I know you're sorry, but it's not nearly enough to make up for what you've done," Victoria continued at breakneck speed. "Because of you, Sylvie believes I betrayed Freya. I don't dare tell her the truth for fear of what she'd do. Finding out would break Morena's heart. I'd tell you to leave, but I don't have that luxury. I need you to help protect us from *Den Valgte*. Ultimately, everything boils down to the same old thing: keeping the pack safe. So we're not going to discuss this any further. It's closed. We're going to lie and pretend everything is just hunky-dory until after I deal with the most immediate threat. But the moot is coming next and who knows what trouble that will bring. So I'm putting you on hold. You'll just have to deal."

"All right." Sawyer pressed his lips together in a flat line of resignation. By force of will, he shut down the pack bond, closing her out. The intense and terrible pressure surrounding her eased.

Victoria exhaled in sheer relief. A part of her was grateful to him for backing off. Now, though, she had no idea what to say to him. Uncomfortable and twitchy, she crossed her arms over her breasts, but it put uncomfortable pressure on her baby bump. The damn bulge, so utterly conspicuous, never escaped her awareness for long. Self-conscious, she dropped her hands.

"What did you need?" Sawyer asked in a tone the color of ash.

She jerked her chin and lurched into an abbreviated explanation. "Sheriff Trash called. The *Den Valgte* prisoners are awake. I'd appreciate it if you'd accompany me and Logan to the jail to talk with them."

"Sure." Sawyer hesitated. "Are you sure Logan wants me along?"

"He complained." She shrugged. "I overruled him. You're coming; it's final."

"Final? Funny, it sounded like you were asking just now." Sawyer bared his teeth, the bite of sarcasm.

Despite the tension, she smiled slightly. "I'm practicing diplomacy."

He snorted. "Diplomacy? That's novel."

"Yeah, well, there's a first time for everything."

"Is diplomacy your plan for dealing with *Den Valgte?*" Sawyer asked with more than a hint of cynicism.

"What're you implying?" Victoria stood straighter in answer to the implicit challenge in his tone.

"Implying? Nothing. I'm dealing in facts." He cocked his head. "Not three days ago, you were furious with *Den Valgte* and that was before they attacked us a second time. I expected more of a slash and burn approach."

"I may have been unnecessarily harsh." Victoria flushed. Creeping heat spread from her throat to her cheeks. Okay, so maybe she'd lost her cool following that last run in. In one fell stroke, she'd denied three of Odin's slain followers the opportunity to be fairly considered for entry to Valhalla. *Because she'd been pissed.* Freya had ripped *Vanadium* from Victoria and severed their ties. She'd just learned Sawyer's shameful secret. And Ráðgríðr had tried to strip Victoria of her status as a Valkyrie. Too much, too fast, temper blown. One hotheaded lapse, however, shouldn't become the standard that defined her entire character.

"*Den Valgte* invaded our territory. They murdered a wolf and a man," Sawyer countered, and she couldn't miss how naturally he used the language of wolves. *Our territory.* Whether aware or not, Sawyer considered himself a member of the Storm Pack.

"We exacted our revenge for their transgressions," Victoria said in a soft voice. "And they retaliated yesterday when they invaded our lands."

"We won." He flexed his fists. For the simplicity of his defense, she wasn't fooled. Sawyer was smart and cunning. He must've thought this through, the same as her, to its natural conclusion.

"And we were damn lucky one of our own wasn't killed in the

process. Next time, we may not be so fortunate. Do you want to take that chance?"

"I don't want anyone else to get hurt." Sawyer clenched his jaws. His psychic defenses slipped. He broadcast across the pack bond sentiment so strong it conveyed thought—*anyone he loved.*

Right then, looking into his heart so full of devotion, it would have been easy to believe Sawyer's remorse was significant. Maybe he'd truly changed in the months that'd passed since he'd murdered Jasper. A part of her wanted forgiveness to be the path they could take. But she stopped herself right there. Scathing skepticism sang through her mind. Victoria deliberately reinforced her shaky defenses. Sawyer and his father had deceived and manipulated her right from the start. She couldn't believe anything they said or did.

"I've been in this position before," Victoria said. "This is the wolf-hunter war all over again. We're outnumbered and outgunned. Every last one of those people we killed today was somebody's relative, friend, or loved one. *Den Valgte* will retaliate and the bloodshed will continue to escalate. Sooner or later, our luck will run out."

"My father is sending more hunters." Sawyer jerked his head to the side, a subconscious sign of disagreement. His aggression carried over the bond loud and clear. She wasn't surprised he wanted to fight. As a Barrett, it was in his blood.

"We're going to negotiate," Victoria snapped at him, losing her frayed temper just a bit. "Aside from the immense irony, your father's followers shouldn't be pitted against Odin's followers. Considering that he's one and the same, that's like a serpent swallowing its own tail. It's just not right."

Sawyer opened his mouth.

Victoria thrust her finger at him. Her tone grew vehement. "Diplomacy has always been the Storm Pack's way. Even when we were strong, going to war was deemed the last resort. My father risked his life to convince your father to sit down and talk. They negotiated a peace that lasted more than thirty years."

"Victoria..." A tick worked on his cheek.

"No. Let me talk." She held up her hand, and he yielded with a curt nod. She took a deep breath and rushed the words. "There are too few of us left for there to be any other option. Granted, we have Logan, but he's so damn young and impulsive..."

Victoria bit her lip on a twinge of guilt at the criticism. Lately, or for the past few days anyway, Logan had gone above and beyond in service to the pack... for her. She couldn't dismiss or evade the memory of Logan saying *"I'm your guy"* like it was a solemn vow.

"What am I—chopped liver?" Sawyer asked.

Victoria flashed a humorless grin at the hunter's sourness. "You're loyal to your father. Let's not pretend otherwise. For now, Jake is willing to protect us but what if he changes his mind? I'm sick and tired of being dependent on outsiders for charity."

Sawyer flushed red. His scent soured; crimson streaked his aura. "You're a hunter, Victoria. That's what that dagger on your arm means. It's a promise."

"It's a promise I don't trust," Victoria countered, speaking over him. He tensed at the insult, but she plowed on. "Promises are made to be broken. Your father has only spared two of his people in defense of my pack. It's not nearly enough."

"It was three," Sawyer grated. Harshness shadowed his features. "Or have you forgotten DNR? He died in defense of our pack."

"I haven't forgotten him. I'm sorry he died. It wasn't fair." Victoria grew heated in the grip of surging anger. How dare he? She regretted the death of DNR, a young hunter who'd perished during the first battle with *Den Valgte*. "I made sure DNR's soul was chosen for Valhalla. It's the best I could do for him."

Sawyer worked his jaws. "I know that. I appreciate it, but I can't help but feel like there should be something more to the afterlife than eternal military duty."

"Oh sweetie, you need to complain to your daddy." Her tone dripped with saccharine sweetness.

He fought but laughter won. He broke into a merciless chuckle. "Fine, you win this round. We'll do it your way and talk. Now, do I have time to rinse off before we go?"

"Yeah, you stink." Victoria grimaced. Okay, that may've been too blunt. She tried to back track. "Ah, that's a good idea."

"Very diplomatic," Sawyer drawled with a throaty chuckle. "I can see you're a natural at this."

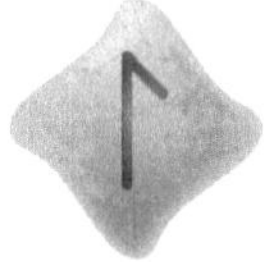

CHAPTER 17

Laguz: **The Water Rune**

THE STURDY KNAPSACK struck the wooden boards of the boat dock with a dull thud. Sawyer bent and dug out a neatly folded stack—a towel and a full set of clean clothing—that he set on the walkway. He straightened and faced out across the lake. Icy fingers closed around his heart, slowing the beat. Beneath the late morning sun, the dark blue water was as smooth as glass, reflecting the evergreen forest and the snow-capped mountains beyond. A vision of pristine tranquility, except its depths concealed unnamed horrors.

"When you said rinse off, I assumed you meant up at the house," Victoria said from behind him. The heat of her breath scalded his skin.

In a static shock, Sawyer's nerve endings tingled and the hair on his nape stood on end. He pivoted and discovered Victoria breathing down his neck. An ironic metaphor since the top of her head only came to his mid-chest. She'd have needed a stepping stool to accomplish the task. He suppressed a surprised start.

Likewise, he refused to retreat. Either action would've signaled his submission. The past few months of living with the pack had served as a crash course in the language of wolves.

"This'll be fine."

"Are you sure? It looks cold." Victoria maintained her proximity, too close for comfort. A challenge except her shuttered expression signaled unease.

"Yeah, I'm sure." As inviting as a hot shower sounded, Sawyer preferred to err on the side of caution. The house belonged to Logan. The male werewolf already had his panties in a twist over Sawyer's very existence. It didn't require flights of fancy to imagine the younger male overreacting to a perceived home invasion. Sawyer imagined getting trapped in the shower—naked and unarmed—with suds dripping into his eyes while a frenzied werewolf lunged for his throat.

Thanks, but no thanks.

"Your loss." She shrugged as though she didn't care, but her strange intensity gave the gesture lie. With the pack bond closed up tighter than a bank vault, Sawyer couldn't tell for sure one way or the other.

He clenched his jaws, hesitating, tempted to call her out on it. His last two attempts to open an honest dialogue with her, though, had gone south fast. Both times, Victoria shut him down completely. So here they were pretend-playing that everything was okay. Trust obliterated. Sawyer owned the fault and he couldn't blame Victoria, however, the platitudes did nothing to alleviate his frustration. A few days ago, Victoria had climbed into his lap, seeking comfort. They'd been falling into something real— each other, maybe—he hesitated to use a word as powerful as love. But now she looked at him with only hurt and mistrust, and it broke his heart.

Grim with remorse, Sawyer shrugged the rifle's carry strap off his shoulder. He caught the weapon in his hands and reached out to hang it on the nearest pylon. Absently, he noted the signs of weathering and made a mental note to paint the wood before summer ended. Likewise, the sturdy boathouse above the pier required maintenance.

"I'll take that. Someone should stand guard while you're indisposed."

Victoria placed herself in his path, extending expectant hands.

He hesitated. Victoria fought with knives, claws, and fangs... and had even twisted healing magic into a weapon once. He had never, however, seen her pick up or use a gun. It begged the question.

"Do you know how to shoot?" Sawyer asked.

"Depends. How broad is the barn?" Victoria grinned, but the tension lines at the corners of her eyes gave lie to her smile. Never in a million year had he seen a woman angrier with him.

"Not exactly reassuring." Sawyer gripped the rifle tighter. The small, irrational worry that she meant to shoot him dead with his own gun bedeviled him.

"Daniel was my lover," Victoria countered with a cutting edge. She held her hands steady in an unspoken demand. "What do you think?"

"That's a good answer." His mouth contorted into an involuntary grimace. Trust had to start somewhere. Sawyer plunked the weapon into her palms. He retained his grip a few precious seconds. "Take care of my baby."

"Yes, sir. I'll have her home ten minutes before curfew." Victoria snapped off a smart salute. When Sawyer released the rifle into her care, she shouldered the strap and hefted it. She performed a press check of the firearm with such easy efficiency that his residual doubts were dispelled.

"Funny."

"Ain't I, though?" Victoria parked against one of the pylons, taking advantage of a sliver of shade the post provided.

With a grunt, Sawyer plunked down onto the wood planks of the walkway. He removed his boots and peeled off his grimy socks, all of which he dumped in a messy pile. His knives received proper handling, each sheath removed and placed with care on the dock. He worked his way up from his calves, growing increasingly uncomfortable with each passing second. He stole a fast glance over his shoulder. Sure enough, Victoria was still staring at him with an unwavering regard. He understood the logic behind maintaining an armed vigil, especially given the attack the prior morning. For logic to hold, she ought to be watching anything but him.

"If you wanted a show, I could've brought a boom box." Sawyer rocked onto his feet and dropped his hands to his belt. He wasn't shy, not by a long shot. Even so, it'd taken him months to get comfortable with the total non-taboo wolf-shifters treated nudity with, but *this* took it too far.

"Dude, did you just say boom box? It's 2011, you know." Victoria asked with a bark of laughter. "How old are you?"

"Older than you. Since when do you say dude?"

"Since I moved to *CAL-a-FORN-eye-a*," she said with a deliberate sneer.

Ah hell, she wasn't going to look away. Sawyer refused to drop his gaze, so he dropped his pants. He forgot about the sheath of throwing knives strapped to his thigh, so his jeans didn't fall far. It ruined the overall effect. So much for the six months he'd spent working his way through grad school as an exotic dancer... Hobbled by his own damn pants, he stumbled and then shuffled to keep from toppling.

Victoria sniggered. "You're killing me."

"Yeah, me too." Cheeks on fire, he fumbled with the strap belting on his knife sheath. All his fingers got fat and turned into thumbs.

A cackle erupted from Victoria, and then she dissolved into a gale of laughter. Mania edged her outburst, the reaction of a woman stressed to the breaking point. She wheezed and huffed, fighting it.

With a growl of frustration, Sawyer finally undid the buckle. The whole ensemble of jeans and sheath plopped down around his ankles. Thoroughly disgruntled, he kicked free of his pants and charged off the side of the dock. He plunged straight into the frigid water, submersed to over his head. The cold slammed his body and a shout rose in his throat which he stifled.

Weightless, he sank through the clear depths while a million bubbles swirled around him. *Laguz*, the water rune, ebbed and flowed throughout the pristine lake. Yet, when Sawyer held his hands before his face, blood coated his skin. The absolute silence and bone-penetrating chill lulled him into numb complacency. Here, his troubled thoughts quieted. He found a measure of peace and fantasized about the serenity to be found if only he could forget himself.

His conscience intruded, lashing at him. Still, he floated through obscurity, hoping for illumination to strike. He needed to make things right with Victoria. The whole situation was classic FUBAR: Fucked Up Beyond All Recognition. He had to figure out some way to fix this thing...

A buried memory coalesced in Sawyer's mind. His old man's voice saying, *"Son, this thing isn't a broken toy."*

Okay, fix wasn't the right word...

Sawyer released a thin stream of bubbles. He wondered what other pithy remark Jake might make. No doubt, one such as, *"You've really screwed the pooch this time."*

"Gee thanks, Dad," Sawyer thought, pursuing the make-believe conversation. The longer he stayed submersed, the more uncomfortable he grew. Pressure built in his lungs; his blood turned sluggish. He fantasized about exhaling, breathing in, filling his lungs with water.

"Giving up is the coward's path," Jake's gruff voice rumbled through Sawyer's mind, far too loud and clear to be a construct of his imagination.

"I'm not a coward!" Startled, Sawyer thrashed his limbs. The uncontrolled motion sent him into a slow spin through the dim water.

"Good," Jake grated. *"Now stop yer bitchin'. You've wronged Victoria. Tell me how you plan to do right by her."*

It required an act of will for Sawyer to set aside his pride. With as much humility as he could muster, he asked, *"What do you suggest?"*

"I told you already once. Now twice. Listen to her."

"That's the trouble. She's not saying anything." Sawyer's sense of urgency built to a crescendo. Lightheadedness suffused him. His thoughts lost coherency, separated by layers of cotton candy.

"Oh, she's talking. She's already told you what she needs. You're just too damn selfish to hear her."

Epiphany dawned over Sawyer. *"I need to make reparations for what I've done."*

Jake snorted. *"There you go. It took you long enough."*

"Thanks, Dad."

"Get it done. Now get your sorry ass to the surface before you force a pregnant woman to jump in after you."

Sawyer's fight returned with a vengeance. A powerful kick propelled him upward. He stroked with his arms and headed for the brightness above, releasing a steady stream of air. He broke the surface and hyperventilated, refilling his starved lungs.

"The next time you want to talk to me, use the damn phone." Jake ended the conversation on the distinctive crash of an old-style rotary phone being slammed into its receiver. Never let it be said his old man didn't have a sense of humor.

Water streamed down his head and long, sodden strands hung in his face. He shoved his hair back and blinked. Once his vision cleared, he oriented toward the boat dock just a few feet away.

"What were you doing down there?" A snarl reverberated in Victoria's throat. The she-wolf crouched on the edge of the dock, holding the edge in a white-knuckled grip. Her trim frame sang with tension, frozen in a diver's stance.

"Thinking." Threading water, he tilted his head back and gazed into her face. Her face was set in a harsh mask that enhanced her austere beauty. The blue of her eyes—the fantastic hue of Arctic ice—eclipsed the whites.

He thought maybe he loved her.

Sawyer asked himself, *What did she need?* The answer came to him then, so simple, so obvious, he felt like a fool. Victoria fought for the pack, sacrificed for the pack—had entered into a marriage of convenience for the pack—strategized and compromised... All for the safety and well-being of her wolf family... who were now his family, too.

"I know how to resolve the *Den Valgte* trouble." A gust of wind kicked a wave into Sawyer's face, and he got a mouthful of water. He spit it out and swam harder.

"Really?" Victoria lilted in surprise. It cracked the facade of her anger, and he thought he spied a glimmer of hope.

"Yeah, really. I need a second chance. I realize what I'm asking is a lot. Do you think you can trust me enough to accept my help?"

Victoria blinked and hesitated. His mouth turned bone dry. At last, she said, "I can't just forgive you. I might not ever be able to forgive you."

"I'm not seeking forgiveness, only for the chance to contribute."

Her face contorted in the throes of indecision. He held his breath, and when she turned away suddenly, his heart broke. No mistaking the meaning of the old cold shoulder. Sawyer exhaled and kicked, propelling himself toward the shore. He didn't intend to give up. He'd find some way to solve the *Den Valgte* problem even if he had to be sneaky about it.

"Hey, where're you going?" Victoria turned back, holding up something small and white in her hand. He squinted but couldn't quite make it out.

"I was gonna get out." He reached water shallow enough that his feet touched bottom, so he stood.

"Not without this." Victoria lopped the oval straight at him.

He snatched it out of the air and almost lost it when it proved slippery. He looked down. Soap—one of the all-natural, eco-friendly bars he kept in his bag. His hopes lifted but he fought to keep them from rising too high. He preferred not to have his heart crushed if he'd read it wrong.

"Are you giving me a second chance?" With a guarded heart, Sawyer raised his eyes to her face again.

She crossed her arms over her chest. Her voice was tight. "I believe everyone deserves a second chance. I wouldn't be standing here now if someone hadn't given me one. But this doesn't mean you're off the hook. You and I have a long way to go before I'll trust you again."

"I'll take what I can get." Overwhelmed with gratitude, Sawyer bowed his head to hide how much he wanted to weep. He cupped his bloodstained hands, filling them with pure water, and reached for *Laguz*, but she refused to answer his summons.

"Hey! Are you listening to me?" Victoria's shout punctured Sawyer's reverie.

He blinked and snapped back to the present. "What did you say?"

Victoria blew stray bangs out of her face. "*I said* you can't represent the pack to *Den Valgte* smelling like you do. You need a full scrub down. That's part of the deal."

"Done." The corners of his mouth turned up in an involuntary smile. Truth be told, lately his body odor offended his *own* nose.

"Do you have a plan for influencing them?" Victoria prowled along the dock. "Right now, I've got nothing."

Sawyer considered as he waded closer to shore. "I'll start by showing off the runes and go from there."

Victoria ceased pacing and cocked her head. "Yeah, that might work."

"It'll work and if it doesn't, I have a backup plan." Confidence flooded Sawyer. He got a good grip on the bar, dunked it in the water, and lathered up.

His thoughts turned to the surprise visit he'd received from his mother. Frigg had specifically mentioned *Gnýrhorn*. It fit, but he found himself reluctant to mention the horn to Victoria. Blowing *Gnýrhorn* summoned the Wild Hunt—and exacted a high price from the caller. Those who rode with Odin's ferocious army never returned. Sawyer wasn't quite ready to commit to the extreme endeavor yet. Not when less drastic solutions might suffice.

"You're not going to tell me what that is, are you?" Victoria's question broke through Sawyer's reverie.

Sawyer startled. The soap slipped through his fingers, forcing him to fumble to recover it while Victoria laughed. Finally, he secured a hold on it again.

"I want to ponder for a while," Sawyer said, and was relieved when she nodded. If she'd pressed the issue, he'd have capitulated but with regret.

"I wish I had scissors." Victoria brought her fingers together in a cutting motion, menacing his hair. From her tone, she was suffering from buyer's remorse, realizing she could've demanded more than a scrub down.

"Fine, but no shorter than my shoulders." Sawyer bared his teeth in a genuine wolf's smile. He foresaw a lot of surrendering to her in his near future. He owed her more than he could ever repay.

Victoria flashed a triumphant grin. "And you need to trim that wretched thing growing on your face."

"A full beard gives a man character." His spirits soared. He took Victoria's willingness to insult him again as a good sign. Things were getting back to normal.

Victoria's snort carried on the water. "That's not character. That's the guy who lurks in dark alleys and leaps out from behind a dumpster to mug you."

"Your diplomacy skills are definitely improving."

Iviðia:

The Troll Women Who Dwell in the Ironwood

THE EL DORADO COUNTY SHERIFF'S DEPARTMENT was a sprawling A-frame building in the picturesque downtown district. It faced the Sierra Pines Municipal Courthouse, located on Main Street amid a cluster of other city government buildings, including the library. Sheriff Trash's white SUV was parked curbside in a loading zone.

Perspiration slickened Victoria's skin, trickling down her temple and jaw, and then her throat. It soaked her nape and back, adding to her misery. Her hair had always been her pride and joy, but these moments were when she considered hacking off her waist-length braid. But worse than the heat was the inexplicable nervousness that prickled her skin. She scuffed the bottom of her flip-flop across the asphalt.

Ahead of her, Logan and Sawyer engaged in competitive bickering, a constant barrage of insults and one-upmanship as they crossed the parking lot toward the front entrance. The lug heads had insisted on traveling in separate cars. At least they weren't trying to kill each other—a definite improvement.

As Victoria passed the front end of the SUV, a glancing ray of sunshine caught the front windshield. She glanced over and then stopped dead in her tracks, staring straight into the glare despite burning pain in her eyes. A woman's silhouette—shadow captured within light. Victoria leaned in closer, convinced it must be her own reflection, an optical illusion. She tilted her head to the side. A chill ran up her spine despite the afternoon heat: the likeness didn't move with her.

Gusty wind kicked up, stirred tree branches, and disturbed debris. The woman whispered soft secrets to Victoria. She strained to hear, cocking her head—

"Vic!" Logan's fingers snapped before her eyes.

"What?" Startled, Victoria jerked her face up.

Logan stood at her side, having closed ranks to hover over her while Sawyer topped the landing of the two stairs leading to the entrance of the sheriff's department.

"What's up with that?" Logan jabbed at her dagger tattoo.

"I don't know. It just lit up." Victoria reached to cover the ache on her upper arm. Heat burned her palm. Her hunter's mark glowed white-hot. Mystical energy coursed through her.

"Weird," Logan muttered. Despite his cavalier tone, the male wolf scanned the surrounding area, searching for hidden dangers. Victoria echoed the sentiment, times ten.

"Is your mark lit up?" She turned to Sawyer. His coat concealed his dagger tattoo, but she could tell from the look on his face that he felt it, too.

"Yeah, but I don't know what invoked it." Sawyer shook his head slowly. "But it's fading already."

"Mine too." Like a fading flame, the hunter's mark on her arm dimmed and then went out, returning to normal. False alarm, maybe? She didn't know what to make of it. Maybe Jake would have the answers she needed... Presuming he could be persuaded to supply something other than a cryptic response.

"Are they prone to premature ejaculation—hunters? Marks, that is," Logan asked, tongue-in-cheek.

"Fuck off." Sawyer flexed his gun hand.

"Sensitive, aren't we? What's wrong? Hit too close to home?"

"Both of you shut up, especially while we're in public." Victoria quelled the urge to grab both of them and smash their heads together. "Let's get moving," she said, but then didn't budge. Her feet were rooted.

"Are you okay?" Solicitousness hung on Logan like an ill-fitting coat. Not his usual attire by far.

"Yeah, I'm fine."

"You don't seem fine, more like dazed and ditzy." Logan turned it snide, needling her, back in his glove-tight smarty-pants.

"The only ditz here is you," Victoria said with a snort. She mustered a small smile. "Do you remember the last time we were here?"

Logan frowned and then grinned. "We broke in through the basement. Is that what's wrong? You're feelin' guilty?"

Victoria preferred not to dwell on their crime spree. "Your uncle was furious..."

He sniggered. "He's gotten over it, Vic. You should too. Besides, it was for a good cause. Truth, justice, and—"

"Yeah, yeah. And your benefit."

"That's the best sort of cause."

Victoria passed Logan and headed up the double stairs. Sawyer held the door for her. She brushed past him without a word. The hunter followed, releasing the door before Logan made it through. Sawyer loomed behind her, so close his heat warmed her back, and she breathed in his musky scent. She sped up, evading him.

At the front desk, a plump, gray-haired granny with spectacles perched on the end of her nose squinted as they entered.

"Asshole." Logan yanked the door wide and barged into the small lobby.

"Prick," Sawyer grunted.

Victoria sped up and made good with her escape.

"Son of—" Logan began.

"Logan Koenig! Aren't you a sight for sore eyes! I'd heard you were back in town. I was so sorry when your father passed away. Felt just terrible I didn't have a chance to tell you before you left." The receptionist sprang to her feet and rushed Logan. Open-mouthed, he pivoted just as the pint-sized dynamo tackled him and wrapped her arms about his waist.

"Mrs. Dawson. It's nice to see you. Uh, thank you." Looking thoroughly discombobulated, Logan patted the woman awkwardly on the back and then spread his arms as though expecting the hug to end.

It didn't.

"I'm not Mrs. Dawson anymore since Mr. Dawson and I separated. Call me Milly." With a blissful smile, Milly stepped back and pinched Logan's cheek, shaking it. She winked. "I'm a free woman now."

Victoria sniggered into her hand.

"I'm going on ahead to talk to the deputies," Sawyer said from the side of his mouth, easing away.

"We'll catch up." She dropped a nod, aware they might be stuck there for a while with gregarious Milly.

"Shoot, that's just my luck. The hottest babe in town becomes available the same day I get engaged," Logan drawled in a voice as smooth as melted chocolate. He flashed a flirtatious smile and wink in return.

"Oh?" Milly rocked on her heels. She shoved her spectacles up her nose.

Victoria bit the inside of her mouth to keep from grinning. A smart woman would've known better than to bait Logan. When he got on a roll, he knew no shame.

"This is my fiancée, Victoria Storm." Logan swept Victoria up in his arms, and she was too damn surprised to even attempt evasion.

"We've met," Milly said. "My granddaughter, Emily, was in your ballet class. She was so sad you quit."

"Emily is a wonderful girl. Very talented," Victoria said through clenched teeth. She hadn't quit her part-time job at the dance studio. The owner had forced her out once Victoria's pregnancy became too obvious to hide.

"Thank you." Milly dropped her speculative gaze to Victoria's stomach. "Is it my imagination, or is there a little trouble in paradise?"

"Logan is a bit premature in announcing our engagement, is all." Fuming, Victoria dug punishing fingernails into Logan's arm. How dare he make her the butt of a tasteless joke? She was just going to *kill* him. "I never agreed to marry you."

"You never said no." He smiled and leaned in close to put his arm around her. His toasty warm breath held the floral notes of sweet citrus candy. Logan was a Tic Tac junkie... and apparently an exceptionally skilled liar.

"True," Victoria ground out. She'd never said no because *he'd never asked*. Taking advantage of his proximity, she tilted her head to better monitor Logan's heart rate. No change. She drew a slow breath, tasting his scent again.

As a rule, wolf-shifters were walking lie detectors thanks to their keen senses. And as another rule, *everyone* who lied, no matter how talented, had tells, which ranged from the obvious to the most minor. Nothing, *absolutely nothing*, altered in his demeanor or his physiological responses even though he was lying like a rug.

"She's determined to make me beg. Tell her she ought to marry me." Charm on full blast, Logan winked at Milly.

The older woman broke into a grin. She gave a sage nod. "Children need a mother and a father, dearie. You should marry Logan. He's a fine young man."

"Thank you, I'm thinking about it." Victoria forced a smile. She played along, determined not to give the gossip mill any more fodder. As an outsider in Sierra Pines, she endured enough speculation about her circumstances and the baby's father from the small-town community already. *This* could only make it worse. People would certainly assume Logan was her child's father... if they didn't already.

She hardly interacted with the townies, anyway. No, it was Logan's talent for subterfuge that disturbed her more. A tendril of doubt and suspicion snaked its way into her psyche and tried to take root. Her morbid imagination whispered, "What if...?" She yanked the weed out and beat it back, determined not to succumb to paranoia. She *needed* Logan, to trust and to depend on, especially in the aftermath of the revelation of Sawyer's betrayal.

"For the best." Milly asked Logan, "Are you having a boy or a girl?"

"Girl." Logan beamed, playing proud papa to the hilt, but then sorrow cast a long shadow over him. "I'm just sorry my parents aren't here to see it."

"Lovely. Little girls are so sweet." Milly clasped her hands beneath her trembling chin. "Your mother and father would've been so proud."

Warily, Victoria rubbed a crimp in her neck, and desperately wished someone would offer her a chair. They exchanged a few more pleasantries before Logan announced their intention to visit his uncle, Sheriff Mike Trash. Milly bid them goodbye, another huge production that involved well-wishing and promises to stay in touch. To her shock, Victoria found herself the recipient of a crushing hug from the fierce granny.

"I can't believe you lied to that poor woman like that," Victoria hissed as they passed through the entrance to the back rooms. Really, she meant to say "I'm going to kill you" but that wasn't what came out.

"I didn't lie. I am going to marry you." Logan grinned, as cocky as all fuck. "I just haven't asked you yet."

Her breath exited her lungs in a peeved gust. Victoria opened her mouth, but they were already through the doorway and on into the bullpen. Sawyer and two of the deputy sheriffs, Gilman and Shaw, stood around the water cooler, shooting the breeze over pro baseball. Their conversation died away as soon as Victoria and Logan arrived.

They exchanged awkward greetings all around. Then both deputies beat it back to their desks, leaving Sawyer, Logan, and Victoria in an awkward ring about the water cooler.

"I'll go find my uncle." Logan grazed Victoria's shoulder. "Wait here."

"Okay." Victoria shoved Logan, and he went. She followed his retreating back, and only when she couldn't avoid it any longer, she turned to Sawyer. Things had been better between them since their conversation at the lake, but they were far from fine. On the upside, bathing had done wonders for his appearance, but he still needed a shave and a haircut.

Sawyer stared back, unflinching and unblinking, with chocolate brown eyes that held a world of misery. His aura was cobalt blue—smooth, hard, and opaque. Every now and then sigils—Old Norse runes—flashed across the surface, visible for only a second before they vanished.

"It may not seem like it, but we're making progress." Sawyer projected diamond-edged sarcasm through the pack bond.

"You and Logan?" Victoria asked, eyeing him. She didn't want to connect with Sawyer. But she'd offered him a second chance—and he'd promised to help her with *Den Valgte*. She wondered, though, if the hunter could be trusted to keep his word. More to the point, would he be able to resolve the conflict? Being a hunter placed a lot of strictures on what and how much he was allowed to reveal.

Sawyer squinted. "I haven't shot him in three days."

"Impressive." Victoria smiled. "How long has it been since you pointed a gun at him?"

"Sixteen hours..." The hunter frowned and cocked his head so his unkempt bangs fell into his eyes. Messy, messy. Her fingers itched once more for a pair of scissors.

"That long, huh?"

"It's tough. I really want to shoot him." Sawyer rolled his shoulders in a sheepish shrug.

She succumbed to giggles. "Believe me—I know the feeling."

SHERIFF TRASH escorted VICTORIA, Sawyer, and Logan to the cellblock where he'd isolated the three *Den Valgte* prisoners. They passed through a long corridor past closed doors marked as the squad and locker rooms. Their footsteps echoed eerily through the corridors and they encountered no one along the way.

It reminded her of the hospital basement.

"Have they said anything?" Victoria asked, shaking off her creepy jitters.

"Nothing other than to demand their lawyer. I've sent for Doc Martens to check them over before they get their one phone call. Of course, it might take him a while to get back to me seeing as how it's a weekend." Mike unlocked and shoved the door open. It creaked on rusty hinges. Once they were through, he locked it behind them.

"Doc Martens?" Victoria missed a mental step. Prior to moving to Sierra Pines, she'd worked as a registered nurse in Arizona. While researching job openings in Sierra Pines, she'd familiarized herself with the name of every local physician who owned a private practice or worked at the hospital. Doc Martens didn't ring any bells unless...

"That's right. Ol' Doc Martens." The sheriff's eyes twinkled with wicked humor.

Victoria grinned. "Is Doc Martens a podiatrist by any chance?"

"He might be. I'm not sure." He winked, and she snickered.

"Do we know anything about them?" Victoria asked.

"I've run their finger prints," Mike said. "The leader's name is

James Reidell. He owns a Harley dealership and is listed as the president of a motorcycle club called Thor's Hammer."

"How apropos." Victoria snorted.

"Reidell has been picked up a few times for drunk and disorderly, but he has no record aside from that," Mike finished.

"The other two?" Sawyer asked.

"More or less the same," Mike said. "One of the two is a carpenter, the other works as a janitor at the local high school. They both belong to Thor's Hammer."

Victoria's skin was crawling, and she didn't know why. Based on a feeling, she asked, "Where are they from?"

"Ironwood, Nevada."

"Ironwood." The word chilled the marrow in Victoria's bones. According to Norse folklore, the *iviðia* raised "giant wolves" that did their bidding. The so-called troll women dwelled in Járnviðr, the Ironwood, and practiced the ancient art of *seidre,* magic concerned with discerning and controlling the course of destiny, which included divination, clairvoyance, prophecy, blessings, and curses.

Logan stirred; his scent soured with unease. "I was born in Ironwood."

"I know," Victoria said, glancing at Logan. She wanted to reach out and offer him comfort, but not in front of the sheriff, and especially not Sawyer.

"What am I missing?" Sawyer shifted his stance.

"Our family has history in Ironwood," Mike said, clearly uneasy with divulging family secrets in front of an outsider.

"Private history." Logan crossed his arms and scowled up a storm.

Victoria pursed her lips, considering the matter. She respected both Mike and Logan's desire for privacy, but they were dealing with a real and monumental threat. "Logan," she began, "Sawyer needs to hear this."

"Bullshit." Logan glared, fire in his amber eyes.

"I'm sorry. He has to know," Victoria said softly, and then

raised her volume. "The Ironwood is home of the *iviðia,* the witches who dwell in the woods. They are known as *dís,* Norns, troll women, *seiðr...*"

"Right, I know my history," Sawyer snapped.

"I'm not interested in what you know. Listen to what I'm telling you." She scowled, waiting to see if he'd interrupt again. When the hunter faced her in grim silence, she continued, "Arik was the Alpha of Ironwood. A witch named Hrafnar used magic to enslave most of his pack. She turned wolves against wolves."

"It was a massacre," Mike said grimly. "Arik got Lori—my sister —and Logan to safety, but he paid a terrible price. They were the only survivors. The rest of the pack died."

"Dad went back and killed Hrafnar. Or thought he did..." Palpable anger radiated off Logan, who stood with his shoulders hunched. His hands closed to white-knuckled fists.

"The witch survived. That's what we were dealing with last February when you blundered into town." Victoria directed the explanation to Sawyer, but reached for Logan. His torment over-whelmed her reluctance. She closed her hands about his fist and cradled it, drawing his tension into herself through the pack bond. Without words, she made a silent promise—she would never reveal the rest of his painful past to anyone. Not now. Not ever.

He gazed into her face and released a long breath. Some tension bled from his lanky frame. Not all, but enough.

"That's enough history lessons for now." Victoria rubbed her fingers across Logan's knuckles and let go. "The relevant takeaway is that Hrafnar probably has sisters. We may be dealing with an entire coven."

"You think they're manipulating *Den Valgte?*" Sawyer asked.

"Maybe. I don't know for sure." Victoria scowled. "But if they're under a witch's influence, it'll make negotiating with them harder. Maybe impossible."

"We'll just have to see how it goes," Mike said. His tone hammered the final nail into the coffin lid. They'd already discussed it to death, and all were in basic agreement. They'd negotiate as a preference; fight as a last resort.

The sheriff halted outside of the entrance to the cellblocks. "Before we get any farther, Sawyer, I'll need you to hand over your firearms. I've made an exception, allowing you to carry in the station, but I can't allow them in the lockup."

"I understand." Sawyer shrugged his coat off and then removed the pair of 9mm pistols he wore in a double harness and passed them to the sheriff.

"Thank you." Mike started to turn away.

"Ah, hold up." Sawyer reached beneath the long tail of his shirt and extracted a 45. He handed it over, too.

"That all?" This time, Mike didn't assume.

Victoria bit her lower lip to stop from busting out laughing.

"Almost." Sawyer pulled his jeans leg up. He had a revolver holstered on his calf.

"Does the phrase 'compensating for inadequacies' ring any bells?" Logan asked, rolling his eyes.

Sawyer surrendered the revolver. "Sheriff, do you need my knives, too?"

The sheriff shifted the armful of weapons along with Sawyer's coat, but couldn't seem to get a good grip. His face flushed, especially his scalp and ears. Finally, with a huff, he dumped the arsenal in the corner.

"That's enough," Mike muttered as he straightened. "We don't have all day. Just make darn sure none of the prisoners gain control of your knives."

"No one touches my weapons but me," Sawyer said in all seriousness.

"We don't need to hear about your special alone time." Logan performed an obscene gesture with his hands—as if there'd been any doubt.

Mike shot his nephew a dirty look. "Now before you go in there, one final check to be sure we're all on the same page. Do you know what you're going to say?"

"Yes, I plan to talk to them. If they are under a *seiðr's* influence, I may be able to detect it," Victoria said. "Based on the little I know, the members of *Den Valgte* are pagan fundamentalists. By their own words, they live and die for Odin. We're going to test their faith."

Victoria winced. *Test of faith.* Gods, but that stung.

Sawyer grunted. His adamant approval traversed the bond.

The sheriff shot a look at his nephew, but addressed Victoria. "That could work... Specifically, what do you have in mind?"

Victoria pursed her lips. Her hesitation stemmed from uncertainty over how much she could say to the sheriff. Technically, Jake Barrett's true identity was a secret—one that hadn't been guarded particularly well or vigilantly lately. Mike may have figured it out already—maybe Logan had told his uncle—or he must at least suspect the truth. Any way she looked at it, however, the revelation couldn't come from her.

"Mike knows. I told him." Logan swiped his palms together.

"You what?" Sawyer burst out.

Aghast, Victoria echoed the hunter. "You what?"

"He needed to know." Wholly unapologetic, Logan shrugged.

"I'm standing right here," Mike said in a tone as dry as the desert.

"Who else did you tell?" Victoria asked.

"Did you take out an ad in the local paper?" Sawyer demanded.

"No. Should I've?" Logan thrust his chin out as though daring the hunter to take a shot at him.

"That's enough, boys." Mike stepped between the two men. "Sawyer, you have my word—your father's secret is safe with me. I have no intention of telling anyone. Besides, who would believe me?" Mike offered to shake on it.

Sawyer knit his brow, and took the sheriff's hand.

Stiffness eased from Victoria's shoulders. She harbored no delusions it was over. There'd be fallout when Jake found out, but she'd deal with it when it happened.

"Ready?" Mike asked.

Victoria squared her shoulders. "As ready as I'll ever be."

Mike used an old-fashioned key on an iron ring to unlock the sliding steel door. It clanked and rumbled as he pushed it open to the cellblock. He stepped aside, allowing Victoria and Sawyer to pass.

"Reidell is on the left."

CHAPTER 19

Ehwaz: The Rune of Momentum

A FROSTY PALL permeated the jail along with the scent of mildew and metal. Walking side-by-side, Victoria and Sawyer entered the central corridor—a short but wide strip between the grilled walls. Watermarked concrete composed the ceilings and floors. All total, the block contained four cells; three of which held prisoners.

"Are you ready for this?" Victoria asked from the side of her mouth in a whisper pitched for Sawyer's ears alone. The she-wolf maintained a rigid stance, radiating palpable tension.

"Yeah, I'm ready." Sawyer reached for the grips of his holstered 9mms but his hands closed on empty air. His lips compressed with grim displeasure. *Right.* The sheriff had confiscated his guns.

Behind them, the mechanical slider thundered and crashed shut. Sawyer instinctively closed ranks with Victoria. Instinct overrode reason. Claustrophobia jangled his nerves.

"Easy there, big fella. We're okay," Victoria murmured, employing the sort of tone people used with nervous dogs.

"Knock it off." Sawyer's mouth tugged into an unwilling smile. Out of morbid curiosity, he stole a quick glance inside the empty cell. It contained a steel sink and commode, a single bed attached to the wall, and a rusted locker.

"Knock what off?" Victoria radiated an aura of contrived innocence. Adding insult to injury, she dropped a slow, heavy thump on his arm... probably because she couldn't reach the top of his head. "Are you saying I should stop treating you like a trigger-happy hothead who's more likely to shoot than talk?"

Zing. Guilty as charged. The woman had his number.

"Yeah, that," Sawyer said with a wry chuckle.

"No need, since I'd never suggest such an outrageous thing."

"That's a win for diplomacy."

"See? I'm capable." She dug her elbow into his ribs, nudging him to create space between them. "Consider yourself managed."

"Yes, ma'am."

When she stepped away, Sawyer checked the paranoid impulse to stay close. The woman had made her desire abundantly clear. Next time, her tactics might not be so subtle.

Their entrance attracted the attention of the *Den Valgte* prisoners. The inmates exchanged a few muttered words as they approached. Reidell, a middle-aged man, occupied the indicated cell which had metal bars rubbed smooth from being gripped. He stood with his brawny arms crossed over his chest. On the other side of the row, a younger man and an older man were imprisoned in separate lockups.

The air crackled with a sudden buildup of electricity. The hairs on the backs of Sawyer's arms stood on end. Beneath Victoria's command, the pack bond energized as she assessed the mystical environment surrounding them. Sawyer understood the magic well enough gain a vague sense of dynamic patterns. She was checking the *Den Valgte* raiders for signs of magic use independent of the enchanted animal skins that the sheriff had confiscated.

Questioningly, Sawyer glanced over and arched his brow.

Victoria shook her head. She faced the prisoners, and called out the traditional greeting. "Hail!"

"Hail," Reidell said, curt and wary. He had dark blond hair streaked with gray; the striations continued through his full mustache and beard.

"My name is Victoria Storm," she said. "I am Odin's Valkyrie and Alpha of the Storm Pack—"

"Those are big claims. Do you have proof to back them up?" Reidell radiated palpable suspicion. He flexed his hands. Extensive Norse-patterned tattoos covered his shoulders and arms, including a large *Mjölnir*—Thor's hammer—the name of his motorcycle club. His robust build belonged to a man accustomed to physical labor. Based on his stance, Sawyer pegged the *Den Valgte* leader as a wrestler.

"My companion is Sawyer Barrett." Victoria rested her hand on Sawyer's forearm. The pack bond pitched with her irritation. The challenge to her authority annoyed Victoria but she kept it off her face.

"Hail." Sawyer stepped up. He maintained a broad stance, at the ready for combat, and endured the keen appraisal of the three *Den Valgte* men as they took his estimate.

"Hail," Reidell grunted the grudging greeting. The man lowered his eyes in a slight but significant deferral to Sawyer's prestige. Reidell's gaze lingered overlong on Sawyer's dagger tattoo, as though he couldn't look away.

Victoria exhaled just a little too fast. Her peevish displeasure surged. "We've identified you as James Reidell, the leader of *Den Valgte*."

"Maybe." Reidell frowned and gave her his attention. "Maybe not."

"Fine, let's try a different approach. Should I be addressing one of these two men rather than you?" She swept her hand to include the prisoners across the row.

Reidell's face pinched. "Speak to me."

"Good, glad we were able to settle that at least," Victoria said with a soft snort. "For the record, we're not the ones behind bars. It was you who trespassed on our lands. We won the battle. *We* have nothing to prove. However, since we wish to open a dialogue with *Den Valgte*, we'll make the effort to establish our credentials to your satisfaction."

"What do you know of *Den Valgte*?" Reidell asked.

"Only what we were told," Victoria said. "That you're heathen and adhere to the old ways. You and your brethren consider yourselves Odin's Chosen."

Sawyer bit his tongue, curbing a rude outburst. Odin's Chosen—the gall of these guys was incredible. Sawyer longed to deliver his opinion on the auspicious claim. He kept quiet only out of respect for Victoria. He owed her his support.

"We are the Chosen. We serve our gods." Reidell raised his hand and touched the Mjölnir pendant on a steel chain over a black t-shirt.

"You serve Odin?"

"You dare question my faith?" Reidell asked, bristling.

Victoria held up a staying hand. "I'm simply asking questions to attain a better understanding of how my pack became your enemy. Less than a week ago, I'd never heard of *Den Valgte*. To the best of my knowledge, we did nothing to initiate hostilities."

The leader stirred. "We came in search of our missing friends."

"Your missing friends—they were two men and a woman named Magdalena?" Victoria asked. "They trespassed on my land, skinned a gray wolf, and murdered a man."

Reidell snarled.

"They're dead," Sawyer said with a degree of pleasure. He earned himself a glare from the *Den Valgte* leader. Try as he might, Sawyer lacked Victoria's proclivity for negotiation.

"We already knew that." Reidell addressed Sawyer. "Why do you allow this woman to speak for you?"

Sawyer hesitated. He traded a loaded glance with Victoria. She exuded pent-up stress, and the last thing he wanted was to undermine her. At last, he said, "Victoria is the leader of the Storm Pack, of which I'm a member. She speaks for all of us."

Reidell grunted but appeared to accept the explanation. He moved on. "The attack yesterday was in retaliation for the deaths of our murdered kin. You may hold us prisoners, but *Den Valgte* is strong. Our brothers will come for us."

"That's exactly what I'd like to avoid," Victoria said steadily. "If the cycle of revenge is allowed to play out, this doesn't end. It escalates. My pack can and will fight to defend itself. We've proven that. Even if you overwhelm us—take our land, murder my wolves, it doesn't stop there. We have people who will avenge us. Do you want a war with wolves? Can you afford a war?"

"I don't want a war," Reidell said after a tense consideration.

"I don't either." Victoria jerked her chin. She poked at Sawyer through the pack bond and asked a nonverbal question—*Are you ready?*

Sawyer nodded.

"What do you want from me? We won't betray our brothers. We'd rather die." Reidell crossed his arms over his chest in open defiance—a strong, proud man. Perspiration beads coalesced on his brow, but he refused to back down. Sawyer found grudging admiration for the other man's stubborn courage.

In the opposite cell, Reidell's followers added their voices.

"Yes, I believe you would," Victoria said. "Your deaths, however, won't give me what I want."

"What is it you want?" Reidell asked.

"I need you to see we're both on the same side—we serve the same gods." Victoria retreated a couple paces, turning the stage over to Sawyer.

Sawyer wrapped his hand around the cord-wrapped haft of his belt throwing knife. Metal hissed over leather as he drew it from its sheath. It sat in his palm, as natural as an extension of himself. The hunter turned to display the black dagger tattoo on his upper arm.

"See this?" Sawyer jostled his elbow.

"Yeah," Reidell said.

"Do you know what this is?" Sawyer asked.

"No," Reidell said in a neutral tone.

"It's called a hunter's mark."

The silence weighed heavy. Sawyer raised the knife and cut a deep slash across the back of his arm from his elbow to his wrist. He hissed through clenched teeth but endured, rock steady. Red blood spilled from the gash in a steady stream and splashed to the concrete floor. The hunter swiped the blade across his denim-clad thigh and then returned it to its scabbard.

"Watch." Sawyer thrust his arm through the bars so Reidell had a clear view. He used his hand to wipe away the hot blood, exposing the injury.

"What am I supposed to be seeing...?" Reidell cast a skeptical glance at the hunter's arm. His skeptical question ended in a startled cry. He fidgeted, performing a sharp double take, and then stared in rapt fascination.

Runes writhed upon Sawyer's skin, pulsating with arcane magic, and swarmed about the gash. The sigils were ancient, painful to gaze upon, yet so powerfully hypnotic that looking away required an act of will. With each passing second, the cut grew narrower and shallower. It stopped bleeding, shrank, and then disappeared altogether.

"Impressive, but it's well known wolves heal quickly." Reidell grabbed the steel bars of his prison and gripped them white-knuckled. His followers echoed his skepticism.

"No tricks. What you're witnessing is more than mere healing." Sawyer raised his hands palms turned up, and summoned the hunter magic at his command. His hunter's mark went nova and the runes rippled on his skin. His strength increased sevenfold as did his stamina and regeneration.

"*Seidre,*" Reidell huffed in awe.

"Greater. These embody the secrets of the cosmos. Odin impaled himself through the chest on the trunk of Yggdrasil and hung for nine days to learn their secrets. Their mastery requires sacrifice." Sawyer clenched his fists and concentrated. He visited each rune in his mind—shaped and named it. It'd taken him months to arrive at the belated realization that he was a god-toddler playing with alphabet blocks. A fragment of a conversation months past filled Sawyer's mind.

In a gruff voice, Jake had lectured, "Runic enchantment makes it possible to reshape reality to suit one's desire. Each rune embodies a primordial force of the universe, and each is a secret. Some will reveal their mysteries easily. Others will be coy. It may take you minutes to master one and centuries to coax another into your care. I suspect you'll take to Hagalaz—disruption—naturally, but millennia might pass before Laguz will give you the time of day."

"Funny," Sawyer bit off. At the time, he'd figured his old man was taking a pot shot at his expense. Now, Sawyer grasped the enormity of his mistake.

"Whatever you do, don't try to force the runes to cooperate. The consequences of misusing or abusing them can be dire."

"Are the runes sentient?" Sawyer asked.

"Yes... and no," Jake said with an enigmatic smile.

Sawyer scoffed. "You do that on purpose."

"Beware turning exclusively to the runes that come naturally to you," Jake warned. "I am Ansuz—knowledge and wisdom. I am the message; however, knowledge without understanding is useless. Stagnation—the trap I fall into time and again. I've learned to choose companions who are disruptive and chaotic—"

"Loki?"

"Loki." Jake grinned. "But a man only needs one Loki in his life. To that end, also seek companions who possess contrary but complimentary traits to your own. Long ago, I wandered constantly, always searching, never satisfied. Your mother gave me a home and family, a place and people to return to when my feet grew weary. She brought purpose into my aimless existence."

"Are you saying I ought to get married?" Unbidden, Sawyer's thoughts turned to Victoria. He immediately dismissed the speculation as impossible.

Jake flashed a toothy grin. "I'm not saying anything at all."

"Such bullshit." Sawyer chuckled, and his dad laughed, too.

"Now, as I was saying—each rune is a unique letter."

"You said they were secrets," Sawyer argued as naturally as he breathed.

"Do you want to learn this stuff or not?"

"Yeah." Sawyer tightened his jaws.

"Then shut up and listen." Jake released a deep grunt. "There are twenty-four runes. Taken together, they compose an alphabet. Letters combine to make words which are also called bind runes. Someday, once you fully grasp the true nature of each sigil, you'll learn to combine them. Short words at first, but eventually longer ones, and someday sentences. This is the language of spellcraft."

The essence of magic.

Power flooded into Sawyer in a rising tide. It pitched and it heaved. He channeled more than he controlled so the excess spilled across his skin and turned his complexion a glossy obsidian. The atmosphere churned with the raw, esoteric forces of creation—an excessive display, downright terrifying, impossible to dismiss or deny.

Sawyer's consciousness zoomed out. He soared to unattainable heights. He plummeted into a bottomless void. He froze; he burned. He hollered at the top of his lungs—a raw battle cry.

All the prisoners backed away from the bars.

"Sawyer," Victoria's tone held a distinct note of warning. She reached for him but stopped herself. Sawyer sensed her gnawing worry.

"Who are you?" Reidell gaped with a rapt fascination.

"I am Aesir—one of your gods."

CHAPTER 20

Hunter's Mark:
Bind Rune to Make a Hunter

"I AM a son of Frigg and Odin," Sawyer announced into the brittle silence, and an odd measure of satisfaction washed through him. It was surprising how good it felt to finally proclaim the truth after a lifetime of secrecy.

Victoria snarled and bristled. Her astonishment pierced the bond. The *Den Valgte* prisoners mirrored her shock but to a far greater extent. The three men backed away from the bars, retreating to the backs of their cells.

"This wasn't what we talked about," she said, hissing. "Have you gone mad?"

"Maybe..." Sawyer's sanity might be in question, but he understood one thing too well—he'd gone too far to back out. He was committed to this course.

"Fine, whatever." Victoria rolled her eyes and sang, "Welcome to the jungle."

"And you call *my* music dated." Sawyer chuckled even as his bones throbbed. His molars ached at the marrow and down to the root. Too late, he grasped his mistake. He lacked the wisdom necessary to command the primordial essence building inside his body. He feared he would shatter into a million pieces.

"I called *you* dated, bub." Victoria gripped his forearm. The vital essence of *Isa* flowed over him, cooling the fiery magic raging within his core.

"Thanks." He exhaled in relief, and his startled gaze flew to her. He wanted to ask how she'd done it—*and why.* Their spiritual connection, however, was too personal to discuss in front of witnesses.

"You're welcome." Victoria smiled with her eyes.

While they'd bantered, Reidell had overcome his initial reticence and crept closer to the bars again. He gripped the bars with both hands, and the bright-white glyph *Ehwaz* lit his soul, signaling his readiness.

"You say you serve Odin. Prove it—take my hand. Swear fealty." Sawyer reached through the bars of Reidell's lockup. Stretched out before him, his arm had the definition of black granite. He barely recognized it.

"What do you ask of me?" Reidell focused the whole of his attention on Sawyer. He lifted his hand but wavered, caught in a crux, probably the greatest challenge his faith had ever endured.

"Everything," Sawyer said, his voice hollow and vast, and not his own. "It might require the loss of your hand or your eye, your life or your soul. You don't choose the price, only whether you'll pay it."

"This could kill me?" Reidell asked.

"It might. Will you die for Odin, or is your heart craven?" Sawyer asked, making it a deliberate taunt. The arrow flew true and struck its target. Reidell scowled, taking umbrage.

"Hail, Odin!" Victoria shouted the battle cry.

"Hail, Odin!" Reidell seized Sawyer's forearm and took up the shout. Their voices blended at a deafening volume, and their souls joined.

In a heartbeat, Sawyer perceived everything about the man before him. Images of James Reidell's past flashed through Sawyer's consciousness. The man's childhood had been difficult—an alcoholic mother, an abusive father. His entire life had been a struggle—marked with harsh defeats and precious few victories.

"You've fought," Sawyer said to Reidell.

"For everything I have." Reidell jerked his chin.

"You've known loss."

"Yes." Reidell's voice cracked. For three years, a wife and a baby daughter shone as the sole beacon in the man's dreary existence, but the screeching crash of a car crash ended their lives. The only thing he had left was his motorcycle club—and his faith.

Unexpected sympathy stabbed at Sawyer. When he'd initiated this exchange, he'd set forth with malice in his heart. Den Valgte had attacked and harmed the Storm Pack. Sawyer had meant to discover what the *Den Valgte* leader cherished most and to take it from him. But now revenge had lost its appeal.

"Are you okay?" Victoria gripped Sawyer's elbow. The she-wolf crowded close, her aura blended with his, her strength reinforced his own.

"I'm good, thanks." Sawyer swallowed around a lump in his throat. Suddenly, he felt small and petty... and undeserving. Sawyer's sins against the pack far outweighed those of the outsiders. Yet, Victoria still treated him kindly, and she'd urged Sawyer to show mercy to the *Den Valgte* men... He only wondered if he was man enough to live up to her example.

"Tell me, am I worthy?" Reidell asked. Remarkably, the man remained steady despite the rigors of having his soul subjected to scrutiny.

"You're worthy." In a small but significant sacrifice of his own, Sawyer let go of his grudge and focused on the spellcraft he meant to undertake.

Sawyer had never made another hunter before. Only his old man brought new members into the fold. Jake had taught Sawyer the basic construction of the hunter's mark bind rune; however, he'd never stated outright that Sawyer was expected or even permitted to use the spell. *Fehu* entered Sawyer's thoughts, casting a fiery glow; the natural starting point for an enchantment designed to delegate his energy to another. The magic came to him in starts and stops. A river of runes ran from Sawyer into Reidell, but then got dammed up.

Reidell's forearm turned black and he grunted in discomfort.

Sawyer drew a sharp breath. In his mind's eye, the shining warrior's prowess sigil coalesced. The bind rune began with *Ihwaz*, the rune of defense. From there, others were laid atop it. It also consisted of *Uruz* for mental and physical strength, *Ehwaz* for swiftness, and *Isa* for will and focus. *Sowilo* extended the improvements to his whole physique, boosting willpower and reflexes. *Ehwaz* served double duty, activating harmony between his mind and body. By the same duality, *Isa* was the linchpin that stabilized the whole dynamic system.

Warrior's prowess—and all its component runes—settled atop the staff of *Fehu* and merged together. The runic magic rolled through Reidell on a wave. The runes entered the man's body and bonded to his spirit. It streamed beneath his skin, passed through his forearm. Too many tattoos covered Reidell's arms; there was no free space for the dagger-shaped hunter's mark.

The magic chose Reidell's *Mjölnir* tattoo, which lit with a fiery glow. With each passing moment, the magic burned brighter, searing the inked Thor's Hammer from the man's skin. Reidell's grip on Sawyer's arm tightened convulsively. It must've hurt like a son of a bitch, he gritted his teeth and endured.

"This is your sacrifice..." The words dragged from Sawyer—a challenge given the intensity of the magic. "Odin permits his followers no conflicted loyalties. You cannot retain your former allegiance to your motorcycle club."

"You would have me forsake my brethren?" Reidell demanded.

"This is not me," Sawyer said, sharp in tone so there'd be no mistake. "Abandon no one—it is your duty to bring your brothers and sisters to Odin. Do you understand and accept?"

"I do!" Reidell bellowed at the top of his lungs. Overwhelmed, he fell to his knees and dragged Sawyer down with him.

Sawyer crashed to the concrete but kept his hold on the hunter initiate. Enthralled by the runes, Sawyer focused on finishing the enchantment. He added *Nauthiz* to deepen the effort and *Thurisaz* to harden the frontiers. *Tiwaz*, the warrior's rune, turned conflict into war, and that should've completed the bind rune. Should've, except it didn't. Reidell's *Mjölnir* tattoo was gone, but his upper arm remained bare of a hunter's mark.

Damn it. Sawyer grunted, gathering the last of his strength. What was he missing? Why wouldn't the mark form? He clenched his teeth and concentrated on the uncooperative runes, envisioning a dagger, the physical symbol of their unity. The magic bucked and twisted. For a second, he got a solid grasp but then it turned intangible beneath his fingers.

Bent over, Victoria squeezed Sawyer's shoulder. Through their psychic bond, she soothed and calmed him. "Stop forcing it. Channeling divinity is like making love."

"Yeah, that's not how I make love." Sawyer's first instinct went straight to resistance. He wanted to fight off her influence even though she was helping him.

"I didn't say, 'Close your eyes and do it for England.'" Victoria muttered something else beneath her breath about men and shoving sticks places they should never go.

"Then what did you mean?" With a grunt, Sawyer turned his head toward her and their gazes locked. Victoria's eyes glinted with paramount annoyance.

"Relax and go to it," Victoria's tone melted to warm silk and slid across his skin. Her voice acquired hypnotic qualities. She called it an alpha's trick—and damn, she was getting good at it.

"I'm relaxed," he claimed in the biggest lie of his life. But then, her badly misquoted lyric hardly warranted a genius reply.

"Then get to it." She dug her fingers into the tense muscles in his shoulders, kneading the knots bunched there.

"Gittin'." It required an act of will and faith, but Sawyer surrendered control. Tension bled from his frame. As his muscles unlocked, pain acquired new dimensions.

"What's happening?" Reidell asked.

Sawyer bristled with irritation over the unwelcome intrusion. His startled gaze flickered to Reidell. Sawyer disliked having witnesses to what he considered an intimate moment with Victoria. It felt like an invasion.

"Shut up." A growl rolled from Victoria's throat. She leaned over Sawyer's shoulder, flattening her chest against his back. Golden radiance shone from her eyes and mouth so bright it obfuscated her features.

Reidell's eyes rounded and he snapped his mouth closed.

Victoria's healing magic bathed Sawyer, warming his skin. Revitalizing energy flowed *through* her into him. It originated from some vast, mysterious ocean that Sawyer sensed at the periphery of his awareness.

The ocean spirit of *Laguz*.

The missing piece of the puzzle fit into place. From *Laguz* came unity; it balanced and bonded the vast hunter collective. A deluge of runic magic overwhelmed and obliterated the dam that'd obstructed the tide. It poured into the clean patch of skin on Reidell's upper arm where *Mjölnir* had once been and filled the void. A scalding hot iron brand in the shape of a dagger formed from the sigils.

Human flesh sizzled like bacon on a fire, and the stench of charred hair and skin permeated the air. Reidell screamed and yanked his hand free. He doubled over, clutching a hand over his new hunter's mark.

"*Now* you are chosen." Sawyer rocked back. Victoria kept him from going over. As soon as he let go, the runic magic drained straight out of him... along with the strength it'd provided. The aftermath left him feeling as hungover as his last drunken bender. Nausea swirled in his gut and the prospect of going down on his knees to worship the porcelain goddess held enigmatic appeal.

"That took a lot out of me." He tipped over, on a collision course with the concrete. Victoria caught his elbow and propped him upright.

"I can see that. Right here." She shoved him against the empty cell.

"Thanks." Sawyer reflexively clutched the bars to stop from toppling, and slouched over, almost bent in half. Every sound rang in his ears. The three *Den Valgte* men were talking over each other at an incoherent clamor. He shook his head, trying to clear it.

Victoria raised her face. Electric blue radiance spilled from her eyes. *Blue, not gold...* She glowed when she used magic, but he'd never witnessed any hue beyond white-bright or glossy gold. Sawyer got stuck on the anomaly. It gave him the creeps.

She leaned in close. Her spearmint-spiked breath ghosted across his cheek. She tucked a strand of hair behind his ear and whispered, "Sawyer, you have to kill Sylvie."

"Excuse me?" Adrenaline swept through Sawyer. He jerked his face toward Victoria. He scoured her face; a stranger stared back at him. Disbelief hung on tight—she couldn't have said what he'd heard.

Victoria arched a fine eyebrow and smirked. She stood close, pressing against him. Beneath the soft cotton of her top, her breasts were soft and inviting. A molten surge of arousal swept Sawyer. Lust turned in his gut like a dagger, and paired unwell with nausea.

"Jim, are you okay?" Both of Reidell's followers shouted at the same time.

"Yeah, I'm fine." On the floor on his cell, Reidell groaned but raised his head. He dragged himself upright, staggered to his bunk, and plunked onto it.

"Shut up!" Sawyer roared at the three prisoners. They fell into startled silence. Sawyer gave his head another slight shake, attempting to stop the ringing. He wrapped his hand around Victoria's wrist and asked, "What did you say?"

"I didn't say anything." She shrugged, looking clueless.

"You said something."

"You're hurting me!" She pouted, thrusting out her lower lip.

With a start of guilt, Sawyer let go of her. His first instinct sent him to an apology, but he bypassed it. The magic had left him as weak as a kitten. He couldn't hurt Victoria with his bare hands when his strength was normal. Something wasn't right. He gritted his teeth and used the bars to haul himself upright. His fight-reflex drove him to assume a defensive stance.

"You said something... a minute ago. What was it?" Sawyer softened his tone to coaxing. Probably not very convincing since his entire body was as tense as a drawn bow.

Victoria frowned. The electric blue glow winked out. "I said that spell seems to have knocked you silly."

"Why would you say that?" Sawyer didn't believe her even for a second. He knew what he'd heard.

"You're disoriented. Now let go before *I* knock you silly. You need to rest a bit longer." Victoria appraised Sawyer with such critical assessment that he started to question his own sanity again. She asked, "Are you okay?"

"Yeah." He jerked his chin and opened his hands. Releasing the bars, he put more weight on his legs, testing them. They held but Victoria hovered like a mother over a child taking his first steps.

A great snort traveled across the cellblock. It came from the elder of Reidell's followers. "What's wrong with him? I thought he's a god?"

"He's a baby god. There's a learning curve." Victoria flipped her braid over her shoulder.

"Ah." The man nodded as though it made perfect sense.

Sawyer narrowed his eyes and took it like a man.

Shuffling footsteps came from the entrance to her row. Sawyer glanced over his shoulder—Mike and Logan stood within the open doorway. The hunter hadn't heard it open. He took the lapse as further evidence of how off his game the magic had left him.

"All right," Victoria said, addressing Reidell and his men. "Now that you're a hunter—or at least a wannabe—you need to learn the ground rules."

"Rules?" Reidell asked.

"Rules. For starters, there's a hierarchy. Sawyer's your boss. Jake Barrett, that's D-A-D..." Victoria aimed up with both thumbs. "Is Sawyer's boss. Got it?"

Sawyer huffed, but at least she didn't add air quotes.

"Got it." Reidell all but grunted.

"Sawyer's a member of the Storm Pack and I'm a hunter." She raised the sleeve of her top to show her own dagger tattoo to the *Den Valgte* men. "We're allies, so no more hostilities. No more killing or skinning wolves or bears. No more wearing stolen hides. Know this..." She crossed her arms over her chest. "If you cross me on this, the repercussions to follow will be your end."

"Agreed." Despite being seated, Reidell maintained a formidable guard.

"With the sheriff's consent..." Victoria glanced over at Mike, her brow arched in question.

Mike tipped his chin.

Victoria continued, "We're willing to consider releasing you as a sign of good faith, but you have to deliver our message to your fellow pagans."

"What's the message?" Reidell asked.

"Tell your brethren what you have seen," Victoria said. "Spread the word. The time of Ragnarök has come and the gods walk among us. Odin is here under the guise of a mortal man. He is calling. I can show *Den Valgte* how to return to the old ways. I can bring your people back to Odin."

Reidell gnawed his lower lip. He wore no masks, only the fervent brightness of a true believer. "My brothers and sisters won't be easily persuaded. They have not seen Odin's son as we have."

Victoria raised her hands. She looked to Sawyer. Only for a split second, but that brief glance betrayed her uncertainty. As Sawyer had expected, converting an entire group of people to their cause would require more than one miracle.

Sawyer drew himself to his full height. Shoulders squared, he spoke to Reidell and his men. "I'll provide all the proof anyone will ever need. Tell your people to gather in Broken Bend on U.S. Route 50. Tomorrow night at sunset."

Victoria turned to Sawyer with an open question on her face. She opened her mouth but then hesitated to ask. Her anxiety snapped like a colony of crocodiles through their empathetic connection.

"I will do as you say." Reidell tilted his head. "What should they expect?"

"I'm the owner of *Gnýrhorn*, a gift from my mother, Frigg." Frigg—it felt weird on his tongue. Sawyer cited his mother's name out of loyalty. He hadn't missed how she went unmentioned. "Tomorrow night, I'll blow *Gnýrhorn* and summon the Wild Hunt."

An awed murmur arose from Reidell and his followers.

Victoria snarled low in her throat and swung on Sawyer. She seized his arm. "Excuse us just a second," she said, dragging him to the corner with the empty lockup. She dug her nails into his skin, dragged him down, and rose on tippy-toes. "Are you insane?"

"That's open to interpretation."

"Damn it, Sawyer." She shook him like a puppy with a toy. "Does your father know what you're doing?"

"You're asking, did I ask permission?" Sawyer bared his teeth. His reputation as a rebel preceded him. In the past, he'd never sought paternal approval when defiance was an option.

"Oh, I know you did. You're such a good, dutiful son." Her sarcasm could've sunk ships, but it failed to disguise her underlying anxiety.

A cat o' nine tails lashed at his conscience. He'd misunderstood —and freaked out—over an imagined instance of Victoria urging him to kill Sylvie. That didn't give him the right to take it out on her.

"Relax," Sawyer said. "Dad knows. You might even say it was his idea."

"Was it?" Victoria looked askance of him.

Sawyer nodded solemnly. He paused, dragging the exact words from his memory. "Dad said, 'Get it done.'"

"All right then." Victoria huffed and righted herself. "Game on."

CHAPTER 21

Berkanan: the Rune of Growth, Fertility, and Becoming

A SENSE of conspiracy hung over Sylvie as she closed her bedroom door and turned the lock on the knob. Nausea swirled in her gut. Her hands shook from sheer anxiety as she read the handwritten phone number off the scrap of paper and dialed it into her seldom-used mobile phone. Her battery had been dead. The charging cable tethered her to the nightstand, but she considered the cell more secure than the landline.

"Goddess, please have him pick up." Sylvie clutched the phone while it rang. She was alone in the lake house; a rare occurrence. Victoria, Sawyer, and Logan had gone to town. Under orders, Morena had taken the wolves for a run along the lake. And Cali Kinkaid stood guard out on the back patio, enjoying a pitcher of lemonade and cookies. The opportunity for complete privacy was unlikely to present itself again anytime soon.

The ringing stopped, and a discernable beat followed. Sylvie imagined the man on the other end listening to the raspy rhythm of her breathing. Self-conscious, she inhaled slowly and sought to steady herself.

"Hello?" Hardened suspicion edged Finn's deep voice. Few people probably had access to his private number and Sylvie's number wouldn't be registered in his caller directory.

"Hail! Alpha Finn, this is Sylvie Thornton, Skald of the Storm Pack." Sylvie took care to address him with the utmost politeness.

Finn was the leader of the White Mountains Tribe, the largest and most powerful werewolf clan in Arizona. Without him, Victoria never would've been able to exert the influence necessary to bring the other packs to the moot. If Sylvie could convince Finn to withdraw his support, the Conclave would collapse.

"Hail, Skald Thornton!" Finn's tone grew light and quick. "What an unexpected pleasure. It's been a long time since we spoke last. I'd received word of your mate's passing." He left the sentence hanging—a spoken question.

"Paul requited himself with honor. His soul is in Valhalla, serving the Einherjar," Sylvie said in answer.

"Hail to the All Father!" Finn shouted.

"Hail *Bági-ulfs*," Sylvie bit off, choosing her reply with great deliberation. Odin had a great many names, one for almost any occasion imaginable. *Bági-ulfs* meant Enemy of the Wolf.

Finn snorted like a mighty stallion. He boomed with laughter. "What is the purpose of your call, Skald Thornton?"

She pressed her lips into a tight smile. "It concerns the Conclave, which is to be held on the night of a lunar eclipse..."

"Oh?" Finn took a cautious turn. Crafty devil, always looking before he placed a foot.

Sylvie drew a steadying breath. "Early yesterday morning before the sun rose, I cast the rune stones and asked, 'When shadows swallow the moon, how will it affect the moot?'"

"How did the runes answer?"

"Ice." Sylvie shuddered as chills ran down her spine.

"Ice?" Finn asked, brusque with wariness.

"*Isa.* I received a vision of a terrible winter."

Finn chuckled. "The Sierra Nevadas have those. Perhaps it is time for the Storm Pack to return to Arizona."

"It was Fimbulvetr. I am convinced the moot will culminate in the onset of the winter of winters." Sylvie understood the jeopardy she was taking even saying it aloud; just like she incurred another huge risk in going behind Victoria's back. In dismissing her skald's advice, Victoria had left Sylvie no other choice.

While Finn considered. Sylvie stared at her hands and concentrated on remaining still. She found it difficult, almost impossible. So much rode on whether Finn believed her. And should Sylvie be proven wrong, her reputation would be destroyed.

"Thank you for the warning, Skald Thornton. I will ask my own seer to perform a divination," Finn said after a hefty delay. Sylvie's chest tightened.

"Thank you for hearing me, Alpha Finn," Sylvie said, doing her damnedest to conceal her bitter disappointment. She supposed she shouldn't be surprised. No one took an old woman seriously. Still, it stung something fierce.

She didn't know the name of Finn's seer. Chances were good he would consult with the scarred priest, Bodaway. The corrupt, vile little man spoke with a forked tongue and only provided advice that served his own interests. Although he was widely despised, Bodaway's status as Heimdallr's priest protected him.

The phone picked up the thrum of fingers on metal. Then, Finn asked, "What did Alpha Storm have to say about this? The Conclave is her brainchild."

Sylvie winced. As much as she dreaded the question, she must provide a blunt and forthright answer. Finn was intelligent and cunning. He'd sort out the complexities. She only hoped he perceived the justness of her cause.

"I regret to say Victoria didn't put any stock in the forecast," Sylvie admitted with great reluctance. "She is determined to go on with the moot."

"I see..." Finn drawled. "I presume she advised Jake Barrett of your vision. After all, the Conclave is being organized largely at his behest—to negotiate a renewed wolf-hunter alliance. What was the Hunter King's opinion of your vision?"

"Victoria didn't confer with Jake Barrett." Emboldened, Sylvie drew herself upright. Renewed confidence kindled her strength. Surely this would work to her advantage and prove her case. Finn would perceive how Victoria had behaved with arrogance and presumption.

"Your alpha presumed to know Jake Barrett's will?" Finn asked in a voice ripe with speculation. His singular emphasis gave Sylvie pause and reason to consider. She wondered if Finn really knew Jake's true identity.

"I can only tell you what I observed. Victoria disregarded my advice to change the date as a safety measure. She made her decision in a matter of minutes and without consulting anyone."

"Jake Barrett is a man of consequence," Finn said.

"That he is." Sylvie kept her inflection neutral.

"In your opinion, did your alpha act as she did from presumption or because she possessed knowledge of Jake's wishes already?"

Herein lay a trap.

She chose her words with precision. "I would not presume to know another's will. If you must pursue the matter, then I suggest you ask Victoria about it directly. However..."

Finn took the bait. "However?"

Sylvie smiled. "My apologies, I misspoke. Weariness has eroded my judgment. The past two days have been trying."

She provided him with a summary of *Den Valgte*'s attack and everything that'd followed, including Victoria's unexplained absence and inexplicable amnesia. She stuck strictly to the facts, but that should be more than enough. It called Victoria's credibility—even her sanity—into question.

"Thank you, Skald Thornton," Finn said once she finished. "You've given me a lot to think about."

CHAPTER 22

Dagaz: The Rune of Transformation

As HE PASSED through the automatic glass doors into the lobby of the Sierra Pines Medical Facility, Logan found himself on a collision course with destiny. Déjà vu seized him, except that wasn't quite right. He wondered if there was a term to define the sensation of running past someone you knew but didn't immediately place. He would've ignored it except a whiff of magic—sharp and pine fresh—stung his nostrils. His stride faltered.

"What's the rush, gorgeous? Don't have time to say hello?"

"Manny?" In solid surprise, Logan performed a full about-face. He halted dead center on the threshold.

Emanuel Luce, Manny for short—druid and nurse—was in his mid-twenties and of average height and build. Freckles dotted his pale complexion, especially across his nose and cheeks. His hair was brown, streaked with bright red highlights, closely shorn on the sides and back, but the top was longish—a collapsed Mohawk worn in a ponytail. A single gold hoop glinted in his left earlobe, although empty piercing holes lined the cartilage of his upper ears.

"Yeah, that's me. What's the hurry?" Manny cocked his head. His tone conveyed concern as well as making an implicit inquiry. Perfectly reasonable, considering the guy worked for Victoria's obstetrician. From Manny's attire, he'd just gotten off work. He wore medical scrubs with a button-down long sleeve shirt underneath.

"Vic is fine," Logan said in answer to the unasked question. He rubbed a finger across his upper lip. He had agreed to meet his buddy, Evan, five minutes ago. Almost anyone else, he would've ignored and hurried on his way, but Logan liked Manny. He could spare the guy a couple minutes, but no more than that.

"Good." Manny flashed a saucy grin. "So, you were coming to see me then? Cause you can't stay away from this hotness..." Manny swept his body in a sassy presentation. "Could you?"

"Yeah, that's it exactly." Logan snickered and waited a beat before he brought his hand up in farewell. "As much as I'd love to stand here appreciating you, I'm in a hurry."

"Where're you heading?" Manny narrowed his eyes and jutted his chin. Aggression embittered his scent. *Interesting.* Logan's rebuff must have annoyed the druid.

"I'm heading to pick up a prescription from the pharmacy," Logan lied, as easily as he breathed. "Sorry I can't stay and talk."

"No problem." Manny frowned. "The pharmacy closes in ten minutes. You'd better hurry."

"Yeah, I'm trying." Logan stepped off the threshold.

"Catch you later." Manny started to turn away but stopped. He snapped his fingers. "Before I forget. I was meaning to call you..."

"Yeah?" Logan fidgeted, mincing his steps.

"I need some help with a ritual."

"What sort of ritual?" Logan refrained from mentioning his un-druidness. A, Manny wasn't an idiot. B, Logan was supposed to be working on being less abrasive... or so the pack kept telling him. Master strategy: Play nice with othersProve his worth as an alphaImpress Victoria.

Get laid.

Manny hesitated, whetting his lips. A war raged on his face until he finally jerked his head. "I'm going to perform a divination. You may've heard—there's a lunar eclipse this week on Wednesday night."

"Yeah, our skald mentioned it." Logan tensed on the rush of excitement, but he strove to keep his reaction hidden.

"It's an ill-omen. It portends a dark night for the soul." Manny's scent acquired tart notes and his respiration grew quick and erratic. Such signs usually signaled deception, but Logan wasn't one-hundred percent sure. The guy might just be stressed out.

"What do you need from me?" Logan asked. Manny's choice of phrasing struck a chord; Sylvie had said the same basic thing. Maybe Logan *should* help out.

"I need someone who can speak to spirits."

Logan hesitated. "I can mention it to Vic."

Manny shook his head. "It's dangerous. I wouldn't want to endanger the baby."

"Good call." Logan grimaced. "Victoria would agree she needs to stay out of danger, but at the first sign of trouble she'd jump in..."

"Feet first," the men said in unison. They traded a conspiratorial look, and then laughed. Any residual hostility between them vanished.

"Maybe you can help me instead."

"Depends on what's involved... and when you need me." Logan harbored doubts about his skill as a spiritualist. Victoria called him a "wild card" which he suspected was her polite way of saying "rank amateur".

"Can I give you a call later and explain more?"

"Sure," Logan agreed, more to be done than any other reason. Later sounded just great. "Do you have my number?"

"Right here." Manny tapped the spot over his heart.

"Hilarious." Logan snorted. "Is everything with you a one liner?"

"I've got some great two liners," Manny returned, straight-faced.

"I'll see ya." Logan flipped his hand and got underway.

The weight of the druid's regard pressed upon Logan's back. For a few seconds, he thought Manny would let it end there. But then the guy shouted loud enough to be heard on the far side of the lobby.

"Are those space pants? Because your ass is out of this world!"

CHAPTER 23

Sowilo: The Rune of Energy and Revelation

THE HOSPITAL'S basement smelled indigo—the color of forgotten places whose very existence had been lost to time. The ultraviolet patina hung like fog over where the modern concrete hallways gave way to a much older structure. It was also where the physical realm touched the transcendent. Here, chilling unease marched with its millipede legs over the flesh of the living, and the dead wandered, ever restless, without respite or terminus.

Logan navigated the darkness, relying on his nocturnal vision. Somehow, he'd gotten lost on his way to the morgue, which was housed in the hospital basement. He recalled it being a right turn off the stairwell entrance and then a straight shot to the northwest corner of the building. Granted, he'd only been down here once—but it was less than a week ago—with Victoria and his Uncle Mike. So, unless the labyrinth-like corridors had reshuffled around him, the morgue's entrance should've been right in front of it. Should've—but wasn't.

"They really need to get the janitorial staff down here," Logan muttered, studying the curtain of spider webs that barred his path. His voice echoed eerily through the concrete caverns. Stranger still, there was no sign of the hundreds of arachnids it would've taken to fill the hallway, ceiling to floor, with the diaphanous drapes.

He started to turn away, reconsidering his path, when the entire mass of webbing trembled. A squishy thud came from behind him. Logan tensed and turned back. The noise emanated from the far end of the corridor, coming closer; a chorus of low, tormented moans.

Logan barred his teeth, scenting death. A snarl rumbled in his throat. The webbing quaked like crazy. An Indiana Jones-sized boulder of ghostly apparitions tore through the spider webs. It had too many heads and too many torsos but no lower extremities. Instead, it cartwheeled along on its dozens of protruding hands.

"Yeah, assume you have right of way, damn rolling rectums." Logan stepped aside, flattening himself against the wall to avoid touching the thing. Ghosts were nothing new to him, but this took the cake. He stared—and it stared back with weeping eyes frozen in masks of perpetual anguish.

"Hate this place. Shit keeps getting weirder." Logan stepped out, brushed a strand of webbing off his fingers, and returned to his original route now that the rolling, ghastly stone had cleared the way.

Ahead, a broken wooden beam thrust from the ceiling. The end bristled with sharp splinters. Logan raised his arm and pushed against the rafter to test its strength. The low ceiling forced him to walk stooped while evading the rubble strewn across the ground. It made for tricky maneuvering. He managed without clonking his skull or tripping, only to put his foot down in a pool of stagnant water. Cold fluid soaked his athletic shoe through. Dankness flooded his nostrils. The farther he traveled, the worse the stench.

With every step, puddles splashed beneath his feet. He scented insects and rodents, including all the offensive byproducts vermin left behind. And mold—a metric buttload of spores.

His nose itched and twitched. He scrunched it, peeling his lips over his teeth. His eyes watered and snot clogged his sinus cavities, seeping into his throat. He fought the sneeze for all he was worth, but lost the battle. A great seizure wracked his entire body, and the bellowed "a-choo" echoed down the bare concrete hallways.

"Now all the monsters know you're here." High and lyrical, the voice originated somewhere in the shifting shadows.

"Then they'd better hide," Logan shot back. He wiped his eyes on the back of his arm. With a noisy slurp, he sucked mucus into his mouth and spat out the gooey mess. The gob landed in the puddle of standing water and sank into the cruddy green scum on top, probably food for the mold. Logan preferred not to think about it.

Evan only giggled.

"It smells like a cesspool down here," Logan grumbled once he could breathe again. Finally, he picked up the odious odor of rotted flesh—the signature scent of the undead. No surprises there. Evan was a ghoul: a carrion eater and a cannibal. Yeah, the guy ate human corpses. Like an alligator, he preferred rotted flesh, claiming it was easier to digest. A disgusting habit, but Logan chose not to judge. So what if his friend was living impaired? Everyone had their faults.

"A werewolf with hay fever... If that's not the saddest thing ever."

"Yeah, I don't have any allergies. Maybe it's the mold. If it's toxic, that might be enough to make me sneeze." Logan pivoted and scanned the passageway, searching for the source of the sound.

Shadow magic concealed Evan from view. The ghoul repelled light and attracted darkness. Inky blackness glommed onto him, as dense as pudding, as malleable as wet clay. He shaped it into a protective shell he carried about on his back like an undead tortoise.

"It's not the mold. It's the magic," Evan whispered in his creepy-cute falsetto.

"What's that supposed to mean?"

"Nothing."

"Bullshit. Why are you hiding from me, man?" Moving with care, Logan picked his way along the tunnel. His shoes were already soaked so it hardly mattered when the standing water rose to his ankles. Narrow-eyed, he scrutinized the darkness.

"I'm scared."

"Why? I've never given you reason to be."

"Not of you."

"Then come out. You're hurting my feelings." Logan pitched a hint of injury into his voice. A cheap shot, but Evan had always been overly empathetic—shockingly sensitive for a dead guy.

It worked. Evan's shadow magic collapsed, revealing the child-sized ghoul. He sat with his knees drawn against his chest, hunched against the base of the wall. Undead didn't age physically, but Evan had the mind of an adult.

"Satisfied?" Evan asked with an angry fist punch at the air.

Logan knelt. He extended his hand and touched Evan's shoulder. The ghoul quivered, but didn't flee. "Better. Now tell me what you're afraid of."

"This place is dangerous. You shouldn't be down here, Logan. I tried to warn you on the phone, but you wouldn't listen."

"Funny, my father said the same thing."

"You've spoken with your father?" Evan jerked his head, glancing up with unmistakable fear in his eyes.

"Yeah, and the more people who insist I stay away, the more it convinces me this is where I should investigate. I'm not leaving until I find some answers." Logan set himself in stubborn determination. His physical stance altered to reflect his resolve.

"Answers to what?"

"To what this place is and whether it presents a threat." Logan kept his suspicions to himself. He didn't want to provide Evan with clues. The ghoul had a tendency to say what he thought Logan wanted to hear at the expense of the truth.

"It's too dangerous to say." Evan moaned and drew his knees against his chest.

"It takes a lot to scare me." Logan placed his hand on Evan's shoulder, offering reassurance. This close, the foul odor of decay clogged his nose and throat. Inescapable. Nausea sat leaden in his stomach, but he quelled the desire to cover his mouth or turn his face aside. For years, Evan had stood by Logan when he needed a friend.

"You're brave. You've always been fearless, even when you were seven and fell into that storm tunnel. You weren't afraid of *me*."

"I was six." Logan grimaced. He recalled that day only too well.

First grade. Back then, Logan belonged to a club along with his friends, Tim Porter, Todd Duvall, and the brothers Dean and Sammy. They called themselves the Black Guard and wore armbands and swore oaths in blood. Oh, Stacy Stone, technically a girl, had fought her way into their ranks. Stacy, however, wasn't afraid of bugs, and played sports just as good as any boy, and insisted she was better than any boy. Since Rule #1 of the Black Guard stated "No girls", they held a secret ceremony to officially make her an honorary boy. Problem solved.

The last day of school prior to the winter break, classes had let out at noon. The Black Guards wound up at Sierra Pine's tiny historic cemetery. They divided into two camps for a snowball fight, using the aged stone crypts for cover. Afterward, they sledded on the slopes of the wooded creek that bordered the graveyard. Hours flew past. When it started to get dark, the other kids left one-by-one until only Logan remained. There was no one to go home to, so he hadn't bothered. His mother had been on one of her drunken benders, and dear old dad was out of town on one of his frequent business trips.

Alone and bored, Logan occupied himself with running an

imaginary obstacle course when he tripped and plunged through a missing grate into the storm tunnels beneath the cemetery. He spent the next several hours stranded. He shouted his voice raw, but no one heard him except for poor dead Evan.

"I broke my leg in two places." Logan grinned despite the general unpleasantness of the memory. His enhanced regeneration hadn't kicked in until he turned eighteen and shifted for the first time. "If you hadn't found me..."

"It was my fault you fell." Evan drew in on himself, cringing from Logan's touch, and his shoulders shook.

"What?" Logan's arm slackened, and his hand slipped from the ghoul's shoulder. "Don't be absurd—"

"I left that grate off the storm tunnel to make it easier when I came back. It was too heavy..." Evan mumbled a handful of other sentences; the rest of the confession was lost to muffled sobs.

"Ah, hell man. Take it easy. Even if you did leave it off, it's not like you shoved me. I wasn't supposed to be playing there alone. I *knew* that—"

"You could've died." Evan lifted his small, grayish face. Tears of slime leaked from the corners of his eyes and ran down his cheeks.

A facial tic jerked at the corner of Logan's eye. He clenched his jaws to stop his mouth from curling. "You saved my life. You didn't have to help me. You could've left me down there."

"Oh, no. I couldn't." Evan shook his head hard. The vehemence of the ghoul's rebuttal rang with discord; off-key and nerve jarring.

"Damn it..." Logan ran his hand through his hair. "Why won't you talk to me, Evan? You don't have any reason to be afraid of me. We're friends. I won't hurt you."

"You told Victoria we're not."

"Not what?"

"Not friends."

"I..." Logan opened his mouth to issue an automatic denial, but it got stuck in his throat. With startling clarity, he recalled those exact words passing his lips a few months back. Heat suffused his face. "So, you heard that, huh?"

"Yeah, I did." Evan pouted; lower lip turned down, arms crossed.

"I'm sorry. I shouldn't've said that. It wasn't true."

Evan studied Logan long and hard. "I understand why you did it. You wanted to impress her. She detests the undead, so you thought you had to act like you did, too."

"It was a crummy thing to do. I'm an asshole." Comeuppance tasted metallic. The true irony resided in the contradiction. At the time, Logan had assumed Victoria would think less of him for claiming friendship with a ghoul. Now that he knew her, he understood—she'd have respected him more if he'd stuck to his guns. Regardless of her personal feelings, Victoria prized integrity and loyalty above all else.

"Yeah, it's okay. You stopped her from killing me. That counts for a lot." Evan used the guy-tone, signaling the conversation was over. He didn't want to pursue emotional intimacy any further.

No problem. Logan didn't, either.

"Evan, tell me what's going on." Logan infused his voice with the resonance of command; a trick he'd learned from Victoria. He'd practiced. The pups and Sophia responded to the vocalization, but he had no idea whether it'd work on a member of the reanimated dead.

"About what?"

"Let's start with this place right here." Logan swept his arm in a wide arc to encompass their surroundings. "What is it?"

"It's a boundary," Evan said with clear reluctance, "between this world and the next."

"You mean the real world and the afterlife?"

"Both are real."

"It's a Hel-gate?"

"I suppose." Evan shrugged.

"Yeah." Logan compressed his lips. *Whatever.* He decided to try a different tactic. "I tried to research the hospital's history on the internet, but my Google-fu failed."

Evan stirred, lifting his head from the cradle of his knees. Scraggly bits of hair clung to his skull. His gray skin stretched taunt across his facial features: bits and pieces peeling off. Only his eyes, great and luminous, were human. "Your father had all the records destroyed."

"Yeah, not surprised." Logan hacked to clear his throat.

"This used to be the Cogley Sanitarium. It was built in 1901. Closed in 1937," Evan said. "The facility was condemned and torn down in 1989. A year later, construction began on what would become the Sierra Pines Medical Facility."

"Sanitarium." Logan's thoughts went straight to creepy horror movies full of psychotic, axe-wielding serial killers.

"They treated tuberculosis here."

"Oh," Logan said, feeling like an idiot. The muscles in his legs ached from crouching. He shifted his weight to stretch out his calves.

Evan closed up again, drawing his thighs against his chest. His voice shrank. "A thousand people died here. Their spirits sank straight into the ground we're standing on and got mired in the muck. The roots of the World Tree are thick in the soil. Poor souls didn't stand a chance. They couldn't escape."

Foreboding filled Logan. "Did you die here?"

"Yes." Evan sobbed. His cries grew strident. "When mama got sick, they sent her to Cogley, but my sister 'n' me went to an orphanage."

"Where was your father?"

"We didn't have one." Evan shook his head, flinging tears. "Then Doris, that's my sister, started coughing and we got sent here, too."

"Ah hell, I'm sorry. I didn't know." Logan's gut cramped. Sympathy and guilt ate at him. He'd known Evan for fourteen years. However, it'd never occurred to Logan to ask about his friend's history... No, untrue. He'd thought to inquire but decided against it. Selfishly, he hadn't wanted to discover the sorts of things that would make him feel bad.

"It's okay. It was a long time ago," Evan said. "There were so many souls trapped here. Gradually, the veil eroded and grew thin."

"This is a gateway to the other side."

Evan bobbed his head.

"Okay, I've got that part." Logan nodded as he talked it through. "There's no way Dad managed this alone. He must've had help."

"You're not going to like the answer to that," Evan said in a teeny-tiny voice. "In fact, you're gonna hate it."

"I don't care. I need to know." A suspicion clung to the periphery of Logan's thoughts—a niggling suspicion that he couldn't dismiss or quash. He turned it aside, but it came creeping back like a rat to the trough. Loki—his father—worked with a mysterious figure known only as the Necromancer. It wasn't *that* far-fetched to speculate that a sorcerer who specialized in death magic had constructed a Hel-gate, was it? Logan only conceived one way to confirm or deny it for sure... and, unfortunately, it meant putting Evan on the spot.

"I want to go." Evan fidgeted, glancing nervously to either side.

"Not until we're done," Logan grated. "Tell me who your master is."

"What?" Evan shot to his feet. "Don't be absurd. I don't have a master. Who told you...?"

Logan surged upright also, rocking back on his heels. "You did —remember? Last week in the hallway outside the morgue you said, 'The master is coming.' Right before you went poof."

"Oh yeah, *that*." Evan contorted in an unnatural whole-body grimace, obviously wrestling with inner demons.

"Victoria says all reanimated undead have a master—" Frustration crawled along Logan's nerves. That the ghoul persisted in lying to him in the face of overwhelming evidence to the contrary was galling. Was Evan protecting the Necromancer? That bastard had tried—and almost succeeded in—destroying Victoria, her baby, and the Storm Pack. No matter the cost, Logan would defend his loved ones.

"Victoria again!" Evan huffed in overblown disgust, but the ghoul wasn't a good-enough liar to cover his fear. A sickly yellow patina hung over him.

The hair on his neck rose like porcupine quills. Logan blinked twice, but the glow didn't vanish. After a puzzled moment, he identified it as the ghoul's spirit. Logan seldom perceived auras—and when he did, he caught only glimpses. Flashes of light and color.

"Stop lying to me! Who's your master?" Logan smashed his fist into an aged wooden post, striking a point a good two feet over Evan's head. The impact knocked a hunk of wood free as well as a shower of debris.

"Please stop! I can't tell you—" Evan wailed and cowered, folding his bony hands over his bald head.

"Is it the Necromancer?" Logan raised his voice to a shout.

"Don't say that name!" Evan hissed like a cornered snake. His nervous gaze flicked about the hallway as though the boogeyman might jump out of the shadows.

"I know my father didn't construct this gateway alone," Logan said, relentless in his pursuit of the truth. "Stir the shit, over and over, and one name floats to the surface—the Necromancer. He's behind the undead armies, and I know he's working with my father—"

"Logan!"

A bright halogen beam cut through the darkness and blinded Logan. He threw up his arm as a shield and turned his face aside. Evan shrieked and bolted, but somehow managed to run straight into Logan's legs, almost knocking him off balance. On reflex, Logan gripped the ghoul's shoulders, holding on despite his determined struggle. Squinting, Logan made out the figure holding the flashlight.

"Uncle Mike?" Logan gawked. His stomach dropped into a bottomless pit. And in the fullness of dread, he *knew*...

"Son, we need to talk," Mike Trash said. "Let the ghoul go."

Disbelief echoed through Logan's mind. His grip slackened, allowing Evan to slip free. Realization outshouted Logan's skepticism. The truth couldn't be denied.

"You," Logan grated between clenched teeth. "You're the Necromancer."

"I'm *a* necromancer." In the face of his accuser, Mike stood there as calm and reasonable as a tranquil sea, wearing his El Dorado County Sheriff's uniform complete with its shiny shield, the image of decorum. "I have influence over the deceased, however, I've never personally used that pretentious title. *That* was your father's idea."

"Actually, it is what you're called," Evan piped up. "Sir."

Mike frowned. He aimed the flashlight at the ghoul, who recoiled from the light. "Evan, you can go. I need to speak with my nephew alone."

"You were spying on me this whole time?" Logan cast a disbelieving glance at the ghoul. Oh fuck, but his friend's deception stung.

"No—" Evan gurgled a denial.

"I thought we were friends! But you were just there to report my every move to my father and uncle?" Logan's cool swirled straight down the drain.

"I'm sorry." Evan hung his head yet still somehow managed to gaze upward. His eyes were full of shame and misery.

Anger burned within Logan's chest. *Deceived and betrayed by his longest held friend and his blood kin.* Stock still, Logan waged a losing battle. White-knuckled with desperation, he kept the beast trapped within a cage of restraint. It battered at the walls surrounding it.

"Evan," Mike drawled with a distinct note of warning.

"*Yes, master.* Evan will do your bidding." Hunched over in a dead-on Igor impersonation, Evan sidled past Logan. On his way by, he leaned in close and whispered, "Sorry. I tried to warn you away."

A rumbling snarl built in Logan's throat. Evan shrank away and beat a hasty retreat.

"Logan, calm down before you do something we'll both regret."

Regret.

Malice in his heart, Logan locked eyes on his uncle. An enraged roar burst from him. Logan *regretted* ever having trusted his uncle. The Necromancer represented a threat to everyone Logan cared for.

The Necromancer had to die.

"Logan, I mean it." Mike placed a hand on Logan's forearm—the tipping point.

Logan lost his tenuous hold on his temper. Rage poured over him. He jerked his forearm free and clobbered Mike full in the face. The sheriff smashed into a wall. Hell bent on murder, Logan lunged for his uncle's throat. Mike rolled aside at the last second and Logan's hands closed on empty air.

Mike scrambled upright and retreated. The sheriff dropped his hand to his holstered sidearm. His eyes bleached solid white, irises and pupils dissolved into a blind man's gaze. But *he saw*, oh he saw all right, the intensity of his baleful glare left no doubt.

Death's loving caress brushed Logan's soul.

Logan launched at his uncle. Midstride, he transformed to a giant wolf, ripping his clothing to shreds. He plunged straight into howling madness. He dropped to all fours, shredding the bits and pieces of fabric as easily as he cast off his humanity. Beast in ascension, the pleasurable burn, and an opportunity to fill the eternally aching void in his belly. Hunger sated for precious seconds.

Mike drew his firearm, firing from the hip. Muzzle flash. The stench of sulfur poisoned the air. An impact slammed into Logan's shoulder. The jolt felt like a hard punch, but no pain penetrated his focus. The man before him was an easy target—prey to be stalked and killed.

Teeth bared, Logan closed his jaws on his uncle's throat only to be cheated of his prize. Trickery... Mike's form grew insubstantial. The sheriff turned transparent. Logan's canines sliced through empty air and clashed together. Denied his prize, he bellowed. Momentum carried Logan straight *through* the ghostly apparition.

He ploughed face first into the wall.

"I'm incorporeal," Mike said. "You can't hurt me. Now—"

Growling, Logan rounded and charged his uncle again. He attacked from behind, going for a bite to the hamstring but scored nothing more than a mouthful of hot air. Next, he took a spine-snapping swipe that sailed through Mike's see-through back.

Mike turned, holstering his ghost gun. "Logan, calm down. Let's talk—

Logan embedded his entire claw up to the wrist in the Necromancer's head space, silencing him. Denied, denied, denied... He tried again and again. With every missed blow, every misplaced bite, the wolf's ire escalated. The little reason he retained incinerated. His temper detonated like a nuke.

"Fine. I can wait out your tantrum." Mike folded his arms across his chest.

Red haze colored the world and fogged his brain. Howling, Logan flew into frenzy. He struck out over and over again. No satisfaction until one of his wild punches hit the wall. On impact, the bones in his claw crunched.

Pain bomb. Fuck.

At last, something to destroy. Double clawed, he pounded the concrete again. Loosened debris rained down on him: mold spores and muck, cement dust and fragments. A hole appeared in the wall, exposing a beam. He hammered at it. The sprinkle turned to a shower.

"Logan!" Mike shouted something else, but the din swallowed his voice.

Thick ribbons of hot drool ran between his teeth. Logan embedded his deep claws in the wood. Splinters crammed into his skin. He dug with all his might. He pushed and pulled, rocking it. The beam creaked and moved... it groaned.

An avalanche descended on Logan's head and back. Stunned, he swayed on all four paws. In a broad stroke, the universe clubbed him over the skull with the felled timber.

Everything went black.

CHAPTER 24

***Wunjo*: The Rune of Joy**

EVERYTHING HURT, even his hair; epic, unreal suffering like the duo Kenny Rogers & Dolly Parton committing the musical turpitude known as "Islands in the Stream."

"Holy shit. What hit me?" Groaning, Logan lifted his leaden eyelids into blinding-bright overhead light. It stabbed at his eyeballs like needles, radiating into his brain. He closed them again, and threw his arm over his face. That careless motion cost him. Lancing agony shot through his shoulder.

"You did. Repeatedly," Mike said in a tone best described as righteously smug. Beyond a doubt, he was enjoying Logan's misery.

"I feel like death warmed over." His head throbbed, a great overripe mass of a melon, and the weight of his forearm threatened to crush his skull. He preferred it to having his eyeballs charbroiled in their sockets.

"No, you don't." Mike chuckled with the confidence of a man

with insight. "Death warmed over is messier," he sniffed and added, "and smells far worse."

"I'll take your word on that." The frenzy and his injuries had depleted his energy to nil, and healing would consume what remained. Likewise, his anger had subsided; a luxury too expensive to afford.

"Is there anything I can do to help?"

"Turn off those damn lights."

Mike's unhurried steps retreated toward the other side of the room. He stopped, and the obnoxious overhead lights dimmed. "Is that better?"

"Yeah." Logan couldn't quite bring himself to offer thanks. Gathering his wits, he took a physical inventory. He rested recumbent, cold steel against his naked back. A thin, scratchy sheet draped over him. He ached all over, but his head hurt the worst. His shoulder came in a distant second. "You shot me."

"I did, and I'm sorry about that. To be fair, you tried to rip me in half."

"I guess I did." Logan grimaced. Too bad he'd failed. Aside from the pain, nothing bothered him as much their inexplicable change in venue.

"I dug the bullet out. It was a standard slug. Nothing special. The wound's already healed up."

"Where are we?" The air tasted dry and sterile; a blend of astringent cleaners and formaldehyde, a dead place. Before Mike answered, Logan supplied his own answer. "Is this an autopsy table?"

"I moved you to the morgue. Unfortunately, it's lacking in comfortable accommodations. The dead, you see, don't tend to be particular."

"You carried me by yourself?" Logan tried to rise, but his spine cramped, bones grating together. He gritted his teeth and sank back. The back of his head struck metal with a solid thunk.

"I called in some muscle."

"Great." Undead laborers had manhandled him while he'd been passed out. "Do you pay them?"

"No. That's the great thing about revenants—they work for free. You may not like it, but you weigh a ton and that ghoul isn't exactly Hercules."

Evan—shit. The blurry memory of Evan's betrayal haunted him. For a couple years there, during the worst time in his life, *that ghoul* had been his only friend. Now he was left with the knowledge that Evan's friendship had been another lie... just like the rest of his miserable life.

"Where is he?" Logan drew a deep breath, gathered his strength, and tried to rise again. The anticipated wave of pain swept over him, but he powered through it long enough to push himself up on his backside. To preserve his privacy, he tucked the sheet beneath his arms, covering his lap. He dangled his legs over the side and hunched over, staring down at the bare concrete floor. The wide, grated drain caught his attention.

"Are you going to puke?" Mike asked in a matter-of-fact manner. As though Logan hadn't flown off the handle and attacked him.

"No." Surprisingly, nausea wasn't one of his symptoms. "Answer the question—where is he?"

"Who?"

"Evan. Stop bullshittin' me. You know his name."

Mike offered a twisted smile. "Evan was upset, but that hardly matters. I can see you care for him. It's sweet but unnecessary. You accused him of spying on you, but the truth is that the ghoul was created to serve you. He can't help but forgive you."

"What...?" Logan reeled. *Serve*—what the fuck?

"Enough of this," Mike said, using the tone of paternal authority. "You're covered in blood and filth. Clean up, dress, eat something. Then we can talk."

Logan opened his mouth to protest.

Mike raised his hand—wait. "That tunnel collapse almost killed you. If you're not already starving, you will be soon. The hungrier your wolf gets, the more irritable and irrational you are. Take care of yourself. Then, I promise you a full explanation."

"Fine! I'll clean up. But I didn't exactly bring a change of clothes." Logan considered his stomach, and found out he was ravenous. It rumbled long and loud. He grimaced in discomfort.

"I managed to scrounge up some scrubs that should fit you." Mike picked up a neat, folded pile of material, and tossed it at his nephew.

"Thanks." Logan snatched it from the air, keeping everything mostly intact. A cursory examination yielded a towel, a blue shirt and matching pants, and open-toed slippers. His mouth contorted but he supposed—beggars, choosers. Yada yada.

"Showers are through there." Mike pointed toward an entrance to an adjacent room. "I'll call the cafeteria and have food sent down while you get cleaned up."

"Where's my phone? I need my keys—" Logan had no idea how much time he'd lost. A sudden sense of urgency heckled him. He'd promised Victoria he'd only be gone a few hours.

"Right here." Mike extracted the requested items and slid them across the slick steel counter to Logan.

Logan snatched up his effects and checked the clock on his phone. He breathed a sigh of relief. Apparently, he hadn't been out that long. The drive to the lake house from town only took a half hour. He still had time before anyone noticed him missing.

Logan slid off the table and landed square on his feet. Moving still hurt like a mo'fucker but his strength improved with each passing minute. He shuffled across the hard floor and rounded the corner into the adjacent room. Lockers lined one wall, a row of benches divided the center, and three shower stalls took up the opposite space. He dropped the towel and garments onto a bench and stepped into the first shower.

Ice-cold water blasted him; a high-pressure spray of liquid needles. By the time he grabbed for the controls, the temperature increased to scalding. He played with the knob until he achieved a satisfactory median. A wall-mounted machine dispensed liquid soap. Logan ducked his head beneath the spray. The runoff turned red. His fingers found a fist-sized lump on the back of his skull, and he winced at his own touch.

"What happened to my head?" Logan raised his voice to carry over the din of running water. It carried through the echoey chambers.

Mike answered from the other room. "That beam you ripped from the wall fell on you. It split your skull. Franky, you're lucky to be alive. You almost killed yourself with your tantrum."

Tantrum. Logan gritted his teeth. Damn it. His uncle had just suffered the revelation of his secret identity. At the least, he should be enduring a setback. Something. So how was it that Mike still reduced Logan to feeling like a stupid kid?

"Why aren't you pissed?" He set about scrubbing away the crud encrusted on his skin. Muck everywhere—in his ears, beneath his nails, between his toes.

"You're a hothead like your father," Mike said in a gruff voice. "Your reaction was expected. Before this whole thing started, I told Arik we should bring you up to speed but he insisted—"

"Son of a bitch! It's a damn conspiracy." Logan cranked the handle, shutting off the water. He grabbed for the towel and rubbed it over his short hair. He paid for the careless gesture in spades when a hand grenade went off inside his skull. He doubled over, grabbing his head with both hands.

"You okay?" Mike stepped into the entrance, standing with his hands at his hips, gunslinger-style.

"Peachy." Logan straightened, taking care.

"Finish dressing. I'll be in the front office, waiting for the food. I told them to give it top priority." Mike left without waiting for an acknowledgement.

"So fucked up," Logan muttered. He stood there and pondered. His life was a twisted, dark comedy, and it kept getting stranger. Mystery enshrouded his entire family... and the double identities. His father—Loki. His uncle—the Necromancer. Logan wondered whether his mother had been a clueless dupe, like him, or had she possessed her own secrets, too? No, he refused to speculate. For the sake of his sanity, his mom needed to remain untouchable.

He'd gotten caught up in contemplating the weirdness, but then his stomach gurgled and his sides ached. Beneath his skin, his wolf stirred. He was hungry enough to eat the moon and... Nope, not going there. Gathering his senses, Logan shook off the mental cobwebs. He finished drying off and dressed. The autopsy room was empty.

Mike waited in the morgue's front office, just like he'd said. A rolling food service cart stacked with covered trays was beside the solitary desk in the corner. Someone had arranged a neat pile of file folders beside the old curly-corded phone and pen canister. In the two times he'd visited the morgue, Logan had never actually seen a member of the alleged staff.

"Does anyone actually work here? Or is this place just for show?" The warm aroma of food hooked his nose and set his mouth to watering. Logan made a beeline for the food cart.

"Oh, the staff is real," Mike said with a slight smile. "I gave them the rest of the day off."

"Yeah? What are they—your disciples?" Logan asked with heavy sarcasm. But before Mike opened his mouth to reply, Logan shot up his hand. "Don't answer that."

"Then don't ask what you don't want to know."

"I don't want to know any of this," Logan muttered, lifting the lid on a tray, revealing a toasted ham and turkey sandwich on a roll. He fell on it like, well, a ravenous wolf, and downed it in three huge bites. The meal hit his stomach, welcome warmth, but didn't even put a dent in his hunger. He finished off the grapes and potato chips, downed an entire pitcher of water, and moved on to the next tray. He continued like that, putting away four full meals.

"You promised me an explanation," Logan said once he'd consumed enough to take the edge off. He kept eating, working his way through a sixth tray, but at a civil pace.

"Well, this is awkward." Mike crossed his arms over his chest, and exhaled so his nostrils flared.

"Ya think?" Logan popped an apple slice into his mouth, sinking his teeth into the sweet flesh. Juice flooded his mouth. He peeled back his lips, revealing the red skin. A childhood stunt, one that'd always made his uncle laugh. He didn't know why he did it, but it produced the intended effect.

Mike chuckled. "I'm not sure where to start."

"The beginning is customary."

"The beginning isn't a fixed point." Mike ran his hand across the top of his head, polishing his smooth scalp with his palm.

"Start with how you've murdered thousands of people! How you orchestrated the *Den Valgte* attack—"

"Hold up. Those are two separate things."

"We're splitting hairs? Seriously?"

His uncle grimaced. "While regrettable, those people in Los Angeles and Tucson had to die to serve the greater good. The army your father and I are building is essential. A necessary evil, if you will. Don't be so quick to judge what you don't understand."

Logan hesitated for a split second. He considered picking it apart, but decided against it. "What about *Den Valgte*? Those bastards almost killed us."

"I had nothing to do with *Den Valgte*." Mike gave him the side eye.

"No?" Logan scoffed, choking on skepticism.

"No." Mike compressed his lips to a flat line. "Your father and I are responsible for plenty of machinations, but orchestrating an invasion of Odin's followers into the heartland of our holdings isn't among them. Why would we do such a thing?"

"That..." Logan cocked his head, tracking the logic. "Makes sense."

"Funny that. How the truth can work to your advantage." Mike flashed a crooked smile. Logan preferred not to guess at its meaning.

Chaos filled his mind—too many thoughts, too many directions. He scrambled to get on top of it all. "Last week..."

"What about it?"

"You brought me and Victoria down here to see the bodies of that wolf and the Federal Wilderness guy. His ghost was super-coherent when he said hunters were to blame. Victoria said it was like he was too lucid. Was that you?"

"Yes," Mike said, pursing his lips, "the spirit was under my control."

"So, you didn't need Victoria's help to communicate with it at all..." Logan narrowed his eyes in realization, and went straight from puzzled to pissed off. "You were just screwing with us."

"It's not as petty as you're making it out to be."

"No? Why'd you do it then?"

His uncle shot a look cold enough to stop the dead in their tracks. "Arik asked me to do it as a favor to him."

"Dad asked you to mess with Victoria and frame Sawyer for murder?"

Mike compressed his lips into a thin line once again. "No. Arik asked me—should an opportunity present itself—to drive a wedge between Victoria and Sawyer Barrett. You see, your father feels the hunter is a threat to her, the child, the entire pack..."

"Yeah, I sorta agree. The guy is a stone-cold killer." Although, sometimes, it was good to have a stone-cold killer on your side... Nope, not going there. Logan shook his head, which sent a fresh wash of pain through his skull.

"I'm glad we see things the same," Mike said, nodding.

"Not the same. You framed Sawyer for those killings." Logan got twitchy. A lump stuck in his throat. Instinct warred with reason. He hated Sawyer with the entirety of his heart and soul, but at the same time, his innate sense of right and wrong balked at the injustice of setting up a man for a murder he hadn't committed. Given Logan's history, it struck far too close to home.

"Logan, it's not like we sent him to prison or put him on death row. We want the hunter gone from our territory. Your father and

I want what's best for you and Victoria—for your sister—for the pack."

Damn it. Logan's mouth puckered at the sourness of hypocrisy. He wanted Sawyer Barrett gone, too, almost enough to just let go and buy into his uncle's rationale that it was all for the best. The one thing holding him back—maybe the only reason for his resistance—was imaging the profound disappointment in Victoria's eyes if she ever learned of this travesty. He couldn't live with himself if he was ever responsible for hurting Vic like that.

"What about everything that happened before? The war you provoked between Victoria's pack and the hunters?" Logan asked, eager to find an alternative topic—any port in the storm.

"That's all history. Much of what happened is regrettable, but I was following your father's lead. He calls the shots." He raised his hands to demonstrate his supposed helplessness.

"Oh, so you're just Dad's obedient minion?" Logan coached his voice, deliberately goading. No matter what Mike claimed, it wasn't all sunshine, lollipops, and rainbows between his uncle and father.

"More like a cooperative ally." Mike smiled but refused to rise to the bait.

"Right." Logan snorted to demonstrate his cynicism.

Mike shook his head. "Focus on what matters. We have common enemies. *Den Valgte*, the hunters."

"Two of those hunters are members of my pack." Not that Logan liked the situation one bit, but sometimes life delivered disappointment.

"I know. Life is stranger than fiction. *Hunters.*" Mike jeered in open derision. "Mark my word, this won't end well. Ah well, it'll sort itself out. What matters is that you understand I'm not a threat to you or your packmates."

"History says otherwise." Logan clenched his hands. An angry accusation sat right on the tip of his tongue. More than anything, he wanted to demand where Mike had been the night the Ironwood witch had enslaved Logan. The bitch had forced him to attack and murder his own mother. *To consume her flesh.*

Distraught, Logan started to turn away.

"History," Mike drawled, "let's talk about history. I've been watching over you your entire life. Take Evan for example..."

"What about Evan?" Logan snapped to attention. The mention of the ghoul's name caught him unprepared. *Stupid.* He should've expected it.

"I made him when you were four." Mike nodded. "At your father's request, because you were always getting into trouble."

"The fuck you say?" The words echoed in his mind.

"You needed a guardian to watch over you from the shadows. He was supposed to remain unseen and silent. If you hadn't fallen into that storm drain, you'd never even have known he was there."

"You enslaved a child's soul to serve me." He growled so harsh his throat ached. He fisted his hands on the verge of attacking his uncle again.

"He was a lost soul, trapped between worlds, doomed to wander forever. This fate is no worse—"

"No worse? He's trapped in a rotting corpse!" Shouting triggered a crippling strobe of pain as the migraine flared like a pulsar. Groaning, he rocked in a self-soothing sway.

Contemplatively, Mike stared into the ether for a long time. Eventually, he asked, "Why does this bother you so much? You've been aware of Evan's condition for years."

"You're telling me that a child's soul is trapped in a rotting corpse, and that it's my fault, but I shouldn't be upset. You seriously don't know how totally fucked up that is?" Logan waited, not really expecting an answer. Through narrowed eyes, he scrutinized Mike, trying to see past the mask to the monster beneath. His Uncle Mike... the man who'd taught Logan to ride a bike, taken him fishing on Sundays, and been like a second father to him. How was *this* even possible?

"I can see you're sympathizing with Evan. Far more than you should. This wasn't your fault, so stop blaming yourself."

Too damn late for that, and the bastard knew it... Logan's jaw assumed a stubborn jut. He hated asking but he had no choice. His obligation to Evan took priority over pride. "Can you do anything to help him?"

"I could terminate the spell that animates the ghoul and set his soul free."

"Free? Or just trapped here as a spirit again?"

Mike sighed. "Logan, all souls wind up stuck somewhere. It's the nature of the beast. Give the word, and I'll let Evan go. He was only created to serve as your chaperone. You're well past the age where you need a guardian. He's served his purpose."

"Fuck no. Evan deserves better than that. He's been your slave for sixteen years." Logan flushed and tensed, struggling against his volatile temper. He wanted nothing more than to resort to violence, but that hadn't worked out so well.

"Technically, he's been yours." Mike cocked his head. "Tell me what he deserves, then? What would be an acceptable resolution to you?"

"I don't know." Logan shook his head as his stomach turned hard and cold.

"What if Evan could live again?" Mike asked after a long pause.

"You could do that?" Tremors passed through Logan. He fought for stillness. In his experience, hope, even a glimmer, possessed far more destructive potential than hatred.

"My dominion is death. Restoring a mortal soul to life using necromancy is difficult. Costly. It requires a sacrifice, one you may not be willing to make." The Necromancer's smile sliced a swath through serenity, the grin of a grim reaper. "Naturally, I have a price for services rendered."

"What's the sacrifice?"

"The hand of a god."

Logan frowned. "I'm not a god."

"No?" Mike arched his brow. "Did Arik neglect to have that all-important father-son talk on the birds 'n' bees? When a daddy god and a mommy god—"

Logan flushed, hot with anger. "My mother was human."

"Lori was my sister." Mike's face went blank and hard as stone. He left the rest unsaid: *And you murdered her.*

Uncle and nephew locked gazes. The unspoken accusation hung between them. Mike's regard held harsh condemnation, as sharp as the blade of a knife. He didn't say anything. That old familiar sickness churned Logan's gut. Guilt. Self-hatred. Depression. He'd carried the burden too long to buckle under its weight. He grabbed hold of the familiar mantra, his exoneration, and repeated it: *Not my fault.*

"I'm not a god!" Logan shouted just to break the awful silence.

"Oh, come now." Mike scoffed, spreading his arms. "I'm a god. You're a god. Our whole family—gods. We can lose a hand or a life. We're all just fragile gods."

Logan huffed in raw disgust. He saw no sense in continuing the argument. "Fine, we're gods. What do you need my hand for?"

"Resurrection requires a sacrifice—the hand of a god, to be specific." Mike returned to the original topic with dogged determination. "Regardless of whatever issues you have with your father, Loki is a god, which makes you one, too. You must've noticed you're different than other werewolves: you don't shift like they do, and silver isn't toxic to you. I saw Thorn on your wrist, so I know Arik must be in contact with you."

"He pops in every now and then," Logan admitted grudgingly.

"So if your father had explained things like he should've, you'd know—"

"Dad explained enough."

Mike scoffed. "Your father never explains everything."

"I've got it." Logan gnashed his teeth. "What's your price?"

"I want your silence. I have to protect this place and my identity."

"No. No way. I won't betray the pack. I won't do anything that endangers the pack." Logan jerked his head, sending a fresh jolt of pain lancing through his head.

"I'm asking for your help in keeping them safe. I've done my best to watch out for Victoria and the pack since Arik left. Her knowing would make that impossible. We both know what would happen if Victoria found out about me—about this place." Mike moved his arm in a wide sweep that encompassed their surroundings.

"Yeah. Vic would tear it to the ground brick by brick." Logan smiled at the twisted irony. Anger and uncertainty bled across his every thought, hampering his judgement. Talk about a swamp of moral ambiguity—should he lie to protect Victoria? Or was it the self-serving, two-faced rationalization of a coward?

"She'd try to kill me—a man who can't be killed. Let's not forget that." Mike crossed the autopsy room to a rolling steel cart that held instrument trays on its two tiers.

"If you do anything to hurt her..." Logan clenched his fists, in the grip of impotent rage. He left the empty threat hanging. Having tried and failed to harm his uncle, words were just words, hollow as the air his uncle could fade into, unless—*until*—he discovered the Necromancer's vulnerabilities. Given time and opportunity, he could investigate. *If* Logan could find him, Arik must have useful information... presuming Loki could be persuaded to part with secrets or tell the truth. He frowned. The longer he thought about it, the worse the plan sounded. Mentally, he painted a big red X over the whole notion of "asking Loki for help."

Maybe Sawyer's old man had answers.

For the first time since learning his uncle's secret, fear visited Logan. He *knew* Victoria. She was righteous and fanatical. She'd go after Mike with guns blazing, consequences be damned. Logan doubted his uncle would demonstrate the same restraint with her that he had with Logan. Victoria—or the baby—could be hurt or killed.

"You know I'm right. I can see it on your face." Mike pushed the cart over to the steel table. One of its wheels squeaked terribly, all that much louder for the bare concrete floor and walls.

"I'm doing this for Vic and the baby," Logan said with undue force.

"And Evan. You're a paragon of virtue." Mike smiled like a twisted serpent biting its own tail. He leaned over the tray and lifted a lid.

A bone saw rested on the tray.

Logan's spine cramped. He swallowed against the bile rising in his throat. Before he changed his mind, he raised his arm and offered his hand.

"I'll keep your secrets—so long as you don't do anything to endanger Vic or the pack. In return, you'll resurrect Evan and free him. That's the deal?"

"That's the deal." Mike said. "Shake on it?"

"Yeah." Logan swallowed his conscience, which like everything else, did nothing to slacken his hunger.

They shook on it over the blade of the saw.

CHAPTER 25

***Mannaz*: The Rune of Humanity**

"HALT RIGHT THERE, buddy! Don't. You. Dare." Cali pointed the glass neck of her beer bottle, taking aim at Sawyer's heart. She leveled a deadly glare down the barrel. The female hunter wore a blue bikini and her curly hair in a topknot.

"What the fuck?" Sawyer coughed up the irate question. He stood balanced on one leg, the other extended over the swirling water of the spa. Rising steam heated the sole of his bare foot. The holsters of his paired 9mms dangled from his fingers. Navy swim trunks sagged on his hips, held in place by the tightly knotted drawstring. Last summer, they'd fit fine. He'd lost weight, although he didn't know how much.

"Did you shower? This spa is pristine. If you leave a ring, I'll kick your ass," Cali said, talking as though she was sixty years older than him instead of six.

"Yes, I showered." His ears burned, and probably his face. Damn it, she'd played the bossy older sister card and he'd walked right into her trap. With a wry grimace, he swore it wouldn't happen again.

"Hot water and soap?"

"Eat me." He set his pistols on the deck and tested the temperature with his toes. After swimming in the lake, the spa was scalding hot. He'd have to ease in.

She snickered. "The new look is a vast improvement."

"Thanks."

"Victoria had her way with you, huh?"

"Obviously." Sawyer ran a self-conscious hand over his hair, which felt a lot lighter, especially in the back. Armed with a pair of scissors and a straight edge, Victoria had taken a good six inches off the ends and reduced his fierce beard to a pale shadow of its former glory.

"The golden blond highlights she added look good."

"Those are natural. I've been spending a lot of time in the sun." He bit back a smart-aleck remark. The female hunter was one to talk—she routinely regaled the frizz of brown curls atop her head as one of the forces of nature.

"Sure, I believe you." Cali laughed from the belly, polished off her beer, and snagged another from the Igloo cooler that sat within arm's reach. "Wow, Victoria must be crushing on you harder than I thought."

His guard came up. "What do you mean?"

She tipped her beer in added emphasis. "She had free license to cut your hair however she wanted, right?"

"So?" Technically, it wasn't true but Sawyer didn't care to quibble.

"So, I'd have shaved you bald!" Cali flashed a wicked smile.

"I'm sure she considered it."

"Victoria's managed to pull you out of that self-destructive funk you'd gotten yourself into. That's a good woman." Cali issued the judgment with the firmness of a judge passing a verdict. Her unwavering stare was loaded with meaning, and he got the distinct impression he was supposed to be picking up on her hidden message.

"Yeah," Sawyer said with a strong nod. He crossed mental fingers.

Her upper lip curled. "You don't have a fucking clue, do you?"

"Nope, not a one."

"Men." She snorted.

"Guilty as charged." With a good-natured grin, Sawyer stepped onto the spa's bench and sat on the edge. Soothing heat penetrated the aching muscles of his calves. A soft groan tore from his throat. "Ah damn, that's good."

"Ain't it, though?" Cali asked with a husky chuckle. In an absent motion, she stretched out her hand and caressed the stock of her rifle that rested on the patio beside the cooler.

Together, they commanded a three-sixty degree view of the surrounding area. After dark, the goddess of the night donned her glittering necklace of distant blazing suns. The summer heat faded, coolness wafted on the breeze, and darkness enshrouded the mountains. Beneath the luminous moon, the swimming pool was smooth and tranquil.

"Damn, it's beautiful out here. Is that romantic or what?" Cali swept her arm in a wide arc, encompassing the spectacular horizon.

"I didn't know you did romantic, Kinkaid." Sawyer pulled his t-shirt over his head. He dropped it onto the patio table next to his guns and knives.

"What're you saying—that I'm not a woman?"

"Me? I'm not saying anything at all." Sawyer shook his head. Oh, no ma'am. He wasn't that stupid.

"You're such a pussy."

"I'm not the one who brought up romance." Sawyer flipped his finger at the cooler on Cali's side of the hot tub. "Pass a beer."

"Catch." She grabbed a bottle and tossed it underhanded.

Sawyer snatched it mid-flight. He glanced at the label which read Sierra Pines Pale Ale. Skepticism reared its ugly head. "A microbrewery?"

"Try it. I promise you'll be surprised."

"You promise?" He twisted off the cap.

"On my honor."

What the hell? Might as well take a chance. Sawyer lifted the mouth of the bottle to his lips and tested it. Its soul was woody, a bit bitter, and held apricot-sweetness.

"So, what do you think?"

"That's good." He wiped froth from his upper lip with the back of his hand.

"I know. I was surprised, too."

"This is nice." Sawyer slid off the ledge and sank chest-deep into the water. A sigh of pleasure eased past his lips. Ah, but it felt good. It'd been too long since he'd indulged in even minimal luxury. But even now, wariness kept him on edge. He scanned the distance for hidden dangers.

"Yeah, it is. I figured I'd landed a cushy gig when I got sent here to babysit the boss's brat." Cali slanted an insinuating glance his way.

Sawyer sneered. "No idea it meant sipping margaritas by the pool."

"Margaritas? Have you been holding out on me?"

"Not so you'd know."

"I'll pick up some tequila and triple sec the next time I'm in town."

"Rock salt 'n' real limes. None of that processed crap."

"Right." Cali threw back her head and laughed.

"Did you get settled okay?" Sawyer asked by way of small talk. In the interests of bolstered security, the decision had been made for Cali to move from the hunters' cabin, which was ten minutes away, to the lake house for at least a few days.

"Yeah, Sylvie put me in a guest bedroom. It's real nice," Cali said, but something in her tone was just a tad off.

"Are you okay with being here?" Sawyer eyed her.

"It's a done deal so there's no sense in whining about it." She shrugged, and her shuttered glare sent a clear message—*Drop it.*

He nodded and did the smart thing: he dropped it. Growing up, Sawyer and his brothers had a saying based on a twisted lyric from an old Jim Croce song, "You don't mess with Crazy Cali Kinkaid."

They sat there for a few minutes, nursing their beers in companionable silence. The hunters had known each other for well over a decade. Ever since the day Jake Barrett had returned from one of his frequent hunting trips with a skinny, frizzy-haired girl with the world's biggest chip on her shoulder. Vampires had murdered her parents. In turn, she'd singlehandedly eradicated the entire nest... and started a fire that'd burned an entire city block to the ground. Hunters fostered her, and she learned their monster-slaying vocation from the old man himself. Cali was Sawyer's sister-in-arms.

"What do you think your dad would say if he could see us now?"

Sawyer pondered. He sat straighter and squared his jaw. *Think mean.* Adopting a glower, he pitched his voice to a gruff growl. "Kinkaid, move over. You're hoggin' the bench. Sawyer, this ain't a damn resort. Fetch your old man a beer."

Cali released a hoot. "Shit! You sound just like 'im."

"One of my many talents." Sawyer raised his hand in false modesty. When she chuckled, he joined right in.

"Do you think we're both losers?" Cali rolled out the question like a red carpet to first-class trouble.

Uh-oh. Sawyer paused with the bottle on the way to his lips. "Losers?"

"Yeah." She cleared her throat. "We're fit, single, attractive— Well, me. You clean up okay."

"What are you on about?" Sawyer sat straighter. He and Cali talked about guns, hunting, and sports—in that order.

"Love. *Les histoires de coeur. Amore.*"

"This again?"

The look she shot him redefined dirty. "I could've died twice this week."

"That describes every week of your life since I met you."

"I can't get DNR out of my head," Cali said with a scowl. "No matter how hard I try, I can't unsee the look on his face as he died. He was terrified."

The sudden change of topic knocked Sawyer off kilter. His stomach dropped. "I'm sorry for what happened to DNR."

DNR, short for Dewey Niles Reynolds, had died in the first *Den Valgte* attack. The young man had been a solider, one of the recruits the U.S. Army had loaned out to Jake Barrett's organization for specialized training in the supernatural.

"The stupid newbie was just starting to catch on. Why'd he have to go and get himself killed?" Cali tipped her beer. Scowling, she averted her gaze.

"It's not fair." Sawyer tensed, expecting her to hurl the glass bottle against the side of the house. He only exhaled once she set it down.

"Fuck fair! It's just a shitty fucking thing that happened! It wasn't my fault." Her hostile glare speared him.

"I never said it was."

"It wasn't anyone's fault." Cali glared as though he'd accused her of murder. She hunched over, bowing her shoulders.

Sawyer drew a breath but thought better of speaking. He wondered—did Cali blame him for DNR's death? Sawyer hadn't been with the other two hunters when Dewey had gone down.

She dropped her chin to her chest and said in a low voice, "I haven't been with a woman in two years. Not since Annie."

Annie—Cali's dead lover.

"Oh." Sawyer's jaws came together with the audible clash of teeth. The dialogue had taken another hairpin turn and this time for the intimate. Awkwardness besieged him. He didn't know what to say but he had to try. "You're lonely. I get it."

"I'm horny and bored. Sierra Pines has shit for entertainment beyond the country club set." She glowered, daring him to comment.

He closed his mouth. From the sounds of it, the woman needed to vent. The best thing he could do was shut up and listen to what she had to say.

"There's that dive bar in Broken Bend but it's full of nothing but truckers and married men from town lookin' to cheat on their wives. It's gotten so bad I'm thinking about riding Logan into Pound Town."

"Are you kidding me?" Sawyer demanded, breaking his self-imposed silence. "You're a lesbian and he's a..."

Cali shrugged and smiled sheepishly. "I'm flexible. The boy is ripped, and he's hot to trot. Enthusiasm makes up for a lot."

"What about South Lake Tahoe?" Sawyer ventured out of desperation.

"Tried it twice. Didn't pan out."

"Reno?"

"Too far to risk it. What if something happened while I was gone?"

"I'm capable of holding down the fort if you need a day off."

She outright ignored his offer. "Logan saved my life."

Sawyer's jaw dropped. "He did?"

Her face set in a mask of strain. "Yeah, the bastard that killed DNR was about to rip my throat out when this huge black wolf came barreling out of nowhere. Logan ripped him in half. It was savage."

"I should've had your back." Sawyer closed his hand to his throat, which was scarred beneath his beard. A bear-shifter had mauled him and left him for dead. The runes healed all physical damage but left the marks—the nature of the magic. Jake bore a patchwork of silvery scars, one atop the other, until no part of him remained untouched. Sawyer supposed it was a window into his own future... should he survive that long.

Cali huffed. "Damn it, Sawyer. That wasn't an indictment. This isn't about you at all. If your fragile male ego can't deal, then just shut the fuck up."

"Sorry." Sawyer threw up his hands in defeat. He kept tight control over his temper. Every time he spoke, he made things worse. As much it galled him, maybe he needed to reconsider his rock-bottom opinion of Logan. From the sounds of it, the male wolf had come through for Cali. That counted for a lot. On a whole 'nother level, his frustration with Kinkaid mounted. This damn conversation had turned into kitchen sink soup. It made his head hurt. He had no idea what they were really discussing, but he suspected Cali understood everything.

Cali released a drawn-out exhalation. "No, don't apologize. That wasn't fair."

"It wasn't?" He perked up. Was that a light at the end of the tunnel?

"No, it wasn't. I've been messed up since Daniel died. I lost so many friends in Tucson... I can't even wrap my head around it. I've been going through a crisis since then."

"I get it." Sawyer nodded, profoundly moved. He'd lost the same people as Cali—lifelong friends.

"I doubt it. You're just a basic dude. You have the emotional intelligence of a xylophone."

He resounded with a mighty harrumph. "I'm at least a sax."

"Bitch, please. You're a pair of bloated bagpipes!"

"I played the French horn in middle school."

"Ooohhh, that's quite... long."

They dissolved into easy laughter.

Cali rubbed her chin. "It'd help with you and Vic, too."

Sawyer lost his smile and his mind. "Say what?"

"Me screwing Logan. It'd be killing three birds with one stone. Just sayin'."

"No. No. Not sayin'." He just about dislocated his jaw jutting it forward. "Three?"

"One, I'd be scratching an itch." She popped up her index finger.

"Yeah, make sure you don't get something that bites."

She flipped him off. "Two, I'd be thanking him for saving my life."

"You deserve better than that."

"The most important thing comes last." She wagged a third finger his way. "While I'm distracting Logan, you can lock it down with Victoria."

Sawyer hit the mental brakes—full stop. With profound suspicion, he asked, "Lock what down?"

She wrinkled her nose. "You two sleeping together yet?"

"No."

"Well, why the fuck not?" She looked at him like he'd grown two heads.

"Victoria and I aren't like that—" Sawyer bit his words off, wriggling free from the compulsion to explain. Inwardly, he writhed with discomfort. His feelings for Victoria weren't an open book. More like an encrypted journal he kept in a locked safe. Even if he'd possessed the ability to set his guilt and culpability aside, Victoria had been his brother's girl... and she was pregnant with another man's child.

"Sawyer. I know you're sick over what happened with that boy in Albuquerque—"

"Jasper." He stiffened. Of course, Cali had been in Albuquerque, witness to his shameful wrongdoing. But this counted as one of the things they didn't discuss.

"Jasper." Cali fidgeted, clearly outside of her comfort zone. She reached and closed her hand on empty air, leaving him with the unshakeable certainty she'd just grabbed his metaphorical wrist. "You're making amends for that. Victoria forgave you—"

"I—" Sawyer got stuck. Technically, second chances and forgiveness weren't the same, but he choked. He coughed into his fist. "Cali, I appreciate the thought, but how is this any of your business?"

"What the hell do you think we've been talking about for the past hour, jackass?" Cali surged to her feet; her fists came up.

Shit. That'd been the wrong thing to say. He also wasn't sure what they'd been discussing, but he was almost positive it hadn't been Victoria. Sawyer set aside his empty bottle and also rose. "Look, all I meant was... Victoria and I aren't a thing."

"What does that mean, you're not a *thing*?" She made *thing* sound mean.

"There's no thing. There's never been a thing. Never will. Victoria was Daniel's girl. My brother hasn't even been gone a year..." Sawyer trailed off, at a complete loss. Cali's sudden and inexplicable interest in his love life left him baffled. She'd never given one fig about who he did—or didn't—date, unless it meant an opportunity to give him a hard time.

"Don't use Daniel as your excuse. He's dead and he's not coming back," Cali said so harshly that Sawyer gaped. She remained standing in her blue bikini and boxer's stance, and he more than halfway expected her to take a swing at him. "You 'n' Victoria are alive. Hunters don't get the luxury of wallowing. There's no yesterday or tomorrow. Only today. You've got to live in the present because life ends just like that—" She snapped her fingers. "Do you think I don't miss Annie? I miss her every single second of every single day. There's not anything I wouldn't trade to have one more day—one more minute—with her. But she's gone and I'm here, so I keep plowing forward. Going through the motions. Because the alternative is to dig my own grave, lie down, and die."

His frustration built, fueling his short temper, but the voice in the back of his head urged him to proceed with extreme caution. He suspected her rant was just the tip of the iceberg. "What the hell is this really about, Cali? Since when do you concern yourself with who I'm seeing?"

She drew a sharp breath and glared. "For the past few months, all you've done is slide deeper into a shithole of depression, Sawyer. I watch you, your father watches you... We're worried sick. Scared you'll screw up in a fight 'n' get killed or worse."

"For fuck's sake—" He started to stand, but she took a jab at him. The force shoved him back down onto the bench seat.

"Shut up and listen." Fire glinted in her eyes and her jaw hardened. All telltale signs of a brooding storm.

Without a word, he plunked down and settled in. Clearly, the woman meant to speak her mind.

Cali's volume dropped, but her intensity redoubled. "Victoria is good for you. Whatever it is, she gets through that thick head of yours where the rest of us fail. So, stop thinking that I give a crap about anything other than keeping you alive. You're wrong."

The rumble of a vehicle engine approached the front of the house, carrying through the quiet night. Sawyer and Cali turned toward the sound. The house blocked the view of the road. The engine thrummed with the horsepower of a sports utility vehicle or a truck. Sawyer was ninety-nine percent certain it was Logan's vehicle. He latched onto the interruption, however, as a handy excuse to extricate himself from the uncomfortable conversation —saved by the bell.

"I'll check it out." Sawyer hoisted himself from the hot tub and snagged his holstered pistols.

"I'm coming with you." Cali clamored out after him and picked up her rifle, shouldering the carry strap. "You're not getting off the hook that easy."

Sawyer crossed the patio, heading toward the side of the house closest to the detached garage. "Look, I appreciate what you're saying and I swear I've got no intention of hurting myself. But you've got to consider what Victoria wants. She hasn't forgiven me for Jasper, and in the past year, she's lost the love of her life and then the father of her child..."

Still out of sight, the vehicle slowed. Its tires crunched when it turned onto the driveway. The engine shut off.

Sawyer ground to a halt. The whole while he grappled with the emotional kraken that Cali had released. He smashed straight into a rude awakening. *Frigg's prophecy—Sawyer's inevitable death.*

Out of distraction, he allowed his uncensored thoughts to spill over into words. "Victoria's already lost enough—Daniel and her mate. It wouldn't be fair to make her endure..."

Cali's face froze into a stony mask. "Endure what?"

A car door opened and shut.

He faltered but managed to finish. "My death."

"Your death?" Cali turned ghostly pale. Then, she ground her teeth together so hard her jaws popped.

"You bastard." She stalked toward him. Her hunter's mark flared to life and his ignited as well. Magic charged the atmosphere.

Shit. A claxon went off in the back of Sawyer's head. He fell back. "Now, Cali—"

"How dare you threaten to off yourself? I opened up to you! I told you how messed up I've been feeling..." Her fist rose, winding up for a haymaker.

"That's not what I meant." He dropped into a defensive stance. His retreat moved them off the even surface of the patio onto tan bark. The uneven edges bit into the bottoms of his feet.

"If anyone's going to kill you, it should be me!" She loosened the punch, and he blocked with his elbow.

"Do you always have this effect on women?" Logan crossed the periphery of Sawyer's vision. On reflex, he turned toward the new threat.

Before Sawyer had a chance to answer, the side of Cali's foot nailed the bridge of his nose. Bones crunched. Blood gushed across his lower face. Pain exploded through his head.

The world spun like a centrifuge.

CHAPTER 26

Algiz: The Rune of Protection and Opportunity

LOGAN HOPPED BACKWARD to avoid having his legs knocked out from under him when Sawyer's massive bulk struck the ground. The hunter hit hard, plowing a furrow through the tan bark before he came to a stop on his side. Seeing Sawyer get his just deserts amused Logan to no end, but he kinda-sorta felt bad for the guy.

"Damn, Dixie, what'd he do to piss you off?" Logan started around Sawyer, but the muzzle of the stub-nosed revolver shoved into his face brought him up short.

"Stop right there." Cali cocked the gun's hammer with her thumb and aimed at his nose. Logan had no idea where the woman could've had the gun hidden, considering she had on a blue bikini. Hell, the rifle carry strap slung across her chest cover more skin.

"Easy, I'm not looking for trouble." Logan threw up his hands in surrender.

"Well, you've found it. Now, mind your own damn..." Cali glanced to the side, and her gaze snagged on his dismemberment. Color drained from her face. She jerked the revolver aside. "Shit, what happened?"

Shit was right.

"It's nothing—just an accident." Logan dropped his arms and thrust the bandaged stump behind his back. He burned with an acute humiliation that was worse than the severe throbbing of the injury. How the hell could he have forgotten his recent mutilation, even for a second?

He'd left more than his faith in his uncle behind at the hospital. The Necromancer had Logan's sacrifice and his silence. In return, Logan had only his uncle's promise to resurrect Evan.

On the ground, Sawyer groaned, gripped his head, and rolled onto his back. In a blood-gargled voice, he asked, "What's an accident?"

"Your face, redneck." Narrow-eyed, Logan appraised the downed hunter. The salty aroma of fresh blood excited his wolf, arousing predatory urges, but nothing too difficult to control. It helped that he'd gorged himself on dry hospital sandwiches a couple hours before.

At a glance, Sawyer's nose was flatter than a Florida swamp. Beneath his skin, busy runes swarmed to repair damage that would've run to the tens of thousands in cosmetic surgery fees.

"Now's not the time for one of your dumbass jokes. Tell me what happened." Cali seized hold of Logan's elbow, immobilizing his arm, and bent to inspect it. Sympathy sweetened her basal scent, taking the edge off the remnants of her anger.

"There was an accident. My uncle was there," Logan lied with the god-given talent he'd inherited from his father. In a twisted metaphor, the explanation wasn't even that far from the truth. "Accident" meant "incident"; his uncle had been present... and the perpetrator. The devil was in the details.

"What sort of accident?" Sawyer dragged himself upright; seated with his legs splayed wide, bark and dirt stuck to his bare skin and his damp swimsuit. Based on the evidence, it was a safe bet the hunters had come from the pool.

"You look like shit." Concern drew Cali's face into a taut canvas, but she released Logan's arm.

"Thanks, Dixie. That's just want I needed to hear." Logan gusted out a forced chuckle. He made a point of ignoring Sawyer's questions. Details would only complicate the lie.

"I'll go get Victoria," Cali volunteered. "She and Sylvie both went to bed an hour ago."

"No, don't do that," Logan said, sharper than intended. His adamancy earned him strange looks from the hunters. To cover, Logan tried to sound casual. "She needs her rest... for the baby."

Cali and Sawyer traded a glance, but didn't argue.

"Where's Morena?" Logan asked.

"Inside." Cali bumped her chin. "She's on watch to make sure Victoria doesn't wander off again in her sleep."

"Vic must be thrilled."

Cali shrugged. "Should I get Morena?"

"No. I'll talk to her tomorrow morning." Logan didn't have the energy to deal with the fit Morena would throw over his severed hand. Worse, though, he dreaded the impending conversation with Victoria.

"Suit yourself." Cali bestowed a final glower upon Sawyer and then marched away. She disappeared around the corner of the house.

"What'd you do to piss her off?" Without intention, Logan offered the other man a hand up, although his heart was divided. He longed to kick Sawyer while he was down.

"Mind your own damn business." Sawyer narrowed his eyes in suspicion. "Do you think I'm gonna fall for that?"

"Not a fake out. I swear." Logan kept his arm extended.

"There's a sucker born every minute." Sawyer tilted his head back, glancing heavenward, and then reached.

"Psyche." Logan jerked his hand aside at the last second, so Sawyer swung through empty air.

The hunter glared.

"I'm just kidding, jackass. Here." Logan seized hold of Sawyer's forearm and hauled the hunter to his feet. The guy weighed a ton.

Sawyer leaned forward, holding the sides of his head. Beneath the drying gore, his nose had dimension again.

"Are you gonna fall over?" Logan asked.

"No."

"Are you gonna puke?"

"No."

Logan retreated anyway. "So, what'd you do to piss Cali off?"

"I didn't listen while she was talking." Sawyer exhaled, lowered his hands, and slowly straightened.

"That's a tough one. Women don't ever say what they mean. They have layers. Like onions but sweeter—Vidalia onions."

"Talk shit like that to Cali and she'll bust your chops." Sawyer retrieved his holstered pistols from the bark.

"Dude, you're the dumbass with the broken nose."

Sawyer scowled and touched his nose. He winced. "True."

Each nursing their own wounds, they headed around to the rear of the house where they joined Cali on the enclosed courtyard patio. She had on a robe and boots, and occupied a patio chair. A silver flask and her revolver were on the table, the rifle slung over the back of the chair.

Logan's nose twitched when the powerful odor of whisky hit him. He sank into the seat next to Cali as Sawyer put on his own robe. Logan watched his rival from the corner of his eye. An insult crossed his mind, but he shoved it aside. Right then, he lacked the energy to mount a solid offense. Better to save it for future use.

So there they were, sullen and silent, for meandering minutes. Logan's despondence bottomed out into a pit of despair. He would've died except that'd have taken too much effort.

After a time, Cali crossed to the cooler and fetched a dripping bottle of water which she then *opened and offered* to Logan. "Here."

His jaw dropped but he accepted it. "Damn, do I look that bad?"

"Like shit warmed over." She resumed her seat and propped her chin on her knee. Her scent held honeyed notes of unexpected sympathy.

Sawyer finally joined them at the table.

"Will your hand regrow?" Cali asked.

"Werewolves don't regenerate limbs." Logan downed half the water in a long gulp. It hit the spot.

"You're not normal." Cali scratched her temple.

That required a retort.

"True, I'm exceptional." Logan winked, and Sawyer curled his upper lip.

Cali ignored Logan's flirting. "I've seen how fast you heal."

Logan stirred. He finished off the water to give himself an opportunity to consider. Truth—he wasn't a normal wolf-shifter. He'd inherited more than a silver tongue and rapid regenerations from his god-father. He also shape shifted differently, although he had no idea why, and the toxic properties of silver didn't affect him as it did most werewolves. Aware of the other's regard, Logan finally offered a reluctant confession.

"I don't know. I've never lost a limb before."

"You also claimed you'd never talked in your animal form." Sawyer made the observation with unwarranted grimness. A fog of distrust engulfed him.

The implicit accusation irritated the crap out of Logan. He bristled. "I said I don't know. What are you accusing me of, redneck?"

Sawyer tensed, leaning forward. He raised his fists, signaling his intent to talk with them. "Just that everything with you is an incomplete story. You got into an accident—where's the damage on your car?

"I never said it was a car accident." Logan bared his teeth. The metal feet of the chair scraped across the patio as he pushed it out.

"That's right. You evaded. You never shut up. Yet everything you say is pure bullshit." With an eager gleam, Sawyer started to rise.

Cali's rifle produced a metallic clap as she slid the bolt. Sawyer and Logan snapped to attention.

"Sit your asses back down—both of you." Cali lashed the command as a whip. "I'll shoot you where you stand. Don't think I won't."

With a pained grimace, Logan dropped into his seat. Sawyer did the same.

"What about tomorrow?" Cali settled the rifle across her lap.

"What about tomorrow?" Logan repeated.

She furrowed her brow. "Tomorrow. You're supposed to be going to Arizona with Victoria. She wanted to give Finn a magic carpet ride on the rainbow bridge. Did you forget?"

"Of course I remember." Logan scoffed while astonishment echoed through his mind. He retained only the vaguest recollection. But yeah, that morning after their trip to the jail, Victoria had asked, and he'd agreed to accompany her. How could he have forgotten?

"You're supposed to be her bodyguard or something, right?" Cali unscrewed the cap off her flask and took a sip. She offered it to Logan. He shook his head.

"Or something," Logan said with a wry smile. He wasn't just a bodyguard, but rather a Valhalla-ordained champion tasked with the duty of defending Victoria's person from attacks and her honor in the event of a challenge.

"What good is a one-handed champion? Can you fight?" Sawyer asked, playing Devil's Advocate to Logan's gloomy musings.

"I can fight." Logan glared.

"Can you win?" Sawyer narrowed his eyes and leaned forward. Brutish intimidation, but he had his point.

Doubt constricted Logan. He shuttered his gaze. "Victoria also said she wanted to avoid confrontations. Dueling is supposed to be a last resort."

"Nothing starts a fight faster than lookin' like you're sure to lose," Cali said, giving voice to a truth that couldn't be denied.

Grim silence reigned. Logan slouched to stop from hunching. A scorpion took up residence within his chest, digging hooked claws into his insides. He prided himself on being fearless, but the prospect of failing Victoria crippled his confidence.

Cali recapped the flask. "Maybe Victoria can heal you. She fixed up my arm."

"She reattached my fingers once." Sawyer flexed the fingers of his right hand while regarding them with a morose scowl. That unmissable aura of "something left unsaid" hung about him.

"Yeah, maybe." The corners of Logan's mouth tugged down. His gaze was drawn toward the French doors that led into the kitchen.

Victoria had once brought Logan back from the dead. All things considered, she probably could regenerate his severed hand. Could a magically regrown hand be considered a true sacrifice? He doubted it. And after what he'd already gone through, he refused to risk Evan's resurrection. Victoria would offer, and he'd have to refuse. It led to even more complications and contortions in what was already a totally fucked-up situation.

"We should come up with a backup plan, just in case she can't fix you," Sawyer hit a beat. "Your hand, that is. I doubt your head is fixable."

"Hilarious," Logan bit off.

"The obvious answer is to cancel the trip to Arizona. Finn might not like it, but he can drive up like everyone else. It's only a few hours." Cali stroked her fingers over the stock of her rifle. Her expression left Logan wondering—who was she fantasizing about shooting now?

"We can't cancel at the last minute. It'd make us look bad," Logan protested. Flaking out would be worse than showing up with a crippled champion. "Besides, Vic wanted the other alphas to see Finn receiving special treatment. It's a prestige thing to remind them that she's a Valkyrie."

"It's also a prestige thing for Finn." Sardonicism ran in a swift stream beneath Sawyer's otherwise bland expression.

"How so?" Cali oozed skepticism.

"Only Aesir and Valkyries are allowed to set foot on Bifröst," Sawyer said. "Anyone else has to be escorted. Victoria made it a point to obtain a special dispensation for Finn and his people."

"How'd she arrange that?" Logan asked. The conversation had taken an eye-opening turn. Victoria had tried to teach Logan how to summon Bifröst, always with the admonishment that it mustn't be misused. He'd tried to call the bridge but failed. Now, he wondered if his lack of success had more to do with his lineage than his having botched the spell.

Sawyer grinned. "She texted my old man."

Cali snorted and chuckled. "Well, at least they're communicating again. When do you plan to tell us what it was you and your father did to piss Victoria off so bad?" She stared through Sawyer.

Sawyer squirmed and changed the subject. "I hate to even say it, but I have to agree with Logan—"

Logan opened his mouth, but Cali thwacked his arm. She said, "You've had your entire life to be a jerk. Take today off."

He shut it.

"What were you sayin'?" Cali prompted Sawyer.

"Only that it wouldn't be smart to cancel Finn's ride on Bifröst. Not only would it make us look unreliable and undermine the prestige thing, but Victoria meant to use it as a bribe for Finn. She's buttering him up so he'll agree to pledge a war party to the protection of our lands."

"That's the first I've heard of this." Logan sat bolt upright. He gripped the arm of his chair. The white-knuckled grip sent pain shooting through his right wrist. A cold shock—he remembered his severed hand.

"We came up with it this afternoon after you disappeared into thin air for hours on end." Sawyer scoffed.

Logan ground his teeth. He balked at the prospect of other

wolf-shifters taking up even semi-permanent residence on Storm Pack territory, but he also understood where Victoria was coming from. The land wouldn't remain theirs for long if they didn't find a way to defend it.

"I'm sick of all the reasons why we can't cancel. Let's start talking about how we'll make this work instead." Cali snapped her fingers repeatedly.

"Simple. I'm the alpha's champion. If Victoria gets challenged, then I'll fight." Logan gathered his reserves... a piss-poor effort. Molasses flowed through his brain, gumming up his thoughts. By the same ticket, exhaustion weighed on him. He ached from head to toe. Hopefully, sleep would improve his condition, but how much?

Cali jeered. "Right now you couldn't manage your fly, school boy. If you try to enter a duel, you'll get slaughtered."

Annoyance flashed through Logan. "Have you got a better idea, Dixie?"

"Yeah, let Sawyer stand in for you as your second."

"I can't," Sawyer said.

"No way," Logan protested simultaneously.

Cali slanted them both a look of raw disgust. "Just because you two can't stand each other..."

"That's got nothing to do with it. It's not personal. Unless there's genuine, provable kinship, I wouldn't be allowed to act as his second. Wolves don't allow outsiders to meddle in their affairs." Oh the irony. Sawyer turned to Logan for support.

"That makes zero sense. You and your father are members of the Storm Pack." Cali drove her fist against her palm.

"It doesn't have to make sense," Sawyer argued. "Werewolf traditions are ingrained, inflexible, and irrational."

Sourness sat on Logan's tongue. He wanted nothing more than to bash Sawyer's head against the table. "Everyone's entitled to occasional stupidity, but you abuse the privilege."

"He's right," Cali said. "Damn it, Sawyer. Shut up unless you have something useful to say."

Preoccupied, Logan rubbed his chin. There was at least one aspect of wolf-shifter culture he knew inside and out: the Norse art of war, including dueling rules and traditions. He had an idea...

"Fine, I'll go with them tomorrow." Sawyer threw up his hands in surrender. "I'll even serve as Logan's second—if they'll allow it. I think you've got misconceptions about what that means, though. If Logan gets challenged to a duel, being his second doesn't mean I can fight on his behalf."

"It doesn't?" Cali's face fell.

"No," Sawyer explained, "A second—"

"Negotiates the terms of the duel." Logan snapped his fingers. *Bingo!* Riding a wave of excitement, he lurched to his feet.

Both hunters looked to him.

A twisted grin turned the corners of Logan's mouth. "I think I know how to make this work to our advantage."

Sköll: "One Who Mocks"
The Great Wolf Fated to Devour the Moon

DOZING in that midway place between consciousness and sound slumber, Victoria drifted on a turbulent sea of troubled dreams. She sought escape but the nightmarish visions held her as a helpless captive until the soft click of the bedroom door jolted her awake. She opened her eyes to the welcome darkness, courtesy of the blackout curtains. She rested on her side, beneath a cool cotton sheet, and listened to the light pad of approaching footsteps. Deep within, her wolf stirred but not with alarm. Welcome. He provoked her—sometimes to anger, other times to laughter—a wild rollercoaster ride. He inspired fright, excitement, confusion... but never boredom.

The bed bucked under the sudden addition of Logan's weight when he landed beside her. His head hit the king-sized feather pillow beside hers so the entire thing poofed up. As soon as he got close, she tasted ashy notes underlying his basal scent. The abnormality set her nose to twitching. She inhaled and confirmed that he was hurting. She stirred in immediate worry, shaken from her drowsy complacency.

"Well, look at this. There's someone sleeping in my bed." Logan ghosted his hand across her bottom over her shorts.

"So now you're a bear?" Victoria smiled before she stopped herself. She should smack him—put him in his place. Their comfortable dynamic hinged on a constant tug of war: he pushed, she pulled; he propositioned her, she insulted him. And so on and so forth... A power struggle rooted in their deepest insecurities. Recently, though—she still wasn't sure exactly when—they'd reached a weird waypoint somewhere between friendship and intimacy.

"More of a wolf," he said with a snicker. "A guy could get the wrong idea—finding a naked woman in his bed."

"I'm not naked," Victoria grumbled for effect. During his months-long absence, she'd moved into his vacant room. Since his return, he'd slept on the floor or the couch. He made no attempt to reclaim his bed, but he never stopped teasing her about it, either.

"A technicality easily fixed." Logan's voice leered, but he hit a strained note. Based on his determined innuendo, his wounds weren't serious.

"You're always inappropriate." She clicked her tongue.

"And you love it."

"Keep telling yourself that." Victoria groaned and chuckled. Pure conjecture, but she envisioned Logan and Sawyer engaging in another scuffle as the cause of Logan's injuries. Like boys on the playground, the pair clashed often and came away with scratches and bruises. She preferred to stay out of it so long as they refrained from killing each other. Eventually, they'd work it out... or Sawyer would leave.

Victoria scowled and stiffened. All of a sudden, her throat tightened, and her chest hurt. She rolled toward Logan and stopped on her side with his arm trapped beneath her. He pressed his forearm against her back, encircling her, and grasped her shoulder. She settled her head in the crook of his shoulder, using him as a pillow. They clung together; shell-shocked survivors of a war that kept claiming their loved ones as its victims. Intimacy, once unknown between them, occurred more and more often, and that terrified her.

"Did you have another fight with Sawyer?" She tried not to nag but criticism crept into her voice anyway.

"No." He snapped out the answer fast but then hesitated. "Why?"

"You're in pain." She rolled her head so her chin was propped on his pec, but the position did nothing to improve her perception into his mood.

"It's called blue balls, Vicky."

She poked his side. "Stop. I can smell it on you."

"Yeah? Well you smell like you've been crying."

"I was." Taken aback, Victoria allowed the admission past her guard. She'd cried herself to sleep—and sometimes she teared up in her dreams. Since she'd never been given to waterworks, she marked it up to pregnancy hormones and tried to dismiss it. Logan had a talent for poking sharp sticks straight past her defenses, though.

"What about?"

"Sylvie and I had another argument. She refuses to accept my break with Freya. It's to the point now where she's openly challenging my judgment on everything. It's a huge mess." Victoria cringed to recall her friend's reaction. She wanted nothing more than to pull the sheet over her head and spend the rest of the day hiding in bed.

Logan delayed a discernable beat. "Can't you just put your foot down? Speaking from experience, I know you're capable of stomping like a rhino... a cute, tiny rhino, but still a rhino when you're determined to have your way."

Victoria chuckled. "I would with anyone else, but not Sylvie. I can't."

He shook his head, but thankfully, he didn't argue. "Bah, give her time. Sylv will realize you're better off without that manipulative elf-bitch."

"Thanks, but I'm really not," Victoria said with a broken laugh. "Without Freya, I'm weaker when I most need to be strong."

"You're plenty strong. Besides, you have me." His voice cracked and his armor with it, exposing vulnerability she imagined Logan preferred remained hidden. In that moment, the darkened room became a blessing.

"I know that." Victoria stroked his chest, pressing her hand over the handprint scar burned into the flesh over his heart. Neither the gloom nor his shirt could hide the mark from her— she knew the exact location.

"It's not just words. I believe in you—"

"I'm turning on the light." Victoria reached over for the lamp on the nightstand. The RN in her needed to perform triage on his injuries.

"Ah, Vic." The bed rocked as Logan surged toward the edge. "Before you do, there's something you should know—"

"What?" After a second of groping, Victoria flipped the switch. Soft light brightened the room. She swung around and halted. Full stop. A ragged gasp tore from Victoria's throat.

His left hand was gone, severed at the wrist, the end wrapped in a fresh white dressing.

Sick with horror, Victoria scrambled across the bed. At her approach, Logan started to cover the bandaged stump of his left arm with his right hand, but aborted the gesture.

"What happened?" Victoria caught his elbow, pulling his arm to her. Too rough; he hissed. She gentled her grip but didn't let go.

"It's surprising how much it still hurts," Logan confessed in a shaky voice. "I expected it to stop once my regeneration kicked in. It's already healed."

"Logan, who hurt you?" White-hot anger flooded her. She would *destroy* whoever had done this to him—rip them to shreds.

"No one." He tugged at his arm, but she held fast.

A repugnant thought sickened her. "Was it Sawyer?"

"No!" He surged, roiling like a restless storm. Tension rolled off him in waves. "It wasn't anyone."

"Don't lie! Tell me who did this to you." Horrified, Victoria bent over his injury. She ripped through the top of the neat dressing, unraveling it from his mid-forearm down. The person who'd applied the dressing had at least basic first aid training.

"I did it to myself."

"I don't believe that."

The last of the dressing fell away. Victoria swept it aside. She grasped his arm, holding him steady, and bent over the injury. His hand had been cut off at the wrist. Like the dressing, the cut was straight and had clean lines, and as Logan claimed, the end of the stump had already healed. Excepting silver, werewolves healed fast and could recover from wounds that were usually lethal to normal people. Hard to hurt, tougher to kill... but they didn't regrow severed limbs.

"I think I can fix this. Did you manage to save your hand?"

"No, it's gone for good," Logan said in a tone heavy with irony. That he found anything about this situation funny—even twisted humor—annoyed her to no end.

"That makes it tougher, but I can do it. I've healed worse." She scowled and fought tears. His suffering upset her more than she could quantify. With an effort, Victoria summoned her healing magic. A shower of sparks flickered on her fingertips and then died. A frustrated snarl ripped from her throat.

"Vic, no—"

"Just hold still. Give me a minute."

Calm... Focus... Breathe deep. She inhaled and blinked her spirit sight into focus. As she'd suspected, Logan's aura retained a bright outline of his severed hand. So long as his life pattern retained the memory, she could do the rest: summon all her magic —call on Odin if she had to—and conjure blood and bone from nothing. Just as the All Father had breathed spirit and life into the first man and woman, she possessed the power to perform a lesser miracle.

"Stop." The strength of Logan's voice bashed through her defenses. He rolled off the bed and moved out of her reach.

"Why?" She blinked, freeing tears, and looked up at him. Undeterred, she pursued him. The room wasn't *that* big—he quickly ran out of places to retreat.

"This was a sacrifice. If you undo it, it doesn't count for anything." Logan's jaw assumed a familiar jut, but he lightened his severity when he raised his hand and wiped tears from her cheek with his thumb.

"What sort of sacrifice?" Her mind boggled. She understood sacrifices—acknowledged their necessity when circumstances called for it—and respected the right of an individual to make one. But she hated unexplained secrets, especially ones that hurt those she loved.

"I can't tell you."

"Why not?"

His face hardened into a stubborn mask. "I gave my word that I wouldn't talk about it."

"Your word?" Victoria repeated, dumbfounded. She couldn't believe what she was hearing. Unfortunately, saying it aloud did nothing to make it more believable.

"That's right."

"Tell me you have a good reason for this self-mutilation? Tell me it was a life or limb decision." She huffed, thin on patience. Her suspicion yawned open like an empty grave.

"Yeah, that." He grimaced. "You've no idea how literally true that is."

"Really." She hemorrhaged skepticism.

"Do you trust me?" Logan's amber eyes caught the light; a luminous, inescapable trap. His charisma pulled her into his depths.

"That's a damning question." Victoria released his injured arm and jerked away. She resisted his allure with her entire strength of will. Since they'd met, Logan had tried to ensnare her time and again. She doubted he was even aware. She'd refused to submit.

"You have my word I haven't done anything that will endanger the pack." From the stubborn set of his jaws, Logan made it clear he didn't intend to volunteer anything more.

Trembling, Victoria sealed her lips. She kept her mouth shut for fear of what she might say. A wildfire of mistrust raged in her heart. Recently, many of the people she loved and trusted had proved themselves liars or frauds, including both Jake and Sawyer. She didn't know who or what to believe anymore.

"After everything we've been through, you either trust me or you don't." His mask of humanity slipped, revealing a lanky shadow wolf. He absorbed light, somehow, so even Victoria's nimbus dimmed where their auras touched.

"I trust you." How could her voice sound so tiny? All sense of security vanished, and she resented him for taking it from her. More than that, it felt like a betrayal. She'd handed him the power to hurt her, only to have him use it against her. She retreated, putting distance between them, propping her back against the headboard.

"Bull." Logan swept his arm wide. He turned away, facing her only in profile. "You don't believe that. Stop lying to me."

"I'm not a liar." Victoria settled into a ready stance, choosing composure over anger. White-blue coalesced in her aura, gathering about her in a cool mist.

"That's a lie," Logan grated. He brooded with angry self-recrimination. All of it, directed inward. "The lies you tell yourself are the worst."

"Logan, why don't you tell me what's wrong instead of trying to start a fight?" Victoria pushed serenity across their psychic connection, a not-so-subtle reminder that it worked both ways.

"I'm not trying to start a fight." He blinked and frowned.

She snorted. "Oh please. Confrontation is the only trick you know. Provocation is your go-to stratagem."

"It is?" His displeasure turned to worry. Poor guy.

Victoria chuckled. "'Fraid so. Your secrets are out."

"Not all of them." He grimaced and opened his mouth, seemingly struggling for words... or maybe it was courage. Victoria sympathized. It took enormous inner strength—and confidence—to admit one's tragic flaws.

She thought it was time to take some of her own medicine.

"You're right. I lie all the time. I lie to protect myself," Victoria forced out, even though it hurt worse than breaking a bone. She'd rather endure crushed fingers than confess the truth passing her lips. "I loved Daniel, and he died. I chose your father for a marriage of convenience, and I told myself feelings didn't matter because it was a sacrifice I made for the good of the pack. But Arik was so much more than I expected. Before I even realized I cared for him, he died."

"Victoria—" Logan raised her name in a loud protest.

She waved him to silence. "I'm a total hypocrite. I lied that night out by the lake when I told you I loved Arik." Tears flooded her eyes and she choked. "I swear, I didn't mean to deceive anyone. It's just the closer I get to my due date, the more I think about what I'll tell my daughter about her father. I can't imagine admitting I didn't love her daddy..."

"I know. You're scared and confused, but don't start her life on a foundation of lies." Logan pressed his cheek against the top of her head. He kissed her forehead. Tingles spread along her nerve endings. Temptation teased her—to wrap her hands behind his neck and pull him into a kiss.

Oh, dangerous... She'd better watch herself.

"You're right. But what am I supposed to tell her then?" She rested against his chest, drew on his strength, and used it to fortify her own. Her insides warmed and liquefied, but far more importantly, she was safe.

This right here, their synergy, represented the pack bond at its best. Logan had the makings of a damn fine alpha. Given some seasoning and a few years under his belt... Years they didn't have.

"We'll tell her we love her. You're not in this alone. I'll be there for her—and you." He stroked his hand over her hair, smoothing it beneath his palm.

She stiffened and withdrew. He let her go without complaint. At a loss for words, Victoria fidgeted. She averted her gaze, so she wouldn't have to look him in the face. There *it* was again: ready-made commitment. It made her so uncomfortable, she wanted to squirm out of her skin.

Earlier at the police station, he'd said he intended to marry her. Now he'd all but declared his commitment to acting as her child's father. She supposed it even made sense. They had the baby in common, as well as friendship and desire. The pragmatic thing to do would've been to just take him up on his offer. It'd be easy. She'd mated with Arik for pragmatic reasons... and look how that'd turned out.

"Logan..." Victoria wrung her hands. A lump formed in her throat. She had no idea what to say but she had to be careful. "I understand what you want, but you deserve better than I can give you."

Logan grunted. His disgruntled annoyance lanced through their empathetic connection. "I thought we'd agreed to cut the shit."

Anger flickered, testing her composure. "Don't get pissy now over being friendzoned. You were doing so well."

"Friendzoned—I should be so lucky." Logan released her and spun away. He threw himself onto the bed again, punched a pillow, and thrust it behind him. He leaned back against the headboard with his long legs stretched out straight. "If you don't want to be with me, just say it. I'm here for you whether we're friends or lovers. But whatever you do—don't treat me like a kid. Don't tell me what I deserve. I'm capable of deciding for myself."

"Did I do that?" Victoria faltered, her confidence shaken. She felt weird, standing in the middle of the room all alone.

"Yeah." Logan flashed a crooked grin. "Condescending is the only trick you know. Patronizing is your go-to stratagem."

"Oh, that burns." She fell into laughter, gasping for breath. Tightness constricted her chest. "I'm sorry. I'll stop."

"You'll try." He glanced down at his wrist stump and winced, then looked up. "Throwing up barriers is your defense mechanism..."

"And being a jackass is yours." She nodded and sniffed, clearing clogged sinuses. "Aren't we a pair?"

"We are." Logan flexed his hand. His handsome features set in an intense mask. "While we're clearing the air, there's something else I want to talk about."

"Yes?" She raised her brow.

He surged off the bed, roiling with restless energy. "You blame yourself for provoking the courtship fight between me and my father."

"Logan—"

"Ut-ut-ut. Let me finish."

She bit her lips, near to bursting with protests.

"What's worse, you believe I blame you too."

"I never said that." Truth—she'd never shared her fear or her guilt with Logan. Not in so many words. But in her own defense, she hadn't had much opportunity to do so.

"You didn't have to. The point I'm trying to make is this: I don't blame you. You don't have anything to feel guilty about. That fight with my father was years in the making. Once, when I was sixteen —before my mother died—Dad predicted the day would come when we'd fight over a woman. He said it would end in death. He wanted me to remember that he loved me no matter what. He made me swear not to forget."

"That's insane." Her head whirled.

"It's the truth. Believe me, I *know* liars." Logan laughed, harsh and bitter. Dazzling clusters of fireworks—crimson and ginger— cascaded across Logan's aura, illuminating the shadows of his soul.

Sudden fear crashed over her like a rogue wave. Victoria's wolf surged, crashing to dominance over her psyche. She bristled, on the verge of a rumbling snarl, and growled in pure wrath. Her knuckles popped, snapped, and reformed, as her hands shifted to claws. Ironically, it saved her. She refrained from smacking Logan full across the face because it would've slashed him. They'd had more than their fair share of misunderstandings, but she'd learned. He wouldn't raise a finger against her, even in self-defense.

Victoria stepped back to give herself room to breathe.

"Do you understand what I'm saying, Vic?" Logan advanced, invading her space. "I'm a natural-born liar."

"I get it." Victoria punched his sternum with enough force to drive him back. Humiliating tears flooded her eyes. "This morning at the police station, you lied to Milly Dawson. Like I wouldn't notice—"

Like she wouldn't notice.

Logan rocked under the force of her blow. His entire tone changed, true to his mercurial nature. "I lied on purpose, so you'd finally know the truth. Please, you have to believe me. I've wanted to tell you for months."

"You've been gone for months. You left us." Victoria snagged on the incongruity, so obvious she should've noticed it already. She probably would've, if she hadn't been working so hard to avoid the truth.

"I left to protect you."

"That makes no sense. If you left to protect us, why'd you come back?" Victoria released a gust of surprise. She snagged and spun on it like a weather vane in a whirlwind. Logan had never before offered his reasons for his absence... nor an explanation for his sudden return. Certainly, she'd wondered... speculated. It didn't make sense. Neither did his claim to have lied in the service of honesty. In fact, the whole convoluted concept hurt her brain.

"I was told you were in danger."

"You're still not making sense," Victoria said, but then, abruptly, the light turned on. She connected an entire line of dots and it formed a big picture. As soon as the fire under her temper extinguished, she crumbled to ash. "You lied on purpose, so I would figure out that you can without getting caught."

"Yeah," he said with flat resignation. "That pretty much sums it up."

"How?" Victoria strove to wrap her mind around it. She already knew the inevitable and obvious conclusion to be drawn, but she loathed to take the last step. She clung to denial, hoping against hope that he'd offer some other explanation.

"You could say I take after my father." Logan flashed a cruel, mocking grin. "You know.... Prince. Lies."

Nausea swirled in her gut. A terrible, terrifying question filled her head. She didn't want to ask, dreading the total loss of her sanity if her worst fear proved true, but it was an impossible burden. She unloaded it as fast as possible. "Arik."

"I'm sorry, Vic."

"No, no being sorry. Admit it. Say it aloud," Victoria demanded the ugly truth. A small part of her wanted to hear him deny it. At any moment, he'd laugh and claim it was all an awful joke.

Logan didn't speak. Rock still, he hunched over in misery.

"Logan?" Victoria closed her eyes. It all made sense now, all of Logan's oddities, from his fluid shape changing, to his silver immunity, to his gift for lying... Of course, the son of the god of lies would excel at deception.

"Yes, Arik," Logan spat out the words as if they were a mouthful of poison. "My father is Loki."

Shaking in the grip of rage, Victoria pressed her hands to her abdomen and panted, fighting a sudden wave of faintness. Arik Koenig, the man she'd chosen as her lifemate, hadn't even been real. Their entire relationship had been based on lies and fraud.

She'd been *tricked*.

"I didn't want you to find out like this," Logan continued to rant. "I didn't want you to find out at all, but you had to know."

"I'm an idiot." Victoria jerked her fist toward her chest.

"Don't." Logan set his hand on her shoulder and squeezed. "I've

known him my entire life. Hell, he raised me. I never even suspected. If you're an idiot, what does that make me?"

Answering that would've been unnecessarily cruel. Instead, Victoria opened her eyes and asked, "How long have you known?"

"Since the night we fought the witch and Dad faked his own death." Logan made the admission with great difficulty, as though each word was torn from him.

"Why didn't you tell me then?" The marrow in her bones froze. *Arik wasn't dead?* Then where was he?

"I was scared."

"Scared of what?"

"Myself." A smirk steeped in self-deprecation twisted his mouth. "Loki fathers monsters—world serpents, death goddesses, giant wolves that consume everything in sight." Genuine fear soured his scent and tainted his aura.

"You're not a monster, Logan." Without hesitation, Victoria charged straight to his defense. It destroyed her to see him hurting so, filled with angst and anger.

"You don't know that for sure. You can't." He lifted his face, eyes wary and lips parted, the vision of skepticism.

She caught his hand and held fast, projecting her conviction across the pack bond. "I do know it. When you thought you were a threat to the pack, you left to protect us. When you found out we were in danger, you came back. You're a good guy. I believe that, and I believe in you."

"I don't even know what to say." He averted his face. Tears glinted on his cheeks. He shook from the force of restrained grief. He clutched her hand, and physical contact bolstered the strength of the empathic connect.

"Take your time." Victoria propped Logan up through the bond, holding him steady until he got his emotions under control. It didn't take long. He squared his shoulders and sucked air through his teeth, visibly calmed.

"Thanks, V." He let go.

"You're welcome." She smiled even as her insides roiled like a stormy sea. She hadn't absorbed the new information yet, or processed the myriad implications. It still seemed surreal—a nightmare she expected to wake up from at any moment.

Her hands closed protectively about her abdomen. A single horrified realization dominated her thoughts, echoing over and over. She couldn't escape it. If Loki fathered monsters... what did that mean for her daughter? Was her unborn baby an abomination?

"The baby's fine," Logan said with disturbing insight.

"You can't know that."

"We saw her Friday on the ultrasound," he countered. "She had one head, two arms, and two legs. She's perfect."

Victoria brooded, at once frustrated with his simplistic and flawed logic. Victoria's child would certainly be a shape changer. They had no way of knowing what the baby would turn into. She was grateful to Logan for making the effort to assure her, though.

She didn't want to ask but she needed to know. Even so, her mouth moved like it was full of marbles, and she couldn't bring herself to use Arik's name aloud.

"Logan, do you talk to... your father?"

He delayed answering for an awfully long time. Prickles blossomed across her skin like a heat rash, and she was both sweaty and itchy by the time Logan grunted what sounded like "Yeah".

"How often?" Her breath hissed. She fumed. Irritation percolated but a far more potent brew of bitter resentment slow boiled. Arik, whom she'd admired and respected, had turned out to be a rat-bastard that had knocked her up and run out on her.

Logan ground his teeth. "Not often. When I first learned the truth, I refused to talk to him, but that didn't stop him. He pops up for father-son chats whenever he feels like it."

"I guess it's nice you get to see him. I'd give anything for one more day with my mom and dad." Victoria struggled to be gracious, but it just about killed her. She supposed, if an upside could be found in this mess, at least her daughter wouldn't grow up without ever knowing her father.

On the downside, her daughter would grow up knowing her father.

"Are you okay, Vic? What're you thinking?"

"I'm thinking the next time you talk to Arik, tell him I'm pissed."

He snorted. "Yeah, I'll do that."

Tell him... I want to talk to him. She bit her tongue.

CHAPTER 28

Hati: "One Who Hates"
The Great Wolf Destined to Devour the Sun

MIDNIGHT FOUND Logan haunting the hallways of his childhood home. He couldn't sleep. He hungered even though he'd just grabbed a snack on his way through the kitchen. His conscience nagged, and coming clean with Victoria about his father hadn't helped because he'd traded one lie for another. Now she knew the truth about Arik... but not Mike Trash, and in some fucked-up way that compounded his guilt. It was one of those times when a guy really needed some fatherly advice from the god of lies.

Feeling like a fool, Logan pushed the door to his father's study open and called into the darkness, "Dad, are you around?"

With baited breath, he waited... listening. He halfway hoped—expected—Arik to step from a shadowy corner. When it didn't happen, he shook his head in self-disgust. A minute passed but no response was forthcoming. Finally, he shook his head again and entered the office. He switched on the architect-style lamp, illuminating the room. *Someone* had cleaned up the computer parts that'd been strewn across the desktop. He located the equipment in a cardboard box on the floor. That little incongruity, so in keeping with Arik's compulsive tidiness, helped reassure Logan that he hadn't imagined his father's visit.

A sharp prick stung his wrist, drawing his attention to the bracelet of thorny vines inked on his skin, and a nettle of feminine-flavored resentment poked at his mind. *Oh yeah...* Logan flashed a brash grin. He *almost* apologized, but the thought of talking to a tattoo proved more than he could handle.

He dropped into his father's executive chair, tipping back. His father's familiar scent clung to the expensive leather. Restless, Logan opened the front drawer and peered inside—pens, mechanical pencils, a legal pad... Boring. He slammed it shut again.

His nose twitched, catching a whiff of an intense menthol aroma—spearmint. Not sweet like candy canes, but astringent as though someone had decided to apply Listerine as cologne. He detected a rising flood of powerful arcana and his wolf burst to the forefront of his psyche.

"What are you looking for in your father's drawers? Does the great Hróðvitnir keep his secrets hidden there?" The woman's sultry voice embodied seduction.

Logan raised his gaze but altered his stance to protect his throat. A tall brunette faced him over the desk. She wore a floor-length blue cloak trimmed in snow-white fur and held a bejeweled distaff. She looked to be in her thirties, but she was hot—straight up Mrs. Robinson.

She had pale blue eyes and a vulture's stare. Not such a turn on.

"Who the hell are you?" Logan shoved the chair out and rose, sinking into an aggressive stance.

The woman smiled in apparent amusement over his display. "I am Grimhild, the mother of the Ironwood coven."

"Yeah, you'd make the MILF list," Logan sneered.

A tic tugged at the corner of one eye. "There is no need for violence—or rudeness. This is merely a polite social call."

"Nothing I have to say to you is polite." A cold layer of fear ran beneath his white-hot anger. Coming here like this... Confronting him in his own home after what an Ironwood witch had done to him... to his mother. Grimhild must believe herself invincible.

"I understand your resentment. My daughter, Hrafnar, located you on her own and proceeded without consulting the coven. She may have mishandled communication with you."

"The harpy enslaved me and made me eat my mother." His lips curled back, revealing his teeth as he prepared to shift straight into his wolf form. In a heartbeat, he could clear the desk and bury his fangs in her long throat. Only caution kept him from taking the leap—his worst fear was losing mastery over himself again.

Grimhild pursed her ruby-red lips. "Mishandled may not be the right word."

"Garbage." Logan exhaled so his nostrils flared. "You must be feeling pretty desperate if you think it's necessary to open a dialogue with me."

"To the contrary, a dialogue has always been the preferable means of communication. Allow me to offer an apology for how Hrafnar mistreated you."

"I don't want your apologies. I want your head on a pike," Logan threw out the gibe, hoping to find the chink in her armor. He'd inherited his father's talent for taunting as well as deceit. What good was his disreputable heritage if he couldn't put those skills to good use?

Grimhild nodded. "Nevertheless, you have my sincerest apologies. Tell me what I can do to make the matter right."

"I want my mother back, bitch." Logan seethed. His temper roiled damn close to the boiling point. A reddish haze tinted his vision while the tactician in the back of his mind lodged a strong protest. The goal was to get under her skin—not to let her under his.

"That is beyond my abilities." Grimhild's unblinking gaze resembled nothing so much as that of a snake. Her cold, hard eyes contradicted her conciliatory tone.

"What do you want from me, Witch Hazel?"

She raised her hands in a grand gesture and spoke with absolute reverence. "The Ironwood coven desires only to serve you. *Sköll*—the Moon Snatcher."

Logan shuddered. Anxiety raked him over the proverbial coals, and it took everything he had to hide his reaction. "Serve me? What is it you think you have to offer?"

"Guidance. We are seers."

"I see just fine." He sneered, but his perspective took a sudden upturn into enlightenment. It occurred to him—Grimhild, the mother of the troll women was *here*, negotiating with *him*, which must mean they wanted something from him they couldn't take by force.

"We are guardians. We can assist in protecting those you hold dear. Your little pack... Victoria and your sweet baby sister." Grimhild smiled, the crocodile showing her teeth. The implicit threat was unmistakable.

"Listen up. Listen close." Crimson menace radiated from his eyes. He rumbled with warning, a snarl that originated in his chest and reverberated in his throat. "If anything—anything at all —happens to Vic or the baby, if so much as a hair on their heads is harmed, I'll make it my life's mission to hunt you and your sinister spawn. There won't be a hag with a drop of your blood left on this earth."

"I have no intention of harming your little pack." Grimhild paled and threw up her arms. The tantalizing allure of fear overtook the minty reek that clung to her. His wolf surged beneath his skin, howling for blood. It required all his control to circle the desk instead of bounding over it.

"If you do..." Logan left the threat hanging. Voracious hunger was the crazed beast that clawed at his ribcage and howled in his belly. With a moan, he parted his jaws. Not quite wide enough to swallow the moon, but a wicked witch would fit just fine in his belly.

"I hear and understand your threat. And this is my warning to you. I have taken Victoria's blood as insurance. If you act against us, I *will* retaliate." The witch halted and retreated no further, signaling to him that her initial reaction had been a reflexive reaction to a perceived threat. He needed to test that, however, to be sure.

"You're lying," Logan accused. Gods, let her be lying. He had no idea how Victoria's blood could be used to harm her. His imagination rushed straight to worst-case scenarios: a magically induced miscarriage or murder... He shook in the grip of fear and anger.

"I'm not. Do you recall Victoria's absence yesterday morning?"

"That was you?" Logan clamped down on homicidal rage and inched around the side of the desk. Cool headedness challenged him. His temper tended to get the better of him, but it seldom worked to his advantage.

"That was me. My magic is powerful. It allowed me to summon and imprison Victoria. She was nothing more than a puppet to my will." Grimhild nodded. Her flinty gaze followed his approach and stood her ground.

"Did you erase Vic's memories, too?" If the witch really did have Victoria bespelled... Everything Vic knew, Grimhild knew, too. *Holy cow.* Logan broke into a cold sweat recalling how close he'd come to revealing Thorn to Victoria. He thanked his lucky stars that he hadn't.

"Yes, and I considered killing her..."

"One hair," Logan said, holding up his index finger, "and I am your enemy until the end of time."

"Then Fortune has smiled upon me because I did not." Grimhild clicked her tongue against her palate. "Now that I understand how important the she-wolf and the baby are to you, I promise: no harm will come to them so long as you're willing to cooperate with us."

"First you want to serve me... now it's blackmail." Another

stride carried him near enough to reach out and touch Grimhild's arm. His hand tingled as it passed through empty air—an illusion.

Thorn lodged a sharp note of disappointment.

Grimhild acquired a smug edge at his failure. "An unfortunate circumstance, but I am a pragmatist. Believe me, this is not how it was meant to be. If your father hadn't stolen you from our care..."

"To hear my father tell it, you witches did the stealing..."

"The Ironwood coven has a divine duty given to us by the Norns to nurture and protect Hróðvitnir's twin sons."

"Twin?" Logan got stuck on the word. Did she mean...? Could it really be true?

"You have a brother," Grimhild said, nodding. "Tristan. He wishes nothing more than to be reunited with you."

"Then why isn't he here?" Logan staggered and caught himself on the edge of the desk. He'd read every bit of surviving Norse literature he could lay his hands on, and conversations with his father had prepared him for the possibility. But still... Knowledge of a theoretical twin and confirmation—those two things were worlds apart.

"Tristan is too important to risk." The witch smiled, confident she held the winning hand. "Believe me, he chaffs at the restrictions imposed upon him, but he understands it is for his own protection—"

"Does he?" Abruptly, Logan decided not to give his hypothetical brother any further credence. It might be a lie. Certainly, it was a distraction. This, however, could be the advantage he'd been looking for—a means of manipulating Grimhild.

"I can arrange for you to meet Tristan. You only have to agree to accompany me to the Ironwood." Grimhild tilted toward him, talking faster.

"Ironwood, Nevada?" Logan coached his manner to curiosity edged with caution. Not a difficult feat, since the feelings were genuine.

"Yes, it's less than an hour from here. If you come with me

now, you could spend several hours with your brother and be home before sunrise. No one would need to be any the wiser."

Logan suppressed a smile. Grimhild must believe him an absolute idiot to assume he'd fall for such a transparent ruse. But then, women did that with him a lot. Victoria had only just started to wise up.

"It's tempting..." He hesitated, playing through the motions of an internal struggle. Grimhild nodded in fervent encouragement. From the intensity on her face, she'd taken the bait. He delayed long enough for it to sink in. "But I can't. We're going to Arizona tomorrow to escort Alpha Finn to the moot."

"The moot?" Grimhild acquired an incredulous tone. He might as well have just declared himself committed to mowing the lawn.

"I'm Victoria's Valhalla-ordained champion—her knight in shining armor. If there's a challenge, I'll duel to defend her honor." Logan brandished a cocky grin and went all in. "Don't want to fuck that up. I'm finally making some headway toward getting her into bed."

"But your hand..." She glanced at his arm with marked concern. Interesting—the first mention she'd made of his recent disfigurement. And she hadn't acted surprised when she'd first appeared. It supported his theory that Grimhild had access to Victoria's awareness.

"Are you calling me a cripple?" He narrowed his eyes and lowered his voice, assuming the air of a hothead with an injured ego. The role came naturally, and the irony wasn't lost on him. Morena would've had a blast lampooning him if she'd been there.

Grimhild pulled herself straight and assumed a placating tone. "No, of course not. I'm only concerned that you could be hurt... or even killed."

"Then I die. I've died before. Valhalla is cool. The days are filled with fighting, the nights with feasting. All the booze and women a guy could ever want."

"Don't be daft." Grimhild oozed icy disdain. "Dying in battle doesn't assure you'll go to Valhalla. You must also be chosen. What are the odds they'll allow Loki's son to pass through the gates of Asgard, let alone dwell in Odin's hall, now that your paternity is known?"

"That's a good point, I suppose." He rubbed his chin.

"You can't fight a duel and expect to win."

"Cali said the exact same thing." He pretended to think on it, but the entirety of his attention centered on the witch—observing and measuring her reactions.

"The female hunter was correct," Grimhild said with earnest enthusiasm. "This injury is too severe, and too incapacitating. You haven't learned the fighting techniques necessary to compensate for it yet."

"Thanks for the vote of confidence..." Logan pouted and delayed three beats. She'd begin to suspect his obtuseness if he overplayed his hand. Loudly, he demanded, "Hey, how'd you know that? Have you got my house bugged?"

"Nothing so mundane." Grimhild raised her chin. "Magical scrying is far superior."

"Huh." He bounced on the balls of his feet, gyrating with frenetic energy. "Well, that sucks but my big sister is the goddess of death. I imagine if I go to Helheimr, I'll be okay."

"The goal is that you should not die at all. You have a great destiny to fulfill." Grimhild's lips curled. She stared down her nose and practically fossilized with contempt.

Logan smirked. "Destiny, schmestiny. I can't lose. I'm a god."

"You are an imbecile." Grimhild pulled back her severe lips, revealing clenched teeth. The skin on her face drew taut, and suddenly she looked a thousand years old.

"Maybe." He shrugged. "But what I'm not is a coward. If there's a challenge tomorrow, I intend to fight, and I intend to win."

"The matter is that important to you?"

"Yeah, it is." Logan thumped his chest He-Man style. "My father raised me in isolation. I'm sure you can guess why." He slanted a significant look. "This is my chance to make a name for myself."

"Fame is a worthy goal. I suppose having you establish yourself as a powerful leader would be a desirable outcome." Grimhild tilted her head. Her face worked as she struggled to come to grips with the whole thing. "And the coven has been concerned Victoria will succeed in renewing the alliance between the wolf packs and the hunters. What is your stance on the matter?"

"As you said, *Victoria* wants an alliance."

"There's no need to be coy with me. What do *you* want?"

"Are you kidding?" Logan scoffed. "I don't trust the hunters any further than I can throw one." He figured he could toss petite little Dixie quite a good distance. Of course, Crazy Cali would beat his ass afterward, but it'd be worth it.

"The hunters are a threat to your pack."

Logan snorted. Yeah, but the hunters weren't nearly as dangerous as the Ironwood Coven. "I'd just as soon punch Sawyer as look at him." Also true. "But Victoria insisted on keeping him around."

"Excellent job of wearing the pants."

"Mind your own damn business." Logan needed to determine whether his inherit talent for subterfuge extended to witches. He figured Grimhild must be as powerful as they came. If he could get a lie past her, then he could fool any member of the coven.

"You are my business." She crossed her arms over her chest.

He released a thin sigh. "Fine. You've finally said something I agree with. I'd love to be rid of Sawyer, preferably in the six-feet-under sense of the word. The guy is tougher than the Terminator, though. I could kill him, but he'd just come back, and he'd be pissed."

"The Barrett men are not indestructible. They have a fatal flaw..." Grimhild's eyes lit and she leaned toward him.

"What's that?" Logan inched closer to her, encouraging the atmosphere of collusion. Of course, Sawyer's fatal flaw intrigued Logan, but not as much as drawing the witch into collusion.

"His heart," she said with a wicked smile. "If you destroy his heart, the runic magic will be unable to resurrect him."

"That's interesting, but it doesn't do me any good to defeat Sawyer in combat if his soul winds up in Valhalla. I need for him to die anything *but* an honorable death, so he winds up in Helheimr."

"There's no returning from Helheimr," Grimhild drawled with canny insight.

"No, there's not. Of course, Victoria and the rest of the pack would have a fit. They'd try to stop me. If only there was some way to prevent them from interfering. And, of course, to replace their memories with some harmless, short-term amnesia..." He eyed her speculatively.

Grimhild fell into stoic silence. She brooded long enough that Logan became worried. Sweat beads formed on his brow. When he refused to wipe his forehead, perspiration stung his eyes.

"You're more diabolic than I expected." Grimhild frowned so her already hawkish features grew sharper.

Logan's heart stopped. Shit, she was on to him... He'd failed to convince her. He tensed, preparing for a magical assault.

"You're trying to manipulate me into offering to help you get rid of Sawyer Barrett. I must admit, I underestimated you."

"Oh, snap." He rolled his shoulders in a golly-gosh shrug. "You caught me."

"Such machinations, however, are unnecessary," Grimhild continued. "I have already stated I am prepared to take measures to do right by you as both restitution for Hrafnar's wrongdoing and to prove the worthiness of my coven as allies."

Logan nodded, pantomiming overeager agreement. Good—he had the stage set. The time had come to go all in. He asked, "Are you offering to help me murder Sawyer?"

"Yes."

"I want you to get the blood of Odin's son on your hands, so I don't wind up framed for acting alone."

"That would be a pleasure." Grimhild smiled like a drawn dagger.

"That means you have to show up in person. The real-life you. No illusions or minions. Help me kill Sawyer and manage the memories of my packmates, and you can consider our alliance a done deal."

"You're asking me to put myself at risk." She pursed her lips.

"No more than I'd be assuming."

"Prove to me you are telling the truth." Grimhild arched her fine brow.

"How the fuck am I supposed to do that? You're the powerful witch. Cast a truth spell. Read my mind like you did with Vic, and you'll see that I intend to honor the deal... Unless you can't?" Logan coached the taunt in a scathing tone.

Grimhild schooled her features to a stoic mask, but a tiny twitch at the corner of her eye betrayed her doubt. Ah-ha! Logan's wolf surged beneath his skin, thirsting for blood. He grew giddy with glee.

"Now you're screwing with me, aren't you?" Logan asked to give her a graceful out. Otherwise, he might be proven too clever for his own good.

"Yes, of course. I was 'screwing' with you. A small bit of payback." She laughed and smoothed her fingers over the snow-white fur that trimmed her cloak. "Now tell me, when and where will this murder transpire?"

"Tomorrow afternoon, after we return from Arizona with Finn and his people," Logan dictated. "The plan is that we'll drop them in Broken Bend and then come back to the house for a couple hours. Sawyer has to retrieve some enchanted horn thingamabob..."

"*Gnýrhorn?*" Grimhild asked.

"Yeah, that." Logan bobbed his head. "Sawyer told the leader of *Den Valgte* to have his followers assemble in Broken Bend at sundown to witness the summoning of the Wild Hunt."

"What will happen when he doesn't show?"

"I'll say he must've chickened out." Logan bared his teeth in a wolf's smile. "The hunters will lose face with the packs and *Den*

Valgte. It kills two birds with one stone. Vic will be upset for a while, but I'll be there to console her."

"An ingenuous plan." Grimhild regarded Logan with undisguised respect. "And then, afterward, you'll return with me to Ironwood to meet your brother and the rest of the coven."

"Absolutely, can't wait." Logan gloried in lying through his teeth. Damn, it felt good. At last he thought he understood his father. Maybe he'd judged his old man too harshly.

"We have a deal." Grimhild started to fade. She turned transparent. "Tomorrow afternoon when you return to the lake house, call my name, and I will be there."

"It'd be easier, and lot more subtle, to send a text. What's your mobile phone number?" Logan asked.

Grimhild sneered. "Those devices are responsible for rotting people's brains. The whole modern world shuffles about bent over them like zombies. It's revolting."

"I take it you don't own one?"

"I have no need. Magic is far superior." She turned her nose into the air and vanished—putting a period on the conversation.

"Good to know." Logan grinned to the nines.

CHAPTER 29

**_Kauno_: The Rune of Fire,
The Torch of Enlightenment**

THE FIRE CRACKLED and popped when Sawyer drove the iron poker into a smoldering log. He added a new piece of timber to the top. The older kindling settled, releasing a swarm of sparks. When the shower settled, _Kauno_—the torch of enlightenment— danced within the lively flames.

The rune's spontaneous appearance took Sawyer unprepared. Contemplatively, he settled on the pine stump that doubled as a seat and dropped the poker. He took a swig of his beer and then set it aside. A pair of unlikely gifts from his mother formed a pile at his feet. _Gnýrhorn,_ an ivory and tawny ram's horn, yellowed with the patina of age, rested atop _Kappiskjǫld_, the round shield. The two artifacts were a puzzle to be solved. It annoyed Sawyer that neither of his parents possessed the capacity to deliver a straightforward message free of guesswork or hidden meanings.

Bending, he lifted the horn and stroked his fingers across the glossy bone. A tarnished brass mouthpiece fitted to the narrow end. Sawyer held the horn aloft, caressing the growth striations with his bare fingers, and slowly turned it for inspection. Despite its impressive heft, he found it difficult to believe the instrument could summon the Wild Hunt.

If everything proceeded according to plan, tomorrow night the heathen followers of *Den Valgte* and the wolves of the White Mountains Tribe would assemble in Broken Bend. Sawyer intended to blow the horn and summon the Asgårdsreien. Odin's ferocious mounted cavalry would descend from the sky and sweep Sawyer up. He would ride with them for the next month... or for the rest of eternity, however long that lasted. Initially, the ordeal had filled him with fear, but the longer he contemplated, the righter it seemed. In his gut, Sawyer had always known he would ride with the Wild Hunt someday. A harrowing trial and maybe, the ultimate sacrifice... Given the choice, he made it willingly. At least he could be assured that no innocents would be swept up in the Hunt. *Gnýrhorn's* power would keep the Wild Hunt tied to the road he called it from.

The truth throbbed in his bones—the Wild Hunt was his destiny.

Heavy footsteps ascended the hillside, crunching dry pine needles and earth. A single person coming toward the camp. Sawyer set the horn aside and picked up his rifle. He expected a member of the pack was coming to visit, but he subscribed to the policy of better safe than sorry.

The pack bond resonated with an unmistakable presence—Logan. The male wolf had a psychic signature like an eclipse; he swallowed up the surrounding light. Even though the male werewolf's lumbering approach had to be deliberate, Sawyer's combat reflexes kicked it to the next level. He tightened his grip on the rifle, shifting it to a ready position, and waited.

A tall, lanky figure manifested at the edge of the tree line. Logan halted and settled into a wary stance with his head low. His eyes strobed deep amber and faded to glowing coals. He kept his injured arm tucked behind his body, shielding it.

Unwilling sympathy stabbed at Sawyer. He didn't want to feel sorry for Logan. The guy was an outright asshole—an angry puppy with a deadly bite. He'd been hostile since the moment they'd met. Although, to be fair, Sawyer had riddled the werewolf full of bullets, but Logan had been asking for it.

They stared in tense, distrustful silence. Without Cali or a common enemy to serve as a distraction, their mutual hostility took precedence.

Logan cleared his throat. "I'm not here to fight."

"No? What do you want then?" Sawyer supposed one concession warranted another. He raised the rifle, so the muzzle pointed at the sky.

"I've got something for you." Logan displayed a clunky black handset.

"A walkie-talkie?" Sawyer cocked his head and raised an open hand.

"Satellite phone. It cost an—" Logan coughed, cutting off the cliché that probably hit too close to home for his comfort. "I don't want to toss it. Not with you standing next to the fire."

Sawyer huffed. "I played center field for MIT."

"The MIT *Engineers*? Oh, that's impressive!" Logan dissolved into snorting laughter. "Well, then. *Here.*" He swung his arm in an underhanded pitch and tossed the device in a fat, slow arc that would've been perfect for T-ball.

Sawyer threw out his hand and caught it. It grated on his nerves that there was no opportunity to show off. A kindergartener could've made the catch. No, he deemed it better to ignore the slight than to rise to the bait. Instead, he glanced down to inspect the sat phone, which was larger and heavier than a smart phone.

"It's got coverage everywhere on Earth," Logan explained. "That's Midgard to you, Aesir, huh?"

"Funny." Sawyer bared his teeth. "I've never been to Asgard. I was born here."

"Kudos for you. Here's the power supply, a spare battery pack, and a solar charger." Logan shrugged a carrycase off his shoulder and slung it toward Sawyer, who snagged the loose strap.

"What's this for?" Sawyer asked, returning his wary attention to the werewolf. He wasn't sure what to make of the gift, so he kept his guard up. Grudgingly, he conceded improved communications was a damn good idea, especially in light of the recent invasion.

"Staying in touch." Logan implied the "Duh" with his tone. "I've got one for Kinkaid, too. I'll get it set up tomorrow."

"I'm sure Cali will appreciate that." It stuck in his throat, but Sawyer managed to force out, "Thanks."

Mercifully, Logan ignored Sawyer's stunted expression of appreciation. The werewolf extracted an identical sat phone from his pocket. His thumb worked over the screen in a typing pattern. "I've already tested the voice-calling feature. I'm sending you a text. Let me know if you get it."

"All right." Sawyer didn't envision doing a lot of texting with Logan, but he bit his tongue. After a minute of playing with the interface, he got the text app open and discovered a text waiting for him.

Logan: *We have a big problem. Don't say anything. Just text. They're listening.*

Adrenaline surged; a jolt coursed along Sawyer's spine. He jerked his head up, nailing Logan with a sharp glance. The werewolf shook his head and mouthed one word: "Text."

Sawyer bent over the sat phone and struggled with the tiny digital keyboard that was far too small for his thumbs. But finally, he hit send. *Who is listening?*

Aloud, Sawyer asked, "Did you get that?"

"Yep." Logan leveled a deadly serious stare at the hunter. "I'm heading back to the house. G'night."

"Night."

Logan left. Sawyer returned to his seat beside the fire and hunched over the phone, waiting in pensive expectation. Thankfully, it took less than a minute before the next text came through.

Logan: *Witches.*

Sawyer: *Witches?*

Logan: *The Ironwood witches. Grimhild, the grand witch-bitch of all time, dropped by for a chat.*

Sawyer hesitated, stroking his thumb across his index finger while he considered. He didn't know about a Grimhild, but his knowledge of the Ironwood coven went beyond what was covered in most books. Reputedly, the troll women raised the giant wolves that would consume the sun and moon... the festive beginning of Ragnarök, the doom of the gods. In the same era, the prophecies said the monstrous wolf Fenrir would break free of his bonds and destroy Odin. Sawyer understood why his old man harbored so many reservations about Loki's wolf-shifter children. No doubt, a great many Asgardians felt the same. Leaden fear settled in Sawyer's gut for the pack he'd adopted. He worried about his ability to protect them from his own people.

Logan: *You still there?*

Sawyer: *Yeah. What did this Grimhild want?*

Logan: *To control me, your head on a platter, the end of the world. Take your pick.*

Sawyer worked his jaws. *That's quite a list.*

Logan: *What can I say? She had ambitions. Not your typical slacker witch who only wants to lure fat children for home-cooked meals.*

Seconds ticked past.

Logan: *I need your help.*

Sawyer: *I'm not sticking my neck out, so you can chop my head off. Sorry, not happening.*

Logan: *Don't be a douche. This is serious. The witch has control of Vic.*

Sawyer sat straighter, muscles bunching. Disbelief defined his initial reaction, but then the vivid memory of Victoria-the-Stranger pushed into his mind. At the jail—that eerie blue glow and her impassive whisper. *"Sawyer, you have to kill Sylvie."* It made possession sound reasonable... even preferable to the alternative.

Sawyer: *You should've led with that.*

Logan: *Yeah, sorry. I never know how to open these sorts of convos. Hey, how're you doing? Seems trite. Whereas, wanna help me kill a witch—*

Sawyer: *Sure.*

Logan: *That was easier than I expected.*

Sawyer: *You said she's a threat to Victoria. She has to die.*

Logan: *We agree on one thing.*

Sawyer: *Tell me more about Grimhild.*

A lengthy delay ensued. Sawyer sweated bullets while he waited. With each passing second, more doubts assailed him, fueling his innate suspicion. He didn't trust Logan, but he had no choice other than to hear the guy out.

Logan: *K, Grimhild. She showed up in my Dad's study about an hour ago. Before you ask, yes, I tried to kill her. I failed. She was using an illusion. My hand passed right through her. Grimmy is using Vic as her eyes and ears and can puppet master her. I believe her 'cause she knew things that only Vic would know.*

Sawyer's hand flexed, clenching on reflex. From the muddled depths of his psyche, something green and mean reared its ugly head. He wanted to demand an accounting of the secrets Logan and Victoria shared. It required an active effort to let it pass.

Logan: *Grimhild threatened to hurt Vic and the baby and the rest of the pack if I refuse to cooperate. She came to negotiate, but the only reason she asked for my cooperation was because she couldn't force it. I've learned to resist their mind-magic.*

Sawyer: *What does she want you to do?*

Logan: *Eat the moon.*

Sawyer delayed his response. Whatever he'd been expecting... whatever he'd known... *this* wasn't it. Regardless of what the legends and lore said, the whole thing sounded absurd. Yet a niggling uncertainty gnawed at him. Gods, giants, magic, and witches were real... so why not a giant moon-munching mutt? At the same time, Logan's casual information dump fed Sawyer's mistrust. The embers flared to flames. But—to be fair—Sawyer would've been suspicious if Logan had withheld information. Either way, there was no winning. The hunter supposed he ought to at least give the wolf-shifter credit for being upfront.

Logan texted into the silence: *Yeah, that was my reaction.*

Sawyer: *She thinks you're Hati?*

Logan: *She called me Sköll. But yeah, close enough.*

Sawyer typed, "And you're cool with just telling me this? Do you know who I am?" Staring at the words on the screen, he endured second thoughts. Besides sounding as pompous as all fuck, the question opened him up to countless snide remarks. Logan lampooned the hunter often enough without being handed new material.

Sawyer hit delete and started over. *I should contact my father.*

Logan: *Yeah, that's great. Go running to daddy.*

Fuck you. Sawyer clenched his jaws. He moved his thumb to close the text app when another message popped up.

Logan: *Did I hit a nerve, big man?*

Sawyer tapped his thumb on the edge of the phone. The whole conversation from the Ironwood witch threat to the revelation of Logan's supposed destiny was like wading through a bog. Each step carried him deeper into the quagmire which was already too thick to escape.

Logan: *Look, if you call Jake and the freaking Hunter King comes roaring into town, Grimhild will scurry back under whatever rock she crawled out from under. We'll miss our chance and she'll come at us again. Whenever and however she wants.*

As much as Sawyer hated to admit it, Logan was right. From a strategic perspective, they had to assess the imminent threat—Grimhild—and come up with a plan for eliminating the witch. There was no room in the equation for ego.

Logan: *Are you still there, man? Stop being such a pussy.*

Sawyer: *We can't pull anyone else in. We take care of this and kill her ourselves.*

Logan: *Yeah.*

Sawyer stroked his upper lip, smoothing his mustache. *Do you have a plan?*

Logan: *As a matter of fact...*

Sawyer snorted. *Yeah, I suspected.*

Logan: *After we get back from Arizona, I told Grimhild I'd call for her help. She's supposed to kill you. To do that—*

Sawyer: *Why?*

Logan: *She'll have to appear in person. Why what?*

Sawyer: *Why after we get back from Arizona?*

Sawyer: *And why is she supposed to kill me? Not you?*

Logan: *Because that's what I told her.*

Sawyer: *Yeah, but why then? You could call her and we could deal with this now.*

Logan: *Look, asshole.*

Sawyer smirked, badly tempted to taunt the big wolf by asking if he'd hit a nerve. Instead, he texted: *What guarantee is there she won't use another illusion?*

Logan: *A, I told her after we get back from Arizona to stall while I come up with a plan. I was making shit up to buy time. If I change things for no reason, she'll get suspicious.*

Sawyer: *K.*

Sawyer nodded to himself. So far as reasons went, it made sense. For someone "making shit up", Logan seemed to possess an uncanny grasp of the intricacies of his tangled web. *That* revived Sawyer's reservations all over again. Was he being lured into a trap?

Logan: *B, I can't guarantee anything. I believe she'll want to kill you in person.*

Sawyer: *Why's that?*

Logan: *She's a blowhard egomaniac. You know the type.*

Sawyer grinned in appreciation. *So you're hoping.*

Logan: *Yeah, I'm hoping. I don't have any way to tell what's illusion from what's real. Do you?*

Sawyer: *No.*

Logan: *Can an illusion even hurt anyone? It's all smoke and mirrors, right?*

Sawyer: *I don't know.*

Logan: *Well, you know as much as I do.*

Sawyer: Next to nothing.

Logan: Sounds like we're ready. I have a dagger, Thorn, that will kill anything so long as you score a direct blow to the heart. Since that's supposedly the only way to kill a Norn anyway, it should work.

Sawyer dropped his hand to the stock of his rifle. He raised his head, scanning the nighttime forest for any lurking menace. Right up until then, the hunter had kept his paranoia under wraps, but a sudden deluge broke the dam. Logan just *happened* to have a magical dagger designed to exploit Sawyer's fatal flaw—too much of a coincidence to be believed.

Logan: I'll give Thorn to you before I call Grimhild. Are you still there?

Sawyer: *So, I'm supposed to stand there with a magic dagger in my hand, and what? Here kitty kitty?*

Logan: *No, shithead. Thorn becomes a tattoo until she's called.*

Sawyer: *Your whole plan is full of holes.*

Logan: *I'm not done but if you've got a better idea, let's hear it.*

Sawyer rubbed his chin, thinking. He had lots of ideas, which all involved contacting his family or fellow hunters for assistance. Considering their self-imposed restriction—not to do or say anything that would alert either Victoria or the witch—he didn't have many viable options.

Logan: *We need a diversion. Something to keep Grimmy distracted so she doesn't see the dagger coming until it's too late.*

Sawyer: *That's easy enough. We start a fight.*

Logan: *It needs to be more staged than just that. It has to look like I'm betraying you. After we get back from Arizona, I'll trade you Thorn for one of your guns. I shoot you and shout to Grimhild to come out to finish you off.*

Sawyer stiffened. Paranoia reared its head and howled at the moon. He jerked his chin. *No fucking way.*

Logan: *Don't be a baby. Getting shot won't kill you. It's easy and impersonal—*

Sawyer shook his head in disgust. Only someone unfamiliar with firearms could call shooting another person impersonal. It was the most intimate of acts.

Logan: *I won't aim for your heart.*

Any residual doubt the hunter harbored vanished —Logan knew.

Sawyer: *How do I know I can trust you? This could be a setup.*

Logan: *It could be. If I planned to betray you, this is how I'd do it.*

Sawyer: *Not reassuring.*

Logan: *What the fuck do you want me to say?*

Sawyer: *Give me one reason to believe you.*

Logan: *I'll give you seven. Vic, Morena, Sylvie, the wolves. For me, eight. My sister is in danger, too.*

Sawyer waged an internal struggle, torn between faith and doubt. Those were damn good reasons, but still.

Logan: *Look, I'd do anything to protect the people I love. But if that's not enough, trust that I hate the Ironwood coven way worse than I hate you.*

Sawyer: *?*

During the ensuing delay, Sawyer came close to concluding the conversation was over. When push came to shove, he and Logan were too damn different to ever be real allies.

Logan: *When I was 18, a witch possessed me and forced me to murder my mother. I ate her.*

"Fuck." Sawyer winced. Sickness and sympathy swirled in his stomach. He'd heard rumors and done research into Logan's past, but the official records listed a bear attack as Lori Koenig's cause of death.

Logan: *That's my worst secret. The last thing I ever wanted you to know. But you have to understand that I'm highly motivated to destroy Grimhild and the rest of her fucking coven.*

Highly motivated. Sawyer swallowed a snort.

Logan: *Do you think I like handing Thorn over to you? I've got no guarantee you'll give her back.*

Sawyer: *You have my word. I don't want your damn dagger.*

Logan: *And you have my word that I won't betray you.*

Sawyer hated the whole situation but he didn't see any other way. *Fine, I'll trade my gun for your dagger. What are we going to fight over?*

Logan: *What do we usually fight over? Don't overthink it.*

Sawyer: *We're in no danger of that.*

CHAPTER 30

Freya: The Goddess of Love and War

Monday Morning...

Hot summer mornings—a time and a mood well suited to sitting and fermenting. Sylvie wiped sweat from her brow and squinted, glancing up at the shining brightness. Rather peevishly, she wondered if Suni, the sun goddess, ever had crappy moments when she just didn't want to rise and shine. Luckily for everyone, the goddess never smirched her sacred duties. Without fail, Suni guided her golden chariot along its designated course through the sky. Nothing short of the great wolf Hati could keep her from her calling.

Sylvie vowed to be like Suni, a source of light and inspiration.

The stag lay on his side, motionless except for the rapid rise and fall of his torso. A final heroic effort drove him to raise his head. When he thrashed, his antlers clattered against the flat-topped boulder. Broken bones of the earth—jagged protrusions of rock—jutted from the mountainside. A swift creek, swollen with runoff, marked its base and the end of the field.

"Shh. You are not the only one who is tired, my friend. You led us on a merry chase," Sylvie said in a soft tone. She stroked her hand over the deer's throat until he subsided again. His strong heart throbbed beneath his tawny hide. She smiled in approval. He had the weight and antler rack of a mature buck: a fine specimen. He'd make a worthy sacrifice. No part of the animal would go to waste: his blood spilled in Freya's name; his flesh butchered to feed the pack.

Bending, Sylvie double-checked the bindings that secured his rear legs. Beneath her touch, the buck quivered, perhaps sensing the wolf that lurked beneath her human skin. The heady scent of fear whet her hunger, but she derived no pleasure from his suffering.

"How long is this going to take?" Morena demanded, bouncing on the balls of her feet. The teenager bustled with frantic energy. Morena belonged to the high school cross-country team. The long, hard hunt to capture the buck had been the equivalent of a warmup workout to the girl.

"It will take as long as is required to perform the ritual properly." Back stiff, bones creaking, Sylvie straightened. When she considered the teenager's energy, envy pinched her insides. Oh, to be young again...

"Yes, of course, but how long is that approximately?"

"It depends."

"No clue?"

"If you have somewhere else you'd rather be, you're free to leave. I'm perfectly capable of completing this alone." Sylvie narrowed her eyes in stern reprimand, a reminder that Morena had begged to accompany her.

Under scrutiny, Morena stilled, ceasing her restless fidgeting. The teen's face underwent the contortions of indecision. After a time, she jutted her lower lip and declared, "I'll stay."

"Good. Fetch me the sacrificial knife." Sylvie jerked her chin to where they'd stashed their packs before undertaking the hunt and capture of the stag.

"We've been gone a long time."

"It hasn't been that long."

"It's been hours." Morena marched off.

Sylvie glanced skyward. Talk of time brought the passage of it to the forefront of her awareness. Based on Suni's position, Sylvie put the time around eight-thirty or so. It'd taken an hour to hike north from the lake house into Desolation Wilderness. Capturing the stag alive had consumed another three. They still needed to perform the ritual and then undertake the return trip... Morena had the right of it—they'd been gone quite a while.

"Are you worried?" Sylvie asked.

"No, are you?" Morena's voice emerged muffled as she bent over their backpacks, rummaging through the contents.

"No, of course not."

Morena stayed silent then burst out, "It's just Sawyer, Logan, and Victoria are leaving for Arizona in a couple hours."

"We have plenty of time to make it back before they leave. Besides, Cali is there. She'll watch over the wolves."

"Okay, if you say so."

"I do," Sylvie said, addressing her adopted daughter's doubts as well as her own. Inevitably, her thoughts turned to her conversation with Finn. The bite of guilt troubled her like the persistent, itchy mark of a mosquito. She had no idea when the little bloodsucker had struck, only suffered the legacy of its visit.

Doubt weighed on Sylvie. She tried to reassure herself. She'd done the right thing in warning Finn. It wasn't a betrayal. Victoria had strayed from the true path. Her mistakes were terrible and sweeping, but Sylvie refused to believe her alpha was beyond redemption. Victoria simply needed to be shown the error of her ways. She could be redeemed.

"Here you go." Morena returned, carrying the knife as well as the hewn maple bowl that completed the ceremonial set. Sylvie had forgotten to mention the vessel, but the teenager had anticipated her needs. Quiet pride filled the skald for her pupil's accomplishment. Someday, Morena would be a worthy successor to her teacher.

"Thank you," Sylvie said, accepting the implements. Like the matching bowl, the knife had a maple handle engraved with inlays of copper and red jasper to form a bind rune. The blade was composed of tempered blue steel. It possessed no magical properties, but served its function well.

She inspected the makeshift altar one last time; everything was in its proper place. For Morena's instruction, she explained aloud, "As we begin, we must offer our thanks to the spirit of the stag to be sacrificed to Freya."

"Why?" The word burst from Morena, but she didn't finish the question. The teenager averted her gaze and bit her lower lip.

"What is it you wish to ask?" Sylvie asked, wondering at the teenager's reaction. The interruption pricked her patience, but also piqued her curiosity.

Morena grimaced. "Nothing, I'm sorry for interrupting."

"Did it pertain to the ritual?"

"Yes, but it's not important. It's probably inappropriate."

"Why don't you leave it to me to determine what's pertinent?" Sylvie flared her nostrils. Her frustration mounted as the teen's evasion wore on her nerves.

"Okay, fine. Just remember, I didn't want to say it." Morena fixed her stare on Sylvie's face.

"Spit it out, child."

"Why are we making the sacrifice to Freya? She didn't ever listen to anyone but Victoria, and now that's past, too. I've tried praying to her for years, and she's never answered. Not even once." Morena spread her hands in a gesture midway between defiance and doubt.

Sylvie felt her jaw drop. Her mouth hung, empty of answers, and her breath vacated her lungs in a great gust. She couldn't believe her ears.

Into the void of silence, Morena prattled on. "I've experimented. I struck out with Heimdallr and Thor—nada. Frigg sent rain once when I asked for a storm. I called Odin once, and he picked up the phone."

"Morena!" Scandalized, Sylvie gasped her outrage. Her mind spun, and she wondered how long Morena had known Jake Barrett's secret. But then in retrospect, maybe her surprise was unwarranted.

"Sorry, I was just joking." The teen gave a swift shrug.

"Well, that wasn't funny!"

"Sorry. All I mean is... we worship *all* the Aesir gods and goddesses, right?"

"That is true." Sylvie agreed with more misgivings than she could count.

"Are we supposed to worship Sawyer?"

Sylvie almost swallowed her tongue. She chose her answer with great care. "I suppose some might, but it'd be unwise. Jake Barrett chose to raise his sons as men. It isn't our place to second-guess or circumvent that."

Morena snorted. "I wouldn't. His head is already big enough."

"Just so." Sylvie smiled despite the seriousness.

"But still, what about the other gods. Do we have to make this sacrifice to Freya? I don't mean any disrespect. I've tried to worship the goddess to please you and Victoria, but it doesn't work for me. Freya's not my patron god."

God—an accidental slip? Or had the girl done it on purpose to test the waters. If so, why had she withheld the god's name?

Gooseflesh rose on the back of Sylvie's neck. She shuddered, and cold sweat poured down her back—all for reasons that defied her understanding. Morena's denouncement hurt to hear. Sylvie had harbored so many aspirations for the girl. Of course, she possessed the self-awareness necessary to recognize how terribly selfish and unfair she was being.

For Morena's sake, Sylvie strove to hide her vast disappointment. "You're not required to worship Freya."

"I'm not?" Morena asked with wide eyes bright with relief.

"No, of course not. You're free to worship as you choose." Sylvie tasted bitterness unlike any she'd ever known. When Morena opened her mouth, the skald held up a hasty hand. "However, since I am making this sacrifice, this is my choice, and I choose Freya."

"Okay." Morena swallowed whatever else she'd been about to say. Her throat worked like a snake downing an egg. She stood rigid with her hands clenched at her sides.

A great and terrible rift divided them.

"Would you like to go?" Sylvie strangled on the question. The back of her throat was raw and scratchy.

"Yes." Morena jerked her head.

"Go." Sylvie gestured and Morena took off like a shot.

Devastated, Sylvie wrapped her arms about herself. She labored for each breath and her chest ached. First Victoria and now Morena... How could she have gone so wrong with her adopted daughters—twice?

CHAPTER 31

***Geirolf*: The Wolf-Spears**

WHITERIVER, *Arizona*

With distinct pleasure, Victoria breathed in deep, filling her lungs. She loved the scent of the desert right after it rained. A strong, musty odor permeated the air along with just a hint of moisture. It was funny, because she tended to think she didn't miss much about Arizona. She preferred cold to heat and forest to desert, but still there were things she missed—the spectacular sunsets and the vast vistas, and the fierce summer storms that were more about wind and lightning arcs than precipitation.

"What's dat smell?" Logan asked, wheezing through his runny nose. His eyes were red-rimmed and watery.

"Creosote." Victoria hid her smile and pointed out one of the rugged bushes growing on the shoulder of the road. It bore distinctive five-petal yellow flowers. "The scent is most noticeable after it rains."

"I hate it." Logan punctuated with another gusty sneeze,

turning his face aside so he wasn't spewing all over her. Instead, he almost nailed Sawyer with a full blast of snot discharge.

"Watch it!" Sawyer evaded, taking a deft step to the side.

"You watch it, jackass," Logan muttered.

"Put a cork in it, both of you." Victoria's ire bounced between the two men.

Logan snorted. "He started it."

"If I throw a stick, will you just leave?" Sawyer shot back. The hunter got in the last word because Logan succumbed to another sneezing fit.

Victoria swallowed a giggle and patted Logan's arm. Poor guy —even his insults were lame today. Sympathy twisted a dagger in her gut. He was still in pain, and trying to hide it. She didn't want to feel sorry for him, but she couldn't help herself. It hurt to witness his suffering.

Their journey on Bifröst had been taken less than an hour. It picked them up in Sierra Pines and deposited them hundreds of miles away in Whiteriver, Arizona. When they stepped off the deck of the rainbow bridge into a community park, an unexpected sight awaited them. The entire White Mountains Tribe had gathered to greet them. Hundreds of men, women, and children. Wolf-shifters, but also human and wolf blood kin.

Alpha Finn presided over it all from a lawn chair throne with his royal court. Finn was a giant, his flame-hued hair a beacon. He wore only trousers and boots. Intricate tattoos covered his bare flesh, including one of *Mjölnir*, Thor's hammer, on his bicep. Finn often boasted his patrilineal line was descended from Thor, the Norse god of thunder, and no one dared challenge him on it. In his wolf form, Finn's fur was bright red, hence, his nickname —Fireball.

"I'm starting to feel like a circus freak. Are they charging admission?" Logan asked from the side of his mouth. Ever restless, he balanced on the balls of his feet and churned his arms. Victoria worried about his ridiculous hyperactivity. He ought to be conserving his energy, not wasting it.

"You'd make a great sideshow attraction," Sawyer weighed in. The hunter had come armed to the teeth. He carried his standard arsenal of knives and firearms. In addition, he wore the red and black round shield strapped across his back. When pressed, Sawyer had provided a curt explanation—"I'm supposed to take it with me to Arizona"—and then refused to say anything more.

"Don't let it get to you." Victoria shot a dirty look at Sawyer, who smirked. She continued, "It's a power play. Finn likes to keep everyone off-balance. My father used to say, 'Finn conducts all conspiracies in the open. It insulates him against charges and confounds the natural schemers who are certain he must be up to something... but can never prove it.'"

Sawyer chuckled in a way that suggested some inside joke.

"Have you got something to add?" Victoria asked.

The hunter opened his mouth, but then hesitated.

"Go on, spit it out." She cocked her head, daring Sawyer with a look.

"I'll tell you later." Sawyer sealed smiling lips.

Victoria's fingers twitched. Curiosity ate at her. She considered pursuing the matter, but then Logan stiffened, staring into the distance.

"Who's that with Finn?" Logan asked.

Victoria followed his gaze—casually, so she wasn't staring. A slender, dark-haired Native American woman was engaged in an intense discussion with Finn. A small child with an intense shock of red hair played at her feet.

"That's Ekta," Victoria said, identifying the woman, "one of Finn's four wives, who are also sisters. I believe Ekta is the eldest."

"Whoa!" Logan bellowed, attracting unnecessary attention. "Four? You're kidding."

"I'm not." Victoria scowled and tightened her grip. It took everything she had not to lecture him again on restraint and respect.

"Four sister-wives. That must be one helluva story." Logan knit his brow but at least he lowered his voice.

"It is, but for another time," Victoria said. "Ekta and her sisters are powerful women from an influential family. They're also Tarak's cousins."

"Tarak is the beta," Logan said, nodding. Prior to their arrival, Victoria had drilled him on the Who's Who of the White Mountains Tribe, and the basics of etiquette. Unfortunately, they hadn't had time to cover everything.

"That's right." In private, she'd warned Logan of the animosity that existed between Finn and Tarak. The two men disliked one another, but a complicated web of familial relationships kept their hostility in check.

"And who's the weasel?" Logan tipped his head toward the gaunt, tall man covered in burn scars who skulked at the periphery of Finn's entourage.

Victoria swallowed rude laughter.

"Bodaway," Sawyer supplied. "He's a priest of Heimdallr."

"He's widely despised, even by his own family," Victoria whispered, taking care not to be overheard.

"Yeah? What'd he do?" Logan asked.

"I'll tell you the whole thing later, but not now. It's a long, sordid story." Victoria waved her hand in dismissal.

Movement in the sky caught her attention. She tilted her head back, following the swift path of a low-flying raven. The bird circled as though looking for a place to land. Victoria surveyed the area and confirmed a distinct dearth of good perches. She took its appearance as a matter of fact. *Of course, Odin was watching.* In contrast, she supposed Sylvie, if she'd been present, would've interpreted it as an omen.

"You're worried about why Finn has called a gathering, aren't you?" Logan asked in a low voice, speaking directly into her ear.

She started, performed a double take, and stared at him suspiciously. "Are you a mind reader, too?"

"Nah." Logan chuckled. "You wear your thoughts on your face."

"I need to work on that." She hesitated before she added, "I'm concerned. He's delaying us, but hasn't offered an explanation other than to say we're waiting for someone."

"Maybe it's time to ask." Sawyer tilted his head back, also following the aerial dance of the lone raven.

"You're right. I'm going to do that." Victoria latched onto the suggestion which had been at the top of her thoughts anyway. She squared her shoulders and undertook a determined march across the open expanse toward Finn. Locked and loaded, and ready for action...

Through the bond, she sensed Sawyer and Logan exchange some mercurial communication. She didn't look back. The men flanked and followed her. It astonished her how swiftly they set aside their differences when circumstances required it.

Miracles were real.

At their approach, Finn rose to welcome them. Ekta remained at his side, silent but keenly observant.

"Welcome Alpha Storm. Do you need something?" Finn asked.

Victoria got whiplash tilting back her head so she could meet Finn's gaze. Ratatoskr's nuts! The man towered over her like a redwood beside a sapling. Lucky for her, she'd gone toe-to-toe with greater men than the White Mountains Alpha. Having stared into the true face of Wodan, Victoria found very little intimidated her anymore.

"Alpha Finn, as I have said before, there is an important matter I wish to discuss with you. Then we must be underway. I've arranged for you and your entourage to travel on Bifröst, but I expected you to be ready. I must return to Sierra Pines."

"I have a good reason for the delay." Finn narrowed his eyes, a clear signal that he disliked being challenged. He worked his jaws —another sign of danger.

"Which is?" Victoria demanded.

"Seamus, perhaps it would placate Alpha Storm to know why she's being asked to wait," Ekta said in a smooth voice. She rested a hand on her husband's arm.

Finn swayed toward his wife. His regard softened. "My mate is wise," he said with a slight smile. He stood tall and proud, shoulders squared, and crossed his arms over his barrel torso—a man as immovable as a mountain. To Victoria, he said, "We are delayed because we are awaiting the arrival of my blood brother. I sent for him yesterday."

"Oh?" Victoria cocked her head and kept a tight rein on her impatience. She expected Finn to play coy and cunning. A wolf, in a word, couldn't change his color.

"Let's speak in private." Finn drew Victoria aside—away from prying ears. Ekta, Logan, and Sawyer joined them. The White Mountains Alpha narrowed his eyes. "Yesterday, I received a rather ominous warning regarding the moot."

"You did?" Victoria schooled her demeanor to a respectful inquiry, but her nerves crawled like a swarm of fire ants. Her gut warned to prepare for badness.

"Your skald called me yesterday afternoon." Finn spoke in a low-pitched voice for her ears only. "She shared a great many troubling concerns with me."

"I see." Victoria clenched his jaws and stiffened. Sylvie's betrayal hurt Victoria to the core, but she wasn't surprised. "Let me guess. She told you of her runic divination regarding the moot, and then questioned my judgement and urged you to withdraw your support."

"That about covers it." Finn smiled, showing teeth. "I see you are familiar with your skald's opinions."

"Painfully," she grated out.

He snorted. "For the record, I have kept the matter to myself."

"I thank you for your discretion." Victoria stood as straight and stiff as a ramrod. Her pride was in tatters; she burned with humiliation.

"I'm familiar with what it means to have dissension within your own house." Finn turned his head, leveling a dark glance at the distant horizon. Then he returned his focus to her and narrowed his eyes. "So, tell me, how much credence should I give your skald's vision? Do you have a good reason for disregarding her warning, Alpha Storm?"

Victoria drew a sharp breath, so her nostrils flared. "Alpha Finn, are you familiar with Jake Barrett?"

"Oh, indeed." His eyes widened. Laughter in his voice, he echoed Victoria's sarcasm of moments before, "Painfully."

"Jake is number three on my speed dial. His son is standing behind me, looking over my shoulder." She jerked her chin. "Do you see him?"

Finn's gaze lifted, following her direction. "I see."

"Do you honor our gods?"

He narrowed his gaze dangerously. "You question my honor?"

Victoria bared her teeth. "You've questioned mine. I am Odin's priestess."

Finn took a step back. He stared in open astonishment. Sawyer edged closer; his heat warmed her skin. His presence was unmissable—comforting to her, and—she imagined—menacing to others.

"I am Odin's priestess," Victoria repeated. It shocked her how easily the declaration rolled off her tongue. After all those months of agonizing and denial, she judged it past time to finally acknowledge the truth. "The moot will convene on the night of the Full Mead Moon. Whether your pack attends, Alpha Finn, is up to you. Let me know if I'm wasting my time here, and I'll be on my way."

Finn opened his mouth. Quiet resounded—an executioner's axe poised to drop. Before he spoke, the faint but distinct whir of a small plane emerged from the distance. Victoria released a held breath. She turned to gaze east with the others. Initially, the airplane appeared tiny, but it grew larger as it drew nearer. The whine of the engine increased until it passed overhead, descending with its landing gear lowered. It landed on a cleared field on the far side of the park.

"Hail, Thor! He's here!" Finn's excited shout broke the stillness. Motion erupted—conversations resumed, and a group of White Mountains warriors headed to greet the plane.

"Thor's on a plane?" Logan asked, drawing a disgusted look from Sawyer.

"Hilarious!" Finn walloped Logan on the shoulder and almost knocked him off his feet. Chuckling, Finn assumed the lead. "Come! I will introduce you to my blood brother, MacTavish. He is the Alpha of Geirolf."

∾

A DIRT LOT served as a makeshift airstrip. Onlookers gathered at a safe distance while it taxied to a halt. Even as the plane's engine died, it kicked up thick clouds of dirt into the air. Victoria found herself caught up in the buzz of excitement that hung over the crowd.

Logan's breath tickled the inside of her ear. "Do you know who the hell this MacTavish is, or what's the big deal with Geirolf?"

"Geirolf means wolf spear. It's an old and distinguished pack that traces its ancestry back to Fenrir. When all the other wolf-shifter tribes were driven out of the old Norselands, Geirolf stayed behind. They chose to fight rather than surrender their ancestral territory." Victoria nudged Sawyer. "Do you know anything else?"

"I'm clueless." Sawyer shrugged.

"At least you understand your limitations," Logan said, and Victoria shushed him.

Fortune granted them a short wait and quick answers. The airplane's doors opened, and a group of rough 'n' ready warriors disembarked. A war party—they moved as one, and their blended auras denoted a powerful pack bond. Victoria performed a quick tally and counted fifteen in total—including two women—all shifters.

Tarak, Finn's beta and second-in-command, accompanied but was not a part of them. He stepped off the airplane last. The muscular werewolf was a full head shorter than the alpha. He had braided black-hair, brown skin, and Apache tribal tattoos on his bare biceps. By reputation, he was a fierce warrior, bloodthirsty and sadistic, and intolerant of outsiders. Years ago, Tarak had sought to claim Victoria as his mate, but she'd evaded his courtship. She strongly suspected he still harbored a grudge.

"Well, if it isn't the biggest eejit I've ever known!" Finn bowled through their ranks, heading straight for a tall, broad-shouldered man. He wore a leather tunic and pants.

"Shut yer puss, fannybaws." The man threw open his arms and charged straight at Finn. The two men collided, chest smashing against chest. Amid a volley of shouted insults, they clobbered each other on the back and shoulders.

"Damn, there are two of 'em," Logan muttered in a tone of open amazement that echoed what Victoria was feeling. "Who'd have thunk it?"

"Not I." Victoria slid him a sly smile.

The Scot, presumably MacTavish, had a wild and bleak charisma. Intricate blue tattoos—a scrolling script in Elder Futhark—embossed his scalp. His entire head was shaved bare except for a thick golden-red braid worn in the style once reserved for nobility. A ferocious wolf covered each shoulder: one grasped the sun between his gaping jaws, and the other the moon.

"You're hours late," Finn admonished his cousin. "What took so long?"

"Loki conjured a storm that grounded our plane for two days," MacTavish complained with a gloomy scowl.

"You haven't changed. Loki isn't always to blame for every thing that goes wrong." Snickering, Finn wrapped his arm around MacTavish's neck and dragged him over.

Tarak tailed them like an ill wind.

"Alpha Victoria Storm, this is my cousin and blood brother, Colin MacTavish. He is the Alpha of Geirolf." Finn swept his arm in a wide arc suggestive of a bow, but he didn't bend.

MacTavish dropped his gaze onto Victoria. She knew the look well, having been the recipient of male chauvinism her entire life.

His eyes widened in surprise and then lit with amusement. Insolently, he surveyed her from head to toe. He parted his lips, no doubt meaning to offer further insult.

Victoria sneered. "Finn, your cousin is a little girl! Where is the warrior you boasted about?"

Into that stillness, a pin dropped. The hot wind blew, and the raven shrieked. Victoria locked gazes with MacTavish, refusing to blink or waver. At her back, both Logan and Sawyer radiated readiness. The men waited in primed anticipation, prepared to come to her defense.

"She has the crack of a lash!" MacTavish burst out at the top of his lungs. He grasped his sides and howled with hilarity.

On cue, Victoria laughed with him as etiquette demanded. Finn joined in, and then Sawyer and Logan. Bawdy amusement poured from the top down and cascaded through the ranks to the lowliest omega. But not Tarak... the beta held himself apart.

They laughed until the humor ran dry.

"Watch out!" Sawyer thrust his arm skyward.

Reflexively, Victoria ducked. A black blur shot past her head, close enough that feathers brushed her face. Astonished, she turned to follow the bird's path as it swooped back around.

"Was it *trying* to hit you?" Logan asked.

"Sure seems that way." On a suspicion, she stepped away from Logan and raised her arm over her head. The raven flew straight at her, hovered on beating wings, and then seized hold of her bicep with its feet. Its talons pierced her skin. She hissed through her teeth, and blood ran from the scratches which healed within seconds. She held stiffly still while the squalling bird climbed up her arm until it found a satisfactory perch on her shoulder.

"Well?" Victoria studied the raven. She halfway expected it to speak, but the corvid only cocked its head and scrutinized her with inquisitive black eyes.

Logan coughed into his hand. "Very a-Poe-priate."

"That was awful," Victoria groaned but cut herself short.

Another hush had fallen. Oppressive attention weighed on her. Everyone was staring, including MacTavish and his followers.

"Is it an omen?" Finn strode toward her. His people parted before him and then closed behind him. They formed a circle about their alpha: men at the inside, women and children on the outside. Spiritually, they were a united whole, immensely mightier together than apart, as was the way of wolves.

"I'm not a *völva*, Alpha Finn. I leave divination to others." Victoria pitched her words to carry to the back of the audience. Through the pack bond, she melded her aura to Logan and Sawyer's, merging their strength. They cooperated, helping her present a united front.

"Ah, a woman after my own heart," Finn said. "I am a warrior, not a priest, not a politician." The alpha glanced pointedly, but not long, at Tarak. "For those who do not know them, our guests are Victoria Storm, Alpha of the Storm Pack. At her side, Logan Koenig, Valhalla-ordained champion..." Oh how Finn rolled *that* off his tongue.

"Hail," Logan said without missing a beat.

"This is Sawyer Barrett, son of the vaunted Hunter King..."

"Hello, it's an honor to meet you." Sawyer raised his hand in a salute.

"That's an interesting accessory you've got there," MacTavish drawled, eyeing the hunter's round shield. "Are you participating in a historical reenactment?"

Annoyance sparked in Sawyer's eyes and he worked his jaws. The hunter had already taken a ton of crap about the shield. Clearly, he hung from a thin thread of patience.

"Sawyer takes that 'come back with your shield or on it' thing literally. I've tried explaining it's all Greek, but..." Logan rolled his shoulders in an exaggerated shrug.

The tension broke—laughter rolled through. At a quick clip, Finn worked his way through every member of Geirolf. Even so, proper introductions required an inordinate amount of time. As the afternoon wore on, the heat worsened. Sweat soaked her shirt, which clung to her skin, Victoria wondered if it'd ever end. At least the raven perched on her shoulder remained silent and still —and watchful.

Finally, Finn moved on to their other business. "This meeting was called on short notice. We are now two hours behind schedule. Alpha Storm, you had a matter you wished to discuss?"

"I do." A leaden mass gathered in Victoria's gut.

"State your business then," Finn said.

"I object," Tarak's voice rang out.

"Already?" Finn scoffed, and competing undercurrents ripped through the White Mountains Tribe and the Geirolf. Some laughed, but others grumbled.

Victoria soured with discontent. She despised Tarak and was glad to have Logan, alert and ready, at her side. Of course, she expected opposition to a female alpha. Male werewolves were nothing if not narrow-minded and macho. To be accepted as their equal, she would have to prove herself.

Tarak stepped into the center of the arena. "Our laws do not allow a female to lead. Victoria Storm is nothing more than an uppity bitch that needs to be put in her place. Yet, here you've given a pregnant she-wolf the respect due an alpha. For months, you've been at her beck and call like a lapdog—"

"I could choose to interpret that as a challenge," Finn said with a toothy smile that was a thousand time scarier than any scowl.

"I'll accept any challenge issued." Tarak crossed his arms over his chest, rooted in the earth. "I will not stay silent."

Victoria speared Tarak with her gaze. Resolve cast her in stone. "If you think you're man enough to put me in my place, Tarak, then come over here and give it a try. I am alpha of my pack and the equal of any man here. I am a Valkyrie, a chooser of the worthy dead. Know this, Tarak Akonye, when you lie in a pool of your own viscera at my feet, it'll be *I* who determines the fate of your soul."

Tarak returned her stare without flinching but color slowly drained from his face. All around, it was deathly silent.

Victoria waited. When her challenge went unaccepted, she turned to Finn. "I have come here today at Odin's behest. I need a war party."

Finn raised his brow, but otherwise gave no sign of his true thoughts. Stoicism defined him. "A war party is a tall order. It would weaken my people's position, so I am obligated to ask, what is your purpose?"

"My pack is small," she said. "We lost a great many warriors in the war with the hunters. I have need of soldiers."

"You have need of soldiers, or Odin has need?" Finn asked with a crafty smile. He watched her with piercing eyes, perceiving far more than she preferred.

"Both." She recognized her mistake in invoking Odin's name, but it was too late to take it back. Disquiet roiled through her until Sawyer settled his hand on her shoulder. His touch soothed her anxiety. Oh yeah, she had Odin's son on her side.

"Funny. You don't look like Odin." Tarak scoffed. A few people nearby sniggered.

"I am a Valkyrie. I serve Odin, and I am his messenger. The Conclave won't be an assembly to negotiate a peacetime alliance." In a burst of anger, Victoria jerked and jostling the raven on her shoulder. The bird dug in with its talons and found a position of better balance.

"Why do you need soldiers for what's supposed to be a peaceful negotiation?" Finn asked.

"Ragnarök is upon us. The signs are all around. This is the axe age and the sword age, when the nations of men go to war. A long winter and time of famine is approaching." Victoria singled out Finn. "Odin is calling. I intend to unite our people as an army to fight for his cause. I need a general to lead them, not some mealy-mouthed politician who doesn't have the balls to deal with dissension within his own pack."

"Feel the lash," MacTavish said with a snicker.

Finn narrowed his eyes and flushed in anger. He gathered himself, as menacing as an active volcano. It was the first crack in his impressive control. *Good.* He needed to get dangerous and grow bold.

Victoria's satisfaction lasted for all of a second.

"Do not listen to the bitch's lies. I will tell you the truth." Bodaway entered the circle. The priest snaked his way to the center.

"What lies are you accusing me of exactly? List your allegations so I may refute them." Grim-faced, Victoria braced for whatever venom the serpent would inject into the proceeding.

"Victoria Storm is a witch and a liar sent to deceive us." Bodaway leveled a single gnarled finger at her. He addressed the crowd, ignoring her challenge. "She has come here with her familiar on her shoulder, knowing many will interpret a raven as a sign of Odin's favor."

"Challenge him," a woman with a voice both ancient and arcane spoke directly into Victoria's ear.

Lightheadedness swept over Victoria, delaying her reaction. The world spun; time stretched into an accordion. Startled, Victoria glanced to the side but found no one there, only the raven. The corvid shone with malice. The crowd burned, caught up in a wildfire of bloodlust. No one else appeared aware the raven had spoken, not even Logan, who stood closest to her, so she assumed its wisdom was for her alone.

"In truth, she is a false prophet," Bodaway said. "If we do as she asks and send a war party to defend outsiders, it will be as Tarak has said. Her goal is to weaken us."

"Challenge him," the raven commanded. *That voice.* It reached straight into Victoria's head, mesmerizing and compelling. She had to obey. The prospect of a duel appealed to her. Logan was there at her side, all set to fight, and she thirsted to see her accusers laid low.

"You make empty allegations without any evidence to prove them, Bodaway," Victoria said, addressing the priest in a voice like ice. She would challenge those who opposed her, but not outright. The circumstances called for cunning.

"Victoria Storm, you said you'd prove yourself." Tarak stepped up and came to the priest's defense.

"I am a Valkyrie, not a witch. Bodaway does nothing more than cast aspersions. Where are his facts?" Victoria shook her head. "I foolishly assumed the charges brought against me would consist of more than baseless lies and name-calling. This is an affront to my honor. Our laws permit me to request a trial by combat. Finn, since this is your territory and your people, I appeal to you for justice."

Victoria infused magic into her voice, imbuing it with the resonance that allowed her to sway the audience. It worked like a charm. She reigned as a queen, and her influence extended even to Finn. Effortlessly, she pushed the raven's counsel onto the alpha —*Make it a challenge.*

"Per our laws, Alpha Storm has a right to a trial by combat." Alpha Finn asserted his authority over his people, a force like the smash of Thor's hammer. The crowd bowed beneath the blow.

"Vic, what the hell are you doing? You said we wanted to avoid a duel at any cost." Logan hissed in her ear. He tugged on her elbow hard enough her joint ached.

"Logan, not now." Victoria jerked her arm free. The rough motion jostled the raven from its perch. The bird took to the air.

"Let her speak." Sawyer cut Logan's next protest off.

"Each side will put forward a champion, and they will fight to the death." Finn crossed his arms over his broad chest. His announcement sent a murmur through the crowd. Some people expressed surprise and dismay; those who'd expected her to back down. Bloodthirsty grins spread on the faces on others. "The gods will determine who is right and just. If Alpha Storm's champion wins the bout, then I will send a war party to serve her."

Inspiration seized Victoria. An idea blossomed in her mind and unfurled into a grand scheme. She dictated to Finn, "You'll send the Wolf Spears."

Surprise flickered across Finn's face. "The Wolf Spears are not mine to command."

"They will be, *General Finn.*" Victoria honeyed her tone, persuasion targeted squarely at his male ego. She called on the subtle but pervasive magic at her fingertips, weaving a siren's song. Visions of honor and glory, wealth and power to carry with him into the afterlife when he'd dine at Odin's table...

Finn's countenance grew cunning. He turned to MacTavish, seeking his blood brother's consent. Victoria's influence streaked like quicksilver through the ambient aura, touching the Scotsman.

After a split-second hesitation, the Geirolf Alpha grinned and spread his hands. "Sure, why not? Let fate throw the dice. If the Norns decree it, the Wolf Spears will pledge our strength to the defense of the lass."

A riot of laughter spread.

"In a contest, both sides must ante up," Tarak shouted, and Victoria stiffened, even though the demand was expected.

Finn narrowed his eyes. "State your demand, Tarak."

Tarak thrust out his chest, puffed up mighty proud. "When I win, Victoria Storm will be exposed as a charlatan and a false prophet. The Storm Pack, stripped of their honor, will surrender their territory. I will claim Desolation Wilderness as mine."

Vigorous murmuring broke out from the crowd.

A snarl erupted from Logan. "I'm gonna tear that smug bastard from limb to limb—"

"Hold that thought." Victoria raised a staying hand. Nervousness fractured her confidence, but she ruthlessly banished it. The moment of choice—a moment of truth... There was no room for hesitation. This was the testing point of her character and competence. She pitched her answer loud enough to ensure everyone would hear. "I accept Tarak's terms, and I name Logan Koenig as the champion who will defend my honor."

"You choose a cripple as your champion!" Tarak scoffed, staring at Sawyer. "Name another—make it a fair fight."

Sawyer tensed, and Logan bristled. The onlookers muttered.

Victoria smiled serenely and locked gazes with her enemy. "I'd have to send a blind, witless child into battle for you to have a fair match, Tarak."

Tarak flushed in anger, and laughter rolled through the mob.

Finn smiled as only a wolf could. "Since Logan is to fight for your honor, he must issue the challenge so that all will know he speaks as his own man."

Profound silence settled; the terrible tension of expectation. Attention centered on Logan, who remained sullen and defiant.

"That's your cue." Victoria prodded Logan. Across a great distance, through a dense fog, she picked up on his reticence. It confounded her. She wondered why he wasn't caught up in the same savage fervor as all the other wolves gathered.

Sawyer's determination thrummed through the pack bond like a force of will—*Do it or I will.*

"I challenge you." At last, reluctantly, Logan stepped up.

"I accept your challenge!" Tarak wailed his fury.

All around, wolves howled. Overhead, a raven cackled a raucous caw. For the world, it sounded like a woman's laughter.

CHAPTER 32

***Ansuz*, Odin's Rune, the Messenger Rune**

THE RAYS of an unforgiving sun beat down on Sylvie's bowed head and shoulders as she poured out her heart and soul to Freya. Her arthritic joints grew stiff; she prayed on bended knees. The blood of the sacrificial stag dried in the bowl while she confessed her sins... all of them.

"Goddess, why won't you speak to me? Am I unworthy? Am I being punished for having aided Victoria's betrayal in some way? I have done my best to help her understand and repent, but she won't listen. She's too damned stubborn. There is only so much I can do. I beg you, reveal your will—one word—I will do anything to make this right."

Hours passed, and her pleas gave way to utter desolation. With her strength spent, she struggled to her feet. Alone and weary, she stood there swaying. Sylvie finally uncurled her clenched fists and let go of her final vestige of hope.

The sun hung low in the late afternoon sky. More time had

passed than she'd realized. By now, Victoria and the men would've left for Arizona to fetch Finn. Their return via Bifröst would soon be forthcoming. Cali would be alone with the wolves and Morena. Undoubtedly, the others were wondering what'd happened to her. If Morena got worried enough, the teenager might decide to come looking for Sylvie.

Sylvie sighed.

"Freya, I would say you've abandoned me, except you were never with me at all. You've never heard my prayers." She croaked because of strained vocal chords and dehydration. The wind kicked up and snatched the last note from her lips, lifted high, and carried it off. She surveyed her once-beloved altar one final time. Going forward, she envisioned no further use for it.

Silence fell, blanketing the wilderness.

"We hear you, Sylvie."

Sylvie tried to wheel around, but her stiff knees failed her. She stumbled but caught herself. Questing, she searched for the source of the young female voice. No one was there.

"We've always heard you," an old woman said, again from behind her.

The third sister announced, "Today, perhaps, you will finally hear us."

Chills coursed down Sylvie's spine. She knew those voices, their diction and speech patterns... Slowly, carefully, she turned to face them. She couldn't afford to show the weakness of her sore body after hours of praying. Not to the Norns. A splash of surprise washed over her when she discovered four women rather than three.

The Norns personified the three aspects of Fate: Verðandi the maiden, Skuld the mature woman, and Urðr the crone. The Sisters Wyrd wore simple robes that belted at the waist. Verðandi and Urðr had their cowls lowered, but Skuld's raised hood concealed her face. But who was this fourth woman?

Sylvie spared the stranger a hasty glance only, because she was unwilling to let her attention stray from the Norns for too long.

The woman stood apart from the Sisters Wyrd. She wore a Navajo-print poncho over a gray mini skirt with over-the-knee boots. Her beauty was stark and harsh like a winter morning. Blood red were her vampire lips and her dagger-pointed nails. She had a bejeweled distaff—the implement of an accomplished *seiðr*. A witch, and far older than she appeared, Sylvie suspected.

"Do you know who we are?" Verðandi stood with her hands clasped before her. When she tilted her head, glossy tresses cascaded over her shoulders.

"Of course. You are the Sisters Wyrd." Sylvie offered them a cautious bow where she never quite let them get out of her sight. "But you, I don't know," she said to the stranger.

"I am Grimhild." She gave a regal tip of her chin and her dark eyes glittered. "I am here as a loyal servant and emissary of the Norns."

Verðandi nodded.

Sylvie pressed her lips together. She chose her words with great care. It never served a person to cross fate. "Pray, tell me, what has earned me this unexpected honor?"

"Your anguish calls to us," Verðandi said.

Urðr cackled. "The skein of your bitterness corrupted our tapestry."

Sylvie lifted a defensive hand and discovered she was trembling. "If I have caused you trouble—"

"There is no trouble," Verðandi interrupted. "We know what it means to have loved and lost..."

Anxiety churned in Sylvie's gut like seasickness. A divine visitation from the goddesses of Fate...? A megalithic storm must be brewing.

Urðr picked up the thread of the conversation. "Our sacrifices went unappreciated. Bitterness gathered upon the boughs of the ancient tree like ice and snow until even our great strength could support no more. We broke."

"We know what it is to be trapped between a harsh past and a grim future," Verðandi said *sotto voce*.

"I don't understand!" Sylvie cried out in immense frustration. Weakness threatened, almost reducing her to tears. She'd already expended the last of her reserves trying to reach Freya. What was wrong with the gods? Were their brains so addled—every last one —that not one deity could provide a single straight answer?

"The day will come when I will have need of you, Sylvie Thornton," Skuld said. "For your service to me, I will never ignore you. I will make you powerful and revered."

Both Verðandi and Urðr shot their sister a dirty look. *I*, it seemed, displeased the collective. Sylvie, however, was beyond caring. After a lifetime of devout prayers, a goddess had at last taken notice of her. She had a purpose after all. One Freya never recognized but Skuld did.

"What would you have me do?" Sylvie asked.

Grimhild cleared her throat and stepped up. "There is an imminent threat to the children of your pack."

"Den Valgte?" Sylvie gasped. Her stomach dropped as she jumped straight to the most obvious menace. She launched into motion, prepared to run flat out across the miles separating her from those she loved.

"Sawyer," Grimhild said.

Sylvie skidded to an unbalanced halt. "Sawyer? What do you mean? He's a member of our pack."

"Sylvie, I'm so sorry to have to be the one to tell you this," Grimhild said with a crocodile's contrived sympathy. "But it was Sawyer who murdered Jasper."

"That's a lie! Please tell me it's a lie." Sylvie staggered. It couldn't be true—*it couldn't*. Sylvie had loved young Jasper every bit as much as she did Morena and the pups. She raised begging hands to Verðandi.

"I'm sorry." Verðandi turned her mouth down in sorrow. "It is the truth."

"Victoria knows and has kept the truth from you this whole time," Grimhild said, "so it is up to you alone to save the pack."

A sharp snap startled Sylvie. She flinched but none of the other women seemed to even hear it. Her last hope of redeeming Victoria died and something deep inside Sylvie—maybe her sanity—broke.

Grimhild extended her arm, offering a slim-profile dagger. Sylvie looked down and stared at the knife—the polished blue-steel reflected bright flashes of sunlight.

"The only way to kill the hunter is to destroy his heart," Grimhild said.

"I understand."

"Swear yourself—heart, body, and soul—to vengeance," Grimhild demanded.

Sylvie accepted the weapon and the geas. "I swear."

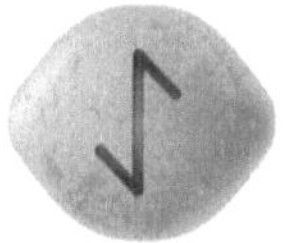

CHAPTER 33

***Ihwaz*: The Rune of Defense**

WHITERIVER, *Arizona*

The air stank of bad mojo.

Summer cast a suffocating shroud over the desert, and afternoon was far and away the worst part of the day. It didn't seem to affect the White Mountains Tribe or their kin, however. The atmosphere bustled with energy and activity. Under Alpha Finn's direction, an arena about the size of a football field was measured and marked off. Spectators gathered on the sidelines, waiting with sharpened anticipation.

Uneasy within his own skin, Logan stood alone in the crowd of his kin. He was surrounded by more wolf-shifters than he'd encountered before in his entire life, more even than he'd imagined existed in the whole world. Yet somehow, contrary to right and reason, Logan shared a stronger connection with the long-haired, redneck hunter than he did with his own people.

Sawyer stood in a tight circle with the man who acted as

Tarak's second, Alpha MacTavish, and Alpha Finn. They engaged in a low, intense conversation, conducting negotiations for the terms of the duel to come.

"Have you contemplated the irony in sending Sawyer Barrett to represent your best interests? Once again, I must applaud your exceptional cunning in choosing the hunter as your second. What better way to allay his suspicious?" Victoria whispered in a voice both sweetly coy and ruthlessly compelling. Command coached in desire.

A sharp sneeze tore from Logan. This wasn't Victoria at all. No, he knew the scent of that foul magic—*Grimhild.* Cold sweat ran down his back. Despite what he'd told Sawyer, Logan worried the witch's mind-magic could influence him. He'd resisted Hrafnar, but how much more powerful was the mother than her daughter?

"What the hell do you think you're doing? We had a deal—no harm to Vic or the baby," Logan ground out from between clenched teeth. He remained turned away from her while his wolf roiled beneath his tenuous control.

"I haven't broken our accord. Mama wolf and baby are safe and sound." Victoria wrapped her hands about her baby bump and gazed down with a creepy little smile on her lips.

"I want you out now." Logan jerked around to face her. He seethed with pent-up rage. He wanted nothing more than to go howling mad—to snatch Victoria off her feet and shake the witch out of her. He didn't dare lift a finger against her for fear that his actions—or Grimhild's—would harm Vic or his baby sister. He couldn't even expose Grimhild's possession without ruining Victoria's standing before the packs. It didn't matter if the rest of them had been chugging the same damn Kool-Aid. People didn't change. They'd cast blame and turn her into a scapegoat rather than accept responsibility.

"Calm yourself. I'll depart soon enough—just as soon as the duel is over." Direct sunlight rendered Victoria's white-blonde hair nearly translucent against her tanned skin. She always wore it slicked against her skull and bound in a braid. Much like her, Victoria's hair didn't like rules; a few stubborn tresses had escaped. Perspiration-dampened strands clung to her throat.

"What happened to you not wanting me to get hurt?" Logan stole a glance over his shoulder at Sawyer and the others. The negotiations continued, but probably not for much longer. The wrist stump of his severed hand throbbed with splitting pain. Reality check—fighting this duel was a terrible idea.

"My concern for your well-being remains unchanged." Grimhild pierced him with a savvy stare harder to look into than the desert sun. "You made your desires clear, however, and winning this duel will fulfill your goal."

"My goal?"

"To earn your name before the packs." She smiled, as wicked as could be, and it wrenched his gut to have to witness that look on Victoria's face.

"Right, my name." Logan didn't give two figs about his "name", but he couldn't argue. He had to own the lie he'd told. Instead, he rolled his shoulders, seeking to ease the excruciating tension from his muscles.

Tarak's second and Sawyer stepped closer and shook, demolishing what little progress Logan had made in the relaxation department. The crowd shushed. The ambient aura resonated with savage expectation.

Finn shouted, "Logan Koenig! We're ready. Are you?"

"Born ready!" Logan raised his good arm.

"*Showtime!*" Victoria wrapped her hands about his forearm. His skin crawled beneath her touch. "Destroy him, *Sköll*. Make your name known to all."

CHAPTER 34

Einherjar: Odin's Elite Army

A LUSTY MIASMA hung thick in the air—one part revelry, two parts hostility, three parts bloodlust. The Wolf Spears in particular reveled in the prospect of combat—loud and rambunctious. Ravens perched on a wire, sounding off in a raucous refrain, blending their voices to the ruckus.

Alpha Finn cut a swath through the crowd as he led the way to the field of battle. Sawyer and the others trailed in Finn's wake. Moving to intercept them, Logan followed an angular path, deliberately striding at a pace faster than Victoria could match. Doggedly, she chased after him, panting. Guilt needled at his conscience. He felt bad, but not bad enough to walk with her while Grimhild held possession.

Finn paused to confer with MacTavish. Then the White Mountains Alpha headed to center field alone. The others halted along the perimeter, joining the hundreds of spectators. Thankfully, Victoria joined Finn's wife, Ekta, at a vantage point reserved for the highest-ranked wolf-shifters and their mates.

Uncertain on how to proceed, Logan dragged his feet. As his path crossed Sawyer's, their gazes clashed. The hunter returned the wolf's regard with an inscrutable, unwavering stare. Trust—a sheet of thin ice beneath their feet; a commodity in short supply. Logan had no way of knowing whether the hunter had negotiated in good faith on his behalf.

Logan sent a sharp note of inquiry across the pack bond—*Is it done?*

Sawyer nodded.

Logan exhaled, grateful for the one saving grace. Maybe he stood a chance of living through this fight after all.

The hunter tossed a scrap of leather at Logan. He held it up for inspection and then scowled. He demanded, "Is this a joke?"

"It's the traditional garb worn by men into a duel. Armor isn't permitted." Sawyer arched his brow as though to signal indifference, but Logan knew the bastard was laughing his ass off beneath that smug smile.

"No fucking away." Logan balled the loincloth and shot it back at Sawyer.

"Suit yourself." Sawyer smirked and closed his fist about the offensive garment.

"Thanks, I will." Logan huffed in mighty disgust. On second thought, though, he reconsidered. Doubtless, he'd have to shift during the combat. He preferred not to ruin his clothing since he hadn't brought a change of outfit. Hastily, he stripped down to his *au natural* state, which earned him hoots and catcalls from the spectators.

"Hold these." Fuming, Logan rolled his clothing into a wad and thrust it at the snickering hyena of a hunter who passed as his second.

Sawyer caught the bundle. "They're only giving you a hard time because you're not wearing the loincloth."

"Oh, and I suppose you would wear the hide miniskirt?"

"When in Rome." Sawyer flashed a swath of white teeth.

"Fine. Give it." Logan held up his good hand, conceding defeat.

Sawyer pitched the wadded loincloth like a fastball. Logan managed to catch the damn thing, but only just barely. The makeshift ball thwacked against his palm with impressive impact. Hell, maybe the beatnik hunter had been telling the truth about playing college ball. Hastily, he shook out the loincloth. The real trouble couldn't be avoided any longer—how to tie the straps with only one hand. Logan would've yanked his own teeth before he'd ask Sawyer for help.

"Do you need assistance?" a woman asked in a strong voice.

Logan pivoted, and came face-to-face with a raven-haired woman. She looked to be in her early twenties but her eyes held wisdom beyond her years. Her cool appraisal made Logan feel like a bride on an auction block.

"I could use a hand. Who are you?" Logan kept his guard up. The last thing he needed was this woman's irate father and brothers... or worse, husband, lining up to take a shot at him.

"Frea. I have neither a mate nor a fiancé. Nor am I in the market for one." If her smile left any doubt, her inflection removed it. The woman found his predicament every bit as amusing as the snickering spectators.

"Good to know," Logan bit off.

"Do you accept my assistance?"

"Yes, please." Mentally, Logan tore up his reservations and cast confetti to the wind—anything to move this humiliating production along. He forked over the garment.

"How do expect to win this fight when you can't dress yourself?" Frea positioned the waistcloth and knotted the straps at his hips.

"I'll win or die," Logan said with too much force. Somehow, though, this stranger had yanked the scab off, exposing his festering insecurity.

"What are you fighting for?" The question compelled a response.

"The people I love," Logan said without hesitation. It didn't even occur to him to lie or refuse. Weird, he *wanted* to provide an honest answer.

Frea smiled in approval. "An excellent response. I confess—I had my doubts about your worthiness. You are a noble champion, son of Loki."

"Thank you." Logan bowed his head, thoroughly humbled. Surprise eluded him. He longed to resort to sarcasm but couldn't summon his wits.

"You have my blessing. The road ahead of you is difficult. Your moment of crisis looms. When your strength is depleted and all seems lost, it will please me that you should find the strength to continue."

Logan parted his lips, on the verge of thanking her again, but his thoughts snagged on the incongruity of her statement. The contrary part of him simply couldn't let it pass. "How is that a blessing?"

"Shh." She stepped back. "Now forget I was here."

"Yes, ma'am." Logan blinked. Blankness whitewashed his mind. He glanced around and discovered he'd fallen behind. The lapse bugged him but everyone else had already moved onto the battlefield. He hurried to catch up.

"Hail!" Finn shouted. A hearty barrage of greetings returned to him, and then a respectful quiet fell. "I call Tarak Akonye, Beta of the White Mountains Tribe, and Logan Koenig, Alpha Storm's champion, to the field!"

"I am here!" Tarak emerged from among the spectators gathered on the sidelines, wearing a loincloth. Even though he stood a full head shorter than Logan, the beta wolf had a much heavier musculature. Scars cross-crossed his body, trophies from prior battles. His unwavering gaze burned with loathing. From the look on his face, the contest could only end with one of them dead.

"Present." Logan stepped onto the arena. Dry summer grasses, flattened beneath so many feet, formed a golden mat interlocked with patches of hard soil.

"Alpha Finn," Victoria's voice rang out clear and sharp from the sidelines. She delayed until Finn gave his full attention, and then she said, "Please restate the concessions and the penalties dependent upon the outcome."

"Very well. Should Tarak Akonye emerge as the victor, Alpha Storm will be known as a witch and a trickster. The Storm Pack stripped of all honor and turned off their lands—"

Cold sweat broke out across Logan's back. Holy Auðumbla—great primordial cow—how had it come to this?

"If Logan Koenig triumphs, then all will know Alpha Storm speaks the will of the All Father, representing him as both priestess and Valkyrie. Should her honor be upheld, her authority will be beyond question," Finn continued.

Leaden weight settled in Logan's gut. A telltale twitch tugged at the corner of Victoria's mouth, and Logan stumbled straight into an epiphany. Abruptly, he understood why the bewitched Victoria had put the Storm Pack's territory on the line. No longer did Logan worry about losing their land. All he could think of was the havoc Grimhild could wreak as a puppet master should Victoria ascend to the status of an ordained oracle. With dawning dread, he understood how cleverly Grimhild had manipulated the situation to her advantage.

"That's not all to be won!" MacTavish released a disgruntled bellow.

Finn laughed from the belly. "Oh yes. Should Victoria's champion triumph, Alpha MacTavish had pledged himself and the Wolf Spears to her service."

"No finer prize has ever been had!" MacTavish shouted, drawing appreciative chuckles from his fellows.

The White Mountains Alpha allowed the outburst to die down before he resumed speaking. "I will serve as the arbiter—declaring the start and end of the fight and announcing the winner. The rules are as follows. When I say 'fight', you fight. When I say 'stop', you 'stop'. You will fight until one of you surrenders, is incapacitated, or dead. Is that clear?"

"Crystal." Logan snapped off a smart salute.

"Yes." Tarak's posture grew militant, and his skin rippled across his torso like a flag in the stiff breeze.

"As negotiated by your seconds, the contest will be fought with weapons made of silver. These daggers are the ancestral dueling weapons of my wife's family. The blades were forged in pure silver by the dwarves of Nidavellir, enchanted to a hardness superior to steel. They cannot be bent or broken. Ekta has graciously agreed to their use here today." Finn bowed to his wife and she returned a regal nod in acknowledgement.

Finn gestured to two men who waited on the sidelines. At his signal, they separated—one approached Victoria and the other Tarak—and presented the open cases. Tradition called for each party to inspect and approve the weapons. Victoria reached into the case and removed a *seax*, a traditional Viking dagger. Held in her shadow, the blade was dark gray. Then she raised it overhead and turned it for inspection. The metal captured sunlight, shone with argent brilliance, and threw bright flashes.

The audience hummed with anticipation.

"Hear me." Victoria lowered the enchanted weapon and held it straight out before her, aimed at the spectators. The magic of the witch possessing her imparted much weight to her words. "Odin as my witness, I speak the truth. Because I am righteous, silver weapons—toxic to our people—will have no more effect upon my champion than steel."

Disbelieving exclamations erupted from all around, followed in quick succession by expressions of shock and awe. Even Sawyer muttered something dark beneath his breath. Logan stiffened in shock at the blatant lie and then the thrill of outrage sang through him. The witch had hijacked his scheme, turning his natural immunity to silver to her advantage. It didn't go down well at all.

Victoria strutted across the field, carrying the *seax* as a silvery standard, and offered it to Logan. He gritted his teeth and accepted it from her, wrapping his hand about the black iron grip. When their fingers brushed, his skin crawled.

Logan hefted the dagger, testing its balance, and found it sublime. It had no guard. The blade curved subtly, an edge designed for cutting and piercing, and ended in a short-clipped point. A work of art. Even so, he would have preferred to use Thorn, but the artifact had to remain a secret for now. Too much depended on the element of surprise. Funny. Even in his absence, Loki crafted clandestine chicanery.

"Make his death slow and lingering, Logan. I want him to suffer," Victoria said in a low, vicious voice. She was a total stranger.

Logan met her gaze, refusing to look away. Fuck, but he hated her like this. Her physical beauty remained unchanged. Normally, she glowed with warmth and seduction; charisma he found damn near irresistible. That magnetism had vanished. That he might never get Victoria back scared him witless. Regardless of what she claimed, Grimhild could keep her claws in Vic indefinitely.

The witch had to die.

The clamor from the crowd increased—a demand for action. For the moment, no trace of the witch's magic hung over them. Their lust for violence was organic to both their wolf-shifter and warrior roots.

"Combatants on the field! Everyone else stand clear!" Finn asserted control over the collected wolves, reining them in. He managed the dynamics of the fragmented and dissentious psychic landscape with deft precision.

"Are you ready?" Finn asked Tarak.

"I am prepared to fight and win!" Tarak raised both arms overhead, fists clenched like a fighter entering the ring. An approving cheer arose among the ranks of the White Mountains Tribe for their champion.

Logan sucked snot and spat to clear his clogged sinuses. For a little while, his allergies had cleared, but they were back with a vengeance. The scent of—what had Vic called it?—creosote polluted the air, almost as noxious as Grimhild's magic. He hated Arizona and everything about it, from the hundred-plus degree temperatures to the lack of greenery. Logan couldn't wait to finish this fight, so he could return to the mountains where he belonged.

"Logan Koenig, are you ready?" Finn crossed his arms over his massive chest.

"Ask the gimp if he's ready to die!" Tarak shouted the taunt, and those in his corner sniggered.

"Let's rock and roll." Logan clenched his jaws and brandished the *seax*. His temper boiled. He swore he'd wipe that smirk off Tarak's smug mug.

"Prepare!" Finn's arm rose over his head. An expectant hush fell.

Time slowed. Logan's focus narrowed so everything around him faded from his awareness. The clamor dimmed and he perceived only his enemy. His muscles drew taut, and he settled into a ready stance. He took to combat as naturally as a snake to slithering. He'd trained his entire life for this; countless hours spent sparring with his father. Arik had honed Logan into a weapon and taught him mastery over all manner of ancient weapons, except, oddly, firearms. During his tenure in Valhalla, Logan had trained with the Einherjar, Odin's elite army. But then, he'd had both of his hands.

Across the field, Tarak adopted a stance wider than his hips, feet staggered and aligned to maximize his leverage. His spine and hips were precisely positioned, and his abdominals were drawn taut. He kept his left arm close to his body, positioned to protect his gut. He held the dagger in a hammer grip, guarding his face.

"Start!" Finn dropped his arm, signaling the commencement of the combat, and the spectators screamed and surged as though they were a single great beast with many mouths. They screamed for blood.

Adrenaline rushed through Logan. The ground was hot and hard beneath his feet. He came off the line at a flat-out sprint, dagger angled for a downward stroke, and charged straight for Tarak.

Tarak held his ground and loosened a fearsome challenge—a roar forged in the heart of the beast. He undertook the change into a wolf. His ears grew pointed and migrated toward the top of his head. Bones snapped and reformed, pushing and pulling beneath the thick gray fur that burst from his skin.

Logan vaulted into the air and twisted while in flight. The world spun. Lightning fast, he altered to the wolfman form that allowed him to retain the use of a claw-like hand. Black fur covered his body, and his size and weight doubled. He pulled out of the spin and landed directly in front of his enemy.

Tarak growled and jerked up his *seax* to defend. He fell back, stumbled, and caught himself. His half-transformed state made every step awkward and painful.

The momentum behind his charge powered Logan's attack. He swung his dagger overhead, putting all his strength behind the blow. The business end of the knife aimed at Tarak's chest; Logan would end this fast with a single stroke before Tarak even finished shifting.

Tarak threw up his arm and parried. The daggers clashed, the metal edges sliding across each other. The short blades reached their ends fast. The beta kicked and planted his foot square on Logan's chest, shoving him back.

Logan staggered but recovered.

Sunlight glanced off his blade. He lunged and slashed. Logan hopped, evading a cut across his abdomen. Heart pounding, he glided across the level earth. Instinctively, he presented his strong side, and kept his bad arm turned away from Tarak.

"Victoria must be desperate sending a cripple to champion her," Tarak taunted in a guttural voice. He launched a powerful offensive, slashing with the knife as he advanced. His movements were strong and sure, following an irregular but measured cadence.

"Finn must be eager to be rid of the village idiot, sending you." Logan settled into a defensive position. He dodged and evaded, retreating across the hard-packed soil. It burned as hot as a stovetop with desert heat.

Disbelief flickered across Tarak's face. The cause wasn't a mystery. In his current shape, Logan was more wolf than man. He shouldn't have been capable of clear speech. "You can speak."

"Surprise, *bitch*. I have a lot of surprises for you," Logan sneered.

"Stop running, you mangy cur. Show me what you've got." Stout and blocky, the man had the solid build of a brick house... and the limited mobility. His compact fighting style relied on superior strength and stamina, but he was slow.

Damn slow.

Tarak swung his *seax* again, the same attack he'd employed already a good dozen times. Logan had committed all his opponent's go-to attacks to memory.

Pouring on a burst of speed, Logan catapulted into a dive. Tarak's silver blade cut a swath through empty air. Before he hit the ground, Logan shifted to human. He tucked his shoulder and rolled past his opponent.

Logan scissor-kicked, cutting Tarak's legs out from under him. The beta crashed onto his back. A deft twist brought Logan to a crouch. Wrestling a larger, stronger opponent meant taking a huge risk. He had one shot at it.

He flung himself across Tarak's chest. The two men grappled. Logan strove to get the upper hand, but Tarak was heavier than him—and as strong as a bear. Logan rasped for breath. Perspiration stung his eyes and slicked their skin, making it harder to get a good grasp.

A fat black fly flew about Logan's head, filling his ear with its buzz.

Dust rose in a cloud, dislodged by their struggle. It settled on his drenched skin, forming a crust that clogged Logan's nostrils. His frustration with the deadlock fueled his effort. He shoved his elbow into his opponent's shoulder and used his good hand, pinioning Tarak on his back.

"Yield." Logan placed the lethal point of the silver knife against his rival's Adam's apple. He dug in. The silver corroded where it touched. Tarak's flesh sizzled and the air filled with the stink of singed fur and meat.

The fly aligned on Tarak's forehead.

"No." Tarak bared his teeth in defiance. He pitted his strength against Logan, trying to break his hold. The two men strained against one another. Tarak's body shifted under Logan as Tarak pushed to complete the change to his wolfman form. His jaws distended into a muzzle as his teeth lengthened to canines.

"You've lost. Surrender." Logan summoned his reserves and committed to one final effort. He stood a chance of thwarting Grimhild's plan, but only if he could win the duel without Tarak's gory demise.

The fly hopped from Tarak's forehead to Logan's temple. He fixated on it—the tiny legs rubbing together in the periphery of his vision. His arm trembled and the knife slipped. The silver blade pierced Tarak's jugular and sank an inch. Blood welled from the wound.

"Never," Tarak snarled in defiance. With kamikaze determination, he lunged toward the blade as though determined to impale himself to prove his unwillingness to submit.

Logan yanked the blade away.

Tarak lurched his head to the side, going for a bite. Snapping jaws closed on Logan's wrist stump, sinking his fangs through skin and sinew, bone and marrow.

Logan howled in anguish.

The world spun. Logan soared and then crashed to the earth on his back, the wind knocked right out of him. Disoriented, he squinted at the menacing figure looming over him—a giant silhouetted against the blazing sun.

Instincts screaming, Logan shifted to his wolfman form. He gathered himself, preparing to launch upright but too late—the dagger thrust downward. Tarak drove the blade straight into Logan's throat, piercing black fur and corded muscle. The blade exited the back of his throat, protruding next to his spine.

Tarak released the *seax* and thrust his arms overhead, reaching for the sky. He shouted, claiming victory. "I am the winner!"

Bright agony ripped through Logan. It lasted only a moment before he spun off into darkness. Distantly, he heard the crowd as it howled and rocked with bloodlust. They chanted their champion's name, "Tarak, Tarak, Tarak."

Logan pushed against the darkness. He couldn't go out—not like this. He refused to let down Victoria, who'd finally begun to trust and depend on him. He couldn't disappoint the pack or his father... and even himself. Failure wasn't the legacy he wanted to be remembered for. Stubbornness allowed Logan to hang on even when pride and anger deserted him. He rallied, rousting from his stupor, but it wasn't enough.

Ravenous hunger tore at his insides—that void in his belly that must be filled. It loathed him and he it. Logan blinked and groaned... and his stomach growled. *Shit*—a bad sign. His instinct for self-preservation threatened everything and everyone around him. Ultimately, famine proved more unbearable than death, and right now he needed one thing above all else...

Air—he needed air. That monstrous burden on his chest —suffocation.

Logan groped for the iron handle of the dagger that protruded from his jugular. He found it—wrapped his hand about the blood-slickened hilt. Clenching his jaws, he tugged but it refused to dislodge.

Abruptly, the audience hushed. Surprise and wonder rippled through the ambient aura.

Desperation bore strength. Logan yanked the silver dagger

free from his flesh, releasing a fountain of blood. His regeneration fed on his rage. Agony twisted in his gut as his body cannibalized fat and even muscle, but his throat healed. Painstakingly, Logan climbed to his feet, retaining his grip on the gore-covered dagger.

Tarak dropped his arms and his jaw.

The black fly alighted on Logan's forearm. He smashed it flat. He was so fucking done with this shit—and done with trying to keep Tarak alive. No more Mr. Nice Werewolf.

Tarak gaped. "Impossible, you're—"

"Immune to silver." Riding an eruption of rage, Logan sprinted, closing the distance that separated them in a blink.

Tarak brought up his claws, but too late.

Logan stabbed with the silver dagger and drove the point into Tarak's belly. The blade embedded to the hilt. Flesh sizzled; the injury smoked.

Wide-eyed, Tarak quivered. He released a great, anguished groan. A trickle of sludge ran past his lips. He doubled over and spewed bloody vomit across Logan's chest.

Grim-faced, Logan took Tarak's weight to stop him from falling. Blood slicked the dagger's hilt so it was damn near impossible to hold onto. Logan clung to it in stubborn determination. He sawed the blade in and out, slicing Tarak open from navel to sternum.

Ropey red intestines spilled onto their feet, and a foul stink worse than skunk permeated the atmosphere. Logan released the blade. Mouth curled in a sneer, he stepped back and Tarak sank to the dry desert dirt that was stained the same hues as his viscera.

Stunned silence greeted his victory.

Victoria strutted onto the field. As she passed Logan, he caught a glimpse of her eyes. Vulture eyes—pale blue beneath a milky film. The color of death.

Logan's soul curdled.

Radiant with triumph, Victoria stood over Tarak, who lay dying in a pool of his own entrails. She spat into his gaping bowels and faced the gathered White Mountains Tribe and the Wolf Spears.

"Tarak Akonye, as Odin's Valkyrie, I declare that you are not chosen for Valhalla." She turned a mean gaze on the onlookers. "Let this be a lesson to all who think to cross me."

Finn came to stand alongside Logan. The White Mountains Alpha cocked his head and said in a low voice, "Calling her the lash may've proven unfortunately prophetic."

CHAPTER 35

Gnýrhorn: "Clashing Horn"

A STORM WAS BREWING.

Towering thunderheads brooded over the Sierra Nevadas, as gloomy as Sawyer's mood. Within the SUV, a volatile argument raged as Logan brought the vehicle to a stop in front of the lake house's detached garage. The moment the front door swung open, the howling wind blasted through the interior.

"Come on, Vic. Don't you think you're being a tad paranoid? If you ask me, Finn and MacTavish are capable of babysitting a few pagan fundamentalists for a couple hours," Logan said, climbing from the driver's seat.

"A, I didn't ask you," Victoria shot back from the front passenger seat while she released her seatbelt. "B, Reidell and his men are more than just pagan fundamentalists. They're—"

"Pagan fundamentalists with guns," Sawyer said, speaking in sync with Victoria. The line hadn't been difficult to anticipate.

Logan and Victoria had been arguing about the same thing for the past thirty minutes or so during the drive to the lake house.

"Precisely." Victoria cast Sawyer a smile. Her blue eyes danced with laughter. Then she hopped from the passenger seat and doggedly returned to her quarrel with Logan. "And C, there's a lot more than just a *few* of them—a lot more."

When Sawyer opened the back passenger door, a chilly gust of wind blasted his long hair and set the lapel of his leather duster to flapping. It carried freshness and moisture—a promise of rain. Gravel crunched beneath Sawyer's boots as he eased from the back of the SUV. He hefted *Kappiskjǫld* off the seat next to him and gazed upon it with no small amount of irony. Lugging the damn shield to Arizona hadn't earned him anything other than sore muscles... Well, that and plenty of ribbing from Finn and his warriors. After a moment's reflection, he leaned the shield against the side of the SUV, because he needed his hands free.

"Hurrying would be prudent." Nervousness threaded Sawyer's characteristic cool. He, too, had been astonished at how many members of *Den Valgte* had turned up in Broken Bend, Sierra Pine's poor neighbor on U.S. Route 50. The tiny truck stop was full to bursting, and more people arrived every hour, even though Sawyer wasn't due to summon the Wild Hunt for hours yet.

"I agree," Victoria said. "I want to make this fast. In 'n' out. No unnecessary delays."

"Whatever," Logan said. "I still say you're getting all panicky over nothing."

"I don't panic," Victoria shot back.

Victoria and Logan exited the vehicle, shutting their doors with a loud bang. Logan took a long stride and then pivoted on his heel. His movements were short and jerky. Aggression glimmered in his gaze—an amber strobe that faded fast. Surly animosity traversed the pack bond—a slip that lasted seconds, but long enough for Sawyer to glimpse the wolf's immense frustration. For once, ironically, the hostility wasn't aimed at Sawyer. They were strange bedfellows indeed.

Showtime.

The two men faced off. Their agreement called for a trade—Sawyer's gun for Logan's magic dagger. For the moment, the SUV blocked Victoria from seeing what they were up to. By now, Sawyer had no clue whether Victoria was herself or Grimhild, but he had to assume the worst.

Without a word, Logan held up his empty hand. A red splash burst from his palm. Sawyer's gaze flew to the wolf-shifter's hand, but his surprise soon turned to sickened fascination. A wooden spike—*a thorn*—pushed through Logan's skin, growing from the inside out. Blood dripped to the driveway. The thorn morphed into a dagger. Even forewarned, Sawyer marveled at the magical manifestation.

Tension gathered in Sawyer's shoulders. He extracted a revolver from the front pocket of his duster. For the life of him, he felt like Val Kilmer as Doc Holliday at the O.K. Corral... *Tombstone*, 1993. When Logan raised his arm, Sawyer worked his jaws. Despite the urgency, Sawyer's stubborn fingers remained clenched about the gun, refusing to let go.

"Sawyer, I want you to haul ass over to your camp, grab your horn, and get back here ASAP. Got that?" Victoria's volume rose, competing with the blustery wind. She headed around the back of the SUV.

"Got it." With a conscious effort, Sawyer summoned the discipline necessary to finally surrender the revolver.

Logan caught the gun, spared it a frowning glance, and then tucked it into the back of his pants beneath his shirt.

Sawyer held out his open hand.

"I want to check in with Sylvie, make sure everything's okay, and get back to Broken Bend straightaway." Victoria rounded the rear of the vehicle, her light steps drawing near.

Logan hesitated. He tightened his grip on the dagger, clearly reluctant to surrender it. From the hardened anger on his face, he looked like he would've as soon run the hunter through as honor their agreement.

"Come on." Sweat beaded Sawyer's brow. He jerked his hand in an urgent demand. Paranoia spiked and adrenaline surged. What the fuck was up—had Logan gotten cold feet? Or changed his mind? Sawyer altered to a defensive stance amidst a swarm of suspicions. A thousand and one doubts assailed him. Damn it. Waiting until the last minute to make the exchange wasn't smart, but then they hadn't exactly had many opportunities. Someone had been with them constantly all day.

Logan grimaced and thrust the weapon hilt-first into Sawyer's hand. He barely had a chance to take the weapon's measure before it vanished unbidden into thin air. Pleasant warmth stroked his wrist beneath the long sleeve of his duster, which concealed the tattoo.

"I want her back when this is over," Logan hissed in a low voice.

"Yeah, sure," Sawyer agreed. Trust between them was still thin. Strange allies, indeed.

"What are you two up to?" Victoria asked, rounding the rear bumper.

Sawyer pivoted to face her. "Up to?" he asked, raising his brow. He strove to school his demeanor to stoicism, taking a page from his old man's playbook, but he was ninety-five percent positive the effort crashed and burned.

Deception made him twitchy.

Victoria ground to a halt. Her blue eyes shone bright with warmth and concern. A dagger twisted in Sawyer's gut. He couldn't tell whether she was still possessed or in command of herself. When he looked at her, he perceived the woman he'd begun to love—not a wicked witch. The only proof he had of the purported possession was Logan's word... and Victoria's uncharacteristically harsh treatment of Tarak.

"What're you guys up to?" Victoria repeated and pursed her lips. Her canny gaze lingered on Sawyer, inflating his discomfort, and then skipped to Logan.

"Nothing." Logan slid toward the edge of the driveway.

Sawyer shrugged but stayed silent. He'd been a member of the Storm Pack long enough to grasp the pointlessness of outright deception. If he lied, she'd smell it on him. Fortunately, *Kappiskjǫld* provided a convenient excuse. He bent to recover it, looping the straps across his forearm for easy carry.

"Nothing? Then why do I smell blood?" Victoria reached for Logan's arm but he evaded, smoothly stepping beyond her reach.

"I may've cut myself." Anxiety flickered across Logan's face. He stood with his maimed arm toward her, trying to keep her from examining his good hand.

"Let me see." The picture of skepticism, Victoria pushed him.

"Don't worry about it. It's already healed." Logan glared in the hunter's direction—a plea? A part of Sawyer was sorely tempted to leave Logan to solve his own problems. The last thing they needed, however, was for Victoria—and hence Grimhild—to notice the missing tattoo.

"I thought we were in a hurry," Sawyer cut in, allowing his pent-up frustration to flavor his tone.

The distraction worked. Victoria pulled around and said, "We are in a hurry."

"Then stop coddling poor li'l Logan." Sawyer used the same "Oh boo-hoo" note of mockery he and his brothers employed when wagging sibling warfare.

"Coddling?" Victoria glared daggers.

"Coddling. You've been mothering him since he lost his hand." Sawyer dropped a nod. When she advanced, he retreated because he considered himself a smart man.

"I don't coddle." Victoria crossed her arms over her chest. The ploy worked—the entirety of her attention transferred to Sawyer. Knowing her as he did, he expected she would take pains to ignore Logan for the next few hours just to prove herself.

Predictable, but so were they all in their own ways.

Relief washed over Logan's face and he mouthed "thanks" over her head. Then he followed through with an audaciously rude gesture. "Go shove that shotgun where the sun doesn't shine!"

"I'm going for *Gnýrhorn*," Sawyer announced.

"Then go," Logan snapped. "Or are you waiting for fanfare?"

Apparently gratitude lasted for less than three seconds with the male werewolf. Sawyer took a stride, lifting his gaze to the distance. He halted.

Fog.

Stray haloed fingers punched holes in the fog, reaching out of the forest. Chills coursed through Sawyer. He turned in place, surveying the landscape. Dense columns of mist surrounded the entire hilltop, rising like hoodoo rocks into the storm clouds.

"That's not creepy at all." Victoria swiped her palms, and searched their surroundings for hidden threats. She edged closer to *Sawyer,* not Logan. Sawyer found distinct satisfaction in being chosen. Proof that on some level, Victoria preferred him... trusted him to protect her.

"Nah, it's fine. When you live at seventy-five hundred feet, weird weather can touch down at any time." Logan shrugged it off.

"Well, I don't like it." Victoria shivered and started around to the front of the house. Sawyer trailed after her, dragging his feet.

The fog crept ever closer.

The front door swung open and Cali emerged. Sawyer pulled up and stared past her, concerned the gray wolves and Morena would come pouring out next. But Cali closed the door behind her, and stood on the porch, grasping her rifle. Her piercing regard sought Sawyer. She raised her brow. He gave a small shake of his head.

Not yet.

"Hey, Cali... what's wrong?" Victoria's greeting began on a normal note and ended on suspicion.

"Wrong? Nothing." Cali probably would've been fine if she'd stopped there... Instead, she gave a small shake of her head, a sign of internal dissonance. "Why do you ask?"

"No reason." Victoria ground to a halt, stared ahead, and then glanced over her shoulder. Under her command, the pack bond roared to life.

Shit. Sawyer tried to quell the mounting alarm but failed. The damnable empathic connection operated as an electric circuit—emotions flowed freely across it, carried to all.

A handgun hammer clicked.

His shoulders bunched and his heart pounded. Hunter magic rose from Sawyer's core like magma pushing to the surface. On his upper arm, his hunter's mark caught fire. A startled cry escaped Victoria as hers lit up also. It took everything he had *not* to drop and draw his guns.

A gunshot cracked, its echo soaring. A strong blow hammered Sawyer in the back. The bullet punched a hole in his chest. A red blossom spread across the front of his shirt a few inches above his heart. Far too close for comfort. The cool breeze whisked the acerbic scent of gunpowder over him.

Sawyer lurched, clutching his breast. *Motherfucker, that hurt.* The bastard had almost shot him through the heart. A groan tore from Sawyer's throat. *Kappiskjǫld's* weight dragged him down like an anchor. He crashed to his knees.

"Whoo! That felt good!" Logan shouted at the top of his lungs, "Get your skank ass out here now, Grimhild!"

Wild arcana bucked and surged, challenging Sawyer's control. Cold fury burned through the hunter. With a determined effort, he gritted his teeth and schooled it, because he had no other choice.

Killing Logan wasn't part of the plan.

CHAPTER 36

Tiwaz: The Warrior's Rune

SAWYER KNELT, doubled forward. His arm jerked free of *Kappiskjøld's* straps and the shield tipped over, landing face down on the ground. Gasping for breath, he grasped the front flap of his leather duster and shoved his finger into the puckered opening—ruined. He glared at Logan. "You're going to pay for that."

"Yeah, I'm scared. Bring it on, douche hammer." Restless pacing carried Logan into Sawyer's peripheral vision. The wolf-shifter radiated terrible tension. He gripped the revolver like it was a snake, holding it away from his body.

Still manning her post on the porch, Cali hefted her rifle into firing position. Across the yard, Victoria whirled and stared. Astonishment crossed her face, and anger chased it. She clenched her hands

"Logan, what the hell are you doing?" Victoria shouted, competing with the wind. Sawyer tasted chagrin. He'd been hoping for concern, but he supposed he and Logan had gone at each other one too many times.

"Grimhild! You said call and you'd come!" Logan scanned the encroaching wall of mist, pivoting on his heel when his search yielded nothing.

Shit. Victoria hadn't bought it. Worry blitzed Sawyer. Heartbeats passed, but still there was no sign of Grimhild. The runes strained against the barrier that prevented them from fulfilling their fundamental function: healing the damage to his body. He could only delay his recovery for so long. Each passing second increased the odds the witch would catch onto their ruse.

"Shoot me again," Sawyer pitched his voice low, taking a chance. He hoped the blustery weather would prevent him from being heard by anyone other than Logan.

Logan swung around. He stabbed at Sawyer through the pack bond—a sharp inquiry. Sawyer nodded his chin, a gesture that could be mistaken for a twitch.

"What are you idiots—" The wind snatched away the rest of Victoria's words. She started toward them; no mistaking the determination in her march. In a few seconds, she'd cross the lawn and have them both in hand, probably to bang their skulls together.

"Damn it." Logan jerked up the revolver and fired at point-blank range. The second bullet caught Sawyer higher on the shoulder.

Pain shrieked. Sawyer lurched, riding a churning crimson sea. A rogue wave broke over his head and the undertow sucked him down. Runes marched across Sawyer's vision. His heart hammered—a low, dense, slow sound. His strength ebbed, sucked down a swirling drain. He doubled over, resting his chest against his thighs and clutching his knees to remain upright.

Sawyer glanced up, squinting through a red gaze. Victoria sprinted toward them; her expression belonged to a woman intent on murder. Logan had big trouble in a little package heading his way. Not that Sawyer gave two figs about the wolf-shifter, but he worried about Victoria getting caught in the crossfire.

Cali jogged along after Victoria, holding her rifle in a military carry. Sawyer registered a split-second of worry over Kinkaid having abandoned her post. She was supposed to keep watch—their sentry and sniper.

"Fuck, you're a tough bastard! Go down already!" Logan kicked Sawyer in the side, demonstrating far too much exuberance for Sawyer's tastes. The bastard had just gone completely off script.

Ribs broke. Agony exploded throughout his chest. Sawyer lost his precarious grip on everything: his balance, the runes, and most of all, his patience. The hunter crashed to the green lawn and landed on his side. The runes busted through their imprisonment and stormed his myriad injuries. Vigorous strength empowered him.

"That's it." Sawyer growled. He'd taken more than enough bullshit. Even though his right arm was pinned beneath him, being a southpaw became a blessing of the moment. Hell bent on revenge, Sawyer yanked one of his 9mms from its holster and shot Logan in the hip.

Blood spurted from the wound. A violent snarl erupted from Logan.

"Damn, you're right. That felt good," Sawyer exclaimed. Better than therapy. He figured he needed more than once session so he fired three more times, clustering the bullets in the Logan's thigh. In Sawyer's opinion, he practiced laudable restraint in not kneecapping the werewolf.

With a roar, Logan threw down the revolver and jumped on Sawyer. He got off another shot that went wide, and then lost his grip on the 9mm. The wolf and hunter grappled, trading vicious kicks and punches. Sawyer forgot everything. The outside world vanished. He poured everything into hurting his opponent and derived perverse satisfaction from the sweaty, bloody struggle.

Locked together, they rolled. Their conflict raged on the metaphysical plane; a psychic blow for every physical one that landed. As Sawyer turned onto his back, Victoria's platinum blonde hair flashed past his vision. Golden radiance spilled from her eyes and mouth, obscuring her features.

Immense energy gathered overhead. As it crested, the alpha released the boom. Nova-brightness blinded Sawyer. A spiritual nuke blasted over him, and the wallop knocked him senseless. He went limp. Likewise, Logan collapsed on top of him. The two men lay like landed fish. Sawyer couldn't draw breath no matter how hard he struggled. For the longest time, blaring filled his ears. He gripped the sides of his head, waiting for the world to stop ringing. After a time, he felt Logan's weight hauled away, and abruptly, air filled his lungs.

Face set in a stoic mask, Victoria leaned over Sawyer. She placed her fingertips to his temple. Warmth washed through his head, clearing out the clouds of discomfort and distress. Sawyer's hearing returned—Victoria's voice the first thing he heard.

"I'm sick to death of the two of them acting like spoiled toddlers." Victoria seemed to be addressing someone out of Sawyer's limited viewpoint. She definitely wasn't talking to him.

Cali chuckled. "Yeah, well, men will be boys."

Sawyer turned his face even though it cost him dearly. His head was an overripe grape about to burst on the vine. It throbbed. His effort yielded an improved perspective, though. Cali lounged a couple feet distant, standing over Logan, who was also prone. Sawyer glimpsed red from the corner of his eye. With a groan, he moved his arm a couple inches until his fingers rested on *Kappiskjøld's* polished front.

Thick fog engulfed them on all sides, restricting visibility to a yard. Nothing penetrated it—not sunlight, moonlight, or starlight. Victoria's pure white halo provided their sole illumination. Not a hint of blue marred her radiance. Victoria was, beyond a shadow of doubt, herself.

The bitter taste of failure filled Sawyer's mouth. With a monumental effort, he lifted his head and aimed a disgusted glare at Logan. Dismay yawned before the hunter, already giving way to resignation. A part of him wondered whether the male werewolf had made up the whole story about the witch. Sawyer berated himself for having been gullible enough to trust.

Faith—always a fool's bet.

CHAPTER 37

***Kappiskjǫld*: Champion's Shield**

TWO FEMALE FIGURES manifested from the mist directly behind Cali. Sawyer readied a warning, but then he recognized Sylvie. Relief washed through him. If anyone could get through to Victoria, it was the skald. But then he saw Sylvie's companion. A woman with a vulture's visage—pale blue eyes covered with a milky film. He hesitated, assessing the threat the stranger possessed.

Those three seconds of indecision earned him a legacy of regret.

"Do it now." The strange woman had a voice like vexation. At the sound of it, Logan turned over on the ground where he rested. Cali jerked and started to turn.

Too late, Sawyer arrived at the stranger's identity—Grimhild.

Light flashed off a steel blade. Sylvie raised the knife overhead and plunged it into Cali's back. The hunter's face drained and her lips turned blue. The light in her eyes dimmed. Without a sound, Kinkaid collapsed into a heap.

"I'm sorry," Sylvie apologized as Cali fell. "I'm so sorry..."

Too late, Sawyer pushed a full-throated shout up from his very core, but his vocal chords froze. He tried to surge upright—and found he couldn't move a muscle. An invisible hand held him pinned against the fresh grass, soft and cool against his back. His hand still rested atop *Kappiskjøld*, for all the good it did him. He could see what was happening only because he'd had his head turned when the paralysis hit.

"No!" Victoria cried out in powerful denial. Her face froze in that shout as she fell prisoner to the same magic that'd captured Sawyer. Within the pack bond, her wolf howled and bashed against the confines of her cage. Sawyer reached out to her; their psyches touched.

"Dixie!" Logan vaulted over Sawyer and landed in a crouch beside Cali's prone form. He bent over and pressed his fingers to her throat, checking for a pulse. "How dare you—she wasn't part of the deal!"

Grimhild sneered. "Logan, you are allowing sentimentality to cloud your judgment. The woman is a hunter. Don't think she wouldn't have turned against us."

"Bring her back now!" A ferocious growl erupted from Logan. He rose to confront Grimhild.

"Her spark is almost out," Grimhild said. "And I'm not a healer."

"Free Victoria to heal her or our deal's off!" Logan rose, baring his teeth.

The witch narrowed her eyes. Her tone grew dangerous. "The terms of our bargain guaranteed the safety of your pack. You're correct in saying the female hunter wasn't part of our deal. It didn't protect her."

Sawyer sensed Cali's life force fading via their hunters' connection. He wanted to go to her, to help her, but he didn't have time. Not to absorb the shock of Sylvie's betrayal, not even to worry for Cali. He had to save *everyone*, which meant getting free.

He strained against the intangible source binding him, but couldn't so much as twitch a finger. His frustration spiraled. He could blink and breathe, but no matter how hard he strained, he couldn't move another muscle.

But he did have his freewill and magic.

"I don't give a shit about technicalities!" Logan shifted his hands to claws, which he raised in menace. "If Cali dies, I'll resist you at every turn. Your life will be a living hell."

"Oh!" Grimhild released a huff, sounding like a fed-up mother dealing with a spoiled child. She waved her arm. "Very well!"

Victoria stumbled and almost fell. A livid snarl escaped from her.

Sawyer wracked his memory for everything his father had told him. Complex enchantments required a real connection to the physical world to render the dynamic magic stable and permanent. To defeat Grimhild, he needed a shield—and *Kappiskjøld* oh so conveniently lay at his fingertips.

"Is it magical?"

"Not yet."

Thank you, Mom. Sawyer centered on *Kappiskjøld.*

"Vic, get over here." A long stride carried Logan to Victoria. He seized her arm and hauled her to Cali. "I know you're confused, but there's no time for explanations now. Later. Can you focus enough to heal Cali?"

"I think so." Victoria glared murder at Logan, but she licked her lips and raised her hands, positioning them over the female hunter. For seconds, nothing happened. Then, a soft glow emanated from her palms and washed over Cali's chest. Silence fell while Victoria worked.

Concentrating, Sawyer summoned the runes into his mind. The magic rushed him, each of the twenty-four symbols clamoring for attention. Too many runes... His mind was awhirl. Sigils tumbled through his consciousness like a flurry of puzzle pieces. *Okay, breathe.* With an effort, he strove for cool headedness... and even achieved a shaky semblance of it. Not much but it'd have to do. Trouble he had in great quantities, but only a thimble of time. He undertook the laborious task of sorting through the runes. He needed to find one suited to his needs—to serve as the basis of a new protective bind rune capable of breaking Grimhild's hold on his body.

Icy *Isa* chilled Sawyer's skin. His hot breath condensed to a vapor cloud when he exhaled. Ah, stagnation... but then *Isa* also provided protection against magical attacks. She represented his predicament and his stated desire—not a bad place to start. He tucked her against his heart and reached for another rune.

Algiz bounced to Sawyer's awareness, vigorous with energy and optimism. It gleefully scolded him to pay attention to signs. He sent it on its way with an unspoken, "Yeah, thanks for that!"

"Can we proceed?" Grimhild took the bloody knife from Sylvie.

"Not until Cali is in the clear. Victoria doesn't need any distractions." Logan's declaration earned him a sharp glance from Victoria. She thinned her lips but otherwise remained silent. Sawyer wondered how much leeway Logan could buy with trust.

"What I need is explanations." Victoria wore a mantle of sternness as she labored over Cali. "What are you up to, Logan?"

"Nothing. Just living up to my heritage. You trust me, don't you?" Logan flashed a grin and dropped a conspiratorial wink.

"It'd better be good—really good." Victoria scowled but didn't lift her gaze from her patient.

Sawyer braced against the sudden onslaught of *Hagalaz*—the stinging hardness of the hailstone. The assault caught him off guard. Hastily, Sawyer threw up his defenses. Irony bit him—he should've heeded *Algiz's* warning. Regardless, he held onto the hailstone; the force of elemental disruption might serve him well in overcoming petrification. *Hagalaz* and *Isa* blended flawlessly.

"It will be." Logan smirked in triumph and told Grimhild, "We're waiting."

"You are an absolute brat," Grimhild shot back.

"Like I've never heard *that* before." Logan rolled his eyes.

"Sylvie, you betrayed us! *Why?*" Victoria turned a look of mixed accusation and hurt to the skald. The moment the healer's attention wavered, Cali's spark dimmed.

An urgent shout built in Sawyer's chest, but his frozen vocal chords refused to cooperate. Within the prison of his mind, he pounded his fists against the walls and yelled at Victoria to focus on what mattered.

"Mine is not the betrayal. It is your treachery that has endangered this pack; you who brought hunters into our midst." Sylvie turned an accusing glare on her alpha.

Grasping the bloodstained weapon she'd claimed from Sylvie, Grimhild stood over Sawyer. Her carrion-eater's gaze fell on him. His skin crawled beneath her regard. Red droplets dripped from the blade and spattered across the back of his hand. His body absorbed Cali's blood and their spiritual connection deepened. Thanks to Victoria's healing and hunter magic, Cali's soul spark brightened.

Victoria grew quiet. Within the pack bond, she gathered strength. "You don't understand—"

"Don't tell me what I don't understand! I understand too much —too well!" Sylvie shouted.

"Silence!" Grimhild stabbed at the air with the knife, spraying him with more of Cali's castoff blood. His thirsty skin absorbed every drop.

Logan rocked on the balls of his feet, and then took to restless wandering, trampling the lawn underfoot. Between his missing front paw and the gunshot wounds on his rear leg, his limp was pronounced.

Desperation sat on Sawyer's chest like a fat cat; encroaching panic threatened to suffocate him. A good half dozen runes passed through Sawyer's thoughts, none of them proper for the protective bind rune he'd constructed. He considered chucking what he'd already built and starting over. Anything to move forward...

Right then inspiration struck, but thankfully without the

harshness of hail. *Raido*, the traveler's rune, leapt to the stage—ready on arrival and good to go. Sawyer pressed *Raido* into place and reached for another.

Perspiration slicked his skin; he sweated apprehension. The richness of runes dwindled with each one as he examined and rejected. Worried, he looked over his metaphorical shoulder at the rejected sigils. What if in his urgency or inexperience, he'd cast off the one he needed? Should he go back and look through the discards?

No. Raido cracked the whip. No going back—forward.

Jera blossomed, soothing his troubled spirit. The harvest, a symbol of prosperity and positive outcomes. Logically, *Jera* didn't serve his greater goal. He closed a mental fist about the symbol, preparing to toss it aside, but the rune restored a sense of peace to his heart. His mind cleared. Trusting his instincts, he united *Jera* with the others, this strengthening the bonds.

His finger twitched, stroking across *Kappiskjǫld's* polished surface. The shield thrummed with the infusion of magic.

Almost there! What was he still missing?

"You are an Oath Breaker," Sylvie ranted at Victoria while Grimhild looked on with a smug smile.

"I am no such thing." Victoria's healing magic flickered out, and Cali weakened. A shout gathered in Sawyer's throat, but his vocal chords again refused to obey him. Relief washed through him when Victoria rallied. Her halo returned.

"Will you be still?" Grimhild demanded of Logan, whose pacing now carried him in revolutions about them.

"No," Logan shot back, and Grimhild released an exasperated hiss.

"You swore to avenge Jasper's murder..." Sylvie's bitter exclamation hitched. "Who is this man at my feet, this child killer you brought into this pack?"

Within his immobile prison, Sawyer faltered. Shame wilted his confidence. He sank into a quagmire of guilt. Hard knots cramped his gut.

"I swore myself to justice." Victoria reached through the pack bond and delivered a psychic kick to his metaphorical backside. She booted him right out of his self-pitying brood. Then, for added measure, she smacked him a few more times. *"Justice."*

Ah, Justice! Sawyer exploded into an epiphany. *Tiwaz* ascended to prominence. *Tiwaz*—the warrior's rune, symbolic of courage and cunning in warfare; it also provided protection. The unbidden sigil locked into place. The protective bind rune blazed to life, and the magic merged with the round shield.

It transformed *Kappiskjøld*—Champion's Shield, an enduring enchantment.

Sawyer was free.

"Are you done yet?" Grimhild demanded of Victoria.

"For the moment. Cali's stable—for now. She's going to need medical care." Victoria raised her hands and shot upright, drawing Grimhild's attention onto herself.

Now or never... Sawyer summoned every iota of magic at his command. His hunter's mark flared into an inferno—and the warrior's rune surged power through him. He rolled and bolted upright. With an act of will, he summoned *Kappiskjøld* to him. The shield leapt off the ground and flew to Sawyer; its straps wrapping about his forearm.

Fog thick enough to cut into slices surrounded him. Through the curtain, he glimpsed Victoria's fleet form as she tackled Sylvie. The women toppled in a scuffle.

Logan's breathing was a heavy rasp—the wolf in the dark.

With a toothy smile, Sawyer prowled toward Grimhild. He was keen for a fight after being restrained for so long. He itched to draw Thorn, but the enchanted dagger had to stay hidden until he got close enough to get a clean shot at the witch's heart. Logan had said Grimhild was supremely overconfident and predicted she'd remain to screw with them... so long as she believed herself invulnerable. Sawyer hoped Logan was right, because so far the guy was batting oh-for-two.

"Halt!" Grimhild whirled, brandishing her bloodstained knife.

She carved a glowing sigil into the air. It transformed into a crackling energy web. The net flew like a dark sail and dropped over Sawyer.

Sawyer raised *Kappiskjǫld* and took cover. The spell hit the shield, crackled like a live wire on water, and fizzled out.

"That tickled. Is that all you've got?" Sawyer shook a shower of sparks off his shield. Never again would a witch's paralysis bind him, and he was resolved to protect those closest to him as well. With a slight alteration, he believed he could extend *Kappiskjǫld's* protective warding to the others. Competing bonds of wolf and hunter magic served as a hindrance to enhancing the Champion's Shield, though.

"Arrogant whelp. You are a stupid child playing in the mud compared to me," Grimhild said with a sneer while she sculpted another sigil, this time using her hand and the blade in concert.

"I've heard pigs like to wallow." The silhouette of a monstrous wolf loomed over Grimhild. Logan's enormous paw swung wide and closed on the witch. The wicked points of the wolf's claw passed through Grimhild's insubstantial form without resistance.

With a frustrated snarl, Logan charged through the illusion, scattering shimmering particles into the mist. Grimhild vanished into the veil again, swallowed whole.

Logan's attack bought Sawyer precious time. He united the twin pledges of his soul and merged them via capricious *Laguz*. She cooperated—this time—but boldly cautioned him not to take her for granted. *Fehu* served as the conduit through which he shared the magic. He reached for Victoria first, figuring she'd be easier than the others since she was already a hunter, and he was right... to a point. *Kappiskjǫld's* protection dropped over her like a mantle.

A startled yelp arose from Victoria, followed by a thunk, and then the pounding of fleeing footsteps. Oops. Sawyer called out, "Victoria?"

Victoria's voice returned strong and clear; she must be close. "Here! I'm fine but I just lost Sylvie. Thanks bunches."

"Sorry." Sawyer winced.

"Did you get Grimhild?" Victoria asked.

"Working on it." Hastily, he fused Cali into the Storm pack and imposed the protective ward over her. He'd apologize to Victoria for usurping her alpha authority... later.

Victoria took up *Kappiskjøld's* magic with the expertise of a trained Valkyrie. "I'm going after Sylvie," she said, and he nodded. She disappeared into the fog.

Sawyer resumed his search.

"Here witchy witchy witchy..." Logan said, singsong. His wolf-gaze strobed; amber radiance cut through the haze. The light cast Grimhild into profile. "Well, lookie here... Kick over some rocks, and vermin crawl out."

"Betraying me was a mistake, Logan. I tried to be gentle with you. I see now, I should've used a firm hand from the start." Grimhild manifested from the mist, a tantalizing shadow that danced just out of reach when Sawyer moved toward her.

"You think you're gonna school me, bitch?" Logan stalked her, crouched close to the earth. The wolf held his head low, protecting his throat, and his tail bristled straight behind him.

"Let's start by muzzling you, mutt." Grimhild etched a variation on the paralysis glyph with her knife. The spell birthed a monstrous fire-hued cobra that coiled before the witch.

The cobra reared its head and flared its hood. It hissed, revealing needle-sharp fangs and bulging venom sacks. Sawyer perceived the snake's underlying energy; binding magic cloaked in a menacing skin.

Another trick.

Logan bared his teeth, thick ropes of saliva sweeping between his canines. A steady snarl issued from his throat. He lowered his front quarters, muscles bunching.

"It's not real," Sawyer shouted, but his warning went unheard.

With a ferocious growl, Logan lunged, going for the snake's throat. His injuries hampered his breaking speed, making him slow off the mark.

The cobra struck.

Sawyer turned *Kappiskjǫld* onto its side and hurled it into the sliver-space that separated wolf and serpent. The shield's edge sliced clean through the cobra's neck. The spell-snake decayed into the rudimentary magic from which it'd come.

Kappiskjǫld embedded itself in the rocky soil. With a resounding clang, Logan plowed headfirst into the unyielding shield. Knocked senseless, he staggered. The wolf expelled a pained moan and his front leg buckled under him.

Sawyer winced. *Oops.* Oh well, such was the cost of war; sometimes casualties fell to friendly fire. Besides, it'd only been Logan's head—nothing he would miss.

Unceremoniously, the shield tipped over and rolled on its rim. Just as Logan raised his head, *Kappiskjǫld* smashed into his skull, knocking the wolf out cold. The shield came to rest propped against Logan; its magic plunged the defenseless wolf straight into the hunter collective with a tsunami-splash. Although it was hidden beneath Logan's dense black fur, a dagger tattoo now marked him.

"Heh." Sawyer braced against the ripple Logan's presence sent through the oceanic hunter connection. Tectonic plates shifted. The earth's crust ripped open, exposing a fiery core. Repercussions would be felt around the world. Sawyer figured he'd be paying the price for *that* for a long, long time.

"Do you think yourself my equal as a magician because you know one trick, boy?" As bold as a bee, Grimhild faced Sawyer over the downed wolf. She brandished her knife, conjuring anew. "Just who do you think you are?"

"I am Veiðimaðr." Sawyer claimed his first true god-name. *Veiðimaðr—the hunter.* Quintessential fire burned in his heart. *Kappiskjǫld* appeared again, strapped to his forearm, leaving his other hand free to wield Thorn. He circled Logan rather than going over. As sure as stones sank, Fate would decree the contrary werewolf to rouse just in time to trip Sawyer up.

"And I am Grimhild." Grimhild thrust her Wyrd-lit dagger toward his chest.

"A pleasure—to kill you." Sawyer threw up his forearm and blocked. The point of her blade slid across the shield, metal upon metal. The unerring precision of the attack—straight at his heart—couldn't be a coincidence. Grimhild knew his Achilles heel. The knowledge didn't frighten him, but it did introduce a healthy sense of caution.

"My name means masked-battle..." Grimhild said as though it should mean something to him. She stabbed, and he parried.

"Do you think I care?" Sawyer put his weight behind the shield and shoved Grimhild back.

"It matters." She slashed and he ducked.

"There are women I have to take shit from," Sawyer said with a sneer. "You're not one of them."

The witch pressed her attack. The hunter maintained his defenses, studying hers. Their fight carried them past the spot where Logan had lain unconscious, but Sawyer dared not spare the attention. Grimhild remained the center of his focus. One slip could earn him a knife through the heart. Throughout, Thorn's essence resonated, awaiting the call to arms. He had but to ask, and she would spring forth. Waiting for the right moment challenged his patience. The atmosphere grew heavy with the clash of combat and the fracas of footsteps.

"I am named after my father, the great god Grimnir." Grimhild's lips grew taut, peeling back in a corpse's rotten smile.

"No." Sawyer faltered. Grimnir—one of Odin's countless names. But this vile-tongued troll woman couldn't possibly be—

"I can see the denial in your eyes, but truth cannot be denied. Before Odin married Frigg, he sired many children on the giantess Grid. I'm your half-sister." Grimhild drove past his guard and hacked at his arm. The edge of her blade slashed a nasty laceration from his elbow to wrist. His life liquid poured forth. A pained cry contorted his throat.

Unreasoning anger clouded Sawyer's vision—and his mind.

No fucking way could this witch-bitch be his sister. A bellow tore from his belly. He swung *Kappiskjǫld* and bashed Grimhild in the chin with the shield. Her jaw crunched, and blood poured from her mouth. The blow toppled her.

"Thorn?" Sawyer raised his hand. Piercing pain emanated from where the tattoo bracelet twined about his wrist. Tendrils burst from the central vines, spreading across his hand and forearm.

Thorn punctured Sawyer's palm, spraying red, the dagger springing into his hand. *Drive me into the witch's heart. I thirst for her life.*

Grimhild lifted her gory face. She froze, her gaze riveted on Thorn.

"Let's finish this." He advanced, holding the dagger level. Deep in his gut, a maggot of anxiety ate at him. His people considered kin slaying to be a terrible crime. What would be the karmic fallout of killing his half-sister?

Why do you hesitate? Destroy her! Thorn's white-hot fury lanced through Sawyer, jolting him to action. Battle rage engulfed him, obliterating reason.

The witch shrieked and fled.

Sawyer loosened a bloodthirsty battle cry and launched into a run, pursuing his prey. The chase led downhill where the forest grew thick on the slope. Visibility remained no more than a few feet. Trees emerged from the thick fog without warning

Nimble as a spider, the witch skittered through the brushwood. A shroud of fog engulfed Grimhild but she couldn't hide. Not from Sawyer. Unerring certainty guided his steps through the old growth. Before Thorn, the trees yielded. Boulders rolled aside. No barrier could bar him, for tonight he was *grennir gunn-más*—feeder of ravens—and Grimhild would be their meal.

He marched, an unstoppable force; the essence of the Asgård-sreien coursed through his veins. His heart throbbed strong, his pulse resounded in his ears, but a primal rhythm drowned those out. He *heard* a ferocious mounted cavalry: the shouts of the soldiers, the fiery snorts and pounding hooves of the horses, and the bellowing of their hounds. The song of the Wild Hunt enraptured him.

The ground beneath his feet leveled out; the forest floor became a beach of smooth, rounded stone. He continued without slowing. Liquid splashed beneath his boots. Abruptly, the fog thinned. Echo Lake stretched before him. Fingers of fog stroked its placid surface.

Sawyer's stride hitched.

Grimhild stood waist deep in the lake—waiting for him. Water —the witch's natural element... and Sawyer's vulnerability. His courage quailed. If he drowned, he couldn't protect his heart.

Sawyer faltered for a stride but he hardened his nerve. His father had taught him never to show fear in the face of the enemy. He taunted her. "Run out of places to run, Grimmy?"

"I chose a strategic retreat to favorable ground." Grimhild's baleful glare said she resented the accusation of cowardice, but her hatred assumed a strange expression. She crooked her finger. "Come deeper, dear brother."

"Standing in a lake won't save you. I can't drown," Sawyer boasted, even though it wasn't the whole truth. He could drown, but the runes would bring him back.

Swallowing bile, Sawyer forged his will to a hammer and flattened fear. He plunged into the lake toward Grimhild. Chilling water rose to his calves and then his knees.

"Oh, but you can drown, and you will, Veiðimaðr." Grimhild made mockery of his true name, which provoked his relentless fury. "Because you'll pursue me into deep water even though you know in your gut that I've won."

"Won?" He scoffed. "Not even close."

Nearby, a she-wolf's howl split the night. In her alpha-voice, Victoria called their pack together. She bayed long and low —*Danger to the pack. Come to me.*

Sawyer missed a step. Their most vulnerable members— Sophia, the pups, and Morena—*should* be safely locked away in the lake house's basement. But just then, Sophia's faint yelp carried across a faint distance, and the pups echoed their mother, reporting their far-flung locations. Sawyer's heart sank. *Shit.* They were running loose through the fog, all vulnerable to Grimhild's mind-magic.

Victoria's howl grew forceful as she sought to gather her strayed followers together. Sawyer felt her summons as a visceral tug. He'd found his place in life with the Storm Pack... and his calling as protector. But as hard as it was, he had to ignore Victoria's command. Right now, slaying Grimhild was the only surefire way to safeguard those he loved.

Sawyer had the heart of a wolf, but the soul of a hunter.

He waded to his thighs. The frigid fluid soaked his jeans which grew heavy, and took a nasty bite from his blood and bone. The life-warmth sapped from his body and his blood ran cold and sluggish. He shivered. The allure of death curled in his nostrils.

"Your pride won't allow you to turn back and that will be your undoing." Grimhild opened her arms like a mother inviting her child into a hug. "The lake will close over your head and swallow you whole. You'll hold your breath till you burst, and then your lungs will flood with icy water. While you're helpless, I'll drag your corpse to the depths and bind you there. You'll revive only to drown again... over and over for the rest of eternity."

From the shore, Victoria shouted, "Sawyer! No, come back!"

"Victoria, stay back!" Sawyer replied without turning. Victoria reached for him across the pack bond, but he shut her out. He raised Thorn overhead, holding her poised for a downward stoke.

"Damn it! Stop! She's trying to—" A vampire wind descended, feasting on warmth and words.

Obeying his gut, Sawyer hesitated. Thirty feet separated him from Grimhild. His advance into the lake had halved the distance between them but for the last meter or so, the gap had remained constant. Trickery enabled her to remain at waist depth even though the water had risen to his chest. Logan had also warned Sawyer to be wary of the possibility that the witch herself would appear as an illusion. The hunter possessed no means of testing it other than to attack.

Thorn's voice hissed through Sawyer's mind, *I sense life force.*

That's good enough for me, Sawyer returned.

"Pathetic." Grimhild sneered. "What good is your all-powerful artifact if you can't get close enough to use it?"

"Close is relative." Sawyer sent a thought to Thorn. In his hand, the dagger shifted to a slender mistletoe dart. He threw, trusting his hunter's aim.

Thorn flew straight and true, struck Grimhild dead center, and sank into her heart. The witch clutched at the dart protruding from her chest. Battle-sweat seeped past her fingers and spread in a red bloom. Shimmering immersed Grimhild's entire form. It faded, revealing—

Morena.

"No." Horror engulfed Sawyer.

Morena coughed blood. Disbelief brightened her gaze. She stared down at the short spear that impaled her and gave the shaft a futile tug.

Roaring deafened him. Sawyer lurched and lumbered through the shallows toward her. *Kappiskjøld* disappeared and became a shield tattoo behind the dagger on his upper arm. He stumbled and fell, soaking himself to the skin. He caught Morena as she sank. The end of the dart banged against his chest.

"Morie, don't die. Please don't die." Sawyer gathered Morena into his arms. His mind raced, incoherent with desperation. One thought ascended—if he could take the teenager to Victoria, Victoria would heal Morena and everything would be okay. He gathered the girl against his chest and struggled toward the shore.

No. Thorn cut through his madness. *I'm sorry. The girl cannot be healed or resurrected. I feed on life force. I have taken hers slowly to give you a chance to say goodbye. Don't waste it.*

He halted, still knee-deep in the shoals.

"Sawyer?" Morena gasped. Red trickled from the corner of her mouth. "It hurts. It's so cold."

"I'm sorry." He met her gaze through a veil of tears. "I swear, I'll save you."

A bloody bubble formed on Morena's lips. The light in her eyes faded to glassy darkness, and she died.

Sawyer broke.

CHAPTER 38

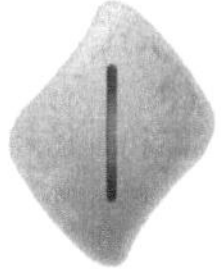

Isa: The Ice Rune

Ice.

Beautiful and treacherous ice immobilized Sylvie's heart.

"Morena was my daughter," Sylvie said in a voice devoid of emotion and as empty as her soul. "How dare you end her life?"

"The girl's death is unfortunate, but she was a necessary sacrifice. Now it will be a simple matter to coax the hunter into killing himself... if his own packmates don't kill him first." Grimhild refused to even look at Sylvie when she spoke. The _seiðr_ kept her attention directed outward.

"This is unacceptable." Sylvie looked on from outside herself— a watcher through the frozen glass.

"It's done. Cease your complaints."

Sylvie pressed her granite lips together.

"Besides, _I_ didn't murder the girl," Grimhild threw out as an afterthought.

"Sawyer was *your* murder weapon," Sylvie said, but Grimhild wasn't listening... or didn't care.

Throughout the drama, a protective rune circle on the hilltop had sheltered the two women. Like a great spider, Grimhild sat at the center of a complex web of enchantment. Multi-colored strands of mysticism flowed from her fingertips, binding her to the weave. Scrying spells enabled her to watch over her victims from a distance. Through illusions and mind magic, she controlled, manipulated, and deceived. Logan, Sawyer, and Victoria were flies thrashing about within the web without even understanding they'd been caught.

As intent as a vulture over carrion, Grimhild tipped forward. She narrowed her pale blue eyes, peering through the smoky mirror which revealed distant images. Sawyer staggered ashore, carrying Morena's body in his arms, and Victoria rushed to meet him. Another farsighted spell showed Logan, more than a mile distant, running as best he could despite his disability and injuries. Since the black wolf had awakened, Grimhild had kept him busy chasing shadows.

"Victoria's not going to kill him," Grimhild hissed her disappointment. She wiggled her fingers, twisting the spell strands, and tightened the focus.

"No, she wouldn't." Sylvie derived no pleasure from the *seiðr's* aggravation. She would never know satisfaction again. But that wouldn't stop her from seeking revenge.

Victoria yanked the mistletoe dart from Morena's chest and cast it aside. Predictably, the alpha conjured healing magic, intent on resurrecting the teenager from the dead. Sylvie desperately wished her success, but knew Victoria labored in vain.

Grimhild zoomed in on the discarded mistletoe dart. She issued an imperious order to Sylvie. "Fetch me that. I'm going to lure the hunter to a watery grave."

Without protest, Sylvie obeyed. She walked downhill to the lakeshore where amid wailing curses and prayers, Victoria toiled at her sorry task, unaware Sawyer had waded back into the lake.

The bloody barb stuck out of the earth, its point embedded in the rocky soil. Sylvie wrapped her hand about its shaft. The artifact transformed into a slender dagger. A female voice sprang into her mind—*Hello, I'm Thorn.*

Overcome with misgiving, Sylvie hesitated. An inexorable sense of wrongness filled her. This weapon was not meant for her. Should she drop it?

Thorn answered the unvoiced question. *I am vengeance. I am wrath. We are well suited to work together... for this one thing. No more.*

Very well. Sylvie started up the slope, but paused. Enough of her humanity remained that she couldn't escape the lash of guilt so easily. Unexpected compassion weighed on her for Victoria, who shared Sylvie's grief over the loss of Morena. Sylvie had an opportunity to make a small act of atonement—she couldn't allow it to pass.

Leaning over, she tapped Victoria on the shoulder and said, "She's gone."

Victoria jerked her head back. She stared with eyes bloodshot and blank, unseeing, but then her gaze focused on Sylvie. She croaked, "Sylvie?"

"I am alive," Sylvie said, uttering a terrible lie. Her lungs still drew breath and her heart pumped blood, but her soul had died with her daughter.

A stony mask dropped over Victoria, transforming her into an ice statue. Cold fury burned in her gaze—and nothing else. For Sylvie, it was looking into a mirror at her own reflection. *A lie.* Victoria still had something left to lose—and hence, a reason to live... and to fight.

"Morena's spark has gone out," Sylvie said. "Let her go. Go after Sawyer. You may still be able to save him."

"Sawyer?" Victoria faltered. The rime encasing her cracked. Further proof that she wasn't as far gone as Sylvie.

"There." Sylvie raised her arm, pointing toward the lake. With a cry, Victoria lurched upright and staggered toward the water.

Sylvie considered helping, but this wasn't her concern—not

anymore. She continued on her way, carrying Thorn, and climbed the hill. At the top, she crossed the mystical circle of protection that guarded Grimhild.

"I've got the weapon," Sylvie announced, raising the knife. She turned it, admiring the silvery blade. It cast its own shimmer, a sliver of trapped moonlight, and the tip was wicked sharp.

Thorn was beautiful—a work of art.

Thank you, Thorn whispered, quivering in her eagerness.

"Not now. I'm busy." Grimhild waved a dismissive hand, but remained intent upon her spell. She didn't even turn her head.

Sylvie scowled over a stab of annoyance. Being so easily dismissed irked her to no end; although, she supposed she ought to be used to it by now. Perhaps there were even advantages to be had in anonymity.

"Sylvie, fetch me that vial," Grimhild instructed with an imperious gesture. It jarred Sylvie from her sulk.

"Morena was my daughter, you festering cunt." Sylvie plunged Thorn into Grimhild's back. The blade impaled the witch clean through the heart and punched a hole in her chest.

Grimhild shrieked and clutched at her breast. Blood filled her hands and gushed through her fingers. Thorn fed, sipping the witch's blood like wine. It took the enchanted weapon a long time to feast on the immense reservoir that stored her immortal life force.

Stabbing the witch wasn't enough. Driven by dissatisfaction, Sylvie shifted her hands to claws and drove her nails into Grimhild's abdomen, hooking her ribcage. The *seiðr's* torso opened with the wet squishes and sloppy plops of a fresh carcass torn apart.

Sylvie ground Grimhild's heart to pâté and then consumed it. The cold meat tasted dreadful as it slid down her throat and lodged in her belly—a most unsatisfying meal. She said to the witch's messy remains, "This is just the beginning of my revenge. The Norns will pay, also. Don't ever think I've forgotten you,

Grimhild, not even for a second. When I'm finished with the Sisters Wyrd, I'll hunt your soul in Niflheimr. There, I'll be your tormentor until the end of days."

When Sylvie searched for Thorn again, the dagger was gone.

Just as well.

CHAPTER 39

Gebo: **The Rune of Love and Forgiveness**

"Sawyer!"

Victoria charged headlong, screaming Sawyer's name, and the world whirled around her. Strain cracked her vocal chords and her frantic search yielded an empire of dust. The contrary hunter was nowhere to be found. She stumbled, positive she was lost and traveling straight at the same time. The thought of Sylvie and Morena held her back. A part of Victoria wanted to turn around—to deal with her betrayer and to continue trying to save Morena. The callous, unforgiving realist at Victoria's core refused to allow the self-delusion. Sylvie and Morena were both dead to her.

No looking over her shoulder; she wasn't going that way.

Digging in her heels, Victoria skidded to a halt. She doubled over, gasping for breath and imposed order over her own internal chaos. Her thoughts cleared and she noticed things. Her surroundings—the cobblestone beach right along the southern side of the boathouse and dock. The worst of the fog had lifted. A

401

few scattered clouds remained, clinging close to the earth. The bright bride of the sky had set; the shining priest hung low.

Two more dawns until the Conclave's commencement. She wondered if Sylvie had been right about this being the start of the end. She wondered whether she'd live long enough to see it. She filled her lungs with cool air, reached through the pack bond, and found Sawyer immediately. He stood with his back to her, waist-deep in the lake. A rush of relief swept away her anxiety and she heaved a sigh.

Sawyer turned slightly, and crimson light glanced off a blade.

Her heart hammered against her breast. Too choked up to speak, Victoria crashed into the lake, splashing up a storm. She headed straight for him. Her approach made a terrific racket that carried across the calm waterfront.

Sawyer pivoted to face her. He gripped the hilt in his fist; blade pressed against his breast over his heart. A dark red stain spread across the front of his torn shirt. Blood coated the knife and his hands. It trickled along his forearms and dripped into the opaque lake.

Victoria roared at the top of her lungs. Her wolf claimed total ascension. Primal instinct ruled. The entirety of her focus locked on the knife. She had to get it away from him before he hurt himself. Hell bent, Victoria rushed him.

"Give me that!"

"Victoria, what?" Sawyer rocked back, raising his arms to protect his throat. The blade flashed. He said something, but she didn't hear him. Because he defended high, she attacked low, using her shortness to her advantage. She sucker-punched him in the stomach and when he bent over, gripping his gut, she nailed him square on the chin.

The blow knocked Sawyer over. He went under with a huge splash. Before he recovered, Victoria shifted her weight onto his chest and went for the knife. Her hands locked on his forearm just below the elbow.

"Give it to me," she grated between clenched teeth. She

strained but couldn't reach because his limbs were too damn long. Her anger leapt and bounced with a puma-like ferocity when he didn't answer. Never mind, he couldn't with his head submerged.

Moonlight glanced off the silvery blade. His willful stubbornness vexed her. *No, infuriated.* The entire purpose in her life became taking it away from him. She'd *kill* him if she had to.

Sawyer tried to sit up. His head broke the surface long enough to gasp for air. Still, he clung to that damn weapon. Infuriated, Victoria shoved him under again, pinning his back against the rocky bottom of the lake.

The hunter thrashed, all limbs flailing. The runes swarmed, buzzing soldier ants to the defense of the colony. The cut over his heart closed. Rushing to Sawyer's defense, the sigils started to meld into that remarkable shield.

"This is for his own good. He can't see straight," Victoria said to the magic. "With this man, bravado and bullheadedness are the same. He's so stubborn he's stupid."

The runes considered her explanation. Their ruckus soothed.

Sawyer lost his held breath. A huge air bubble burst to the surface along with a muffled shout. He inhaled water and convulsed.

Victoria grabbed his arms and hauled Sawyer up. He broke the surface and vomited water. Terrible coughing wracked his chest—fluid forced through his nose and mouth. While he recovered, she seized his forearm and yanked it up. No sign of the knife... She checked his other hand and found it empty, too.

"What'd you do with it?" Victoria shook him hard enough to rattle the teeth from his mouth.

"Do with what?" He sucked snot to clear his airways and spat.

Gripping a fistful of hair, Victoria stood over him. "The knife. I want it. I'm not going to let you kill yourself."

"I'm not trying to kill myself," Sawyer protested. "Stop! Will you let go?"

"Not until you give it." She yanked hard on the roots, punishing him.

"Ouch. Fuck, knock that off." He reached for her wrist, so she thwacked him across the back of the head.

"Give me the knife."

Sawyer bellowed like a pride-wounded beast. "Damn it! I'm not trying to kill myself and even if I was, you couldn't stop me!"

"I have to try!" She cuffed him again, venting her harrowing frustration.

"I murdered Morena." He hung his head, hiding beneath his hair. The weight of his shame and guilt crushed him. A scourge of self-hatred blasted her across the pack bond.

"Grimhild murdered Morena. I witnessed the whole thing. The glamour fooled me, too, Sawyer. I was close enough to stop you, but I didn't. This is on me as much as it is you." In her heart, Victoria carried the knowledge that if she'd been closer than Sawyer, Morena's blood would be on her hands. She wouldn't have hesitated to deliver the kill stroke.

He shook his head in adamant denial. "I murdered Jasper, too. This is who I am—a slayer of innocents."

Shattering silence descended. The truth hurt; a thousand tiny lacerations to her already broken heart. Victoria thrust his head away, releasing his hair. She broke on a sob. Tears slid down her face, dripped from her chin and cheeks. She sniffled and hiccupped; her throat so parched it ached. Oh, the irony of suffering dehydration while standing in a vast lake.

"Do you want the knife to kill me yourself?"

Victoria gasped. Outrage thrilled through her. She drew back her arm and delivered a ringing slap to his cheek. His beard softened the impact, but the blow turned his head. Afterward, she hyperventilated and stared at her hand as though it were a squid that had acted of its own volition.

"Yeah." Sawyer worked his jaw from side to side and touched his bloody lip. "I had that coming."

Warmth swept her face. "Give me the knife, so we can have an adult conversation. Please? All this wrestling and drama... it's not good for the baby."

No, she wasn't above playing that card.

He gave a guilty start and flexed his empty hands. "Why are you convinced I still have the knife?"

"Because I know you, Sawyer Barrett." She pinned him with her best don't-give-me-shit stare which she'd been practicing in preparation for motherhood.

The corners of his mouth split in a sheepish smile. He rocked sideways, shifting his backside, and reached beneath him. His hand came up with the recovered knife, which he offered to her.

"Here."

"You were sitting on it this whole time?" Victoria accepted the knife.

"Yeah. And before you ask—it was uncomfortable."

She almost... *almost* smiled. Nothing felt real. Their whole interaction possessed a nightmarish quality. After Grimhild had released Victoria, a tsunami of missing memories had flooded back, plugging all the amnesiac holes in her mind.

Morena was dead; nothing could change that. Victoria had been here so many times before that the concept of survivor guilt had lost all meaning. People died. Life went on—laughter and tears. The arduous march of days as they blurred into weeks and then months...

Most importantly, Victoria lived on *to fight*. Battle was the one constant certainty in her existence. The next combat always awaited just around the next corner. Tomorrow or next week... or possibly two minutes from now. Grimhild might very well be waiting for the bell to ring, signaling the start of the next round. Maybe. Victoria thought it far more likely the vaunted Queen of Burgundy and Ljosalfheim had met with a messy ending on the business end of that knife Sylvie had taken from the beach.

"Can I have my knife?" Sawyer asked.

Pursing her lips, she considered. She flirted with the temptation to pitch the weapon into the watery depths, but it would be a senseless waste. Ultimately, she returned the weapon to its scabbard on Sawyer's belt. Futile gestures aside, the hunter would live or die because he chose to do so. No one could force him to live. As Sylvie had said, Morena was gone and there was nothing Victoria could do about that. But Sawyer was still alive and kicking, and she had to try to save him.

Would Sawyer let her help?

"Are you going to hurt yourself the second I turn my back?" Victoria asked, voicing her worst fear.

"I don't think so." His long frame was strung tight on a rack of tension.

"But you really don't know?" she pressed.

He shrugged and held up his hands, palms toward her, fingers splayed. "I have blood on my hands. Do you see?"

She glanced down. His hands were clean. Glibness flitted on her tongue but she bit it. A healer should never leap to conclusions without a thorough examination. She closed her fingers about his wrists and altered her vision, peering into the spirit world. Innocent blood stained Sawyer's soul. Understanding lit her mind. He required cleansing—not easily obtained. Souls required delicate handling. Do not machine wash. Do not dry clean.

Victoria held up white-knuckled fists. Her arms trembled—her whole body shook. She *knew* what saving Sawyer required, and it was all on her. Forgiveness. Sawyer needed it. Victoria had already denied him repeatedly because she couldn't forget Jasper, the boy she'd lost in Albuquerque. Recently, she'd lost a hell of a lot more than loved ones, though. Without mercy, Victoria replayed the litany of names in her head: Daniel, her parents, and dozens of packmates in Phoenix; Jasper; Rand; Paul; Arik; Freya —*yes, even Freya*—and now Sylvie and Morena. Soon, she'd be adding Sawyer to the list if she refused to let go of her grudge.

She couldn't stand to lose Sawyer, too.

"Give me your hands..." Victoria held hers out expectantly.

"Okay..." Sawyer grasped her hands in his own. "Why?"

Victoria didn't answer. She reached for Odin, remarkably at ease in her new role as his priestess. Her difficulties had been all on her, barriers she'd erected—grief over what she'd lost, reluctance to embrace change, sheer stubbornness, and even a failure to recognize what was right under her nose. Oh, and she mustn't forget, she was still unbelievably pissed with Jake and had no concept of how to reconcile that.

Anger, ironically enough, enhanced her connection to Odin. Divinity flowed through her. Its brilliant radiance suffused both her and Sawyer. The nova-bright nimbus lit up the early evening with fireworks reflected off the water.

Still, she faltered. Something held her back, and she didn't understand what. With each passing moment, her frustration mounted until she fought tears. On the verge of screaming, Victoria sank her teeth into her lower lip hard enough to draw blood. The coppery heat brushed her tongue.

Jake? In desperation, she built the prayer in her mind, struggling to put her confusion into words. In an unexpected act of kindness, Jake answered before she finished.

Relax and go to it. The rest will follow.

That's it? A soggy giggle escaped Victoria. Tears dashed down her cheeks.

That's it. Jake chuckled.

Gee, thanks. Where'd you hear that corny line?

Oh, I may've read it somewhere...

That'll teach you—don't believe everything you read.

The god of the gallows laughed and laughed. Energy flowed easily through Victoria now. She wielded the torch and seared the taint from Sawyer's soul.

"What are you doing?" Sawyer shifted, restless beneath her ministrations. The heat blistered his skin, but he bore the discomfort without so much as a whimper.

"Removing the bloodstain." She released him, watching in silent fascination as the industrious runes set about healing the burns. "There. All done."

Sawyer stared at his hands, his face stony. Freed of the fault, his aura shone with the purity of polished gemstones—ruby and sapphire. He double blinked. Always a skeptic at heart, Sawyer accepted nothing at face value. He turned his hands, inspecting them from all angles, rubbed his palms together, and looked again.

In a voice rife with skepticism, he said, "It can't be that easy."

"It's not. I can purify your soul. I can't heal your heart. I can't take your guilt or your anger..." She would've absorbed his burden, too, if she were able, because she loved him. Victoria stumbled to a full stop, reeling. *She loved him...* and not just as a friend or member of her pack. How had this happened? She guarded her heart fiercely against romantic entanglements.

"I don't deserve this," Sawyer was protesting, whatever he'd said before lost forever to the annals of history.

Victoria focused so she didn't miss anything else.

"Sylvie was right. I deserve punishment—"

"No." Victoria cut him off with harsh severity. "Sylvie's quest for vengeance resulted in Morena's death. I saw Sylvie—" She jerked her head toward the shore. "While I was trying to resurrect Morie, Sylvie warned me to come after you."

"She did?" Surprise glimmered in his brown eyes.

"Yeah." Victoria clutched that tidbit to her heart. It didn't excuse what Sylvie had done, couldn't redeem her, but it was something. "She took the weapon that killed Morena."

Curiosity pricked her about the enchanted weapon—what was it, where had it come from, and why did everyone seem to understand it except her? But those questions could wait.

"What did she want with Thorn?" Sawyer's volume spiked with alarm.

"I don't know... but if I know Sylvie, Grimhild is toast. Sylvie loved that girl like her own flesh and blood." Victoria clenched her jaws. No matter what, she didn't have a shred of doubt that Morena's murder would turn Sylvie against the witch.

But Victoria shared blame in Morena's death. Bitter regret hung over her—a burden she would shoulder for the rest of her life. In hindsight, she saw all the things she'd done wrong. So many mistakes. It was too late to fix the past, but she could rectify one glaring error.

Carefully, she rose while Sawyer remained seated in the rocky shallows. She stroked his forehead, pushing back wet bangs, and pressed her lips to his forehead. "I forgive you for Morena's death —and Jasper's."

Sawyer flinched as though she'd struck him. "I don't deserve forgiveness."

She cupped his jaw and lifted his face toward her. The anguish there shocked her. Hot droplets dashed down his cheeks and clung to his beard. Her lips parted in dismay. She'd meant for forgiveness to be a kindness, not another cruelty.

"It's not about worth. It's about healing. This is as much for my own good and the pack, Sawyer. Sylvie has shown me the cost of clinging to blame. We lost Sylvie and Morena today. I can't lose you, too, so I'm forgiving you for everything. I want a clean start."

A powerful sob wracked Sawyer. His arms closed around her and he clung for dear life. Victoria stroked his hair and shushed him like a babe while he cried it out. The man grieved like he fought: brutally and with all his strength. The break lasted seconds, releasing a deluge of grief and guilt before he recovered his composure. In the aftermath, Sawyer splashed cold water across his face. He kept his head bowed and briefly turned his face into her throat. His hot breath caressed her skin.

"Thank you," he said in a prayerful voice.

She nodded, blinded by her own tears. "Promise me you won't leave."

He stayed silent long enough that she got scared. At last, he said, "I can't make that promise. I'm supposed to be blowing that damn horn and riding off with the Hunt in an hour."

"All right then." A rough, stuttered chuckle escaped Victoria. "Promise you'll come back."

"I promise I'll return or perish trying." Sawyer crossed his heart. "Good enough?"

"Yeah." She tried to nod but the clattering of her teeth made it impossible. Now that she no longer channeled divinity, she was suddenly freezing her ass off. Shivering, Victoria wrapped her arms around herself. Abruptly, she gained self-awareness. They'd been submerged in snow-melted water for who knew how long. Sawyer must be miserable, too.

"Your lips are blue. Let's get out." Sawyer clasped her arm.

"Okay." Leaning on him for support, Victoria slogged toward the shore—each step required monumental effort, and the same held true for Sawyer. She raised her face and spotted Logan—shifted to human—in the distance, lolloping downhill toward them.

Logan met them on the river-rock beach. With tears streaming down his cheeks, he dropped to his knees beside Morena's body. He gathered the teenager into his arms, hugging her to his chest. "Damn it, kid. Why didn't you stay put where you were safe?"

"We were stupid to think she would," Sawyer said, and for once Logan didn't argue.

"Grimhild?" Victoria asked, her voice strained from overuse.

"Ding-dong. Sylvie got her. I didn't know what to do so I left her to her kill." Logan slit his throat with a finger-knife. Instead of looking at Victoria and Sawyer, he stared into the distance.

"You did the right thing." Victoria shuddered. She couldn't take another death. Not today. Which left her with a big problem—what to do about Sylvie—but at least the decision was one where she could procrastinate, at least for a while.

"What now?" Logan asked. He might've said more, but something on the dock snagged his attention.

"Now we get back to work..." Victoria started accounting. She had too many tasks to remain idle. She would prepare Morena's body and conduct her funeral. The living, however, took priority. They needed to get Cali to a hospital. Sawyer should collect *Gnýrhorn* and make haste to Broken Bend where the wolf-shifter packs and *Den Valgte* awaited their return.

Sawyer followed Logan's gaze and the hunter, too, stared. He muttered, "Well, fuck."

A raven's distinctive refrain pierced the evening.

"What are you two looking at?" Victoria turned and found her answer.

On the boat dock, an enormous eagle-sized raven sat atop a pylon. A second bird perched atop the next post down. Both watched through shiny black eyes.

Huginn and Muninn.

"What do you want now?" Victoria huffed, marching forward. If Jake dared make *another* demand of her right now...! *Oh, Lord Odin, hear my prayers and accept this fine offering.* She thrust her middle finger, aimed at the sky.

Both ravens spread their wings and bowed.

CHAPTER 40

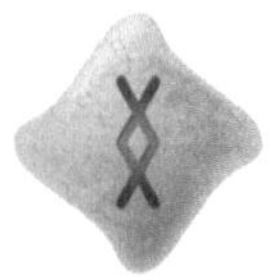

Ingwaz: The Rune of Peace and Harmony

Deadness entombed Logan.

A nurse with a rhino-complex herded Logan from the ICU. He delayed long enough to glance over his shoulder. Cali Kinkaid rested in a hospital bed as motionless as a corpse. She lived, but remained unconscious. The hospital staff claimed all her vital signs were stable.

"Visiting hours are tomorrow between eleven a.m. and eight p.m. You can call the Intensive Care desk to inquire into her status." Nurse Rhino bumped Logan, using her bulk to get him moving again.

"Thanks." Logan hoped for relief at the news or annoyance over being bullied, but he felt... nothing. Absolute and utter numbness formed a void around him. Maybe he had died in the fight with Grimhild—his soul had left his body, whisked away to the underworld. And then Uncle Mike had decided to reanimate

413

his corpse, leaving consciousness without the capacity for emotions.

He must've looked pretty damn pitiful, because Nurse Rhino's round face crumpled and she placed a heavy pat on his shoulder. "Your friend will be fine. She's hanging in there."

"She's tough." Logan didn't know the exact specifics of how hunter magic worked, but he had confidence. It annoyed him, though, that Sawyer had an army of those little solider runes, but Cali didn't.

"There you go. On your way now." Nurse Rhino thumped his back once more and then shoved him through the automatic entrance to the ICU. It shut and locked behind him.

Temptation heckled Logan. He wanted to smash the heavy security doors to smithereens, but it would've accomplished nothing other than to get him arrested. Besides, busting up a part of the hospital would draw unwanted attention and require awkward explanations.

On cue, his sat phone beeped that he had a new text. Logan checked the message, expecting it to be from Vic. It wasn't.

Mike Trash: *If you're done in the ICU, can you drop by the morgue?*

Logan jerked his head up, searching the walls and ceiling for eyeballs. He found none. He texted: *Are you spying on me?*

Mike Trash: *Of course not. The hospital simply has certain built-in security features. The morgue?*

Logan: *Busy. I promised Vic that I'd go straight over to Broken Bend as soon as I finished up here.*

Under the direction of Alpha Finn, assorted wolf-shifter packs were gathering there along with the members of *Den Valgte*. All of them waiting for the main event, when Sawyer would toot his little horn and summon the Wild Hunt. If he'd had more time, Logan would've loaded "Ride of the Valkyries" onto his phone and set up some Bluetooth speakers... The main event was less than an hour off, though, so it was a delay he couldn't afford.

Mike Trash: *It's about our deal.*

Logan grimaced, and his resolve collapsed like wet tissue. His conscience dropkicked him right in the gonads. Abruptly, his apathy vanished. He gnawed his lower lip, checked the time, and typed: *K, but I don't have much time.*

Mike Trash: *Ten minutes. Promise.*

Logan: *I'll be right down. Presuming the ducking basement doesn't swallow me alive.*

Mike Trash: *I'll make sure you can get straight through.*

Logan: *On my way.*

~

LIFE GOT weird when visiting his uncle—AKA the Necromancer—at the city morgue—AKA portal to the underworld—started to seem normal. Just another day in Sierra Pines; bang on strangeness. This time, at least, getting here had been uneventful. He hadn't gotten lost or knocked himself senseless.

Logan shoved open the door to the morgue's office and peered inside. The lights were on and the front desk, as always, unoccupied. After a momentary hesitation, he entered.

"Hello?" Logan called, his voice echoing.

"We're in here." Mike's voice emanated past the heavy swinging doors that led to the autopsy rooms.

Logan stared at the entrance, deliberating. It might be a trap, but he didn't think so. For one, too obvious. For another, Mike gave every indication of being satisfied with their agreement.

No guts, no glory. Logan charged straight through, using his elbows to shove the doors open. It allowed him to raise his arms in a defensive stance. Before he cleared the entrance, he asked, "Is that the creepy 'we' or the royal 'we'?"

"Is there a difference?" Mike stood with his back to Logan. The sheriff's bulk blocked the person seated on the autopsy table. He held a penlight at shoulder-level, presumably aimed into the face of his patient.

"Depends. How much inbreeding are we discussing?" Logan stalled in the doorway, still wary of a trap. He sucked in a sharp breath, seeing with his nose. He sorted and identified the customary odors, eliminating his uncle's basal spoor and the astringent brew of morgue chemicals. It left a single living person: male and young.

"Everything looks normal." Mike clicked off the penlight, dropped his arm, and stepped back to reveal a boy of nine or ten who looked like he'd stepped straight out of a Nineteenth Century lithograph.

"Am I really gonna live, Doctor?" The boy asked in a hauntingly familiar soprano-pitched voice.

Logan tripped over his own feet. His heart smashed into his chest and then his throat. He stumbled, a hair shy of performing a face plant, and stared at the kid in helpless fascination. Nine or ten, the boy had light skin, a Crayola shade of deathly pale to be precise, and shaggy blond hair beneath a caramel-colored newsboy cap. His white shirt, buttoned to the throat, brown wool coat and trousers, and worn loafers. He held the newspaper carry satchel slung over his shoulder against his chest, his thin fingers wrapped about the edges.

"Don't be a smart ass," Mike snapped in crisp reply.

"But my ass is the only smart part of me," the boy shot back. But he cringed when no one laughed, betraying his bravado.

"No truer words." Shaking his head, Mike swiped his hands together.

"Evan?" Logan's eyes rounded till they watered.

"Yeah?" Evan tilted his head, gazing up into Logan's face.

Logan lost his words. The kid had haunted eyes: ice-frosted marbles with gravestone-shaped pupils floating in the ice-blue irises. No matter the power of the magic that'd restored his life, death had marked his soul.

"We had a deal: your hand and silence in exchange for Evan's life." Mike smiled, near as cold as the frozen Arctic. "If I'm nothing else, I'm a lawful devil. I keep my bargains."

"And his freedom." Logan's gaze remained locked with the boy's.

"And his freedom." Mike clucked his tongue. "Although, I have warned Evan... If he should reveal my true nature or this place to outsiders, the consequences will be dire."

Evan cringed again and whispered, "I understand."

"Good," Mike said. "From here on out, he's free of my command. For the rest of his natural life, however long that is."

"It'd better not wind up prematurely shortened." Logan glowered and left the threat hanging. Frankly, he didn't know what he could do to hurt his uncle, but as sure as Loki lied, he would overturn Valhalla and Helheimr in his quest.

Mike frowned, suggesting mild offense. "Now, now. No need for threats."

"Funny. I heard you make one ten seconds ago."

"Logan, let's not get nasty. We're all family here." Mike spread his arms.

"Yeah, I'm still unclear on the specifics of how that works." The whole damn thing hurt his brain. Questions popped up faster than he could smash them down—a maddening game of whack-a-mole.

"It's a discussion for another time." Mike clasped Logan's shoulder. "Now take Evan on home 'n' get him settled. He's been through an ordeal."

"Home!" An incredulous squawk burst from Logan.

"Stop talking about me like I'm not here." Evan pushed off the table and landed square on his feet. Upright, he stood right around the five-foot mark; taller than Victoria, but the top of his head only came to Logan's sternum.

"I don't know anything about kids." Logan squared off with his uncle.

"Then now's a good time to learn." Mike flashed a your-problem-now smile. "Want my advice? Take him home and let the ladies deal with him."

"Yeah, that'll go over great. It's no wonder you're still a bachelor, Unc." Logan scowled in disgust. He stomped his feet. The jibe stung precisely *because* there were no "ladies" left to take Evan home to. No more Sylvie and no more Morena...

They exchanged a terse farewell. Oddly, it wasn't the tensest family moment Logan had ever endured with his uncle. So far as things went in relative terms, their warmth barometer hovered in the near-affectionate range.

The walk out with Evan proved a hundred times more uncomfortable. At least the labyrinth-like basement burped them out onto the central stairwell without any issues. Logan took the lead, glancing over his shoulder at frequent intervals to make sure the boy trailed behind him. Their footsteps echoed, rising through the concrete cavern. In silence, they reached the ground floor and entered the lobby via the elevator bay.

Some balding guy manned the reception desk, talking on the phone. Assorted staff and patients scattered throughout, going about their business. As edgy as a coyote on the sly, Logan headed toward the nearest exit. With every stride, he expected someone to shout out, challenging his right to be walking out with a ten-year-old kid. When the automatic doors swooshed open, a rush of cool night air blasted across his face, chilling the perspiration beaded on his forehead. As soon as he set foot outside, he released a held breath with a conspicuous gust.

"Tell me about it," Evan muttered. "Fuck, I need a smoke."

"You won't live long if you keep that up," Logan said, biting back a stronger rebuke. He'd be damned if he'd allow his misadventure into foster parenting to turn him into someone's maiden auntie. Double damned if he'd sacrifice another hand.

"Whatever." Evan rolled his eyes.

"Fuck, you've got the brat thing down like you trained for it." Logan charged across the parking lot toward the garage where he'd left his car. He kept his stride long and fast; the kid could keep up... or not.

Evan dashed after him and pulled alongside, complaining the whole time. "Yeah, well as you and everyone else seem to have forgotten, I'm over a hundred years old. Trapping an adult mind in a child's body is just the twisted sort of joke the master gets off on."

Logan skidded to a halt just outside the garage's ground-floor entrance. Snarling in frustration, he swung around. "He's not your master anymore."

"No, I suppose you think you're my master now?" Evan leveled a baleful glare from beneath the tilted brim of his cap and the shaggy crop of blond bangs that hung over his forehead.

"No, of course not." Logan fumed, quite at a loss for words. The perfect cutting retort crossed his mind, but he bit it back out of a stunted sense of decency. Evan had suffered incalculable trauma for decades. If being a reanimated ghoul that had to dine on rotting flesh to survive and being forced to serve an evil Necromancer didn't count as a cause for PTSD, then nothing did.

"What's your plan then, Logan?"

"I don't know! I don't have a fucking clue! I've been making it up as I go along—" Logan tried to gesture with his missing hand, and then winced. He dropped his arm, but too late. The boy fixated on the bandaged stump until Logan itched with discomfort; however, he remained still through sheer force of will.

"That's the trouble. You didn't give this an ounce of thought at all. You arranged to have me resurrected, but it didn't occur to you to ask for an adult body?" Evan asked, dripping sarcasm.

"Oh, grow up!" Logan shot back. "You're over a hundred years old. What's ten more?"

Evan glared.

"I'm sorry. I screwed up." The apology left a bad taste in his mouth, but he spat it out anyway. What was owed must be paid.

"Don't apologize! You stupid jerk!" With a shriek, Evan flew into a childish rage. The boy pummeled Logan with his fists. He landed a harmless gut punch before Logan brought up his arm in an automatic block.

"Knock it off!" Logan backslid, lest a careless movement might harm Evan now that he was a living child. The former ghoul's temper tantrum left him bewildered.

"No! You knock it off! I hate you!" Evan threw another flurry of glancing punches. A brackish scent clung to him, sharp and sorrowful.

"Stop. What the fuck's wrong?" Logan retreated further, a step that carried him off the curb. He dropped a step but landed square on his feet. Roughly, he caught the boy's arm and held him easily at bay.

"This! You!" Evan's fists flew harmlessly through empty air because he couldn't reach, but that didn't stop him from trying.

"What'd I do now?" Logan didn't miss the high note of desperation in his own voice. He clung to his wit's end, unable to conceive of what else he could do or give to make right of this mess.

"How can you not know?" Abruptly, Evan ceased his attack. He repeated the question, tears streaming down his cheeks. "You chopped off your hand for me, you stupid son of a bitch. I pushed you! It was me!"

"What are you talking about?" Logan let go of Evan. His brow knit in consternation. He understood all the words but nothing the boy said made a lick of sense.

Evan choked on a sob and continued in a strangled voice. "Your uncle forced me to serve as your guardian. I watched over you for years. I had no one to talk to; no one to play with. I resented you. I wanted to hurt you, so I pushed you."

A lightbulb clicked on.

"Wait," Logan said, "Are we talking about that day—"

"That day you fell into that storm drain and broke your leg." Evan nodded furiously. "Hurting you gave me the excuse I needed to talk to you without the master becoming angry.

"First off, he's Mike or Sheriff Trash to you now. You've got to get that straight. If you slip up in front of Vic, it's all over."

"Yeah, I've got it." Evan took an angry swipe at his face, smashed his nose with the back of his hand, smearing tears and snot.

"Second, that's what this huge fuss is all about—a broken leg? I've broken more bones than I can count on one hand." Logan shrugged as his lips twisted in a farce of a smile. One hand—ironically, all he had left anyway.

"You're not angry?" Evan jerked his face up. Distrust waged a fierce war with hope, and his slender shoulders shook.

"Nah, it's fine. We're good. This is a time for second chances. You, me..." Even Sawyer? Logan paused, putting it together in his head. He found himself nodding because the concept resonated. Redemption. Victoria had started Logan on his. Paying it forward felt good. *Right.* Maybe Sawyer deserved a second chance.

CHAPTER 41

Asgårdsreien: The Wild Hunt

THERE WAS a strange pleasure to be had from standing in the middle of a twisty mountain highway. Sawyer straddled the double yellow line that divided U.S. Route 50. He wore _Gnýrhorn's_ carry strap slung over his shoulder, but his hand kept returning to the cream-hued ram's horn. The growth grooves gave it a distinctive, bumpy feel that seduced his fingertips along exploratory paths. He found the repetitious action soothing and had taken to strumming it.

Before him, Victoria took part in a circle chat that included the _Den Valgte_ leader, Reidell, Alpha MacTavish, and Alpha Finn. The blonde she-wolf put her hands on her hips and her volume rose. "Warn your people to stand at least five hundred feet back from the shoulder of the highway when the Hunt rides through."

Silence stretched out.

Sawyer bit back a smile. Wait for it... Who would it be?

"And if they don't?" Finn dared ask.

423

"Then the Hunt exacts a sacrifice and takes your man," Victoria snapped. "Finn, do whatever the hell you want. It makes no difference to me."

Finn huffed and grinned, baring his teeth.

"Unless it's a member of the Wolf Spears. MacTavish, keep your people behind the safety lines. Do you hear me?" Victoria demanded.

"Aye, ma'am! I'll make 'em toe the line." MacTavish had an infectious laugh which pulled the others in.

Reidell chuckled. "I'll spread the word."

The evening roiled with energy and expectation. Alphas Finn and MacTavish returned to the area north of the road where their people gathered alongside other wolf-shifter packs. Over the course of that day, a good half-dozen other alphas and their entourages had arrived early for the Conclave. In total, they numbered fifty-to-sixty. Reidell headed in the opposite direction and joined the four hundred-something followers of *Den Valgte* who congregated in the vacant lot amid the shambles of the former Fireside Inn. Best guess, Sawyer figured visitors outnumbered Broken Bend's resident population at least twenty to one. He doubted the poor pit-stop town had ever seen the like.

Victoria strode to Sawyer. When she tilted her head back, moonlight fell on her face. She had dark circles under her eyes. "They're restless," she said. "We can't delay much longer. Sherriff Trash gave us two hours to clean up our 'chemical spill'. It's been three."

"I'm ready to go. How much longer do you want to wait?" Sawyer refrained from reiterating the obvious—which Victoria already knew. He should go now. The *only* reason they'd postponed this long was because Logan hadn't shown yet.

A frown pinched her forehead, and she gnawed her lower lip. "Five more minutes?"

"Five more minutes," Sawyer agreed because he disliked the thought of leaving her alone. Hell, he didn't want to leave her at all. So, every excuse, every stolen minute, became a special memory to take with him when he left.

Victoria dug out her phone and placed a call. Their gazes locked, and they stared into each other's eyes while it rang until it went to voicemail. She shoved it back into her pocket. The sudden motion set her to swaying on her feet.

Sawyer reflexively caught her shoulder. "You okay?"

"Yeah, I'm fine." She steadied and righted under her own strength.

Sawyer clenched his jaws and accepted the lie. No good would come from calling her out on it. They were both dead tired—heart and soul—faking their way through everything as though it was okay. Sawyer kept returning to the long walk he'd made from the lakeshore with Morena's body cradled in his arms. He was alive; she was dead. He'd gladly take her place if it meant she would live again.

"I don't want you to leave." The admission burst from Victoria with the fervency of a confession. She focused on him with unwavering intensity. Her startling bluntness put Sawyer off balance. For months, they'd danced around their mutual attraction, but never acknowledged it.

"This is my destiny. My entire life, I've been called to the Hunt." Sawyer deliberately offered the words that would ease her burden. A part of him didn't want to go either; a greater aspect of him felt compelled to this. Summoning the Wild Hunt wasn't about his wants or needs, but about making amends... and discovering his heritage.

Victoria sank her teeth into her lower lip. Conflict wagged war across her countenance. They'd reached the point of no return. But people who left with the Asgårdsreien never returned... and they both knew it. The chances they'd see each other again in this lifetime were slim to none.

Sawyer waited and watched while Victoria agonized. He marked the exact moment she reached her decision. A remote, grim mask dropped over her and her blue eyes turned hard. Sawyer knew the look, having witnessed it countless times from his father—the pragmatic face of a general.

"I *need* this army," Victoria grated out with excessive force. "We're going to war."

Sawyer nodded, and dismissed his final lingering doubt about their course of action. Where Victoria led, he'd follow. If she demanded a sacrifice, he'd make it. Their futures would remain intertwined, their lives dedicated to a shared purpose; no matter how long or far their paths diverged.

"Whatcha thinking?" Victoria rested her open hand on Sawyer's chest, stroking him. His foolish heart jumped and then raced.

"Clowns to the left, jokers to the right." Sawyer flashed a cocky grin.

"Here I am, stuck in the middle..." Victoria chuckled. Expectation shone in her eyes. For what, he had no clue, but he hated to disappoint her. He suspected he would anyway.

The silence grew uncomfortable.

"I've been meaning to ask..." Sawyer said just to break it.

"Yeah?" She frowned in clear frustration. Now there, at least, was a familiar reaction.

"Back when Grimhild had me paralyzed, how did you know I needed *Tiwaz* to complete *Kappiskjǫld*?"

Her brow knit. "I don't know what you're talking about."

"Sure you do. You must. You put emphasis on justice." A golden glow haloed Victoria, an aspect he'd always assumed she derived from her association with Freya. He knew now that it originated from Victoria alone.

"Oh, that." Victoria licked her lips. "I was trying to warn you that Logan meant to jump Grimhild. Tyr is the god of justice."

Sawyer scowled, considering false assumptions. Based on recent experiences, he'd molded his expectations about Victoria on *Laguz*, but her aura manifested none of the deep blues or greens inherent with an affinity to the water rune.

"Tyr has one hand. As does..." Victoria nodded, encouraging him to finish.

"Logan." Sawyer shook his head, chagrined to realize how badly they'd miscommunicated. In light of new facts, their being alive became a matter of happenstance. And if he set aside everything he *thought* to be true, what did that leave?

"Are you saying that I inspired you?" Victoria's voice lilted with laughter. A lively school of runes shaped like a child's drawing of fish—diamonds with tails—swirled through the radiant depths of her aura.

"Inspired is a strong word," Sawyer hedged, stupidly fibbing to a woman who could smell lies. He squinted at her nimbus and looked closer to be sure.

Othila—the rune of home and hearth—overlay her soul.

"I did inspire you!" Victoria's smile stretched to a grin. "That's so sweet. No one has ever considered me their muse before. Do you think—"

Sawyer claimed her mouth in a rough kiss, tightening his hands about her shoulders. Initially, her lips yielded in surprise with alluring softness and he took what he wanted; every stolen second all that much sweeter for its forbidden nature. A raider's kiss: worthy of a would-be Viking voyager. The pleasure he derived from the illicit wickedness shocked him to the core.

Scorching heat set his senses on fire.

Victoria raised her hands, and he hardened in anticipation. Oh, for the love of mystery. The next seconds would reveal whether she welcomed or resented his advance. He halfway expected to wind up laid-out flat, eating pavement. The moment her fingers brushed his throat, ghosting across his beard, he braced.

An impatient grunt emanated deep in Victoria's throat—a threat and a demand. She caught his hair and tugged hard, pulling him down. Sawyer bowed to her will and bent further, even though it crimped his neck to come down to her level. He'd have preferred to lift her to his, but he remained mindful of their rapt audience. The kiss gentled, no less passionate. She took as much as she gave, and he horded every precious second as the charm to take with him into the savage trial he faced.

"I love you, too," Sawyer said, breaking the kiss. It ended, as all things must, on a bittersweet note. Wetness glistened on Victoria's cheeks and Sawyer's entire world had altered forever. She was the hearth of his heart, the beloved he'd return to... if he met a home-coming at all.

He didn't say goodbye.

Victoria pressed her hand to his heart again, overlaying the imprint branded into his flesh. An ironic smile twisted her lips, and then she allowed her arm to fall. Without a word, she walked to the north side of the road and joined Logan on the shoulder—the bastard had finally shown up at last. The strangest mix of conflicting emotions to ever exist struck Sawyer. A dagger's twist, a double-edged blade... Relief because Sawyer didn't have to leave Victoria alone. Logan would be there with her. And envy for the exact same reason.

Jealousy stabbed Sawyer in the heart when Logan raised his arms and Victoria walked straight into his embrace. She wrapped her arms around his waist and pressed her face to his chest. The male wolf and hunter locked gazes across the distance that sepa-rated them... a gulf which, ironically, wasn't as wide as it'd been a few days ago.

"Good luck!" Logan shouted, and threw up his middle finger in a singular salute, positioned discreetly behind Victoria's head and out of her view.

Fuck off.

Sawyer laughed so hard it hurt. Mid-chuckle, he raised *Gnýrhorn* to the heavens, filled his lungs with breath, and placed his lips over the mouthpiece. He had no experience with musical instruments, aside from the French horn in sixth grade and a disastrous six-month obsession with drums in his teens. His worst fear was that he'd blow the damn thing and no sound would emerge.

Worry proved unnecessary.

A rolling roar blared from the horn. A freezing gale blasted down out of the formidable north, shoving stormy thunderheads before it. Dark clouds stacked in the sky, roiling with the turmoil of flash and fury. Their blackness hid the moon and the stars. A few fat droplets of rain plopped down; an ill omen of the torrent to follow.

Thor's playground.

Sawyer craned his neck, lifting his face to the heavens, distantly aware his many watchers did the same. He turned his gaze to the south, and onlookers mirrored his action. With dreadful expectation, they waited, one and all, for the Hunt's arrival.

They waited...

And waited...

Sweat beaded on Sawyer's brow and ran down his back in cold rivulets. He tightened his grip on *Gnýrhorn*, considering whether to blow it again, but his mother's instructions had been strict and specific. One long blast—no more, no less—summoned the Asgårdsreien.

Just when he'd decided they wouldn't come, the Ride of Asgard descended on the winds of the storm. Baying hounds ran at the forefront, heralding the arrival of Odin's mounted cavalry. Fierce warriors wore the visage of madness. Flames burned in the eyes of their steeds, whose hooves sparked lightning across the sky.

Their clamor—the all-consuming battle rage of the berserker.

Thunder on the earth, the Wild Hunt touched down on the black asphalt of Highway 50 amid a shower of sparks. The ground shook as if in the grip of a quake. They aimed straight for Sawyer. He braced, squared his stance, and stood his ground. His courage quailed, his heart pounding so hard it threatened to explode within his breast.

The riders parted. A massive, magnificent eight-legged horse the color of driven snow emerged from the pack to lead the charge. *Sleipnir!* Sawyer's nerves surged with exhilaration and terror. He moved in measure, stepping to the warhorse's left side.

The horse bore down on Sawyer, drawing nearer. The world narrowed and even the deafening din of the cavalry faded. His focus tightened to the flared nostrils and all-too-intelligent consideration in Sleipnir's gaze. Not just a horse, but a god who cast judgement on the merit of the rider to sit in his saddle.

Woe to the unworthy.

Sawyer cast fear aside. As Sleipnir bolted past, the hunter lunged and grasped ahold of the front edge of the saddle. The racing horse yanked him off his feet. For a few seconds, he dangled by his fingertips, his legs flapping behind him. Leather flew from the steed's withers, whipping at his eyes with a painful sting.

With a mighty exertion, Sawyer dragged his chest across the horse's back. He reached for the reins but found only thick mane. The beast bucked beneath him, tossing him into the air. Still clutching strands of Sleipnir's mane, Sawyer careened through the air. He fully expected to crash to the pavement, only to get trampled beneath the hooves of the riders behind them.

He smashed into the saddle. A pained grunt expelled from his chest and he bent over, enduring a wave of crippling nausea. Oh well, he really hadn't wanted kids anyway.

Hello, I'm Sleipnir. Amusement flavored the friendly greeting that popped into Sawyer's mind. Yes, the horse was laughing at him, and no, there wasn't a damn thing he could do about it.

"Sawyer," he managed. "Thanks for not throwing me."

I find it difficult to believe Odin didn't teach his son to ride, Sleipnir said in a voice rife with skepticism.

"He tried. I didn't want to listen." Sawyer added another monumental stupidity of youth to his very long list.

Sleipnir snorted. *Jake warned me about you. You'd better hold tight. As we take to the sky, the ride will get rough.*

Sawyer clung on for dear life.

CHAPTER 42

***Raido*: The Traveler's Rune**

IN THE MOMENT, Sylvie's top priority was leaving. She wanted to be gone before the others returned. To that end, she hastened her steps. She carried a pack containing her clothing and her rune chest. The rest of her worldly possessions, she would abandon.

Located in the hallway off the kitchen, a small closet was sandwiched between the laundry room and the pantry. It contained a great many brooms and mops as well as the trophies Victoria had taken from the witches she'd slain—a wolf's head amulet and a staff.

Sylvie switched on the light and entered the cramped room. She bent to place a bundle containing her altar, every single precious piece, on the floor. The effort of stooping cost her. Her old joints popped and her spine creaked, but the physical ravages of age paled in comparison to the erosion of her soul.

"I have given years of my life to your service, Freya, and to the Storm Pack, for whatever little value you or Victoria have placed on that." Sylvie intended the words to commemorate the transition of her life, but bitter acrimony crept into her voice. She drew a sharp breath and finished, "But I can serve you no more."

From a nail on the wall, she removed the wolf's head amulet and placed the rawhide cord over her head. The moment the metal touched her skin, powerful protective magic rolled through Sylvie. The talisman didn't burn her despite being made from silver.

A twisted staff leaned against the wall beneath the nail. Sylvie wrapped her hand about the coarse cane and took it up. Its enchantments remained unknown to her, but she would figure it out.

Sylvie passed through the kitchen where Sophia and the pups haunted the refrigerator. Wild things—wolves shouldn't be kept indoors like domesticated dogs. Lately, though, with all that'd been going on, the pack's gray wolves had been kept confined—their freedom restricted—all too often. In her final duty as mother to the pack, Sylvie tarried long enough to feed venison steaks to the wolves who gulped their meals down within seconds.

The four gray wolves trailed Sylvie to the front door. The house was completely silent other than the click of their nails on the tile. They stood huddled together, ears flat and tails tucked. In their own way, they understood the significance of Morena's absence within the pack bond.

From the open entryway, Sylvie looked back upon them with sorrow. She regretted the distress her departure would cause them. In all this, they were innocent of wrongdoing—just victims... the same as Morena.

Sylvie chose them as her witnesses for the Ritual of Severance, which must be performed before her family, cutting all her family obligations before she undertook the journey of the *völva*—a wand carrier—and seer. From this point forward, she traveled the road to revenge.

The Sisters Wyrd had best beware.

A tear rolled down her cheek as she said her final words to her family, "Sophia, my beloved pups, my time with this pack is over. Your children are more than half-grown. They must yet learn to hunt, but you are more than able to teach them. Know this—my heart is heavy, brimming with regret, and I will miss you. Once I leave here, I will wander the world for the remainder of my days. I don't know where my travels will take me, but I expect the settling of scores will guide my steps."

She turned her back on her old life and shut the door quietly behind her.

The End.